ske.

This book should be  the

SKELMERSDALL

Maeve Crawford was born in Sheffield where she spent all her childhood. Educated at Marcliffe Grammar, she worked as a secretary in Sales Promotion and as a Medical Records Officer.

Now living in Scarborough, she is married with three children.

Her interests include complementary therapies, poetry and writing for pleasure.

Published by

**MELROSE
BOOKS**

An Imprint of Melrose Press Limited
St Thomas Place, Ely
Cambridgeshire
CB7 4GG, UK
www.melrosebooks.com

FIRST EDITION

Copyright © Maeve Crawford 2006

The Author asserts her moral right to
be identified as the author of this work

Cover designed by

ISBN 1 905226 69 1

Printed and bound in Great Britain by:
CPI Antony Rowe, Bumpers Farm,
Chippenham, Wiltshire, SN14 6LH, UK

SILENT MENACE

Maeve Crawford

To my family for their patience and support and to my
friends for their encouragement.

INTRODUCTION

An only child of a single Mum, Ellie became a victim of homelessness at 16 and made a momentous decision to live in a silent world, choosing not to speak. This led, not to a life of despair or despondency, but to a journey of hope, excitement, opportunity and endurance, and eventually to a devotional love for Gary who carried her safely through a hazardous environment.

Touring Europe in a converted bus she was protected and nurtured by seven members of a rock band who discovered that she had a natural affinity to smooth out the wrinkles of continual abusive conflict.

Yet she had a past of perjury and maliciousness and a trial which came back to haunt her and further episodes were to prove how events in her life were controlled by her inability to speak.

The hardships ended when her beauty was captured by the paparazzi in Milan and the nomadic culture gave way to a life of fame and fortune.

However in the background Gary was waiting, trying to cope with a debilitating disease for which there is no cure, and at the height of her success Ellie chooses to recover her voice, to shelve all her plans and return to England to care for him.

Choosing to have a child by donor was to produce a mixture of anxiety and pain yet the overriding concern was for Gary, despite his betrayal. Overwhelmed in violent and

1

insubordinate misery Ellie learns to cope with the trauma of his illness and the effect on her life.

Mavis Crawford. 2005

CHAPTER ONE

"Silence seldom doth harm." (Proverbial.)

It was 2.30 in the afternoon when Moira emerged from the Court House, exactly four hours after stepping out into the bright, sunny streets of Durham. The trial was over and she had stayed behind just long enough to castigate the Counsel for the Defence with the kind of remark which would not have endeared her to him.

Moira did not wait for the doors to swing shut but slammed through them, pinning her shoulder bag against the frame. She wept, ready to explode, but was spared close scrutiny from court officials who had seen it all before. This was, for some, the centre point of human misery and today this wretched feeling of disbelief was seeping into her whole being.

Lisa was in desperate need of reassurance. Her mother was ignoring her, striding down the steps, tossing her blonde hair in exasperation, her daughter hot on her heels.

'Mom. Stop. Listen to me. I'm sorry. I know how much you cared for Phil. I didn't want you to be hurt but I told it as it was.' Moira grimaced, gripping her arm. Lisa turned on her, struggling to remain calm. 'He is guilty, you know he is, he has no respect for you or anyone.' She checked her pace. Her mother moved quickly away. Lisa plucked up courage. 'You have never really trusted him, have you?'

Moira strode towards the car park, her stiletto heels clicking on the asphalt and rested her long slim fingers on the car handle. Icy cold eyes looked hatefully at her daughter. 'Don't you ever shut up? You are 16 for God's sake, you know nothing about life.' Her fist clenched, inches from Lisa's face. 'All I hear from you is endless chatter, nonsense I can do without. Make yourself scarce. I want to be on my own!' They stared hard at each other, hostility rising between them.

Lisa sighed. 'I'm going to see Gran.'

Moira's tone was spiteful. 'You can do what you bloody like!'

Lisa would allow her mother a cooling down period. It had happened before. Her mother would again point out that she was a true example of her Gran who was tolerated rather than liked and respected rather than loved. But Lisa had a special affection for Gran and because the old lady took pride in preparing Lisa for adult life and embodied her right to the status of Grandmother their relationship was close. Yet there was much more to it, this bonding that meant so much to both of them.

As tired as she was Gran listened to Lisa's graphic account of the evidence. Herself incapable of fuss or exaggeration, she marvelled at the articulate way Lisa gave details of the trial. Lisa's expressive blue eyes were full of light. Tendrils of fair hair brushed against her flushed skin and she had an endearing habit of gently sliding it behind her ears. She smiled often and talked incessantly.

'Gran, I'm not sorry for what I've done. You taught me all about honesty. When I was giving evidence I could feel the hatred and I was scared but I was also privileged to feel able to stand there and feel confident that justice was being done.' She made no drama of this. It would be a subject for the gossips to mull over for a long time but Gran approved of every word. The buzz in the city would die down soon enough.

****

Moira was standing in front of the kitchen window, one hand clenched by her side and in the other a bloody Mary. Venetian blinds shut out the afternoon sun and the room was in semi darkness. It was easy to make out that she was angry and her eyes were red with weeping. 'You have ruined my life.' Lisa sensed that the confrontation was far reaching. 'Everything I have wanted you have taken away from me. First Tony, oh you couldn't let that go could you?' She slumped into a kitchen chair.

'Mom, let me explain.' Moira rose unsteadily. Lisa was tall but her mother, despite her lack of height, had bitter enmity to add to her strength and pushed her away. Lisa persisted. 'I didn't want you to get hurt again. I saw him with her lots of times. Everyone knew, even at the gym; it wasn't fair on you.'

'Don't you see!' Moira mocked her. 'I knew, my wide circle of acquaintances knew, but it didn't matter. I needed him. Just as I need Phil.'

She helped herself to another drink. 'And you have done it again, only this time Phil won't be back for six years, will he? Did you think about that when you were giving evidence, so prim and demure?' Her eyes narrowed. 'I am on my own again.' For a moment she remained silent whilst in a spurt of neatness she arranged a bunch of dahlias in a vase on the worktop. Composed, Lisa whispered, 'Mom, Phil took the car after he had been drinking, drove at speed, knocked down a young woman and left her to die. And you expected me to keep quiet? What sort of person do you think I am?'

Moira reached for the scissors and snipped off the stalks. 'He said he was innocent.' Lisa was regaining her nerve.

'Well he would, wouldn't he?'

Moira whipped round, she hated her daughter's flippancy. Her face was contemptuous. 'You must take me for a fool. Your mouth will be the death of you. Learn to keep it shut.' She poked a finger at the slim figure before her. 'You have caused me no end of trouble with mouthing off, perpetrating slander and lies against people I love. I want you out of my life.'

Lisa felt sick. Her stomach churned, her throat felt choked and dry. This was not fair. It was so sudden. She was in shock. This one-sided love was what she was used to; sulkiness and reserve was what she had grown up with but in the complicated world of her teens this was disconcerting. Tears were welling and she braced herself. 'I don't want to leave you; you're upset. Anyway, I have nowhere to go.'

Moira sneered. 'You can go and live with your Gran. You always were her little pet, her little darling, someone to spoil, to mould. You are grown-up now, well able to stand on your own two feet. Out!' She pushed her roughly towards the door leading to the hall and as Lisa turned to plead with her she felt a sharp pain above her right eye. Moira had lost control; she had lashed out. The scissors fell to the floor.

Lisa vomited. She climbed the stairs, her whole body shaking. Her room looked exactly the same as she had left it that morning. Posters covered the walls and fluffy bears and dolphins were scattered indiscriminately on, in and around drawers.

She wept, gathering armfuls of clothes, sweeping toiletries into a backpack and thrusting a diary, notes and a bank book into a money bag. Her mother was screaming at her, 'I never want to see you or hear your voice again.' Lisa halted in the hallway but was forced outside. The large oak door slammed behind her.

It was difficult to assess what to do. A backward glance at the house caused her to wonder. Would she ever return? Would she want to, to the pent-up anger and the drinking and the bad memories and the outrage of innocence?

She was aware as the damp grass on the green seeped into her shoes that there was a cool breeze and how unsuitable her clothes were. 'Dress smartly for the trial,' Moira had told her. Her skirt and blouse were flimsy and she pulled her coat tightly round her slight frame and shivered. Her head ached as the bump over her right eye became inflamed. This was a ridiculous situation to be in. In the last eight years she had borne as good-humouredly as she could the cruelty and vulgarity of her mother's lifestyle but she had never thought of leaving home. At times she had been suspicious of Tony and afraid of Phil and she was frightened now.

Would she be able to make Gran understand? Gran's view of life, her respect for honesty had rendered herself at odds with people. Her observations, her love of truth had ruined any illusions she had of a decent relationship with her daughter and Moira hated her.

'I never want to hear your voice again.' Her mother's scream echoed in Lisa's aching head. Why bother to speak? Why try to explain anything, to anyone. Words. 'In your own words,' the Prosecutor had said. She had processed them into lies. 'And after all what is a lie? Tis but the truth in masquerade.' Lord Byron featured high in her studies, but would she be returning to college? Lisa thought not; she had made a decision. She would never speak again, not until Phil was released from prison; she was solely to blame for his conviction and there was a price to be paid. It was fully intended and fully dreaded.

She had to go somewhere. It was barely 4.30. Should she take a bus? No. There needed to be a considerable distance between them, not just a stone's throw, but somewhere away from suspecting, inquisitive people and good intentions which are for ever going wrong. It was a long walk to the rail station. The monitors displayed the destinations; she would pick one at random – Sheffield.

The grey-haired, hefty gentleman at the ticket office smiled as she scribbled on a piece of paper "Single please". That was easy but it was only the beginning.

In Sheffield so many people were bustling around, dashing and weaving, pushing and jostling their way across from the station to the bus terminal. Everybody with somewhere to go. There was a deli and in the warmth of the waiting room she ate her sandwich and drank her Coke, and listened to the chatter. In the distance came the sound of a guitar and she moved nearer to where a solitary figure, tall, intent on his strumming, his guitar strung across his lean shoulders, played a popular melody. His brown hair was cropped short and he had a solemnity, rare in one so young, Lisa thought.

Her contribution to his collection of coins clinked in his bag. He smiled without looking at her. Lisa sat opposite him for quite a while, her right hand cupped over her eye. It was sore and she felt conspicuous perched on the hard bench. Was this the right thing to do? Ought she to go back and put an end to this ridiculous pledge? A door slammed behind her, shops were closing. It was time to move.

Slowly she rose, lifted her bag and straightened her back. There was no point in rapid movement, she reflected; where should she go? The purpose of her being here was still obscure but she would stay with it until it bored or frightened her. Her thoughts had distracted her and the guitarist had gone.

At the far end of the station she saw him striding away, his ragged jeans overlapping his boots and wearing a coat decorated with colourful symbols. Was he homeless? If so where did he go? There was only one way to find out and that was to follow him. He moved quickly up the steep flight of steps and Lisa almost had to run to keep up with him. He became aware of her when the sound of her heels echoed on the cobbles on the approach to the cafe. It was dusk and the murmuration of starlings gave life to the starless sky. The thin blouse and linen suit had provided little warmth and the cool night air was causing her to shiver. What, she wondered, had happened to her self-respect?

He pushed the door, holding it open for her. The warmth in the cafe was comforting. Patiently she stood by the long counter and waited. Chips were bubbling in the pan and a few customers were seated at plastic tables on battered unmatched chairs all needing a coat of paint. Pasties, pizzas and cakes were neatly stacked in covered containers and piles of crockery stood in readiness against a white brick wall. She studied the room too attentively, she realized; it was one way of gathering her thoughts. 'Hi!' The assistant waited. Lisa opened her mouth to speak and remembered; her eyes widened then she pointed to the pizza. 'Chips?' he asked. Smiling, she shook her head.

Settling in the corner, she considered her situation. In cash she had enough for a week perhaps but there was sufficient in the bank. Gran's gift of an endowment 'for when you reach 15 and university or whatever you decide to do' would tide her over.

Gary had been preoccupied. This was his time with his friends; when he discussed community projects and homelessness schemes. But his curiosity had been aroused by the girl sitting by the window. Alone, bedraggled like a straw in the wind. Vulnerable maybe. He hardly expected to be so concerned but he was. She carried little in the way of baggage; her clothing was unsuitable and her eye was turning a bruised blue. There was excessive concentration on her face as she stirred her tea. Gary was inquisitive, but more than that he wanted to help.

Propping his guitar on the chair, he approached her table. He leaned over and pondered the girlish twist of her hair in the fold of her neck. Quietly he asked 'Are you alright?' He waited, no answer came. 'You see,' he continued. 'You passed three cafes on the way and I have a feeling that you followed me here. Am I right?' Lisa looked down at his slender fingers on her arm, the hands of a stranger, and swallowed hard. Her lack of experience caught her unawares but she had to be bold. Raising her hand to her throat she shook her head. It surprised him; he frowned. Fumbling for her diary, she scribbled "I can't speak!" adding "but I can hear very well." Gary puffed out his cheeks. 'Thank God,' he smiled.

'Is it a temporary thing?' Lisa held her palms outwards, shrugging her shoulders. She sipped her tea slowly, averting her eyes; she needed time to think.

'What's your name?' He waited.

'Where are you from?' She pressed her lips together.

It was obvious to him that she was anxious and apprehensive.

'Are you running away?' The diary remained on the table.

'I'm Gary.' The attempt to be friendly was ineffectual. She rubbed her hand over her eye. Lisa hated being rude. She would have to respond in some way. Was he being curious or benevolent? 'How old are you?' There was no urgency in his voice. Was this the starting point, she wondered? Gary studied the contour of her face as she turned away from him. What was it that he had reckoned over the years? If you want people to be comfortable in your company, keep your distance. He suddenly sat back in his chair. Indecisive blue eyes met those of a determined grey. Lisa's finger reached towards her mouth and reassurance was needed.

He called across the cafe for Tiz. A slim girl with closely cropped hair and numerous ear- piercings sat beside him. Gary smiled. 'I think this young lady is in need of a friend. I am trying to establish what we can do to help her. She is not able to speak but perhaps we can determine what she wants.'

Tiz was obliging. 'I'm Teresa but nobody calls me that. Just Tiz. What can we do to help?' A change of name, that's a start, thought Lisa. Her name was Elise but no one called her that either. She made her first decision; she would be known as Ellie.

Tearing a sheet from her diary, she stifled a sob. Why did she want to cry? It might be the chance for a new beginning; no one should waste tears when making a fresh start.

"My name is Ellie," she wrote. "I am 16 and I want to do something more with my life. I am putting the past behind me. I have nowhere to go!" Tiz handed the paper to Gary.

'No problem.' He patted her hand reassuringly. 'You are among friends. Now we will find you somewhere to stay.' How peculiar, mused Gary, that this silent waif could have made such an impression on him.

****

The party was in full swing when Ellie and Gary arrived.

A journey through dim streets and narrow cobbled ginnels led them to a terraced house in the city centre, very safely secured with mortice locks and shutters. This was to be her home for two nights, then the occupants moved on, no reason was given. Ellie tried hard not to smile too appreciatively; she wanted to stay alert. She had no misgivings as yet but she was shrewd enough to realize that she needed friends.

During their short walk Gary had made polite and informative conversation and this dumb game of hers was beginning to excite her. She reminded herself that she was pleased not to have spent the night on the streets, that something to do with pride would stop her from being pursued by unscrupulous people.

Her bed was hard. Lumps of straw dug into her and it was so narrow that she shoved it against the wall and during the night bitterly regretted it. Dampness from the walls created dark stains on her borrowed sleeping bag. The entire life of the street had joined the party downstairs; she dare not venture out of her room for more blankets. She was cold and hungry. Still, she sighed, I shall be here for the rest of the night, longing for a hot breakfast, but safe.

Ellie slept for less than a couple of hours. Sometimes she would pace the room or stare out of the grimy windows. The noise was deafening, like Atlantic rollers bursting in her ears. When she heard the door open she did not look up at once. When she did, she froze. Four youths, uninvited and unwelcome, half fell against the worm-eaten chest, belching and staggering. She drew herself up, covering her body and, folding her arms across her chest, made for the door. 'No need for that. Go back to bed. You are perfectly safe with us.' He at least appeared sober. 'We're turning in now.'

Ellie backed away from him; she couldn't shout. She drew herself up to a greater rigidity and stared hard into deep brown eyes. He looked serious and boyish. 'It's OK, really.'

It was the smell of toast and the dryness in her mouth that coaxed her out of bed. She strode over the four bodies, stretched out like contented cats, gently snoring, fully clothed and odorous. They lay on a moth-eaten carpet weaving dreams of life.

Ellie sat down at the table littered with cereal packets and cartons of Soya milk. The two girls at the sink stared at her in amazement. 'Hell,' followed by an expletive which would become as familiar to her as breathing. Jan, a tall blonde, wearing a hideous skeleton tee shirt which hung from her scraggy arms, repeated herself. 'Hell, I'd forgotten about you. I'm supposed to give you a message.'

There was a pause whilst she returned the pan to the stove and searched through the pile of papers near the sink. 'Believe me there is so much to do in this place and I'm running the whole damn show.' She sniffed. 'I have it.' The note was covered in cooking oil and some words were smeared and difficult to read. Ellie was to wait for Gary until 5pm.

There was little conversation or contact. Jan was flushed and stressed out. Ellie was practically ignored. She ate her cornflakes, enjoyed two slices of toast and marmalade and drank three cups of tea. Jan's companion, wearing a gilet and torn dungarees, took Ellie's hand in hers. 'I am no judge but you don't strike me as being silly. I think you have good sense. How old are you? Sixteen? You don't always know why things happen but when they do you can either accept them or drive them away!' Ellie removed her hand and smiled. She was not attracted by physical contact from a woman, her mother had never held her hand since babyhood but it had never been an issue; she was unable to explain why.

Nobody suggested that she clear up the mess after the night's celebrations but she did. She was grateful for the hospitality despite the unsatisfactory sleeping arrangements and the vulgar companions. A lukewarm bath soothed her itching (she blamed the straw) and her eye felt a little better despite the loss of sleep.

'You're tired,' Gary remarked. 'Sorry. I didn't know about the party.' Ellie had thought of him as a street musician, even a beggar, but sitting with him in the cafe where they had met the previous evening she realized that he had many sides to his nature. He had an obsession with homelessness, condemned cowardice and laziness, and spoke with authority on the economic plight of nations. His hands accentuated his finer points and Ellie noted the strong contours of his face and his small, even teeth.

There was lighthearted gossip among the group of friends and amusing and pleasing topics. They shared a pizza and salad washed down with fruit juice. It was hard not to join in the discussion and harder still not to appear bored and for those who were unaware that Ellie did not speak she must have appeared to be ignorant or stupid. However, the sense of Gary's friendliness dispelled any doubts.

It wasn't an easy thing to do – to return to the cold, austere house with the straw mattress and the stained bath. On the whole she thought this was quite proper until something could be sorted out. Ellie put out the light, said her prayers and slept.

'What do you know about the music scene?' Gary asked indulgently. Leaving the house she had bid goodbye to Jan and her friend and at about eleven accompanied Gary to the bus station. It appeared to her that music and politics spread jointly through his life. There was so much she wanted to know and simply by listening to others she gained an inkling of his ambitions to help the underprivileged.

Beneath all his activities of debate and self-assurance, however, she sensed a sadness. There were long silences but he tried to amuse her and she marvelled at the generous way he treated her. No one had asked her for money and her contribution to the cafe bill had been refused.

Yet here he was again playing to the crowds in and milling around the terminal. She should go to the market, he suggested, buy some warm clothing from the charity shops and some decent footwear. 'I'll meet you back here at 6pm.' She refused his offer of £20 and tapped her bag. 'Take care of it, be careful,' he warned.

Ellie loved the market. Coloured fabrics, coloured fruits, coloured awnings, coloured people, Sheffield was alive with shoppers. Stallholders yelled their wares, barrow boys flirted with customers, old women shuffled, headscarves tied securely under their chins, and old men grumbled and shoved everybody who got in their way. There was laughter and sarcasm and biting wit.

She purchased three sweaters, two pairs of jeans and a waterproof jacket from a charity shop and a pair of Doc Martens from a sale. Her mother would have been appalled; a leper colony would have been preferable to a charity shop. Words were not necessary; everything she required was hands-on, easily available.

In Woolworths she chose a postcard view of Derbyshire along with a book of stamps and posted it after watching tiny children at play near the fountain. Gran would not judge her. The bitterness she felt for her mother was raw and it was to Gran that she owed an explanation and it was important to let her know that she was safe.

'Ah, that is what I was afraid of, a shopaholic.' Gary pursed his mouth. He would argue that he had seen prettier girls, girls with lovelier eyes and a naive elegance but he hadn't. She turned heads. It occurred to Ellie that there was no reason why she couldn't settle here as he carried her bags and his guitar to the cafe.

Perhaps they had mistaken her lack of speech for shyness but his friends' reaction to her slowly changed. She thought at first it hardly mattered but she did not want to offend anyone. Her clothes made all the difference. The well cut, smart city suit, the chiffon scarf, the high-heeled shoes, the velveteen blouse were discarded, replaced by tee shirts and jeans. The bags were strewn about the floor of the cafe and she agreed to a swop. One sweater for one pair of tartan trews.

It amused her when Gary spoke to her as if she was a child, touching her arm as if wanting to protect her. Yet he would be in no more than the mid-twenties. He had some good news for her. She was to stay with an elderly woman for a short period until something more suitable could be sorted out.

Bella was wizened, bombastic and deaf. She was reluctant

to divulge her age other than to say that she was pre-Titanic. Everything about the terrace house was old, from the faded paintwork to the peeling woodwork, but Ellie was grateful for a decent bed and clean sheets. Her bedroom had the feel of olden times. Photographs were displayed over the bed and a clock which was an hour slow was the centrepiece on the bookshelf. It reminded her of the little boy who preferred the clock without the pendulum because, although it didn't tell the time, it went more easily than before.

Unusual carved ornaments sat proudly on what her Gran called a whatnot and between the two sash windows a small tea table covered with a crocheted cloth was home to a huge Toby-jug. The wooden bed was covered with a knitted spread arranged in squares and the floor was scattered with rugs of various sizes. Lavender pillows were neatly arranged on the ottoman. A collage rested on the mantel above the black iron fireplace facing the bed. This was to be her room for the time being. To Ellie it was a step back in time. She was surrounded by the sight and smell of decay; she shivered; she would wither away here; she was 16, this was not what she was used to.

Gary consoled her. 'The house has been sold. It won't be for long.'

'She's very thin,' Bella shouted. Her hearing aid whistled repeatedly. 'I'll make sure she gets plenty of good wholesome food inside her.'

Halfway through the meal Ellie rose from the supper table. The burning sensation in her chest wasn't easing. She held her hand to her stomach; this gesture implied that she was full. It had nothing to do with her discomfort. The cafe had provided healthy vegetarian food but here she was being given fatty, cheap cuts of meat, stew that had been on the simmer for days, and pigs' trotters and brawn. In the two months Ellie had been here her attempts at presenting Bella with a number of pasta dishes such as spaghetti and macaroni had failed miserably and on the last occasion she spat it out quite forcibly, cursing under her breath. Her favourite black pudding appeared on her plate.

Now Ellie was unhappy. She had tried to escape from this, having things forced upon her. Yet she was so grateful to have a roof over her head and to feel safe. Now the whole place seemed to hurt her. How could that be? Bella did nothing now but knit and cook, and after shopping and cleaning Ellie was bored. Most of all she missed having friends and especially Gary.

The greater part of her wanted to look for work. This thought led her to gather up all her courage and enthusiasm but the search for a job was difficult. The domestic agencies preferred older people, the restaurants were put off by her silence and hotels wanted all night cover.

Bella snored loudly in the rocking chair. Was it the thought of growing old that alarmed her? Was the abundant evidence of ageing in Bella frightening? Was the polishing of furniture and the dusting of bric-a-brac the only thing that mattered? Plus the routine of washing and ironing?

Gary, as always, walked too fast for Ellie. Perhaps it was madness, he admitted, to expect a young, lively girl to live with an old woman. It wasn't ideal but it was a safe house and he knew that the two of them were kind despite their incompatibility. However, the good news was that Jan had taken overall charge of the cafe and had offered Ellie a job in the kitchen. Actually it was an opportunity to repay her dues and for Jan to assert herself. 'You're a demon for work,' she laughed appreciatively.

The curious tactics of some customers were a puzzle to Ellie. Bas frightened her. A skinhead with large hairy hands and each finger tattooed with a letter. In her naivety she was a while figuring out that it spelled "bastards" and soon realized that his rages could easily spin out of control. He could not tolerate criticism. She was also perplexed by talk of Criminal Trespass and Protected Intending Occupier but Gary explained it in that gentle tone she had grown used to.

She settled happily in the spare room above the cafe and thanked God for His timing of this intervention. Tiz was the first to offer friendship. Together they spent the whole afternoon in the Art Museum and observing at first with only half an interest Ellie soon became aware that Tiz derived much pleasure from discussing Romanticism. 'Do you like art? It is something I've always enjoyed!' She moved slowly around the gallery. 'Thanks for coming.'

Boo (whose real name was Bonita) was dark skinned and agile, half Spanish and excitable. In contrast to Tiz, who wore her hair closely cropped with numerous piercings in her ears, nose and lips, she had black hair which hung in a thick plait down to her waist. But it was Fab (who confessed to being Amanda) who was to be the one to bring heartache to Ellie. A student of philosophy specializing in Fabianism, a political doctrine which favoured gradual social progress and change, she explained at length to Ellie. Gary was unimpressed and quietly told her so.

What they did best was to play together in a band. They succeeded in achieving two or three gigs a month and practised in the old chapel hall. Gary was a shrewd and tactful organizer but they were yet to take the world by storm.

Rev played drums. He could often be seen on his haunches, his fingers drumming to a tune in his head. The naevus which had been removed from his neck had left an unsightly scar which stretched across his throat. The mild jibes about a hangman's rope compelled him to wear a choker and because it was usually white he was christened Rev. It actually suited him.

Bas was overcharged with energy. His stamina as the lead singer was remarkable. He would jerk his whole body and pace the length of the stage with sheer pizzazz. Often he would spring alive with anger, his eyes would narrow and he would explode.

Over the months Ellie had time to study her companions. 'We don't discuss our private lives,' Boo declared, 'but we know lots of things about each other!' Somehow they found it easier to talk to her now that she whisked around the cafe tables and mopped the floor. The young men teased her, the women were vigilant and Gary was amused when her cheeks flushed and her eyes flashed.

****

'He seems to have some hidden axes to grind,' Rev was complaining about Bas. 'He has no right to turn down the tour of Ireland. I say we go ahead anyway. This reluctance to change, inability to mix with other bands, it's a bit childish.'

'He's right you know,' Boo sighed. 'We are pretty well-known over there, we can manage him.'

'The crux of the matter is we can't get a word in edgeways with Bas around. He never really stops being a front man and he gossips.'

'Gossip is natural!' commented Boo.

'The bearer of gossip lets out secrets,' added Fab.

"Oh, yes," Ellie would have agreed to that!

Gary waited until Ellie's head appeared over the counter.

He leaned over. She had been replacing cans and her face was red with bending. He startled her. 'Do you have a passport?' She shook her head. 'No, I didn't think so. I'll get you a form.' Here was the short cut to her ambition to travel. Was she going to Ireland? She gave him a cheeky smile. It was all very well and she was excited at the prospect but she had so little to give in return. Having no demands on life meant that she could take so much for granted. Still, she was capable of contributing to the kitty and she paid her rent for the small room upstairs and felt as much as anyone that she belonged.

She watched the turn of his head as he walked towards the door and then looked at her folded hands across the worktop. She gripped them tightly. How she longed to speak but instead mouthed "thank you". 'Oh, yes,' he paused with an afterthought. 'The Punx picnic will be our next gig. It's August 1st at Nottingham!'

'Punx piss-up, you mean,' shouted Bas.

'For you, maybe,' muttered Boo.

Gary's patience was more than usually overtaxed when the date of the picnic drew near. Everyone talked about it, everyone wanted to take part, everyone wanted centre stage but no one wanted to organise. 'What is there to organise anyway?' Bas snorted. It was impossible to take him seriously, the ill-mannered lout who had neither good looks nor good sense but could smell trouble a mile off and shoved his way through major disturbances.

Ellie was amused to discover that some women found his volatile moods attractive and he turned out to be an excellent lyricist. Fab wasn't sure about her commitment any more. 'It never occurs to anyone that I have a life apart from this poxy band.' Her bright red hair, tucked neatly under a bandeau, shone beneath the fluorescent light in the cafe. 'I've been hanging around with you lot for two years and the total sum of my life is a bed-sit in a crummy block of flats.' This was no moment for self analysis. No one was listening and no one cared.

Rev poked his fingers down his collar. 'The only thing that matters is to believe in what you are doing. I want to outrage the world, make people understand about injustice and torture, and this is the only way I know how.' He drummed his fingers on the plastic table and tapped his feet.

Cheddar was new to Ellie. A little odd, with piercing blue eyes and a constant sniff. 'He's a roadie, really,' Boo explained, 'but a qualified electrician so he's good to have around; sound checks and that sort of thing and an excellent guitarist; always backs away from the stage though. No confidence.' Ellie sighed. The intricacies of life on the road escaped her.

Cheddar spoke lazily. 'How are we getting to Nottingham?' Gary grinned at the earnest, boyish features.

'National Express.'

'Bloody Hell,' they chorused. 'It takes years, all round the houses, through all the villages. No way.'

'It's cheap.' Gary looked charily around him. 'You could hitch.'

'We're hitching.' Boo smiled at Tiz. Ellie looked expectantly. "You are coming with me?" Gary straightened his back. 'Maybe another time.'

CHAPTER TWO

"Speech is silver, silence is golden." (Proverbial.)

There were hundreds of wild, noisy participants when Ellie and the band arrived at the park. She had this preposterous notion that it was a free-for-all; she did not believe that sharing a room with twelve sweaty bodies was a good idea and she tried to make this crystal clear to Gary. He did not reprove her; how could he? Considering the frustration of her silence all he could do was to take into account her feelings and avoid confounding her.

'Well, you sure come alive when you are drunk.' Fab cuddled up to Rev. She embraced him, kissed him and buried her elfin face in his neck. Others were lolling on sleeping bags drinking scrumpy. Bas was naked apart from a pair of boxer shorts. Gary was sitting with his back to the wall, his eyes closed. Ellie felt it necessary to absent herself; the sweat and the smell of alcohol was a sickening and menacing reminder of Phil. Gary raised a bottle to his lips.

She had never kissed a man; not the sort of kiss that took your breath away or set the heart racing, or fed the sensual imagination with the tip of a tongue. Nor had she wanted to until now. Rev and Fab were locked in their own world. It was the sounds, not the sight that was providing the stimulus but she had to brush them away. She mustn't weaken, not yet.

Gary for a while avoided her eyes then slowly moved

towards her and took her arm. There was a gentleness about his touch as he led her down the stairs and into the street. It was this action that warmed her heart, an act of accessible love, a love that made her content and happy. There was no need for words; there was mutual understanding in their eyes. It was this show of respect that made her realize how lucky she was and because of it she felt protected.

They walked hand in hand past the derelict houses, past a small clearing set among car repair shops and a brick factory. She knew him as a man who was naturally attracted to helping the underprivileged, unable to resist appeals for help, but little about him personally. Ellie liked clear- cut situations.

A chilly breeze blew through the darkness and she moved nearer to him. "How old are you?" she mouthed. He looked into her large, deep blue eyes.

'Twenty-four.' He waited for more questions. "Was he married? Where did he live? With anyone?" He walked in silence for a few seconds. She was waiting in anticipation and the breeze danced through her fair hair and wisps settled on her pink cheeks. He shook his head, almost amused at her.

The city was waking up, buses spewed out fumes, the street cleaner sprayed the gutters with chemically treated water and the dark gave way to the first oyster-shell moment of dawn. Ellie wore a dignified expression, almost aristocratic, Gary thought, as he told her that he had a flat in the city, that he was unmarried, lived alone and was willing to answer any questions. Somehow he felt that he could not throw away such a chance as this.

It had occurred to her that she had begun to sentimentalise about Gary. There was no need. Reason had always dominated her emotions; there was plenty of time. The simplicity of his lifestyle comforted her. Together they returned to the revolting shabbiness of the crumbling building and the empty cigarette packets and beer cans littering the floor. Bas passed a grimy hand across his watery, bloodshot eyes. Ellie had this vision of a nomadic tribe of homeless alcoholics and she laughed silently. She felt intoxicated by the early morning sunlight as it filtered through the tiny blackened windows, and even in this room felt at peace. There was nothing to do but sleep.

****

'Is it true?'

'You have to be joking.'

'Where the hell will we get the money from?'

'A bus, you must be out of your ******* mind.'

There were obscenities, half amusing, half exasperating, coarse scatological language from the men and sarcastic, caustic comments from the women. Gary leaned against the window. Bas waited for his reaction. He looked around, his face was set with grim determination.

Ellie turned the cafe sign to "Closed" and bolted the door. She was tired this evening. They were long days, 8am till 8pm, but she had two free days each week, free meals, a comfortable room and a wage. She had written a long letter to Gran. 'I feel that I am my own person now. I have a job, good honest friends and feel that my life is taking shape. You once said that a kind word is like a Spring Day. I have heard lots of kind words, so please don't worry about me.' She described her friends and reassured Gran that she was in good health. She did not mention the pledge of silence. This would be too much betrayal of emotion.

The friends were arguing, undistracted by the few remaining customers. 'I understand what you are saying,' Gary acknowledged. 'All I object to is that you went ahead without any discussion.'

'He's had an attack of madness if you ask me,' jeered Boo.

'Wait.' Tiz was sympathetic. 'It would be great if we could all travel together. At least we would all arrive at the same time and we wouldn't have the pantomime we had in France last year.'

'Because,' grunted Cheddar, 'Fab had this thing with the Gallic charmer who spent half the night in the can.'

'Can we get back to the business in hand?' begged Gary.
Rev requested a hearing. 'Hang on. Bas has bought a bus
...'

'No. I bloody haven't, it's a coach.'

'Oh, my God. How old?'

'1970.'

A chorus of 1970 rang in Ellie's ears as she put away the
cutlery. She smiled with amusement and loosened her hair.
It hung tousled against her flushed cheeks. Her blue eyes
searched for Gary and he glanced at her affectionately. Rev
dragged his chair away from the table and opened the
door for the last of the customers to leave. Boo made a
spiteful remark about Bas and his frame of mind, and he
did something quite extraordinary. He kissed her full on the
mouth. 'Ugh,' she gulped, wiping her lips with the back of
her hand. She rose to her full height, anger surfacing in her
dark eyes. Suddenly Gary raised his voice as Boo gripped
her guitar case and beat Bas forcefully about the head. Ellie
grabbed Boo by her long plait and pushed her into a chair.
Pinning down her shoulders, she faced her and wrapped her
long legs around Boo's knees. The Spanish eyes grew darker
and bigger and her obscenities grew louder until Ellie flung
herself on her knees before her and hugged her. It was over
in seconds and crying bitterly, Boo left the room. Ellie could
offer no words of comfort. Bas nursed the abrasions to his
face; sometimes he carried his grudges a bit too far. He
stood up. 'Leave it,' demanded Gary.

How extraordinary to feel this way, observed Ellie. To
her this was almost a flashback but she did not want to
remember the incident all those months ago. 'OK,' said a
gentle voice enquiringly. She stopped shaking.

'Well, what next?' Bas continued even more vehemently.
'This coach is pre-motorway and built like a brick shithouse.
Mustard has checked out the engine and the chassis and all
we need to do, he says, is to check the injector pipes for
leaks.'

'Who is this Mustard then?' asked Rev.

'He's a mechanic, you remember him from Sprung Rhythm, ALF in prison for a while.' Gary pressed his palms together.

'How much?'

'Well, nothing really.'

'No.'

Bas was eager for more involvement. 'It's on loan.' Gary knew that it would mean relatively less problems if they were all together and he and Bas both put their best efforts into the group. 'Mustard, he would no doubt be collateral, right?'

'We might as well take a look.'

'It's on the rec just behind Ma Bella's.' They stormed from the café, both girls linking arms with Ellie, and Boo insisting that Bas was dangerous and that she wouldn't stand for his insulting behaviour much longer.

It had been a day of intermittent sun and rain. The dull comfort Ellie had gained from Bella's hospitality was brought home to her as they approached the row of gloomy, run-down houses – decay that can neither be mapped nor defined as slums.

It was a case of wading through large puddles of oil and sludge and her sense of absurdity when she saw the vehicle caused her to stop dead in her tracks. Surrounding it were broken cars of all descriptions; wrecks, insides scattered among piles of bricks and tiles and mounds of grass – home to nuts and bolts and rusty doors. Ellie looked in bewilderment towards the men.

'I've seen much worse,' Rev enthused, kicking the tyres with his heavy boots.

'It's a lousy sickly green,' berated Tiz.

'Look. It's serviceable; we don't want any of your psychedelic colours; it's a pull for the police,' argued Bas.

Gary had risked crawling underneath and paused with his foot on the step. 'We'll see what Mustard has to say before we decide.'

The mechanic arrived within half an hour. He walked towards them with shoulders hunched and with a slight limp. His hair and beard were ginger and he had a kind, rugged face and a confident air about him. 'Hi, ladies,' he beamed.

Gary shook his hand. 'What do you reckon?' Somehow there seemed to be an unspoken agreement, nothing was decided in words but the looks which passed between them belied their intentions.

'My general rule is this.' Mustard straightened his back. 'Don't buy anything foreign and if it works, leave it. I'm dead keen to see this on the road. If I'm in any doubt about the engine's efficiency I'll let you know. Must admit it looks OK to me.'

'Bas said it was a coach,' Tiz whined.

'He lied,' Boo snorted. Gary was one for compromise, a shrewd judge of character. He allowed his friends their eccentricities but they all had to fit in with one another. As the men drove off Boo stared after them gloomily. 'We'll be a bit congested. I'm not sharing with Bas; he's got some filthy habits.'

'Oh, come on, you must,' Tiz pleaded.

'There's no must about it; if Gary wants me in this band then we'll have to come to some understanding.'

Boo fiddled with her hair; her dark eyes flashed under the street lights as she struggled to keep her footing in the rough road up to Ma Bella's. Even more green paint had disappeared from the ramshackle door and dilapidated windows since Ellie was last here. The threadbare cleanliness was so pathetically obvious in the sitting room and she remembered the kindness which was shown to her and felt uneasy inside. Yet how could she run away from a guilt that didn't exist?

Ellie made tea and cut thick slices of malt loaf. 'No, I'm not tired.' Bella was adamant. 'I get upset, you know. My eldest daughter rarely comes to visit me. It's the life they lead, you know,' she sighed. "If only you lived a little nearer," they say. Well, I don't and that's that!' She shoved a loose strand of hair under her scarf and her hearing aid crackled like a firework. 'What about her?' She pointed an arthritic finger at

Ellie in the kitchen. 'Contrary Miss. She could have stayed, you know. I said to Gary, she won't get far not being able to speak.' She considered this for a short while. 'Poor lass.' She rocked gently, her gnarled hands clasped together. For the remainder of the visit she slept, gaping like a goldfish, and they drank their tea and ate the malt loaf, left the kitchen tidy and added coal to the fire.

'Is it right you are in trouble with the law?' Gary enquired.

'Naw, not any more.' Mustard shrugged. 'I went to Leeds, squatted and was charged under Section 10 Criminal Law Act.'

'That's the Obstructing Officers of the Court, right?'

'Yeh, it's a tough one and I had a rough ride but I must admit I was lucky not to be convicted. I'm clean to tour.'

****

Cheddar had a grin of amusement on his face. He had occupied a whole table in the café, covering it with sketch books, coloured pens and rulers. It was after 8pm and the cafe was closed. Many thought his name was as a result of his grin but Tiz assured all and sundry it was because he cheesed everybody off, particularly this evening.

'I'm the one at the Art College,' she said peevishly. 'I should be the one doing that.'

'It needn't be a bone of contention,' pleaded Rev. 'There is something of your own that you can do.' Boo giggled.

'It's like colouring class at kindergarten.' Bas made a move from his seat by the door and Boo slid between Rev and Mustard.

'Look,' Cheddar put his hands firmly on the table. 'We have to plan our layout of the bus. We want a scaled down drawing of the first floor plan.' Ellie sat opposite. A little of his exasperation melted. 'So,' he continued, 'everything and everyone has to be catered for.'

Bas arrived with the alcohol and they gave him their

undivided attention. Cheddar continued. 'We have to include all vertical structures and match the fittings to them. I shall be asking for any reasonable suggestions!' He stood up and folded his arms.

'I'm thinking of the time when the old converted fire engine got stuck in the bog near Fort William after we had cruised halfway round Scotland with a 15 degree tilt! It murdered the suspension,' roared Rev. His laughter was infectious.

'Yes, well,' mocked Cheddar.

'Bunks, how many? Do we need a fire? A pot belly stove will burn just about anything. Furnishings, cupboards, seats, worktops, floor covering, windows? Ideas on a piece of paper, pronto. Let's get going.' Everyone was talking at once and fighting like toddlers over highlighters. It worried Ellie that they might consider her pampered and purposeless so she wrote on her pad, "I can sew."

'Brilliant,' praised Tiz. 'We'll have curtains.'

'Oh, God,' groaned Bas, 'and colour coordinates and scatter cushions.'

'Piss off,' swore Boo. Bas and Rev cavorted around the room, hands on hips.

'We can have floral flounces and dusky pink drapes,' Bas lisped and Rev, quite taken with Bas's fluttering eyelashes, purred and gently pushed his arm. 'Oh and a frill at the bottom of my bunk.' This was greeted with general laughter. It was a lively and hilarious evening, Bas burnishing his wits and Rev seemingly enchanted with this paunchy camp skinhead.

Jan appeared in the kitchen doorway, leaning against the door jamb. 'Well I'm so glad that you are all having a good time. Can anybody join in?'

'Steady,' warned Boo as Jan staggered across the room.

'I am steady,' giggled Jan. It would be impossible to say how much alcohol Jan consumed. Ellie found it strange that she drank so much. Perhaps it was to break the loneliness of losing her dungareed friend who had disappeared overnight and Ellie could offer her little solace. Drink was poor compensation but it saddened Ellie to see her and was a disturbing reflection of her Mother's behaviour. She knew that Jan's responses were slowing down; she could see it in her daily routine and she was becoming careless. Jan was not yet middle-aged but the inner change was in her expression; her face was pale and her speech dull. Often she coughed and croaked throughout the night. However she was smiling as she sank into the chair.

Gary appeared shortly before ten. He stared at their jubilant faces. 'They're on their best behaviour,' Jan slurred, which told him that they had settled down after some uncivil disruption. He looked at them each in turn like an anxious hostess checking the dinner table and poured out a beer. He had a calmness and an influence which was so understated and Ellie was beginning to realize how much she missed him when he wasn't around. Yet she knew so little about him. They gathered around the tables to discuss the lasting advantages of having their own bus, the extravagances and the fund-raising. Gary produced a selection of tee shirts featuring a Dark Horse logo – a black horse with a sprinkling of grey on its coat, a roan on a white background. On the reverse a list of dates and venues was recorded.

In the beginning Ellie had not been impressed by their music, or their gigs. The nights seemed to drag on and the cacophony of sound continued to whistle in her ears well into the next day. She found it hard to defend herself against pogo dancers, sweat-infested bodies, leapfroggers and Doc Marten stompers. She was continually sticking to the floor or finding herself pinned against the bar. The arguments and fights were nonsense induced by politics and liquor. Then she discovered her niche. She was given the job of rubber-stamping at a small table by the door, secure and out of the way. She had never imagined the variety of tattoos. Often they didn't match the faces. Red roses entangled with green vines she would assume belonged to a female and a skull, a death's-head, a reminder of inescapable death, would conjure up a morbid male. Both sexes had the cephalic interest; most wore black.

At first there was a mistrust and mystification about punks but she was becoming better informed and was she right in assuming that it was a world apart but none the less a colourful aspect of anarchy?

'Is that it? Have we finished for tonight?' Gary threw back his head and stretched.

'Exactly,' yawned Bas. 'Let's have another drink.' The group declined. Jan had slipped down into the chair and the side piece was sticking into her face. Boo and Tiz lifted her gently, balancing her body between them, carrying her into the lounge and onto the sofa. The consequences would surely be felt in the morning. It was left to Ellie to cook the breakfast.

'I have something for you.' Gary leaned over as Ellie was tidying the menus and setting the tables for the following day. 'Your passport.' Ellie smiled delightedly. She studied it in great detail. "For Ireland?" she mouthed. 'No.'

She frowned. She wasn't going with them! She pushed back a wispy fringe. 'You don't need a passport for Ireland,' he mused. 'It's for later. Take good care of it, always keep it safe.'

****

'You haven't told me whether it's alright to move it,' grumbled Bas.

'No, because I don't know. We're waiting for Mustard. He has the contact.' Gary sighed. Ellie looked out of the cab window. Here on the recreation ground the litter was strewn around the bus. Scraps of food, cans, and plastic bags held down by sludgy puddles, cardboard boxes, small crates and dollops of dog excrement. Plus a supermarket trolley – not an enchanting environment. She had left behind a clean breath of well-lawned gardens and privet hedges, where the neighbours became agitated if the road was unswept and a street light was unlit. This was how they lived. She would be different. She looked round in curious wonder.

Behind the driver were four seats, two more opposite and

the rest upended and ready to be removed. The carpet was several shades of green, stained and spattered with chewing gum. All the windows, bar one, were intact and one of the skylights looked perilously on a tilt. She pointed all this out to Boo who brusquely insisted that these faults were no obstacles and she should have seen what they had had in the past.

'Yes, it's in a state of neglect but we will soon have it out right.' Tiz clambered in with a handful of drawings, dropped on her knees and pulled out a tape measure.

'I only want to say,' she hinted, 'that we have to go rooting tomorrow. I think that's the plan anyway.'

"Rooting?" Ellie turned it over in her mind.

Gary elucidated. 'Scavenge, whatever is going free.' He couldn't have known what she was thinking but somehow he seemed to be a man who had mastered the art of observation, a man who was discreet and understanding. He was writing in a small notebook. She watched him deep in concentration and wondered how much he understood his companions and how much they understood him.

Mustard arrived clutching two large holdalls and unsteadily climbed in through the emergency door. 'Grief, the amount of stress I put my body through. I've been in the loft more times this morning than I've ever been before. Up and down like a whore's drawers.'

Boo glanced in disgust. 'Dustbin language.'

'Did I say that aloud?' Mustard said apologetically. 'Must admit didn't mean to offend.' Boo had been joking, obscenities were two a penny. Ellie was reminded of Gran's disapproval of bad language and it was hard to imagine how Gran would deal with the change in her lifestyle. Ellie wrote regularly, at times economical with the truth, adding, "I'm keeping all my wits about me."

'Are we ready now?' Mustard coaxed the bus over the pitfalls and crevices and around small heaps of bricks on the rec and onto the road. Everything in the bus shook and rattled; it was noisy and had a tawdriness about it but Rev went on and on about potential and efficiency until everyone was convinced of its durability. 'It would be a good idea to tell us where we are going,' groaned Boo, slipping and sliding on the decrepit seats.

'To the cemetery,' shouted Bas.

Some things haunt you always, decided Boo and a graveyard was one of them. She was totally forbidden to enter one as a child and the taboo had stayed with her. There were no flowers on the graves. She deplored the state of the headstones and the air of decay around the epitaphs. 'Don't say we're staying here?' Her face turned white and her dark eyes burned.

Bas swore. 'Course not, stupid, we're going round the back.'

Once or twice Mustard veered off the narrow road, then with a strong grip on the brakes brought the bus to a halt outside a chapel. It was well over a hundred years old. A huge, carved wooden door led to a small entrance containing a monk's bench and original wall carvings. Stone arches had markings of faded murals but few of the original windows remained. A blue and gold painted statue stood between two ornate candlesticks.

Maggie had moved in when the chapel had been modernised but was now finding it all too much.

She was a sparrow-like woman, her sallow complexion due to too much artificial light. She made them tea. 'Your bus will be safe here. It will be a pleasant change to have some company, somebody to chat to. Keep it under the tunnel. The noise won't bother me; it sure as hell won't bother them.' She pointed towards the tiny windows of the sitting room and, on rising, swore from the vagaries of her rheumatism. 'You know you youngsters are so lucky. I've left everything too late. I have pain constantly all through my body and I regret many things. Can you imagine, to be born, to live and to die in one city, never to know what is over the horizon? Mustard is the only person I see from one week to the next.'

The theme of melancholy spurred them into action. Despite her disability, she hugged them in turn and Mustard recovered from his embarrassment and with grim reluctance pecked her on the cheek.

****

Rooting was quite an arduous business. Ellie was kitted out with well-worn jeans topped with a multicoloured jumper dragged from the sixties. High on the list were skips and neglected gardens. One held disastrous mistakes of DIY and the other contents of plastic bags which never found their way to the dustbins. They each carried a pair of marigolds and baby wipes.

Tiz selected an area of unkempt terrace houses. 'What are we looking for?' demanded Boo. She had cancelled a couple of customer appointments at the salon despite the necessity of seeking approval from her boss. It was alright for Tiz, she was an art student and had weekends off, she moaned. As for Ellie it seemed that she could come and go as she pleased. Gary, apparently, had little power to refuse. 'It's quite simple,' she observed. 'I should not be envious. Ellie is unable to speak, has yet to grow up and, for her own safety, had to be protected.'

It was necessary to climb the fence to look into the skip. The crow cawed, disturbing the quiet of the cool evening. In the foreground were the weed-choked railway lines and it became clear that trespassing was in order. Ellie had the longest legs. She sat astride the fence clinging on to the support and jumped. It was no great effort and she landed in thick grass. She squatted for a moment but in that short time knew that something was wrong. Behind her came the sound of heavy breathing. So close that she could smell the fetid breath and something prodded painfully into the small of her back. She clasped her hands in front of her and pressed her lips tight. She daren't call out. There were vigorous movements behind her and cries of enticement from Tiz and Boo. 'Come on, Boy. There's a good dog. Fetch.'

'By morning you will have forgotten all about it,' Tiz praised. 'You were so cool. Honestly.' In the light of the street lamps Boo studied Ellie. 'We slipped up a little, sorry; it's not usually that dangerous.' There was a pleading look in the sombre eyes. Ellie, remembering the chaos that followed, began to smile. They had caused upheaval to the occupants when the dog leapt over the fence after the stick, Tiz fell against the gate, which split in half, the children screamed as their pet rabbits hopped onto the main road and a swerving car hit a wheelie bin. Had it been worth it?

'We don't have a lot of time, the cafe will be closing soon,' informed Tiz.

'Well I'm not going to the cemetery, that's for sure,' insisted Boo. They picked up the stainless steel sink top and staggered on, saying little. Composed until Tiz giggled and Boo burst into laughter. They didn't find it in the skip but at the top of the garden and it was their prize for ingenuity. It was becoming clear now to Ellie that nothing was off limits.

Half a mile from the bus renovation work was in progress. Up to now the girls had done well; a daily reconnoitre and rooting had produced planks of plain pine and plywood. The past elegance of a department store was being torn apart. The exquisite pillars were cracked and discarded, the chandeliers dim and grooved in dust. The skip stood in readiness for their destruction. Boo was in a mischievous mood. She whistled through the cracks in the tall hoardings and pushed her small fingers through the holes, rocking the slats to attract attention.

Hard hatted and hard-faced, the foreman appeared, his deadpan expression unfathomable. Tiz closed in beside her, hopeful and amenable, whilst Ellie gave a reminiscent shiver at the thought of fences and their undoing. It was a course of reassurance that Ellie could remain silent, for on this occasion she would most definitely have had something to say.

He was arrogant; his cold blue eyes were deeply set in a coarse, tired face. There followed a long, unsavoury argument. The nasal grey hairs and moustache trembled as he snorted his disapproval, 'Scroungers, the lot of you.

What do you take me for? Has nobody ever told you to find work like anybody else? **** off.' There were more obscenities directed at Boo. She bristled; Tiz stepped forward, grabbed his moustache with both hands, and tugged. 'Screw you!' she retaliated and pushed him with force against the boards. There were shouts of approval from the men on the scaffolding and the girls walked away with heads held high.

'Whichever course we adopt it never seems to work,' Tiz grumbled to Rev. He leaned back from his drawing.

'I've never let it get the better of me but there are times when male ammunition is fired at us from all angles. There are even snipers on the battlefield. They creep up on us using their bloody tool as a weapon.'

'Don't I know it,' agreed Boo. 'I've carried it with me a long time.' Gary was finishing his pizza. The atmosphere was hollow. Supper was over and Ellie found it hard to keep awake.

'What are you anxious about?' queried Gary.

'I'm not, not here.' Tiz sighed. The cafe was warm. The sweet smell of Jan's plum tobacco drifted through the sitting room door. Tomorrow it would be lavender or peach. Gary pushed away his plate and put his hands behind his head. He often did that, Ellie observed.

'We're just disappointed that we came back empty-handed, that's all. It's there in the skip just waiting to be taken,' pleaded Boo.

'We've plenty to be going on with. Don't let it get to you,' Gary appealed. 'When there is an opportunity we'll move it.'

'Bastard,' Bas had gone. He responded fiercely to instances of oppression; he thwarted danger if there was any chance of a satisfactory conclusion. There may be grief but there was a sudden exodus and as the door slammed there was a clatter of heavy boots as Mustard, Cheddar, Rev, Gary and the girls chased after Bas. His one fanaticism was for the band. He was rowdy and he was proud.

The sky began to darken. Tiz was lagging behind; she

was less agile than her friends and her stomach hurt. She slowed to a halt. She had only the vaguest idea what would happen but she hoped for everyone's sake that the building site was deserted. 'With you in a moment,' panted Tiz.

The months were sliding towards autumn. Leaves were enticed from the trees by the late summer wind and the bushes were shedding their leaves in favour of berries. She shivered a little in the fading light; the rain had been little more than a tiny drizzle. Now she set off forcefully behind them. She heard them approaching, a noisy trundling of wheels, the brash tones of Bas and the softer murmur of Gary and tinkling, almost like the sound of a harp. As they came nearer a thump, thump of wood was audible and she was choked with relief when they came into view, unharmed and unaccompanied. Piled high on a supermarket trolley was the insulation that they needed. Three rolls of thick polystyrene which could be sandwiched between plywood for the roof and walls. This would keep them cosy and warm whichever country they chose to visit. Bas, in character, had defied authority and the girls too. They were dragging planks of wood, stopping at intervals to rearrange the weight. Rev smiled. 'How do you know when to change course, Tiz asked me. I'll tell you, Boo. First you ask, then you plead, then demand and when all else fails, take. Here.' It was a chandelier, large and circular with lustrous glass pendants and the wind sang between the hanging crystals.

'Yes, I hear you,' Maggie spoke dully, shuffling painfully towards the door. The frame supported her fragility as she unbolted the grille. She wondered each day how much longer she could go on living alone. She had not requested or encouraged visits from Social Services and the ingratiating politeness of the District Nurse annoyed her. She intended to remain at home as long as possible. She could hardly care for herself but Mustard's friends had brought sunshine and some independence into her life, and whilst they were around the desperation and weariness seemed to disappear.

The men worked hard on the bus. Tiz especially was well informed. Above the clattering and banging and profanities she explained that all they needed really was the framework, plywood, formica, brackets and lots of glue. 'Screw it and glue it,' she smiled.

'Aye, lass,' sighed Maggie. 'You make it sound so easy. But I tell you what, if I had my time over again I'd go with yer.' The girls listened over supper whilst she discussed her free insurance policy and pondered on her remark 'If it isn't enough to bury me then somebody else will have to find the money.' Ellie found it morbid. It must feel like an entombment surrounded as she was by headstones and Angels of Death.

The sound of hammering on metal continued and the impatient altercation of men working under pressure ceased only when they sat down to eat their supper.

Ellie stretched out on the battered sofa under the window. The light was fading and she was barely able to see Gary's face, but she could tell from the strained tone of his voice that he was exhausted. Perhaps he was ill? Did her loss of speech mean that she was more observant, more intuitive, more perceptive? She felt close to him despite his frequent bouts of aloofness and regretted her lack of experience with the opposite sex. Listening was what she did best; her knowledge of the group was gained by what they said to and about each other. They teased her, advised her, warned and complimented her – and when they included her in their plans she viewed this with a realistic fondness but of Gary she learned little.

Worthy causes and self-help strategies for the homeless seemed to take up most of his time yet she had little idea of his accomplishments. He was looking at her over the top of his can of beer. It was the end of a very long day but he took comfort in seeing Ellie rested and warm and winked at her. He also took note that the line of her profile was beautiful.

'Tomorrow we're taking the bus out for a trial run, if that's OK with everyone?' He stretched his arms above his head.

Mustard yawned. 'Must admit things are going well, can't

ask for more.'

'Girls,' Bas dictated. 'We want some water containers, five gallon, if possible with taps.'

'Is that all?' sneered Boo, tossing back her long plaits.

'Yes, well,' Bas pouted. 'We don't care, do we Rev? You use all the water, you girls with your bits and pieces.' He continued in a falsetto. 'Somebody has pinched the wipes again.' Rising from her chair, Boo swiped the back of his head. 'Moron,' she clipped. 'We like to keep extremely clean even though we live with pigs.'

CHAPTER THREE

"Silence is a fence round wisdom." (Proverbial German.)

Mustard viewed his bus with a realistic attitude and decided that there would be no roof racks, cow catchers or air horns. He regarded it as his bus because he knew a great deal about the mechanics; they couldn't manage without him. How many mobile mechanics were there who had his skills and made a living from travelling to festivals and doing the circuit and had enough money left to last through the winter? Meantime he had to keep the old girl on the road. It was regrettable that after the Irish tour it was due to be loaned to another band but he would be driving anyway.

Through the window he watched his passengers approach. He winced as needle-sharp pains shot up his leg. Referred pain, his GP told him. It didn't help knowing what it was but he had to put up with the discomfort for the time being; it would not help for them to know about it.

They were a mixed bunch, he reckoned. Boo easily upset and superstitious, Tiz strong and confident, and Ellie with her delicate sensuality and wide-eyed innocence, mixing with the masculine medley of musicians.

Ellie looked about her. There was an abundance of activity in the churchyard. Grey squirrels were darting and pigeons were homing in the broken tiles in Maggie's chapel. Cats skulked behind the hedges and crows hovered and alighted on the giant oak. Boo could not and would not look at the crow. She regarded it as a harbinger of death and disaster and scuttled into the bus. 'There will be a funeral in the near future,' she shuddered.

Bas was his usual flippant self. 'Course there will, silly cow, this is a cemetery, isn't it?'

Gary was quiet, businesslike, opening letters and thoughtfully scribbling. 'Right, before we go, one piece of news. Fab will be joining us on the tour.' There were gasps of despair. 'Oh no, you have to be joking. All we will hear will be philosophical arguments about every trite subject that comes up,' argued Tiz.

'She has a strong voice,' claimed Gary.

'Oh, she's not singing, surely. Anyway she doesn't know the songs.' Bas was incensed.

'She can learn,' Gary continued. 'Kindly remember she's done it before. What is the problem? There is plenty of room.'

Boo sniffed, focussing on Bas. 'His problem is that he has to share the vocals. You are sad, do you know that?'

'Whose idea was it, anyway?' hollered Bas.

'Mine.' Rev rose from his seat at the back of the bus. 'Mine, actually,' he repeated. 'The best arse in the business.'

'That figures,' Boo interjected. 'Well, if she starts playing up like last time, she's out, OK?' Tossing her head she dropped heavily into the seat next to Mustard.

'Must admit she's a lively one,' he murmured to himself. Boo frowned.

'Wait until we're in each others' armpits 24 hours a day,' Tiz grumbled.

In a quiet back street in the shadow of a brewery they picked up Cheddar. He was wearing black trousers with innumerable zips, a tee shirt embellished with ACAB and a black woolly hat, set so far back on his head that it was hardly worth wearing one at all. His attitude was pessimistic from the start. 'Sounds like a pit full of rattlers.' Having expressed his opinion he sat down next to Ellie. He smelled of garlic.

The contents of the bus were sparse but once the rest of the furnishings were properly installed, swore Mustard, the ride would be as smooth as a baby's bottom. 'That's gratifying to know,' breathed Tiz.

They took the road to Rotherham. Ellie edged away from Cheddar, who pressed his body to hers and spoke softly in her ear. She turned to look out of the window. Throughout the neighbourhood for miles on every side there were signs of regrowth and new buildings. In the middle of terraced housing grassland had been planted and trees were taking root. It was not her idea of country but in all directions, like the strand of a vast spider's web, were patches of green. Suddenly towering gaunt and impressive a building of vast proportions was a dream realized in the preservation of steelworks.

'This is Magna,' exclaimed Rev. 'Can we have a look?'

'At some crummy old steelworks? I don't think so,' complained Boo.

'And what you say goes, does it?' challenged Bas. 'What would you know about furnaces, anyway?

'My grandfather worked in the rolling mills; it was bloody hot, hard dangerous work. I vote we take a look.'

'What made me think that you come from a slightly superior class?' Boo's sarcastic comment infuriated Bas.

'Shut it.' He moved menacingly towards her and she retreated, her shapely arms crossed in front of her heaving chest. 'Bastard,' she spat at him.

Ellie understood that their relationship mirrored so clearly the strength of obstinacy and their wilfulness but in a general way they channelled it evenly. Bas didn't like being lectured. Had he met his match in this impetuous, fiery woman?

Once the bus was parked, the general idea was to enjoy the experience and it proved to be exhilarating and worthwhile. Air, Fire, Water, Earth. Unlimited adventure and amazement. All that was objectionable in Bas seemed to melt when they reached the water world with the mist and the rain. He made for the Supersoakers and the hydrogen rocket and fired the water cannon at human targets, and the tiny boy with the golden hair and deep blue eyes attached himself to Bas like a limpet.

'Who's he?' Tiz asked as they made their way to the Big Melt. The noise broke upon the hearers with an effect like that produced by the exploding of a paper bag, which has first been inflated and then burst with a stroke of a hand. The boy shrank from them and bellowed. His face reddened and puffed with indignation. Boo knelt to stroke his hand, Rev bent to pick him up but he struggled to be free. The calm tones of Gary did nothing to quieten the yelling and when Mustard grabbed his arm, the boy pulled frantically at his beard. There was a thunderclap as the furnace burst into life and for some moments the child was struck dumb.

Ellie was secretly amused. Where was it she had read, "I sound my barbaric yawp over the roofs of the world?" He started again.

'This is bloody ridiculous,' moaned Bas. 'It's interfering with my time and galling me no end.'

Boo quipped with condescending pity, 'You don't understand kids. He's frightened. We'll go look for his parents.' The men bowed out, striding in the direction of the cafe.

At the lost child point he was reunited with his fearful and trembling mother, who hurriedly took delivery of her protesting infant. 'Wallace, don't you ever run away again.' Blissfully aware of their incredulity at such a title, Tiz exclaimed, 'I bet they have a dog called GROMMIT,' and doubled up in peals of laughter.

Mustard took a long time over his Yorkshire pudding, scooping out the vegetables, which found their way into his beard and dribbled onto his collar. The inflatable restaurant was overflowing with children, all tending to rouse Bas into a state of anger. He scowled with impatience. Boo draped herself into the opposite chair. She looked him full in the face. 'What? What?' he enquired in a voice of increasing exasperation. She shrugged her shoulders and walked away.

'Let's go,' sighed Gary. 'I wish these barrels were bigger.

Do you think they'll do?' Tiz bounced off the back seat of the bus to inspect.

'Great. They fit in nicely under the seat. These are the ones from the pub, are they? How much did you pay?'

'A wink and a smile,' Boo pouted.

The interior of the bus was bright and compact. Provision was made for everyone's convenience and comfort. It had cupboards and bunks, plates and crockery, and sufficient space for musical instruments.

The shadows between the graves were forming peculiar patterns on the grass and in the soft light from the tiny windows of the house Ellie felt quite at ease. She was partly actuated by curiosity and a vague yearning for something that would give meaning to her life. By this time she felt that she knew the girls quite well and her first disparaging impression of the punk scene was beginning to wear off. A glance at Gary, kneeling in the corner by the driving seat, reminded her that here was a good-natured, determined man and one that she could trust. There was a half guilty feeling, a vague feeling of surprise when he caught her looking at him, and she turned away.

'We start painting tomorrow, Gary, is that OK?' Rev had his hair spiked. 'Let's paint it silver and green.'

'Like a Venusian, you mean?' smiled Gary. 'And have everybody claiming their free cup of tea. You must be joking.'

'How about grey and a smattering of white? We'll put it to the others.' Tiz had yet to decide what type of paint she would use for the horse. 'I may use Latex. On the passenger side so that it is a declaration of free spirits to others when we are abroad.'

'And a logo,' chipped in Rev. 'Don't forget that.'

Mustard was full of good nature, tuning the engine, rechecking all the pins and joints under the vehicle, checking the springs and brake cylinders, and boring Ellie with all manner of oil changes and new filters. A favourable wind was blowing away the fumes and little beads of sweat were gathering around his moustache. Suddenly he rose on one leg; he called out, grimaced and limped away. Boo glanced at Ellie. 'Don't look so worried, there isn't a lot to do now.' Her dark plaits were peppered with white blobs of paint and her cheeks were red with exertion. She hammered the lid on the tin of paint and beamed.

It had rained since early morning, a gentle drizzle at first only to build up to a downpour and the sky was overcast. Gary had intended to discuss details of the Irish tour but somehow it had been abandoned in favour of a Self Defence Course for Women, albeit a crash course version and for the benefit of Ellie and Fab.

The chairs and tables had been stacked against the wall and the cafe was warm. The indescribable look on Jan's face, one of almost deep hostility at being disturbed on a Sunday, forced Boo to whisper fussily to Tiz, 'Perhaps we should go?'

'Stuff that,' she replied with a contemptuous toss of her head, and Jan slumped in a corner clutching a glass of vodka.

Fab identified herself with Siouxsie from the Banshees although she looked nothing like her and wore bifocals. However, she dressed almost identically. Boo and Tiz could not decide who should take the class. They argued. Gary, treating the matter with sensitivity but with firmness, suggested that they divide the lesson into two halves. Bas barked. 'Get on with it!' and Gary retired, squatting on the floor strumming his guitar.

'We will begin with loose clothing and bare feet.' Tiz's tone appealed to the group of giggling girls. Ellie arched her eyebrows in unaffected surprise. 'We will deal first of all with aggressive elements on the dance floor. Now Ellie experienced this which is why she is on the door instead of enjoying herself with the rest of us. It may look combative but while you are dancing, it's not!' She ran her fingers through her shorn hair.

'If you fall down somebody will pick you up,' Bas grunted.

'Like hell, they will.'

'Dancing is enjoyable,' ventured Boo. 'If it's a political band it's exciting. I get quite breathless. If the fellas shove you then you shove them back. If it gets physical then you boot 'em.'

Rev intervened. 'You're not supposed to scare the shit out of Ellie. Get on with something constructive.' Tiz hesitated. There was a long silence.

'Well,' Tiz began again. 'I usually begin with verbal strategies but I can do that another time with Fab. I'll concentrate on body language!' Ellie had never acknowledged the value of self exploration; asserting herself had never become an important part of taking control of her life. Yet she would not be here today if she had failed to defend herself against a man intent on violation. It was her extremely keen strong will and her natural hotheadedness that had saved her and punished him.

Now here she was being taught how to defend her boundaries by moves, wrist grabs, clothes' grabs, strikes and stances. In the corner Gary had stopped playing. He could not imagine the fresh- faced girl before him fighting her way out of trouble; what he did see was a gentle gazelle moving with a kind of bewildered frustration in a world without words.

Now it was Fab's half hour of martial art and a grim side of female confrontation became obvious. There was anger surfacing when Rev suggested she should join the band; there was jealousy from Bas when she was asked to sing and there was an underlying feeling that she had been asked to come along as a comfort blanket, an expression Boo spat out with derogatory bile. Tiz was suddenly hostile, aggravated by Bas shouting and waving his arms about, and Mustard, pleasantly intoxicated, shuffling with agitation, cheered him on.

Fab was a match for Tiz. Removing her glasses with a cool, defiant gesture, she faced her opponent. Bringing up her knee she drove out her foot, hitting Tiz's knee with her heel and the real fight began. Suddenly Bas flung his strong arms around Tiz and in a bear hug scooped her up. Fab burst into a storm of frustrated weeping and in her distress appealed to Gary. Yet the assurance was needed by Ellie. With these images in mind would she feel confident to travel with them, to trust them?

Her natural buoyant spirit had responded with withdrawal and she sank into the seat next to Jan. It was time to sit down and take stock. She had never been at ease with physical contact but when Gary leaned over and squeezed her hand she felt a strengthening bond. Gradually the large blue eyes lost the uneasy, apprehensive stare and her face resumed its serenity.

He spoke softly. 'Often relationships are turbulent and disturbing!' he stated. 'Sometimes a bit volatile but on the whole this is what keeps the band alive and challenging.' He was so very different from the others, she thought. She pursed her lips in a child like gesture. 'Still prepared to come with us?' The smile lingered for an instant, then she nodded. The truth of this description was to remain with her for many years.

CHAPTER FOUR

"Sweet is the Silent Mouth." (Irish Proverbial.)

The bus bore on its passenger side Tiz's painting of the horse. A roan, a black stallion with a sprinkling of greyish hairs on its coat and in large letters of black paint the words "Dark Horse".

'Mustard, admit it, it looks very impressive.'

'Wonderful,' chimed in Boo.

'Great,' echoed Rev and Cheddar.

'Yes, it is,' agreed Fab and Bas added, 'Bloody fantastic!'

Gary and Ellie nodded their approval. The men were like proud fathers seeing their offspring for the first time, glowing with admiration, conceit and delight. They were tired.

In the hall they had practised until well past midnight and the itinerary was finalised and personal belongings, food and instruments packed securely.

Maggie waved them off, twisting her walking frame into the asphalt path and laughing at Bas until tears ran down her gaunt cheeks. Ellie sat next to Fab listening attentively to her sole interpretation of the battle of survival in which they were all engaged. They were on their way to Liverpool. Exhaustion had given way to excitement and whilst the men occupied the bunks the girls were happy to view the wooded countryside and chat. Ellie would have argued with Fab. How could she agree to non-confrontational social progress

and change when she was ready to fight to the death with
Tiz? At first Ellie had been nervous over her inability to
articulate but there was a confidence emerging and it had
dawned on her that her other senses more than compensated
for her refusal to speak. She was gaining in knowledge and
in the silent arguments formed conclusions which couldn't
be misinterpreted. It was pleasantly one-sided. They knew
so little about her but she was learning more about them.

Cheddar was becoming irritated. He seemed to have held
on to a likeable boyishness but he was exasperated over
something. Tiz and Boo were making peanut butter and
tomato sandwiches for the ferry journey. Fab was spreading
liberal scrapings of garlic on poppy seed plaits and Ellie was
packing fruit in plastic containers.

Cheddar trundled to the rear of the bus. He poured water
into a plastic cup and swallowed two tablets. He was afraid
of being seasick. Ellie sat beside him; beneath his long, black
hair his complexion was wan and for a moment he looked
startled. She laid a hand on his arm. "You will be alright,"
she mouthed. She was almost like a doctor sprinkling
her patient with perfume instead of administering strong
medicine. The girls nudged each other and stared. Ellie's
role was defined, she was the carer.

The fresh invigorating sea air tore into their hair and
faces. The surge and swell of the Irish Sea challenged them
on deck. Cheddar shared serious and tender moments in a
quiet corner of the ferry with his head on Ellie's shoulder
and his hat pulled well over his eyes.

She was aware that Gary was regarding her shrewdly. He
was finding it hard to keep his balance. 'Want something to
eat?' She shook her head. 'Later?' She nodded and watched
him walk away, a calm, gentle man. Had he ever been
affected by the stormy waves of life? Fab's philosophical
nurturing was creeping in.

The boisterous public exhibition by Bas in the ferry
restaurant was related to Ellie and Cheddar on the way to
their squat in Dublin. 'He is so ignorant, the pig,' divulged
Boo. 'Do you know what he did? Stole somebody's meal.'

'A great deal of smoke from a small fire,' laughed Bas.

'Rubbish, he had paid for that meal.'

'And he didn't want it, he was spewing all over the place.'

'You are disgusting, do you know that?' Boo glared. Bas smiled, unaffected by the feisty glare in the dark eyes.

At the squat in Dublin, Beck had a smoker's hoarse hack of a chuckle. She had struggled manfully, she pointed out, to become self sufficient and in the long row of uniform terrace houses she had created a home. On the messy and grimy street she had painted her house a forest green with a white step and a shamrock-styled knocker. Once, she said, her life had been collapsing all around her but 'I crossed the water and Ireland now has my ears, eyes and soul.'

The meal she had prepared was delicious. They listened in rapt attention as in serious and sentimental tones she described a life filled with emotional turmoil. 'My advice to you all,' she whispered, 'is this. If you learn only one thing in your lifetime, let it be this. That you alone are responsible for creating your own happiness.'

Somehow what Beck had said mattered to Ellie. It struck a chord. The most important aspect of her life was her feelings; her nightly prayers triggered moments of self-doubt yet she was convinced that she was moving in the right direction.

They slept comfortably on mattresses in two rooms. Cheddar offered Ellie a bar of chocolate and lay beside her. She pushed him away, and he mumbled that he wanted to be close to her. She would have been less eager to dismiss Gary. The rain bounced off the sills as gentle snores consoled her.

'The most instantly talkative city in Europe, that is what the writer V.S. Pritchett dubbed it,' encouraged Gary as they set out to discover Dublin before the evening gig. No one was paying attention. It was a great city, abundant with shops for the girls and beguiling with its Georgian architecture and to Bas's delight, numerous public houses. They explored the majestic cathedrals, embraced the welcome of the people and soaked up the atmosphere in the park where they squatted on the grass and ate their picnic lunch. They took numerous snapshots and posed outside "La Stampa". They remained relatively well behaved, enjoying the warmth and vibrancy of the heart of Ireland.

Ellie concluded that the Irish never allowed their religion to prejudice their temporal interests or mar their worldly pleasures. Quite different to her upbringing with Gran. Ellie had not entered a church since leaving home.

The gig was in a small village north of the city. They wore their Dark Horse tee shirts and were prepared for an evening of lively punk without morons or chinners, derided Bas. Having his wits about him was essential; he considered himself to be the muscle. The venue was heaving. An overheated cellar where the ventilation was non-existent and the air smelled of trapped cigarette smoke did not appeal to Ellie. She sat next to a middle-aged man with a clean-shaven, freckled face and red hair. Loud and demonstrative, he shouted encouragement to the musicians even though the cacophony of sound deadened anything he said. Gary approached him and shook his hand.

Ellie stepped outside into the fresh air. She breathed in slowly and found a small patch of green, a veritable oasis in the black smoke-shrouded desert around. Away from the cellar shelter she sat on a large tree trunk and hugged her knees. Gary should be out here, drinking in the sweetness of a Gaelic evening. She was a little reluctant to admit that she missed him when the gigs were over and he wandered off by himself. She had resolved not to be too inquisitive or to be in any way a liability but this didn't rule out any notion that she shouldn't be concerned. Perhaps he was tired. Maybe the odd stumble was overindulgence and yet she had never seen him drunk.

The clouds scurried across the face of the full moon and the wind sighed as it shuffled through the grass and she shivered. 'Here you are.' Cheddar threw his arm around Ellie's neck. She rested close to him slipping her hand in his. 'We've finished our stint and are packing up. Want a drink?'

****

'Mavourneen,' Aggie greeted Ellie with enthusiasm. Blinking through thick spectacles, she pecked her on the cheek. 'A kiss and a cup of tea, one to warm the heart, one to warm the body.' No one else received this sort of treatment. Aggie weaved wonderful shawls and sweaters and opened her traditional Irish house to wandering musicians of all nationalities.

There was a rich aroma of newly baked bread stacked in a central open hearth. The house had just two rooms, a living kitchen and a bedroom, and most of the furniture was pushed against the walls, leaving the main floor area free.

The girls prepared a vegetable stew whilst Cheddar and Rev grabbed bottles of Irish whisky from the bus. 'Ah,' Aggie licked her lips 'Usquebaugh.' They had driven only forty miles from the gig and already Gary was flagging. It was a short walk to the byre and the hole in the wall and Tiz claimed the bed recess rather than a sleeping bag as she was feeling unwell. Aggie offered her a hot plate from the oven and an Irish stone which, she claimed, had healing qualities. She wrapped it tightly in linen.

'Must admit there is something in these superstitions,' observed Mustard. 'Do you know why I wear an earring? To protect me from drowning.'

Ellie was tired but was kept awake by the celebrations in the cottage and the constant trips to the back of the byre. Boo and Fab, carried along by roars of laughter and a chorus of Galway Bay, decided to join them. It was Ellie that cooked breakfast. Mustard was fine. He knew he had to drive to Killarney and had slept in Aggie's bed. Aggie slurped her porridge and wiped her spectacles with a sweep of her apron before adjusting them on her nose. Boo bought one of her colourful shawls and Gary, running his fingers through his hair and looking slightly pinched, removed the collection of empties. He looked up into Ellie's face and she flushed. She held his gaze. She's not making it easy for me, he sighed. Aggie waved a subdued goodbye.

'Heaven's Reflex,' announced Gary and turned to Ellie. 'Its beauty has earned it this nickname.' The vivid blue of the Lakes of Killarney reflected the craggy mountains above and the group of young people recovering from a night at the gin palace as Tiz chose to call it whereas Bas referred to it in more robust terms, relaxed on the grass.

'Let's take a track through the woods,' challenged Gary.

'No, you're on your own mate.'

'Sod off.'

'Are you taking the piss?'

'You have to be kidding.'

'No thanks.'

Inactivity was voted in. 'Just you and me then, Ellie.' Before she could resist he linked her arm in his and led her away.

Why did he feel that he was on delicate ground? They sauntered through the sprawling woodland. He thanked her for helping with the chores. He would have liked to say how the sweater complemented the blue of her eyes and that the jeans she was wearing could have been made for her rather than being an off-the-peg cast off in a charity shop. A gleam of comfort dawned; she had made no attempt to drink alcohol and she was popular with everyone in the band. He knew them well and they were aware that she had never posed a threat to them. Whatever happened in the future she had people she could rely on.

As they walked with the sun on their backs and the cushiony turf beneath their feet he began to feel relaxed and affectionate. At the moment he reached for her hand Cheddar spoiled it by lumbering after them. He was running and tying his hair in a ponytail at the same time. Digging deep in his pocket he produced a bar of chocolate, separating several links of chains between his legs. Ellie shook her head. He pushed the bar nervously into her hand with a squeeze but with just the slightest touch of defiance she handed it back. Her colour had heightened. Gary suggested an ice cream and they sat on a bench watching the red admiral busy among the sedum. Cheddar studied Ellie as she curled her tongue around the cone and she smiled as the ice cream dripped down her chin. She began to laugh soundlessly. Cheddar wiped it away with his hand. It was a tender moment but were these untried waters into which she was about to plunge? A knot twisted in Gary's stomach as he watched her run back to the lake with Cheddar in hot pursuit. He strolled; he had scarcely been prepared for so much fatigue and there was a long way to go.

As he looked down at the sparkling waters of the lake he understood why this had been an inspiration to artists for countless years and how easily the romantic heart can be stirred. The sky had a soft look and the smell of the fields was sweet.

'Don't misunderstand me, Tiz, you are brilliant as an artist but what you are asking is really more than we can cope with.' Gary leaned forward in the bus. 'I often wonder whether you yourself really believe all the things you preach but now you are asking me to put money up front.'

They were on their way to the Dingle Peninsula. 'Explain it to me once more.' In her eagerness Tiz rose from her seat. 'Last night, at the gig in Killarney, I met a mate from Bradford. I've known him for a long time. He runs an Independent Library of personal beliefs, ideals, Indian philosophy.'

Gary interrupted. 'I would have thought that was Fab's department.'

'Oh, no,' Tiz appealed. 'It has nothing to do with her.' She lowered her voice. Fab was asleep in the lower bunk, Bas snoring loudly above her. 'The library covers a broad range of issues including social alternatives, which I know you have considered, Gary. Nuclear issues, animal rights, conflict resolution.'

Gary waved his hand as though pleading for a brief delay. 'OK, I'm sold on the theory. Now what about the practical?' Gary quizzed.

The bus pulled up at the traffic lights. Mustard stretched his arms above his head and yawned. 'OK, Mustard?'

'Yep, we've a while to go though.' Ellie left the passenger seat to make drinks. She slid past Gary and for a moment he lost concentration. It concerned him.

'Anyway,' Tiz was enthusing. 'They want me to design

logos for various groups and have asked me to submit sketches. Gary?'

He regained his composure. 'How much will the initial outlay be?' He heaved a sigh as her voice became appealing.

'Oh, not much. I'm sure you will agree that it will be good publicity for the band and all I require are basic materials and, if possible, access to the internet. It would speed things up a bit. I have the ideas and the commitment.'

'I know,' Gary acknowledged. 'Let me think about it.'

Ellie made them herb tea. She sat beside Gary and gave an involuntary sigh. When they looked at her she gave them her usual enthusiastic smile and Gary realized that she was uncovering an experience the depths of which he was unable to explain. He was anxious for Ellie's approval on every decision he made. Why? He was satisfied that he was doing the right thing by having her with them. In many ways she was innocent yet with an intelligence that gleamed through her silence, and had a dignified awareness of the pitfalls of the punk scene. Perhaps he wanted to prove by example, the programme of self-help and mutual aid given to the homeless and underprivileged of the present day society. Perhaps he simply needed her approbation.

It was impossible to avoid close contact on the bus. Boo, a stickler for cleanliness, indicated that her smalls had to be washed daily, usually in the tiny bowl under the sink, towelled dry and hung on a line above her bunk. Ellie was taken by surprise at some of the things Bas had to say about it. His vulgarity was met with a chorus of coarse plebeian remarks and Cheddar doubled up with laughter. He rolled off his bunk and onto Fab, who awoke with a start. Boo was incensed. She fumed and raged at Bas, lunged at him and fought like a tiger.

Mustard slowed the bus almost to a halt: this temper tantrum made no more impression on him than furious waves upon a rock. Gary stood calmly by. 'Pack it in, that's enough. You are behaving like little kids. For God's sake, you'll injure each other.' He may as well have poured oil on a blazing fire and the sparks flared up again. Without warning the bus swerved and Fab was thrown against the sharp corner of the sink.

It was Ellie who produced the first aid kit and attended to the wound in Fab's arm. Fab's reaction amounted almost to hysteria but Ellie remained calm, stroking her head and covering her with a blanket. Indicating that there would be no need for stitches, it was obvious that there was this emphasis of caring in her nature and this added another step on the road to belonging.

Bas retired to the back of the bus. His red face swollen with anger he surrounded himself with cans of lager. He continued to stare at Boo. 'Bitch, stupid f****** bitch. You are bloody mad, you are.'

'You should be locked up,' she spat. Mustard stopped the bus.

'Sorry, couldn't stop. Must admit you had a right go at one another.'

'Are you OK for tonight Fab?' Cheddar called out.

'Is that all you care about?' yelled Tiz. 'Can't you see she's in shock?'

Ellie made tea. Postcards of Killarney were pinned to the cupboard above the sink. She was reminded of Kate Kearney's cottage where they had spent time at the Gap of Dunloe together, happily browsing through the souvenir and gift store, taking a snack and visiting Moriarty's with the wonderful display of Waterford crystal and Belleek china. There had been no sign of quarrels then. She would have liked to have stayed longer, to have explored the quiet, empty countryside and taken expeditions to the east of the lakes but they had to move on.

Again she had sent postcards home to Gran. What on earth would she be thinking? She chose them carefully, always written with reassurance in mind, describing her friends in glowing terms.

She missed her. She hardly ever thought about her mother.

She felt Gary's arm about her shoulder. 'Thanks, Ellie. You

are a little wonder, do you know that? I hope you are OK
with us. I realize that it can't be easy but I'm here for you.
Remember that.' He smiled. The clear, trustful eyes met his.
'Did you like Killarney?' Ellie nodded. Mustard had returned
to the driving seat and everyone appeared to have recovered
from the ordeal. 'Peace, perfect peace,' Gary sighed.

"Fine manners and fine words are cheap in Ireland"
wrote George Bernard Shaw. Maybe so, thought Ellie. My
fine manners are there for all to see but my fine words are
concealed and silent, and the urge to speak becomes less.
She was no longer frustrated or stultified; by listening she
was learning and speech brought anger and resentment.
With Gary she experienced a speechless happiness; he cared
for her and with a simple confidence she cared for him. Was
it obsession or passion? She didn't have an answer.

CHAPTER FIVE

"A close mouth is as good as a priest's blessing any day."
(Proverbial Irish.)

An Daingean (the Irish name for Dingle) was heaving in the heat of the afternoon sun. They honked their way through the one-way systems into the large car park of the market town and relaxed. They had four hours before the gig, with the full intention of exploring Dingle. Fab had recovered from the fight. 'Tough as old boots,' declared Rev. It was hardly heartfelt sympathy but it was the best he could do. Wearing a ragged tee shirt which hardly concealed his paunch, Bas strutted ahead carrying a can of lager and chanting. Boo, her long plaits catching the sun, adding a tinge of blue, mingled with the inhabitants; many with their dark eyes and hair, a result of their long history of friendly trade with the Spanish.

'His name is Fungie,' Tiz announced.

'Who?' enquired Fab, adjusting the dressing on her arm.

'The Dingle dolphin,' Tiz continued. 'Let's book a boat trip out to see him.' They scrambled down a walkway but Gary was finding it difficult to keep his balance. Whilst the rest of the party forged on ahead, Ellie clung onto his arm, scared that he was in danger of stumbling. He smiled despite the drawn look on his pale face and sighed. 'Just a little bit under the weather, nothing to worry about.' Her look of concern was obvious. She put her hands round his waist to steady him. His surprise was equalled by his anger and indignation at her evident sympathy. His expression was guarded. 'Look, I'm OK Ellie, don't fuss.'

After an hour Gary felt the need to sleep. The girls went in pursuit of Fungie and the men in search of a pub. He awoke to the hysteria of disturbed gulls and to the warmth of Ellie's hand in his. The grass was soft beneath him and the sun warm against his face. He was aware that perhaps she had been watching him sleep, studying him closely, and Ellie was one of those people who can see as much at a glance as many would discover during a prolonged scrutiny. Resting beside him, Ellie was glad that he accepted her the way she was; she would be a fool to risk scaring him away. Oh for a world of constant sunshine and loving indulgence, Gary thought.

Mustard found them first. 'Must admit this is one hell of a nice place,' he enthused. He scratched his beard at length. He had a round, ruddy, almost jovial face and Ellie, who was no longer phased by his vague utterances, pushed him playfully.

'Do you know what they told us?' Tiz was relating. 'When you book the boat trip and Fungie doesn't appear you get your money back.'

'Well, there you are,' snorted Bas. 'It's probably a rubber one like "Jaws". They can do anything nowadays you know to fool the punters.'

'Oh, and you would know, I suppose?' rubbished Boo.

'You moron!' Bas made a feeble move towards her. 'Like the tee shirt?'

'Only a shroud would look good on you,' spat Boo.

Gary had been occupied with the guide. 'Right, now we eat. O'Riordan's Cafe who, according to this, have an enlightened veggie menu. Then the gig, then the camp.' Fab's eyes widened behind her specs.

'We are actually staying on a camp site?'

'Don't you ever listen to what anybody says?' sighed Rev.

'Oh, shut up, you,' replied Fab with a sheepish air.

'That means, Ellie,' smiled Tiz, 'a long scented shower and clean clothes.' Not a muscle in Rev's face moved. He threw himself forward with his elbows on his knees and supported his forehead with his hands.

'Oh, please, that sums up women really. Always washing; we don't smell.' 'That,' said Boo haughtily, 'is a matter of opinion.'

Ellie jumped up. She understood that there are people who give little thought to the act of taking a bath or shower or changing into clean clothes but for her it was a compulsive necessity. Strip washes within the confines of the bus were never satisfactory despite the blanket curtain and it was difficult to kick away the struts of propriety.

O'Riordan's was full. They chose a small cafe packed with tourists. Bas's offensive tee shirt, Rev's multicoloured hair and Tiz's numerous tattoos did not deter the waiter from giving them excellent service and a table by the window. Once again they were in good spirits.

Kerry lamb and beef in Guinness was being served on the opposite table. Rev turned up his nose. This was probably the first time Ellie had been tempted by meat since leaving home. She had been so long without it and it smelled and looked so appetizing. There were no rules to say she had to do without but she had eagerly fitted in with the others and was now able to contribute her black-eye bean casserole with confidence.

The elderly man with the succulent meat dish adjusted his spectacles and smiled at Ellie. She returned his smile. She saw in a moment the mistake she had made and when he called the waiter over she straightened her back and lowered her eyes. From the kitchen the waiter appeared with a small portion of beef in gravy. He hovered. 'The gentleman requests that you try a little.' His brogue was endearing. She hesitantly pushed the plate away. There followed a long silence.

Rules are not always cut and dried. Ellie's cheeks grew hot and her fork clattered to the floor. 'I'm sorry,' Gary rose to his feet. 'The young lady is a vegetarian.' It was well-known to the group that Bas did not suffer meat eaters gladly. The vague thoughts that had come to Ellie once or twice on this subject were taking shape in her mind. "Do you think we could eat in peace? You don't see me shoving platefuls of veggie lasagne under folks' noses." Bas leaned over, grabbed the plate and plonked it in front of the man, spilling the contents onto the tablecloth. Ellie found herself on delicate ground. It seemed that she couldn't avoid trouble despite never opening her mouth. It was obvious when Bas returned to his seat that he had an indomitable appetite for aggression; and it was not about to change. He swore repeatedly. Gary moved forward but hesitated. For a moment his mind was confused; he completely forgot what he was about to say. There were symptoms, warnings he had to be aware of that he had to fight but what were they? With shaking hands he pushed back his hair and walked hesitantly out of the cafe and into the invigorating air of Castlegregory.

It concerned Rev that there was a shortage of punks about. This was remedied as soon as they approached the gig, a timber roofed pub with picnic benches and hammered copper tables. It was busy. Gary had recovered after a long nap on the bus and they unloaded the gear carefully along the flagstoned floor and onto the raised dais in the corner. Putting the finishing touches meant a sound check and everybody hated it. No one was interested, no one had the patience to work at it, it was boring. Cheddar came into his own at times like this. Uncultured, not very bright, but blindly enthusiastic. It mattered to him a great deal.

Fab was at her best. She sang raw, coarse lyrics which Ellie found harrowing but which Boo argued were a significant part of her education although unbecoming to a philosophy student. They were headlining, they played well together yet their individuality shone through each number.

Gary was setting up an interview with a DIY hard-core Punk Zine and Ellie was concerned at how tired he looked. Could the scene in the cafe have started a chain reaction? But then when he smiled his grey eyes crinkled at the corners and he laughed at the reporter's quote by Frank Zappa,

"Rock journalism is people who can't write interviewing people who can't talk for people who can't read". How many months, years perhaps of silence lay ahead for her?

A touch of eccentricity, even a little madness, caused Rev to remove his clothing down to his boxer shorts embroidered with an Irish shamrock but he retained his dog collar. His proud Mohican shone brightly. "The drum does not make as much noise as the mouth", isn't that what the proverb says? Not in Rev's case, Ellie thought.

Mustard had slept in the bus. The girls were enthusiastic about spending the night at the camp site even though dawn was just a few hours away. The roads were quiet and wove between gently undulating green and brown hills. A faint sigh of relief rose from Boo. 'Imagine,' she simpered. 'A warm shower and clean clothes.'

'Huh,' grunted Bas. 'Tell you what, do my laundry for us, will yer?'

Boo adopted a distant somewhat tight-lipped look and Fab uttered sneeringly, 'Sod off!' He threw a large plastic bag in her direction and Ellie moved down the bus, slipping in next to Mustard. Jumping from her seat, Boo strode towards Bas and emptied the contents of his bag over his head. His jaw dropped and his eyes narrowed. He visibly reddened. Tiz moved to the sink, placing herself between them. Flushed and sweating, Bas exploded. 'You stupid f******.' Gary raised his hand. He felt that this was too much prevarication to be ignored. He needed to control this cluster of unruly tearaways. Bas was a hard nut to crack.

'Come on,' he urged. 'We've had a good time so far. Don't let's rock the boat; we are dependant on one another. It's no big deal, washing clothes.' Bas could only groan. Rev's face lit up with relief as with a fine show of reluctance Bas picked up his clothes and returned to his bunk. Cheddar slept and sniffed – even in sleep he sniffed.

The pure, cold light in the sky hung over the quiet of the camp site. There was no one around. Set back among tall trees were the shower cubicles and in front, standing in a row, were red geraniums in huge pots. The girls could hardly contain themselves. Tonight, as close friends, they could wash away some of the psychological baggage that each of them carried.

Ellie thought of Gran. 'You can't clean up the world with soft soap, it needs grit,' she would say. The group were noisy. Cheddar was singing. Ellie was relieved that their mild flirtation was over. At least she assumed it was. They returned to the bus to a sleep born of happy weariness. Bas was swinging his newly-washed laundry over his head to remove the excess water and hung it over a line. 'Silly sod washed it in the shower,' Cheddar informed Tiz. 'Danced on it like a dhobi wallah.'

'Well at least he won't smell like a polecat any more,' replied Boo.

It was decided that they would remain at the site for a couple of days. Gary had for some time been waiting for an opportunity to discuss finance with the group and in particular Tiz's request for cash for her library venture. Conflicting loyalties, resentments and antagonisms had been put on hold. It would take time for Bas to overcome his sense of irritation and his anger. Monies from the gigs had always been distributed fairly and Ellie had no problem with doing whatever was asked of her.

Gary steered his course with his own charting; she was aware of this, but dependancy always cuts both ways and it was difficult to know who was depending on whom.

The sky was cloudless and the whole landscape was bathed in sunlight. They sprawled on the grass close by the bus. Ellie had cooked a vegetable stew and bread pudding. Boo, still wrapped up in superstitious mysteries, insisted that the Irish used to dip the hand of a dead man in the mixture to make sure that the butter churned.

Ellie studied her friends discreetly. Mustard sat apart scooping up large chunks of vegetables, soupy liquid running down his ginger beard. He chomped loudly. His was a humour nicely marbled with absurdity and his repeated phrase of 'must admit' no longer got on her nerves. Cheddar had little faith in everyday living, freedom was the way forward, anarchy had its place in his workshy approach and yes, she had to agree, he did cheese them off at times. She had anticipated a closer relationship but was relieved now that it hadn't materialized.

Rev's approach to life was uncomplicated. He enjoyed it. His character was a marvellous combination of eagerness and patience. His clothes were a passionate declaration of his colourful outlook, his slender frame deceiving. 'In gyms people have to pay to be physical instead of being paid to be physical,' he had panted at Ellie after a long solo on the drums. He had the energy of three men, she decided, and the women loved him.

Boo was plaiting her long hair, chatting to Tiz who was busy cutting her toenails. She was frank and obstreperous with a dignified firmness, a perfect foil for Bas. 'All women have their whims,' he quipped at her when she rebuked him for washing his feet in the washing-up bowl. Boo painted Tiz's toenails bright red. Tiz wore very little under her shorts and tee shirt and her left arm was completely covered with Celtic tattoos, beautifully done but which mystified Ellie.

Touring was a very hungry business. Ellie stepped carefully over Bas's legs sprawled over the carpet of wild flowers, and collected the dirty dishes. Bas was of an uncertain character, notoriously quick-tempered and unpredictable. He would scorn, chide and bully and his manners were, to say the least, rude. His last comment to Boo, 'Beans again, lass; I could blow away the horns of a bullock,' resulted in a barrage of abuse and handfuls of soil aimed at his head.

'Your conversation is filthier than you are yourself,' Boo shrieked.

'He thinks he is behaving in a perfectly natural manner,' complained Fab.

'Fabianism is what Fab is all about,' divulged Gary. 'Gradual non-confrontational social progress and change. She sang well'

Bas, the front man, dismissed her, considering her simply decorative. She had an impish and attractive face. No matter how large an audience she had never felt inadequate and flirted openly with anyone who took her fancy.

'Everything happens in perfect order,' she intimated to Ellie. 'If we live without challenges we tend to stagnate and stop developing. Life then becomes monotonous. Don't you agree?' Ellie, of course, had a character to uphold. No one expected her to answer, but a nod or a shake of the head would suffice and she was after all a sounding block. No one expected her to have an opinion.

Gary had found a section of wall against which to stand; he was using the mobile phone. No one else could be bothered with the constant interruptions and inane chatter. It was evident to Ellie that this tenacious man with a cursory approach to illness was ill. She knew that he was vehemently opposed to drugs, aware that he drank little alcohol. His paleness was a sharp contrast against the healthy tan of his companions and he was painfully thin. She looked beyond him at the acres of flower fields scattered with clusters of trees. As she moved towards him he was shaking and his look was almost reproachful. 'Hi, Ellie.' Grinning weakly, it was almost as if his smile had become fixed. He explained, 'Tomorrow we start early for Galway and The Burren. We do one more gig, move onto Dublin and then head for home.' She indicated that he might be tired. 'Yes, a little. Can you man the stall tomorrow? We don't have to take all our tapes back with us although we have sold quite a few. You are a star, Ellie. You have cooked all the meals, cleaned up and done all those invisible supporting roles. I won't forget it.'

There would be things which Ellie would never forget. Later she recalled how he would lose control of his hands, how they would twitch and he would clasp them tightly to him. At times his delicate health would strain to breaking point but with consistent, stubborn insistence he refused to give in.

The leg which Mustard had been treating for some time had flared up again. He had caught it in the driver's seat and with a violent wrench pulled it free. 'Can't drive. Not tomorrow anyway.'

'You're bloody awkward,' taunted Bas.

'Don't be such an arse,' pouted Tiz. Profanities sailed backwards and forwards.

Fab sulked. 'We can't miss the Galway bash.' Rev drummed his fingers on the bottom of the bunk. Mustard sank down groaning.

Ellie finished the dishes. Mustard lay flat out on the bunk, hands behind his head and cursed. It is peoples' attitude to others that makes them what they are, Ellie had decided. What they made of her actions was their problem. With a jar of warm aromatherapy oil she approached the bunk. It had a hammock middle but undeterred she motioned Mustard to remove his trousers. Suddenly he became nervous and difficult. Ellie smothered a laugh and with unblinking blue eyes pulled hard at his belt, then at his jeans. He struggled, his beard shook with exasperation, his moustache quivered. The girls giggled and threw themselves at him, removing his boots and yanking his jeans around his ankles. His indignation was slowly subsiding, his resistance already weak. The leg was bruised, small blue abrasions were appearing on the tight skin and gently Ellie massaged the warm oil into the joint. Sometimes when the only comfort is the warmth and concern of others it is heaven sent. There was only a momentary cry of pain and then Mustard relaxed. Of course from that moment everything changed. Masseuse was added to her accomplishments and Gary was in her sights.

It was the night that brought the melancholia. Lying in bed, listening to the deep breathing, gentle sighs and an instant silence it was Ellie's time for taking stock. She had always seemed to yearn for some elusive aspiration, now she felt that she was straddling worlds, dark and light. She prayed for Gran's wisdom. Often Gran had reminded her, 'Don't be afraid of your feelings but always be wary of them.'

The night air was filled with the fragrance of flowers and dreams of Gary filled her with longing. She felt unable to stem the hunger at these times when heavy breathing provoked her inner senses and desire was hidden in her whole existence. She was aware of a striking similarity between herself and Gary; it appeared that neither had been able to establish roots. Well, maybe because he was older he could lead by example and yet, in just a few words, she could turn his world upside down. How much effort is needed to shake off weariness and uncertainty, she wondered?

CHAPTER SIX

"A shut mouth catches no flies." (Proverbial.)

This was an important time for Ellie. She snuggled deep into her sleeping bag. Would her companions remember? Would they care that tomorrow was her 17th birthday? She fell asleep, listening to the wind rustling the leaves outside her open window.

She awoke to a gentle rocking and stifled laughter. If there was the slightest sign of confusion in her mind it was now. Was she at sea? She could hear rushes of water dousing the windows and pelting against the sides. She pulled herself up slowly onto the pillow and found herself alone. She had overslept and they were washing the bus. Quickly she dressed and opened the door onto a wild, romantic landscape where the morning sun shone through the trees and sparkled on the water.

The men were vigorous in their scouring. Bas, on top of the bus, scrubbed down with impressive thoroughness. The painting of Dark Horse was treated with reverence and the wheels especially were given a drenching. Cheddar was compelled to clean the windows but there was a general feeling of good humour and sarcastic bantering.

Patches of woodland were threaded with clear streams and here the girls were doing the laundry and hanging their smalls over the bushes. Boo's tendency to fly off the handle was further provoked when Rev, making his way gingerly

down the hill to refill his bucket, returned to the bus with
her panties and hoisted them on a pole.

Ellie searched for Gary. There was a sudden sprint up
the hill and each in turn wished her 'Happy Birthday' and
hugged her. She cast a bright look of surprise at the circle of
faces. 'Secrecy is a large part of the pleasure,' hailed Fab as
they climbed into the bus to give her presents. Here, thought
Ellie, was an ark of friendship, a cave filled with the treasure
of kind intentions. They would always be there through
the years to come even when time and circumstance were
between them. She was secretly amused at their antics and
yet often surprised and alarmed at their attitude towards
one another. Would it not be better if hearers, like herself,
were to examine themselves and follow their example?

Gary appeared in the doorway. Impatience gnawed at her
like a piranha; she wanted this day to be special, her first
birthday away from the mental brutality and indifference
in her life. He took her hand and in it placed a book.
'Happy Birthday, Ellie. I hope you like it. I saw you reading
"Treasure Island", so I assume that you will like his poetry!'
It was beautifully bound – "A Child's Garden of Verses" by
Robert Louis Stevenson. It was worth all the time searching
through bookshops just to see the smile and the fresh glow
gained from a night of dreamless sleep, or so he imagined.
He could not have imagined her thoughts.

"Does he consider me still a child? We will see." In the
lay-by above the fields which spread out beneath like a quilt
of heaven the bus gleamed and sparkled in the noon sun. Tiz
and Fab prepared vegeburger and leek, tomato and cashew
nut crumble. Bas, Rev and Cheddar kicked a ball about and
Gary and Mustard planned the tour of Galway.

'Can I ask you a favour?' Boo stared critically at Ellie.
'Can I do something with your hair?' The look was
appealing and she laid a sisterly hand on her shoulder. Ellie
had never changed her style in years. It was straight and
fair and usually tied back. Why not? It was hardly likely to
go wrong. She was a hairdresser after all. She inclined her
head in polite assent and they sat on the long grass beside

the running water; running water that constitutes a magical barrier that no spirit can cross, according to Boo.

Ellie joined her companions for lunch with plaited, beaded hair and gilded lacquer. Gary's eyes widened; he was confronted with the appearance of a lovely young woman but he was discreet and merely smiled.

They had six hours in which to explore Galway. Once the bus was parked they walked the patchwork of narrow, winding streets; visited the brightly painted shops and listened to the mixture of English and Irish. They sauntered around the Salmon Weir Bridge over the short River Corrib on its way to the Atlantic, and took numerous snaps. Tiz held the camera. There was always a great deal of preparation and posing. 'For Heaven's sake get on with it,' Bas protested. He lifted up his shirt, revealing his ample stomach.

Boo elbowed him. 'Shift!'

'I'll stand next to the draggled peacock.'

'That's you. Ellie, if he hurls insults, ignore him.'

Their path took them through long grass which held many a tick and summer midges until they came to Galway Cathedral. To Ellie it was sacred; she was filled with wonder and awe.

Bas shuffled on the steps and strode off with Mustard at his heels. Gary held Ellie's arm and it was almost as if he was drawing a polite veil over their friendship. The action was rendered more beautiful still by the excitement of entering God's house whether it be a cathedral or the tiny chapel in which she had played hymns on the old piano every Sunday.

Now as she stood and gazed at the Stations of the Cross she understood why it was such a wonderful blessing to have people believe in you. The two figures sat very close in a cushioned pew; one regretting her foolishness and the other wondering how many more years of normal life lay ahead. Both had important decisions to make but one was more poignant and painful than the other. Ellie prayed for both of them.

Encouraged by his warmth, Ellie drew close. She closed

her eyes, entertaining the hope that Gary would cultivate some sort of relationship. She was 17; she knew her own mind and recognised the deep feelings within her heart.

A gentle nudge from Tiz drew her attention to Rev. He was wearing a long, black coat – similar to the soutane worn by priests – which flowed and flapped behind him. On his head he wore a black beret which sat untidily on his thick hair. Where had the Mohican gone? It appeared he was having a serious discussion with two nuns. Did they assume he was a priest, suggested Fab? 'It's the white collar,' simpered Boo. 'They are walking together. Surely they realize that priests don't have spiked jelled hair and long fingernails?'

'They are coming over. I'm off.' Tiz was flushed.

'Hang on,' giggled Boo. 'They are bowing to each other.' Rev's action was full of dignity. The nuns turned and moved slowly away. 'You don't half fancy yourself,' taunted Boo as Rev approached casually. 'What on earth did you find to talk about?'

Rev grinned. 'We discussed venial sins and the Eucharist.' There was a long silence as they left the cathedral. The sun shimmered on the river below. Bas stumbled towards them, drink in hand, with Mustard limping painfully behind him.

'What is venial sin?' enquired Fab.

Rev drew himself up to his full height. 'It's a sin that is not fully evil and does not deprive the soul of God's grace.'

'And how would you know?' rubbished Bas with a cold swagger.

'That's for me to know and you to find out.' Bas lunged at him but the challenge changed into a chase across wide meadows carpeted with thick tall grass.

The meal in the bus was sparse. Hummus, baked beans and cold pasta. Wishful Ellie, delightfully cheerful and blissfully aware that her beaded hair was quite alluring and unusual for her, was prepared for a lively evening.

Gary found her mischievous and she coloured his world when he had to shove memories and dark experiences out of his mind. The change in her appearance was an inevitable progression into his world and yet he dare not make plans. Not yet, he could only wait.

They drove towards the Connemara region and within the bus shafts of sunlight cut through to illuminate a soft, shining landscape of hills and streams. Good-natured, light hearted Cheddar had been missing for most of the day but was reluctant to say why. Yet Ellie was conscious of pain in his eyes.

On a sprawling farm the groups formed. Dotted with pools and rivulets of water the land was a mass of bodies; it was a popular venue and the bands had been arriving for days. It was the most exhausting, exciting, boisterous gig yet. Fab was fierce. In the flush of her success her performance became passionate and not to be outdone Bas was fast and furious. Between them they stirred the crowd into hysterical energy and competed with enthusiasm.

Ellie was aware of a sharp pain to her head. In the pit in front of the stage she gradually found herself crushed among the dancers, spitting and jostling until elbows drove her towards the ground and she wanted to scream. Covered in perspiration she clenched her fist; she could hear her heart thumping and there was an empty feeling in the pit of her stomach. Stage divers leapt and vaulted and plunged over the heads of the crowd; they were lifted high and spread-eagled and bodies were pushed and edged onto safe patches of grass. Her head was buzzing. In her ears the whining feedback grated.

Cheddar recognised the top of her beaded plaits as she was sent sprawling across the grass. He pointed excitedly to Gary and shouted. A beam of pain irradiated Gary's face. He had been a watcher in the shadows, taking a break, and Ellie had almost been crushed.

Her brown eyes blazing with vitality, Boo jumped from the stage. Their gig was over, others were taking their place. Ellie had recovered sufficiently to congratulate them for she was beginning to realize that this was no noisy, unhinged punk group band but a well-organized set of musicians who composed all their own songs and performed well. She had discovered a new expression, "pit etiquette", which meant that, in future, she would stay well clear of the stage.

'These damn girls,' derided Bas as he and Mustard settled down with half a dozen cans. In a semicircle they sprawled on dry grass around the bus and relaxed. They were in good spirits – as much a part of Ireland as the trees and the birds. The outburst was aimed at Tiz and Fab who had acquired a couple of men with circuitous intentions to escort them to the nearest copse. Boo was in a heated argument with Cheddar for failing to keep an eye on Ellie and Rev was desperate for a bit of peace and quiet. 'I'm off for a walk.' His long hair, lank and wet with sweat, shone in the setting sun. 'See you at the pub.'

'At least we don't get verbally abused any more,' commented Tiz. 'I once read that being a female on stage is a licence for being heckled. Well, maybe it is predominantly a male world and we have this whole body image issue, but what the heck, we can be as good a guitarist as a man any day.'

'I like the aggression and competition,' enthused Fab. 'We are more dedicated and the music scene can be a daunting place for a woman but we are strong because we have to be. We are cautious because we are surrounded by morons at times but,' and she cast an impetuous eye at Gary, 'when it all comes together and we have equal treatment in an integrated environment it is all worth it.'

'Must admit, that just about sums it all up.' Mustard hardly opened his eyes.

'You read too much,' Bas slurred sarcastically. The captive young men were suitably impressed but were bright enough to remain silent, especially in the company of such vibrant, exciting and talented girls.

Ellie had squirreled away several vegetable pasties, Irish soda bread and yogurts. She felt no anxiety in the warmth of the countryside and yet the deep concern for Gary raised its head as he appeared wearing an exhausted, anaemic look. Ellie steeled herself against the hurt and pain in his eyes. He was a difficult man to fathom. When she smiled at him she was relieved to see the despondency had lifted, if only fleetingly. Was he a helpless victim of some narcotic? No, she did not believe that was possible. Was there some wretched secret that he was unable to dispose of? She could identify with that. Whatever it was it was changing him. Yet his pale face was focused and after the meal he thanked her, apologised for the danger he had put her in and suggested they all retire to the pub.

Ellie cleared away the dishes. She shuddered to see Bas in the act of raising a half bottle of whisky to his lips. It was a little after nine. The daylight hours had withered to half their summer glory but the evening was still young and they were ready to celebrate Ellie's birthday.

The pub came highly recommended. Mustard drove the bus into a charming little town of old houses huddled under a ruined mill surrounded by a mill pond. The pub, although very old, was excellently preserved but had maintained its scruffy smoke-tarnished veneer and was heaving at the seams. Gary instructed them all to keep together and the young men, somewhat enamoured of the girls, escorted them in.

There were three rooms downstairs. One was taken over by the bar behind which stood a huge, whiskered middle-aged man whose face assumed an expression of injured dignity when accosted with, 'Say, come on, Pat, we're dying of thirst here.' The words were almost deadened by the music. It came from the adjoining room and Rev was burning with curiosity. The drums, the pipes, the fiddle and the mandolin reverberated throughout the room; he couldn't wait to be served. It was left to Gary and Bas and two pretty colleens to sort out the beers.

The room was large with lacklustre curtains and windows opening out onto the street. Hammered copper tables and ripped leather-topped stools were pushed into corners and a piano took pride of place in front of a black iron fireplace with loose painted tiles. Whilst couples were dancing an elderly woman was putting finishing touches to a knitted garment in the nook. All the tables were occupied; people sat on them, stood on them, danced on them.

'Don't keep giving me not really, is it yes or no?' A deep voice held court. Tiz was in an altercation with a man. 'Mad,' he muttered. 'You are stark, staring mad.' Thrusting his mean face forward, he punched her arm. She recoiled. His hand covered her mouth, his fingers splayed across her cheek. She pushed his away; his hand sought the glass perched precariously on the sill.

Tiz spat, 'Nobody does that to me. I wouldn't be in this scene if I couldn't take care of myself. So f*** you.' His anger was mounting.

'Go on then, show us what you are made of. All that Sapphic so-called inclination, all that tribade shit.' He brought the glass into violent contact with the table edge and it smashed to pieces on the floor.

Bas was instantly by her side. There was a scuffle, nothing more; no one invited needless pain and Bas, on his own admission, had not had a real fight for ages. His youth had been spent in constant aggression with his father who had eventually left home but his legacy meant that he was well able to take care of himself. Nothing, according to Bas, is more important than a father who keeps his word.

'What the hell was all that about?' he barked.

'He insinuated,' complained Tiz. 'He suggested that I was a lesbian.'

Bas hollered. 'So what? Like hell he did. He's filled his last tub of coal.'

'Where did that come from? Sour-tongued and sarcastic but never humorous,' Tiz mused.

The man meanwhile had disappeared. It was a chilling incident. Bas was in hot pursuit. Later when he returned with bruised knuckles and a smile of satisfaction his remark to Tiz, 'There's no need for thanks, it's my pleasure,' was followed quickly by:

'She wasn't going to thank you, anyway,' from a sarcastic Boo.

The landlord appeared, shoving his way to the centre of the room. 'Refreshments will be served in the next room directly but in the meantime we will spare no pains to oblige our friends with some authentic Irish ballads.'

The mood had changed. Customers were conversing and Gary, with Ellie by his side, was in deep discussion with a couple of young Welshmen. His ability to rivet his listener's attention never palled and they debated the Celtic influence in Wales and the band's successful visit to the Mumbles. Ellie would have liked to join in. She and Gran had been there and to the Gower Peninsula. She remembered the chapel and the great hall of Oystermouth Castle and the wide bay with the long promenade. Now, clutching her glass of orange, all she wanted was to sit. Perhaps it was the after effects of the pit experience but she felt justifiably furious that she had allowed it to happen.

The ballads over, there was a scramble for food. Then came the problem. Vegetarians are particular. Anything which is obviously meat can be avoided; it is the sneaky covering of paste under mayonnaise and pasta with chicken disguised as cannelloni which causes concern. Rev and Cheddar (so dissimilar in many ways) probed and peered at each dish and sandwich. They settled for colcannon, an Irish dish of mashed potato and cabbage. 'It's bubble and squeak, really. We used to have it every Sunday night,' claimed Fab.

'Where have you been, anyway?' enquired Boo.

Fab gave a cheeky grin. 'Just talking. Scenting the talent as the fox scents the poultry coop. What about you, Ellie, are you OK? You look pale.'

They walked round the table following each other in single file, paper plates balancing precariously as they scanned the food for seconds. Ellie paused. Did they realize the depths of her isolation, the frustration she felt? She had taken great pains to hide her anxieties but even as a child had always wanted to know what lay around the bend in the road. She needed some air.

There were shadows between the trees as Ellie stepped into the street. Just two forlorn trees fighting for light between a small factory and a high wall. Time and weather had worn down a stone obelisk in the market place and surrounding it were wooden seats on which young people were chatting.

She did not protest when Gary joined her; how could she? He spread out his hands as if to apologise or perhaps to wonder at her intentions. Behind the tiredness there was a deep sense of satisfaction, there was no sign of a frown and his eyes were clear. While she had silently thanked the strangers all around her, while she had relied on her girl friends at all times, in her heart she knew that she felt some deep affection for Gary. 'If you cannot face a problem you can't resolve it,' Gran had said. What should she write in her next letter? That she was falling in love? That he was a little older. That she knew nothing about him, well hardly anything. Most important, would he ever forgive her for this deception?

He went on at length discussing the itinerary for the next few days. Then he studied the ground for a moment, and looked up at her. 'Are you enjoying yourself?' The breeze had brought colour back into her face. 'Shall we go back?' He pacified her by whispering 'Happy Birthday' and with her arm linked in his they left the peace of the street for the din of the public house.

The name of Dark Horse acted like magic on Cheddar. He had been in a bit of a stupor watching shadows move across the floor. Pat, the whiskered barman, approached. 'It is to be observed,' he began, 'that when in Ireland you do as the Irish do. What we do is drink and sing and play music. In that order or all at once. You take your choice.' The accent thick and rich concluded. 'However everyone must do their bit and we'll have no shirkers.'

Was anyone listening? There was even more noise and more people – the food had been cleared and an overspill of regulars occupied the bar area. 'Right!' Pat cleared his throat. 'We'll start with Sean. You will notice that the eats have gone; that's because of the English. It's unlucky, so they say. Sing at the table, die in the workhouse.' Boo nodded in agreement. Sean reached for the pipes. 'Sorry, Sean, we will have the Irish toast; all raise your glasses. May the road rise to meet you and may the sun be always at your back. Right, Sean.'

After the Irish had performed – dancing, singing or playing an instrument – Rev played on borrowed drums and Boo and Tiz sang one of their own compositions. Gary gave his rendition of Galway Bay after which Pat pointed to Ellie. 'I'm sorry,' Gary began. 'Ellie doesn't play. As it is her birthday perhaps we can excuse her.' Ellie moved slowly forward. Something flickered in the depths of her eyes. There was an impulse within her; she was goaded into doing something she hadn't done in a long while. As she approached the piano there was a lull. It may have been her graceful composure as her nervousness was tempered with exhilaration, or her calm expression which turned heads. She lifted the lid and hesitantly began. "Ar hywd a nos", a Welsh tune. "All through the Night". It echoed around the room and the Cymric tones from a lone Cambrian sobered the audience into reflection. Ellie could only play hymns yet it did not seem inappropriate even here. The fiddle and mandolin picked up and the rest joined in.

It was too late to stem the emotion that Gary was feeling. He seemed to be struggling; his body trembled and his mind was wandering. The glass beads in her hair matched the sparkle in her eyes and he could only look and wonder. It was a few moments of magic. To appreciative applause she blushed as Gary took her hand and led her away. He would have cause much later to reflect on this evening, the atmosphere, and on the music, and he would blame the charm of Ireland with its beauty, its mystery and its enchantment, for the potent medicine which his ailing body needed.

The applause was followed with a chorus of "Happy Birthday". Bas and Fab led with their interpretation of "Wild Rover" amidst frantic clearing of empty cigarette packets and scraps of food which littered the tables and floor. No one could be persuaded to leave until Pat had bestowed on them the Irish blessing. 'Now all raise your glasses.' His voice rose:

'May you have food and raiment,
A pillow for your head.

May you be forty years in heaven
Before the devil knows you're dead.'

It was a rowdy, hilarious group that stumbled and fell
in the direction of the bus. Mustard awoke with a start; his
visit to the pub had been a short one, mainly to eat, and
he had caught up with some sleep. He knew their moods.
This had been a rewarding and beneficial tour; the response
from other bands had been appreciative and sales of tapes
had doubled. Bas rubbed his hands with gratification as he
fell into his bunk.

Rev removed his trousers but the girls appeared to be
indifferent to his maleness. It was with a quiet insistence
that Fab was put to bed before she collapsed in a heap. Tiz
and Boo shared a bunk, giggling and whispering until they
too slipped into silence.

CHAPTER SEVEN

"The saving of a man is the holding of his tongue."
(Proverbial Arabic.)

During her first days Ellie had been coy and reserved, but with little privacy and the minimum of home comforts the way to survive was to give in to threadbare cleanliness and honest humour. They were crammed in the bus and bodies were hot. Half dressed, she washed as best she could in the tiny bowl. Cheddar was asleep on the floor after vowing never again to get drunk.

Further down the bus Gary and Mustard were quietly reminiscing. 'Last year about this time,' said Gary, 'we attended the Feile An Phobali, the Peoples Festival in West Belfast, and it was brilliant although very political and we got to play in the sidelines despite being blanked by the headliners. There was an abundance of traditional folk music and visual arts but it's not something I would put them through again. I bring this up because your European tour is political, isn't it?'

Mustard leaned back in his seat rubbing his leg. 'Must admit it's a lot different when it is global. You don't expect to persuade everybody round to your opinion. And anyway there is always somebody with a dogged determination to drag you down.'

Gary sighed. 'People generally give little thought to their closeness of culture and politics but it is simply a gut feeling, you just go that way.'

The conversation, although brief, had been arduous for Gary. Overcome with fatigue, he splashed cold water on his face. He felt as if marauding armies were attacking his arms and legs.

He felt sick although he hadn't eaten a great deal and had drunk mostly water and a couple of cold beers. They were almost home. Itineraries are never straightforward, there is always doubling back to do; you follow the gigs, not the road, he declared. Removing his jeans and tee shirt, he slithered into his sleeping bag and curled up on the floor.

Ellie was conscious of a hunger to hold him. Her thoughts were running wild, rolling back and forth inside her head with the persistence of a tide. She was unable to concentrate on anything other than Gary. In her daily chores nothing seemed to prove sufficient distraction. She knew right from wrong, of course she did, but she also knew what she wanted. She was old enough, she was 17 and he bought her children's books. It would take only one word to turn her life around yet in her heart she knew that her silence was the saving of her.

Ellie resisted all temptations to mull over the day's events; her prayers were short. Her dreams were of rich valleys and countryside where all the hills dip into the sea. She was oblivious to the deep snores and grunts of Bas, Rev's steady breathing and the sniffs and wheezes of Cheddar.

In a few hours they would be setting out for home. Rev was a law unto himself, a person who travelled round the world with his eyes wide open, unblinkered, observant and rational. He read a lot. When he wasn't buried in a book he was out on one of his walks that could stretch for miles. He turned over in his bunk and opened his eyes. Ellie caught a softness in them she had never seen before but then he smiled and dropped off to sleep.

Pat had made the pub's washroom available to them in the morning and the bus was parked a little way across the green.

With the exception of Rev they trooped across the cobbles, Boo clasping her toiletries, her long hair loose. Bas followed in his boxer shorts, chasing her across the street, hopping as the gravel cut into his bare feet. There was a free-for-all in the cobweb-covered shed and the water was barely warm. Modesty was an old-fashioned preoccupation; there wasn't the time or space to cultivate good taste. By the time the wandering boy had returned it was time to move on.

There were few demands on Ellie. It was her choice to shop, prepare menus and cook the food. She was never sure at what age memory begins but Gran always let her help with meals, unlike her mother who generally wanted her out of the way. 'We are almost out of Calor Gas,' exclaimed Tiz.

'I think we should have enough to see us until we get home.'

The day had brightened. Ireland, a country of dramatic weather changes, had turned the sombre cirrus clouds into a sparkling jewelled sky. The morning had been a mixture of sun and rain painting leaves with a copper glow.

They sat on a tarpaulin eating their vegetable curry and rice. This was no ordinary life; no one knew of the terrible struggle this important decision had cost her. She wanted to laugh and sing, to discuss and argue, to interrupt and cajole, to talk. There was a moment of emptiness when she felt she had something of importance to say. This sacrifice was not for the love of her mother or for the hatred felt for Phil, despite the recurring nightmares of his lurking figure in her bedroom. This was for her and her peace of mind.

Finally when everything moveable was packed away, instruments safely in cases and "niggles put to bed" as Gran would describe it, they began their journey to Athlone.

It was time to write postcards. Ellie had no desire to inflict any worry on Gran. If she was on a vertiginously steep slope she would hide it from her. She wished to remain virtuous and responsible in her eyes and still wanted the comfort of blood ties.

Bas was being questioned on the subject of toilet rolls.

'Look Bas,' Tiz was nagging 'You brought them in, didn't you? You stole them from the pub.'

'Bloody hell,' he stormed. 'Half of them were littering the floor, along with empty cig packets and goodness knows what else.'

'We don't need them, that's rotten, that is,' Tiz snapped. Boo glared at him. She occasionally struck out for herself. 'You,' she pointed a finger, 'are a jerk. It's morons like you that get us a bad name. Is it any wonder that we're ostracized?' Her eyes flashed.

'You look great when you're feisty,' Bas taunted. 'You'll make someone a fair rumpus of a wife.'

She whirled on him. 'Marriage does not enter into my scheme of things,' she protested so *** off!'

Ellie was amazed that these intelligent people could fly off the handle so quickly but Gary had the answer. Wages. 'It has been a great tour, fantastic gigs, sales of tapes and tee shirts are up and we are in pocket. So now it is pay-out time.' Tiz and Gary divided the cash on a small table wedged between the seats. It was done efficiently and without disagreement. 'The band receive the lion's share,' Gary explained to Ellie. 'It works out well usually. Let me know if you don't agree.'

'By the way, Tiz,' his expression was benevolent. 'There is money there for your venture with the Bradford library. It's a start. Good luck with it.' Tiz had simply put the idea on hold but Gary, as usual, had taken her seriously.

'You don't mind?'

'Just make sure we get a mention,' he replied.

'It is impossible to wind down after such a hectic time,' echoed Fab. 'Although I daresay it's back to the humdrum world, we can do it all again next year.'

'Says who?' questioned Bas. 'I don't remember asking you to join us.'

She turned on him, shaking with tension 'Do you know what, Mr Halitosis, you're jealous because you don't have the stage to yourself.'

'You have expressed just what I've often felt,' encouraged

Boo and the stressful atmosphere was close to breaking point.

'Must admit,' hollered Mustard, 'things are getting a bit hot in here. What say I stop for a bit and we all go outside and cool down?' The opportunity passed, there was a smell of rain in the air and as the road began to climb the storm broke. Lightning leapt around the sky, rain poured in torrents, forming rivers which swept towards them and Boo was hysterical. She rolled herself into a ball and squatted at the rear of the bus. Fab and Tiz crouched beside her. 'I'm so scared,' she whimpered.

'You're alright.' They rubbed her arms and held her head. Boo was pale, her dark eyes wide; her whole body trembled with each flash of lightning. She cried out at each clap of thunder. Bas drew the curtains. He was muttering words of consolation.

This was a rare moment, not a tremor of misgiving. Cheddar sat through it all with indifference. Ellie felt a sickness in her throat, she was scared too. Not with the intense dread or fear Boo experienced but she would have liked a little reassurance. It was as if her tongue was glued to the top of her mouth. The magnificent spectacle was being watched by Gary and Rev. 'The anger of the Gods,' suggested Gary, 'but don't mention it to Boo. She is swamped in superstition as it is.'

Everyone around Boo was treading softly even though the storm had passed and the sun had reappeared as the bus turned to follow the river. Fab had forgotten the quarrel; in her cheery, self- possessed way she attempted to analyse Bas psychologically, putting the whole thing down to his persona. She regarded the disagreement between them as purely jealousy.

'It would be good if we could stop soon,' Rev hinted. The clouds had rolled away and in the distance he had spotted a large marquee. 'We might just as well stretch our legs.' It was quite normal for the girls, particularly, to be inquisitive. The marquee was in the middle of a field surrounded by a dozen or more cars. Were they trespassing? Surely not, thought Tiz. She led the way.

'It's a ceilidh, must be,' she whispered. No one could have anticipated the beauty of the colours, the fragrance of the flowers and the aroma of the candles. Their feet were soaked after walking over the fields, but they were made welcome by a fair young man in a smart suit and maroon cravat. They stepped onto a red carpet and into a Celtic ceremony of marriage. Tiz was beginning to regret her foolishness. They couldn't gatecrash such a felicitous occasion, could they? Their clothes were most unsuitable for a wedding. They were seated at the back, all of them, apart from Bas who remained standing at the entrance.

There was an air of suppressed excitement. Surrounding the chairs was a circle made of stones. They were handed an order of service which explained that the circle represented a "wholeness and eternity" and a natural cycle night and day, sun and moon. Songs were interspersed with poems and candles, symbolizing fire, water, air and earth, were scattered around. Bas was becoming uneasy. 'Same as Magna really,' he informed Cheddar, 'only not as loud.'

The bride wore a simple white dress, the bridegroom was tall and wore grey; they drank milk for youth and wine as an emblem of their adult lives. Ellie was fascinated. How could anyone imagine rocky ground ahead when the path of two lovers appeared as smooth as velvet? Rev's attention was drawn to the refreshments on the huge trestle tables in the corner. Bas stood stiffly in the doorway. When the couple exchanged water "for the time they die and return to their natural state" Gary stole a glance at Ellie. If only life was all faithfulness and happy marriages, he thought. If only we were all given the chance to find out. The hand fastening was followed by the couple kissing and jumping over the broom; the stepping into a new life together and sweeping away any bad luck for the future. Well, thought Tiz, Boo could easily relate to that.

The Irish are a warm, gregarious, competitive race. It is irreverent to refuse their hospitality and these celebrations were not confined to close friends and neighbours. In a countryside of such rich valleys it injected life and enchantment into the lives of anyone choosing to stay.

Bas met his match in the best man (or someone who was his equivalent) and sadly the drinking competition was short-lived. Bas lay in the long grass. His last drink had had the effect of dismantling his perceptions utterly. The idea that this was the way to live was the determinism Bas stood by. Put all you have got, risk all that you have into the moment, live without holding anything back and don't care about the result. He was paralytically drunk. Unceremoniously he was dragged across the grass and propped up against the wheel of the bus. Mud clung to his face and clothing and the girls swept past him with an air of loathing; apart from Ellie. Alcohol, unsocial behaviour, arrogance and Bas could not be separated. Ellie could laugh at his warped sense of humour, could sympathise with his sense of gross vulgarity, for who was to say what lay behind the gruff exterior. Might there not be the potential for a decent Bas?

The final touches were being put together for the last stretch before home. Ellie was carried along on the floodtide of this enthusiasm for it wasn't too difficult to imagine the seclusion of her own room and a hot bath. Boo was levelling a pointed finger in the direction of Bas. 'What are we going to do about him? It's time we were going.' Equipped with a bowl filled with soapy liquid, she tripped down the steps, knelt beside the still heavily inebriated Bas, and carefully washed his face. Several pairs of astonished eyes watched her from the bus. Unabashed she sponged the front of his shirt and wiped his hands. She had her audience and Bas was in no position to complain.

Rev and Cheddar settled him in the bunk. Boo shrugged her shoulders; her eyes were speculative. 'Not a word,' she said. The light from the full moon poured in brightly through the bus windows as the friends settled down for the night. Ellie mused for a while in the moonlight over the perplexities of her life and how easy it was to be friendly and absorb the positive aspects of the punk scene. She had understood it to be an ugly life. Why, when she was discovering that it had a caring, sharing side which was almost beautiful?

Dublin was a welcome sight. Cheddar was becoming increasingly agitated and bit his nails incessantly. Rev's question, 'Are you OK? Have you had your travel pills?' was rewarded with subdued responses. Once aboard the ferry he became restless and began to panic. He shook with agitation, unsmiling and ungracious. 'Oh, come on,' pleaded Boo. 'It's not that bad, a bit choppy but, you know, we can find a quiet place.'

'It's more than a bit choppy,' dismissed Bas. 'Have you looked out across the sea? It's like a tidal wave.'

'It's all in the mind,' offered Fab, rubbing his arm. 'It's simply a complex you have really; ignore him.'

Gary's tone was reassuring. 'Come on, Cheddar, remember how well Ellie looked after you last time.' Cheddar stood his ground. 'I'm not leaving the bus!' There was a chorus of suggestions.

'Now look,' Fab's tone was motherly. 'Maybe you have had a bad experience in the past but I am sure it will pass.'

'Hell,' mocked Bas, 'this is no moment for self-analysis.'

Cheddar sat down abruptly. Bas heaved him up, grasping him around the waist, turning him and pushing him towards the door. Cheddar breathed deeply half a dozen times as he arrived on deck and fell into a window seat. His extreme attitude got him nowhere. The entire performance had been sorted, smiled Tiz and suggested that it was now up to Ellie to keep an eye on him. 'The floors have shifted,' he uttered and turned to her with a pathetic stare. She cradled his head and as she held him close his lean, youthful body appeared frail and vulnerable.

The waves lifted, heaved and pushed against the vessel and the howling wind drove everyone from the decks and away from the doors. Cheddar's head fell forward; there was no cry for help, no further talk. He was still. Ellie looked for friendly familiar faces but none came. Passengers held onto each other and inebriated youths stopped to ask if she was alright. Finding themselves the centre of attention Cheddar slept while Ellie could only nod or shake her head. The significance of what might be happening was all too clear. This was the border of somebody's life.

It was not the first time she regretted her silence. With a disgusting reflex Cheddar tossed his head and as the ferry rose high in the water he landed on the deck. He threw up all over her shoes, causing her to retch, and swallowing was painful. When Gary appeared his soothing voice calmed her. Bas was harsh and unsympathetic. 'Best get him to the sick bay,' Gary suggested.

'What?' Bas was dismissive. 'Naw, we haven't far to go. He'll soon get over it.'

'I doubt it.' Cheddar passed out. 'Off you go, Ellie, thanks. We'll look after him.'

Ellie's desire for a shower was threatening to open the floodgates of her phobia against dirt. The girls were gathered in the rest room. 'Oh, hell, Ellie. We didn't know you were sick. Come on, we'll help you clean up,' soothed Tiz. Language is elastic but hers was limited. However, she convinced them that it was Cheddar who was on his way to the sick bay and the reinforced group were quickly on their way to join Bas and Gary.

The sea was rough, the wind whipped up the waves, forming patterns like corrugated sheets. People were reeling like tops, holding on to anything that was fastened down. Ellie had been praying; she would hate anything to happen to Cheddar. He talked comparatively little and was often a source of annoyance to all of them. His ablutions were often at their most urgent in the middle of the night and Bas had growled in a spate of vulgarity when he had failed to secure the door and the rain and wind swept onto the occupants, soaking the sleeping bags. Some of his topics were inane and even childish but Mustard always jumped to his defence and with quick gestures and a nervous movement of his beard would calm things down.

The questions implied rather than asked by the doctor had produced various responses from the group who had insisted in piling into the bay. 'He isn't taking drugs,' Gary was heard to say. 'He hasn't had any alcohol for hours; he isn't on any medication as far as we know.' Ellie, trying to eavesdrop, could only hear snatches of conversation above the loud gusts of wind. With suspicious curiosity the doctor asked if someone could check his pockets. There was an awkward pause. Cheddar was out cold. Rev appeared in the doorway. 'I'll do it.' Cheddar had numerous pockets and a variety of zips. It was quite a relief to discover an empty foil strip of Stugeron in his jacket.

Ellie remembered on the journey to Dublin he had at least eight tablets left. Had something happened in Connemara? He had appeared troubled. Had he overdosed? No, the whole idea was intolerable. The nurse positively smacked her lips as she spoke. 'Are you sure this is all there is? These are travel pills, hardly the usual OD prescription!'

'There's nothing else,' Rev replied gravely. 'Is he going to be alright?'

The doctor had been thorough. 'Sure, we'll keep him here under observation for a while; will someone stay with him?' It was Rev who sat with the kidney bowl at the ready and as the group turned to leave the nurse laughed and turning to him cheekily said, 'Let's fasten all his zips and tidy him up shall we?'

No one was more capable of saying the most cutting and venomous things than Bas. With a flourish he slammed the bus door and seated himself next to Mustard for the journey from Liverpool. 'He's a complete waste of bloody time, you know. He gets a share of the pickings and what does he do? Not a fat lot. Sound checks, yes, I'll grant you that but as far as any lugging that's way out of his league.' Mustard's beard was bristling as he concentrated on the road ahead and his lips tightened beneath his moustache. He liked Cheddar and felt sorry for him. Bas carried on unfolding a full catalogue of mistakes due to Cheddar on the tour in spite of Cheddar lying within earshot and in no position to defend himself.

Ellie was seated on cushions beside his bunk holding his hand. He had been half carried from the sick bay by Rev and Gary who looked tired and austere and complained of dehydration. Slowly Gary moved to stand behind Bas. 'What's your gripe, Bas? The tour has gone smoother than most. Why wait till now to have a go? And Cheddar, of all people?'

'Because Bas is an arse,' called out Boo.

'A pleb,' seconded Tiz.

'I'm coming to it,' Bas growled. There was a sudden movement from the back of the bus as Cheddar staggered to his feet. Ellie tried holding onto him but he fell forwards, banging his head. Bas's revelation had been stopped.

When everyone had settled down and Cheddar was resting once again Ellie replaced Bas in the seat next to Mustard. She liked riding up front, she enjoyed watching him drive, she felt sure that she could drive the bus with a little tuition. Mustard talked about all sorts; Ellie was a captive audience. His long association with the ALF had brought about his arrests on more than one occasion; he had written songs about animal cruelty which the band had included in the tour. She would miss him. She would miss them all, sighed Ellie, but Gary especially.

Damp sheep, huddled cows and the strong overwhelming smell of pig slurry deteriorating on the air introduced them once more to the English countryside. Conversation was beginning to flag. Their own beds were a welcoming prospect, they were all tired and needed a break from each other. They were in search of space. 'It happens after every tour,' Gary had told Ellie way back in Ireland. 'We get on each others' nerves, small incidents get blown out of all proportion and words are used which should never have been thought of. Everyone agrees that they are never going to do it again. But they do. Rev has the answer, he disappears, have you noticed? Goes for long, and I mean long, walks. I used to be able to do that.'

Had she set anybody's nerves on edge, Ellie wondered? Gran used to say that she filled the house with her imperfect singing. Well, it couldn't possibly be that. Perhaps there were some rules she had broken inadvertently. Well, if she had, no one had thought to tell her about it.

They had a short rest at the American diner: stainless steel and Stars and Stripes. Rock and Roll music played on a juke box and Tiz and Rev jigged to "Staying Alive" whilst queuing for seats. They had frugally restricted the intake of food on the bus; this was their last meal before getting home. Cheddar refused to join them.

At the next table a young child was completely taken with Rev, staring with bright blue eyes, dribbling and cooing with each mouthful of food. The wonder of babies, mused Ellie, something she looked forward to, and yet she was to discover that nature is not always so well disposed towards conception.

Bas was soon restored to favour; he settled the bill and snatched a handful of tomato sauce sachets on his way out.

CHAPTER EIGHT

"See how great a forest a little fire kindles, and the tongue is a fire, a world of iniquity." (*James Ch 3 v 5 & 6.*)

It was one thing to renounce, in moments of extreme anger, all the comforts of a home, but quite another thing to settle for the discomforts of lack of privacy and modern facilities. Yet this phase of quiet defiance had opened up a new world and evoked a confidence which had previously escaped her. And as the weeks had run into months Ellie had felt ready for anything. Her relationships had not been corroded by lack of comfort.

Gingerly Cheddar lifted up his head. Sheffield had a distinct smell, he recalled. Smoke and spumy steel furnaces, soot and rolling mills were locked in the past but the shadows of factories still clung to the blanket of dust even though modernisation had washed away the debris. It was not unpleasant, it was home.

He was evidently still drugged but was the first to be dropped off. He was helped to his front door by Mustard and greeted by his mother who was in a shrunken sweater and had a bust which reached down to her waist. The house was listed for a clearance scheme, claimed Tiz as they waved to him through the window. 'They could rehouse them anywhere,' she said. 'Could be miles away.'

It was the turn of Fab to gather up her belongings. She had been pleasant and amusing and wanton (according to Boo) and kind to Ellie. She would peer in a scholarly manner over her glasses and quote Socrates. 'When I do not understand I prefer to say nothing,' she told Ellie, who hoped she wasn't alluding to her. There was a rush of hugging and goodbyes. Bas, who had woken from a hard sleep, only to find girls milling around him, was far from impressed. His vulgarity was hardly offensive any more; it was too late in the day.

Boo was disturbed. She had hoped to leave the bus without the scrutiny of Bas. The little fantasy she had of never having to sleep near him and listen to his grunts throughout the night was coming to fruition. Her departure with Tiz was to be a frantic one. Mustard pulled up. Bas leapt out and assumed a dramatic pose. The girls struggled with the backpacks, the guitars and Boo's beautiful shawl purchased from Aggie. Bas gave a subdued snort, wrapped the shawl around her and lifted her and the luggage onto the pavement. Her black eyes flashed. She attempted to struggle free but it was hopeless. She wept with frustration and Bas let her go. Tiz treated this show of macho exhibitionism with contempt. She even went as far as to express her disapproval by kicking his shins. 'See ya,' she grinned.

There was no point in lying to himself. Gary was relieved to be home. He was weary. There had been moments of tension, situations had to be defused on occasions and he had held all his emotions of fear and anger inside. His ability to remain reasonable was still there; he was grateful for that. His health had rallied for a time at least.

The bus stopped by the Wicker Bridge and the River Don murmured past. It was approaching 9 pm and mist hovered over the water. Bas clambered down the steps and Rev patted Mustard on the back. 'Thanks, mate. Cheers,' and they were gone.

There was so much Gary wanted to say to Ellie; she was fun and interesting; he admired her; she gave him all the support and encouragement that she could, but he had left it too late. Yet how could he ignore the flickering in the depths of her eyes when she looked at him? Or explain his reluctance to let her get too close?

Even before they crossed the bridge and drove under the viaduct they could smell the acrid smoke. What they saw stirred such fear and anger and, as the bus turned towards the road and the cafe, their feelings were of disbelief. The cafe was a blackened shell; the smoke furled in last gasps through the scarred roof. There were no windows, no doors. Twists of metal lay inside the entrance and sodden debris covered the street. Fire had gutted the inside of the building and embers gleamed like the eyes of the mythical salamander. Fire engines were preparing to leave and men were rolling hoses and shouting last minute instructions.

Ellie stood in the doorway of the bus surrounded by her belongings, her presents neatly packed in a plastic bag clasped in her hand. Tears rolled down her cheeks. She didn't see Gary approach the fireman or hear what conversation took place; she didn't see him kick out at the trivet or the masonry scattered around the pavement, or the pain and anguish in his face. It had been a furious blaze. She buried her face in her hands and dropped to the floor.

It was as if Gary suddenly refused to function. Between Ellie and Mustard, back on the bus, he would not be drawn. His eyes followed every movement of activity out in the street; the neighbours closing their doors and the firefighters poking at the ashes for the last time. Then, almost as if someone had switched on a light, his mind was clear. Then he could no longer keep his feelings to himself. His distress was evident. Jan had been taken to hospital badly burned. She was alone. It was difficult to imagine her suffering, Ellie sobbed quietly, and it would be an anxious wait to see how Jan progressed. The strong smell of smoke, charred wood and the oppressive pall reminded them that they had to move on.

'Ellie,' Gary's thoughtful tone almost stopped her tears. 'Do you mind staying with Maggie? Mustard and I, well, we'll stay on the bus overnight after we have been to see Jan. I can't see any other solution for the moment.'

There was a half-injured look on Mustard's face. 'You can stay on the bus with us if you want, Ellie, if you don't want to be on your own.'

'Perhaps, yes, maybe that would be a good idea!' invited Gary. 'I would like to point out that I am not thinking straight.' She clasped his hand and shook her head. "Maggie", she mouthed.

When they met at the breakfast table next morning Maggie was showing signs of frustration. 'I'm on me beam ends, waiting for news and explanations,' she wailed at Ellie. 'You would think they would come and let us know.' It was hardly, thought Ellie, that so little happened in Maggie's life that this drama, however dreadful a tragedy, was food she could feed on for a long time.

Ellie hadn't slept very well. Maggie moved about a lot during the night and Ellie had become used to the sound of traffic and other people. Here her room was above the front door which was hardly discernible beneath the shade of the heavy porch. A Virginia creeper clung to the stone walls and spread around her bedroom window. Maggie reminded her of Gran although lacking the spruceness and tact. Gran's advice that you shouldn't jump into an opinion all at once, you should rely on experience, would not have pleased Maggie. Here she was again with someone much older, someone desperate to throw questions and have them answered only to be met with a female Trappist monk. Maybe when she was old she would open a talking shop where people met, not to play whist or to listen to music, or to become members of a historical society, but simply to talk.

'It is not quite clear what happened,' Gary reported. 'Anything could have caused the fire – an electrical fault, a chip pan, even a lighted cigarette. They have investigators there now.'

When he talked of Jan he hesitated. 'She is burned mostly on her face, neck and shoulders, but her hands too are bad. We weren't allowed to see her but we have left a message and flowers. Tomorrow she may be moved to a burns unit; at present she is in Intensive Care.'

Maggie's face was a study of perplexity and sympathy.

'You can stay as long as you like, love,' she declared and patted Ellie's hand.

'We have three days before we loan the bus to another band so if we could leave it here until then, Maggie? We have to clean it up a bit.' Gary requested.

The light of the September evening was lovely and persistent. Along with Mustard, Gary and Ellie squatted comfortably on the old sofa under the window. It was with some trepidation that they watched Maggie slowly make her way to the kitchen, grasping the furniture with one hand and balancing her stick with the other. Everything in the house was showing signs of ageing. It could be so modern, so welcoming, thought Ellie. The chapel was a conversion but had still retained many of its original features such as the door and mullioned windows. Few wanted to live here and although it had all modern amenities very few wanted to visit for long periods either. There had never been any question of Maggie being in danger but Ellie would not be happy to have Gran live here alone.

Gary announced that he and Mustard would be purchasing a van and would Ellie like to go along, they would give her a call about 9am. 'His friends speak very highly of him,' Mustard was heard to say as they closed the heavy door behind them.

"It is plain why some furniture or leather when artificially aged is called distressed," groaned Ellie to herself as she approached the bath. Maggie had insisted she tried it out. 'You don't have to lift your legs, just walk into it and sit down. You can use my loofah if you like and my Castile soap that my daughter sent me last Christmas. Social Services had the bath put in for me.'

Ellie arranged her own toiletries on the stool and stepped into the bath. She caught sight of her reflection in the tarnished mirror and giggled. What if the girls could see her now? She removed her hair beads and gently shampooed her fair hair. How she would have liked to turn the clock back, she sighed; she would have been stronger, firmer with Jan when she drank so much. It was too late now. She slipped

into her pyjamas, made cocoa for supper and lay on the bed
wondering about the future and worrying about Gary.

****

'Let's not be hasty about this,' Mustard was protesting.
'Car salesmen are a special breed in my opinion. Some are
hucksters, some dishonest and aggressive; most are not but
it takes one to know one. Must admit I've met them all.' He
pulled the bus expertly into the showroom car park.

'What's he doing?' the grease-covered mechanic asked
Gary.

'Sorry, can't help you there.' Mustard grabbed discarded
pieces of rag and disappeared under a white van.

'He can't do that here. Not until he has a word with the
boss. You'll get me the bloody sack.' He snatched the phone
off the wall, not knowing for sure what he was going to say.
Gary leaned towards him. 'I think he is thinking of buying
the place.' He replaced the phone with a sideways glance
at Mustard, who moved about the showroom as if he had
taken charge.

A small, hot breeze ruffled the bunting and carried the
smell of coffee from the adjoining garage. Ellie appeared,
her shirt hanging loosely over pale blue shorts, and smiled.
Kneeling, she stroked a black and white kitten and carried
it to the low wall where she sat cuddling it, and holding it
close to her face. The concept of Ellie's gentle fondling was
inflaming Gary's imagination but Mustard's shout of 'Over
here' had prompted the mechanic to remove himself from
the pit and join them. He had found what he wanted, he
informed Gary; time for a test drive.

The mechanic showed vigorous reluctance. 'What about
security?'

Mustard was shrewd. 'For goodness sake,' he protested.
'There's a bloody great bus there. What more do you
want?'

They arranged the purchase of a white Peugeot van from
a salesman who Ellie presumed had done some heroic deeds

in his day as he was adorned with so much jewellery an Olympic winner would have been outshadowed. There had been little haggling. 'Don't you understand the problems that face a man like me?' grumbled the salesman. Mustard replied in so low a tone that it was completely lost on him but the bargain was struck; they were to pick it up later.

There were many lovely parks and gardens for people to enjoy nearby and Gary decided to pick up drinks and sandwiches from the supermarket and show them where he had spent his childhood. 'Abbeyfield Park,' he mused. 'Once had a pond with swans and a playground with a long swing thing like a shamrock; I can't remember the name of it now.'

'Was it called a shanty?' offered Mustard.

'Maybe. We used to stand at each end like Volga boatmen.' It concerned him that he was becoming more forgetful. They sat in the warm sun watching a game of bowls, driving off wasps from their food.

'See those rocks that are broken and rotten? We built a fort with those. I'm surprised they have survived!' Now they had been chosen as a home for rockery plants, the blue moss phlox, the yellow stonecrop and the bellflower, all familiar from her mother's garden, remembered Ellie. She had much preferred to be gardening than in her mother's shop. Sometimes her feeble protests worked but usually she was expected to work at the alterations on Saturday and have them ready for Monday. It was a boutique, her mother insisted, not a shop. She was drawn only to people with a show of wealth on their back. She could easily spot disreputable people, she observed, and held court in the thickly-carpeted, fashionable corner of the mall. Ellie was a huge disappointment to her and she told her so. 'When I need you to talk to customers you clam up on me. It won't hurt you to be sociable whilst you are waving the tape measure about.' Most of her clientele were pretentious snobs, like her mother; she did not miss her at all. In her present world of multicoloured lights her former life was one of shadows – obscure.

Mustard winced visibly as he rose from the bench; his leg was troubling him again. Ellie motioned that she would give him a massage before he left for his tour. It was the least she could do. Gary yawned. He could easily have fallen asleep but he had promised to visit Jan.

Whether it was the peculiarity of Maggie's appearance that disturbed Ellie or her inability to understand what the symptoms meant but it was obvious that something had to be done. Maggie was slumped in her chair, her frame on its side, and she was dribbling. Gary had been dropped off at the hospital and there was only Mustard to call on. Ellie ran towards the tunnel where the bus was parked and it wasn't long before he was taking charge and the doctor had been called.

It came as a shock to Ellie. Who would look after Gran if she was taken ill? Who would be there for her? For eight years Gran had taken care of her; is this how she should be repaid? Had she been respectful, thoughtful, caring enough? She was not a bad girl, just a good girl who had acted badly.

When Maggie had been safely tucked away in bed and instructions had been given for her medication, Ellie pulled up a chair beside her and wrote a long, apologetic letter to Gran. She looked at the pale, wasted, time-ravaged face on the pillow and held her hands. A slight stroke, the doctor had said. Nothing major; she could cope. Mustard was near but only for one more night.

It was a relief to see Tiz and Fab again. Boo was definitely not going to set foot in the cemetery even to visit Maggie but Tiz hastened to explain that they had sent toiletries. Gary arrived with news of Jan; she was out of Intensive Care but not yet ready to be moved to the burns unit. He hadn't shaved for a few days and Ellie, who had escaped for a short while from caring for Maggie, helped clean the bus, all the while keeping a close eye on his stumbling movements. He certainly looked tired but to keep sane he had to be in control.

Sometimes the cemetery seemed to engulf her. During the

day there were birds and squirrels, a family of hedgehogs and the occasional stoat, but the silence of the night matched her own silence and now poor Maggie had a glimpse of what the loss of speech entails.

It was almost midnight when she heard it, an unfamiliar thumping, scraping sound coming from her bedroom. She hadn't been upstairs since Maggie's illness; she had slept on the sofa. Her nursing care was taken over during the day; it was simply that someone had to be in attendance. She pushed away the duvet. There it was again. Was someone breaking in?

She picked up Maggie's walking stick. Whoever it was wasn't going to go away. It might be a feeble attempt but she had to protect Maggie. She trod each stair carefully, stepping up and waiting. She couldn't decipher the sounds, or even be sure that they were human. She reached the landing and held her breath. Lifting the old-fashioned latch, she prodded the door with the stick. What now? The door creaked open slowly and she paused.

It came at her swiftly, directly, then around her shoulders. Then another and another and it took all her efforts not to scream. Like a blind person she waved the stick in front of her probing at obstacles then retreating. Bats. The scream froze in her throat. She slammed the door shut. None had escaped as far as she knew. With heart thumping she almost fell down the stairs. Ellie had come this far without facing any severe constraints; nevertheless the episode unnerved her. In the hallway she flopped into a chair. There was a sound at the front door. A gentler knocking, a gnawing, rubbing sound. Ellie fixed her eyes on the letterbox. It was difficult to ignore the tapping and it was a graveyard. It was too much. She couldn't be so heartless as to forget that Maggie was relying on her. All she required was a little pampering and security.

Trying hard to conceal her fear she tackled the number of locks that secured the heavy oak door then breathed a sigh of relief when it creaked open to reveal Harry, the hedgehog. He had called for his milk and cat food. With so much on her mind she had forgotten to feed him. She began to giggle.

Mustard calmly appraised the situation with regard to the bats and they had, as he had rightly deduced, returned to their home in the chapel roof. 'They are only pipistrelles,' he mocked. 'They won't hurt you; they are probably more terrified of you than you are of them. Anyway,' he quipped, 'keep your windows closed,' and his beard quivered as he shook his head and smiled.

His last evening had been a sombre one; she had massaged his leg as promised and he and Gary had finished the last of the beers as the bus was now ready for the journey abroad. There would be no one to share the great impenetrable silences of the night when Gary returned to his flat.

"What sort of creature am I?" muttered Ellie, "to be afraid of the dark?" He had lied to her, her stepfather, about Moira's house being haunted; about vampires and ghosts and the evil eye. She was eleven years old and the supernatural was unknown to her. She had been taught about goodness and truth. It was deliberate and sometimes she would carry the thoughts to bed with her and panic in the darkness. When she had her mother all to herself she tried to explain all her fears but she was accused of exaggerating and lying. There was no sympathy. 'I might adopt you,' he taunted her as he sidled into her bedroom to say goodnight. 'Do you know what adoption is? It's a form of abduction sanctioned by law,' and he patted her head.

It was the rage boiling inside her that persuaded her to tell her mother about his affair with the girl at the gym. 'Everyone knows about it and they are laughing at you. You have a business to think about; it's the talk of the town.'

She was a child, her mother reminded her. 'Be careful what you say.'

It was degrading to watch her mother plead and when he eventually left the hate Moira should have felt for him unloaded itself on Ellie. She was shamed out of tears by her strong mother and more and more cut herself off.

CHAPTER NINE

"A shut mouth makes no enemies." (Proverbial Irish.)

"Well, this place is certainly putting its stamp on me,"
Ellie decided, a remark Gran was known to use often. She
needed some fresh air. Drops of rain were falling as she
walked towards the tunnel and the bus. The wood pigeons
and songbirds were in good spirits and as she looked at the
tombstones it was not a morbid fear she felt but sorrow.
Abbeyfield Park came to mind; surely cemeteries are merely
public parks in which people happen to be buried. Her
situation seemed safe enough.

She paused by the slimy pond and rested in a lean-to
whose walls and roof were painted with a strange mixture
of greys and greens. Several stones and lumps of wood
had been thrown onto the water and the statue had been
despoiled, leaving one arm severed at the elbow. A small
mound had been marked by a pile of pebbles.

Ellie needed this time to herself, these few moments
away in the fresh air. Of the many visitors that morning the
District Nurse had been the most welcome. She had a round,
friendly face and fat arms that wobbled when she applied
cream to Maggie's bottom. It didn't seem to matter that Ellie
was there, in fact she was asked to stand by with talcum at
the ready. 'It's not as if you can go into training for grief,'
she told Ellie. 'I've just left a poor soul who is devastated
by the loss of his old lady. You are alright though, Maggie

love. Soon have you back on your feet.' Ellie was only too thankful she was being looked after.

The meals on wheels arrived shortly after, followed by a Physiotherapist who sat beside Maggie, took some time to evaluate the situation, had a cup of coffee and a chocolate biscuit, and cheerfully left.

Ellie approached the bus with a heavy heart. It would be like saying goodbye to an old friend. Mustard was alone preparing flyers with coloured paper and a marker pen. 'Early to bed, early to rise, ain't never no good if you don't advertise,' he chortled. She pointed to his leg. 'It comes and goes.' There was comfort in knowing that the bus would be returned and in the meantime they would take delivery of the van. Mustard entered the chapel house quietly to take his leave of Maggie. He shook his head sadly. 'See you soon, take care.'

****

'Our purpose is to take you to Bradford, visit your library, do the deal and visit the One in Twelve,' Gary explained. Tiz had an interview and they were due to play a gig the same night.

Boo was sitting upright on a settee where the broken springs were plainly visible through the stained cloth. In the corner were piles of magazines and a threadbare carpet lay dangerously near an antiquated electric fire. This was where Bas and Rev lived. The landlord was reluctant to spend and not even Bas could persuade him, and he had tried. It was a hurried decision to meet here and memories of the cafe were still raw. When the subject of Jan was raised Boo moved away with tears in her eyes. But what delighted them all was that she was improving.

Ellie offered to make tea. The trickle of water that ran idly from the tap would take an age, she muttered, so she filled the kettle in the bathroom which was remarkably clean. Cheddar was absent; he had a severe cold proffered Fab. 'Could be something nasty.' They had a pizza delivered and pulled faces at passers-by who stared openly through curtainless windows.

'There is nowhere to hang 'em,' complained Bas. 'Anyway, they fell to bits when we tried to put 'em back.' As the night grew darker the city became a rowdy area filled with drunks and the noise of car sirens and slamming of doors.

'It isn't unlikely that the van could be hit,' said Rev with forewarning.

'Not while I'm sat here,' bellowed Bas. A fine, misty rain, without a breath of wind greeted them as they left.

They had been thrown together quite a lot, Ellie and Cheddar. He was very conscious of the role they all had to play within the group and although he would disappear when the time came to clear the stage he would blend in relatively well. It was when they rattled round the corner close by the Anglican Cathedral, the chalk white gleam of its frontage in the night reflecting back at them, that Fab was heard to say, 'He's sleeping in a car.'

'Who is?' mumbled Tiz, flat on the floor, both legs up against the side of the van.

'Cheddar,' divulged Fab. 'His father, or so-called, threw him out. He had nowhere to go so he is bunked up in an abandoned car.' Tiz straightened herself.

'Like hell he is, how do you know?'

'Gossip grows out of its own accord,' she quoted.

'Give me strength,' spat Tiz.

Gary pulled up. 'We've got to find him. Anyone got any ideas?' There was a long silence. Boo sighed.

'Aw come on,' Gary appealed. 'Give us a clue, Fab.'

'Somewhere off City Road, I think.' There wasn't time to double back, it was getting late and the girls had work in the morning; late nights never worried the men. But this was an emergency. For over an hour they scoured the streets and were on the verge of giving up altogether when Ellie pointed to a lean, familiar figure about to climb into a rusty wreck of a car.

'What the hell do you think you are doing?' Cheddar faced Gary with a blank and dreamy expression. There was no recognition, no surprise.

Ellie stood there motionless, suddenly she felt calm. 'Being young and inexperienced is no excuse for stupidity,' ranted Tiz. He was bundled into the van along with two large sacks of clothing and a carrier bag full of cheap wine. Waif-loving Ellie nursed his head in her lap; this was getting to be a habit. 'God, he's stoned,' Tiz warned. 'Where are you taking him?'

'Where do you think?' Bas was not pleased to see him nor enthusiastic about having a sickly youth full of illegal substances on his premises. He vented his fury on the furniture, knocked over a table and sent a buffet flying. He would have plenty to say on the subject in the morning.

From a place near the fire Ellie watched Maggie sleep. 'She rallied round almost as soon as you were out the door,' declared Dot. She was a grotesquely fat woman of about 60, wore her hair swept back from her face and ears, and over her flowered cotton dress hung a cardigan which had seen better days. 'Every day's the same to me,' she grumbled to Maggie. 'A day looked like a week to me but that is what happens when your family desert you.' Ellie wondered how she managed to consume a chicken leg, two pickled onions and two slices of brawn while hardly stopping for breath.

Maggie was sitting up in bed, her head slightly on one side but fully aware of what was going on. The colour had returned to her pinched cheeks and the only sign that she had of the stroke was a little droop at the corner of her mouth. Dot accepted the £5 note which Ellie gave her without looking up from her plate, so engrossed was she in removing the wizened skin from the chicken bone. Gary later drove her home.

****

Bas was in good voice. He had listened over his evening meal to Cheddar's detailed and disturbing episodes over the past days. How his mother had to meet him in the laundrette to give him his Giro; how some dealers had accosted him until he had chosen to slip into the Police Station claiming that he had lost his dog; and how he had paid 20p in a Superloo in order to have a wash. Bas left it all behind. This was the place to be, belting out in the pub with one or two songs on the Karaoke. Here his friends could treat him to a pint or two and a joke shared where the respective merits of jobs, politics and football could be thrashed out.

He liked his work. Scaffolding was where you were seen shirtless in summer and a great viewpoint for vigorously sizing up the girls. On football he remained neutral. 'I'm a darts man, me,' he would boast. This pub was his home from home; here he took pride in his own skill, his opinions, his macho image and virility. Tonight was a charity darts match. He elbowed the women aside and lurched up the stairs.

There was a distinct air of change about the place since he had been away; he couldn't quite explain the feeling of misgiving but there were a few newcomers hanging around the bar. He mentioned it to Charlie, a capable barman adept at pulling pints and holding conversations with more than one person at a time without actually having eye contact. However he did take a breather. 'I'll tell yer what, Bas, you have to keep yer eyes peeled. They've got some lively ideas up their sleeve.'

'Like what?' Bas wheedled.

'Like there's plenty of brass to be made.'

Charlie pointed to a pasty faced youth standing at the entrance to the games room, one hand resting on the pool table. On an emotional level Bas's feelings were simplistic. He had opinions for or against, he was either angry or calm, happy or miserable, he hated or he loved and despite the amount of alcohol he drank the strong passions never varied. He sang karaoke, enjoyed several jokes with the lads, but still the niggle persisted and he watched the surreptitious offloading of drugs and the smug expression on the dealer's face. He knew that something had to be done. This was his patch. He waited. The opportunity came; the dealer made a move. Bas followed him into the beer garden and into the ginnel. There were no words between them; Bas spun him round and head-butted him. Two hands were not enough to express his feelings. His feet found his shins and the steel toecaps cracked against the bones. When the knee came in contact with the groin, Bas left him rolling in agony. As he told Charlie later, 'If they do this shit in public they don't care any more. They're hankering to be done.'

'First of all you need to come with me and see if this is what you want.' Gary had called to collect Cheddar and take him to the Foyer, a drop-in centre for young people needing support. Gary was closely involved as a member of the Housing Support team. It had taken a while to wake him. Gary had knocked repeatedly, yelled through the letterbox and finally peered through the window. Cheddar was on the battered couch pushed against the back wall from which the crumbling plaster had fallen onto his coat which covered his face. He almost fell as he opened the door, calling out what sounded like a puppy's insolent yelp.

'I'm alright here,' Cheddar protested.

'I don't think so. You don't have a bed and you need looking after.' Gary put an almost fatherly hand on his shoulder. 'On the other hand it is none of my business unless you want it to be.'

Cheddar retrieved his trousers from the far corner of the room. He looked a picture of exhaustion and had to be persuaded to wash before climbing wearily into the van. The bistro at the Foyer served good food and cheap drinks, a charity which catered for young people between the ages of 16–25. 'There is no reason why anyone should be homeless,' rebuked Paula, sitting beside them whilst Cheddar made light of the cheese and onion flan. 'I might point out that there is a shower facility and then we can fill in the appropriate forms.'

'She seems OK,' muttered Cheddar, 'but I don't know about the forms.'

'Nothing to worry about,' assured Gary. 'You will have a senior worker to help you through the early stages and then we will find you somewhere suitable to live. Sound alright?'

Gary had also resolved to improve Ellie's lifestyle. Maggie was recuperating at the chapel house and Ellie was very comfortable (the hot water in the bathroom was a bonus) but she needed sparkle and zing in her life and, he suspected, a job. There was a vacancy at the cafe on Victoria Quays; he would see what she thought about it. The sight of her face lighting up was the answer he wanted. Ellie understood this to be one of the reasons for his unpredictability and absences and she had missed him so much. She had put a brave face on all that might lie in the future and could not imagine it without him. Would he understand her longing for him? She doubted it.

Victoria Quays is only a few minutes' walk from the centre of Sheffield. It was ll.00am and Ellie was due for her interview. She was nervous and Gary held her arm as she approached the canal basin. She didn't know quite what to expect but when she saw the sun glinting on the colourful boats and the glamorous shops on the waterfront she thought of Gran and her love of canals. 'A word is better than a good present' she would say. Ellie had words to say but would not say them. If she did they would not be about three appearances in Court, of perjury, or times marred by violence but instead she would describe the yellow water lilies floating like apples of gold on the gentle lapping of the water. Gary had hesitated, then cautiously moved forward a step at a time over the cobbles. 'I just thought it sounded an interesting place to work,' he grinned.

June, the Manageress, took an instant liking to Ellie. She recognised that she was shy and a little nervous but not timid. She had a natural beauty and June appreciated the absence of body piercing and the neat way she wore her hair. She said as much to Gary, forgetting that Ellie could hear. 'Can you cook, love, or would you prefer to work in the stillroom?'

"Whatever," she mouthed. June went on to explain that they had a staff of four who usually agreed to disagree and could she start on Monday?

As they walked home through the refurbished arches she

was dazzled by the gowns in the bridal shop and the beauty of this historical canal basin. She lifted her face and kissed Gary on the cheek and felt that somehow she was drowning in influences. Here was a man of propriety, of courtesy, not pretentious or weak-willed like the men her mother chose. In her mind she was aware that she was often childish but in her heart she knew she was a woman. Gary did not return her kiss, instead he drew back from her. 'Should I have warned them how mischievous you can be? Can I trust you to behave yourself?' Why not. Everyone had believed in her so far. Maggie was out of bed and in front of the fire when Gary drove Ellie home. She had some news.

****

Rev was in a serious state of panic. 'Have you any idea what could happen now? There will be gangs of them descending on us wanting retribution. They'll want money and their pound of flesh. They'll knock the living daylights out of us.' He paced the room. 'What the hell were you thinking of, Bas? Well, me, I'm off. Sorry mate, I'm scared shitless.' When the tap at the window intensified to a knock and then a clattering of the letterbox Rev shot upstairs. Bas opened the door cautiously to Gary. He related the whole sordid incident of the dealer over a can of lager. Rev joined them looking decidedly sheepish but Gary spoke to him calmly without histrionics until in a sudden urge to appear normal he began to pile a number of the *Big Issue* magazines onto a stained wooden bookcase.

'Where is he now?' quizzed Gary.

'In the hospital I shouldn't wonder. The cops were there in no time.'

'You saw them?'

'I called them.' Bas straightened his back. 'I wanted him caught with the stuff still on him. It will be some time before he's back in circulation, I'll tell you. No need to go flying off anywhere, Rev, don't go and wallow in fear and dread.' It did not take too long before Rev had relaxed enough to drum his fingers on the greasy arms of the battered armchair and close his eyes. They were going to Doncaster tomorrow anyway.

'Who would have a front of a house hidden in Virginia creeper?' protested the daughter with the Castile soaps. She arrived by early morning train. 'From London,' she moaned. 'It was a nightmare all the way and I had booked my seat.' Ellie had spring-cleaned the house in one day 'to put things right' Maggie had requested. 'She's a fussy little Madam.' The larder cupboard had been the untidiest, one that Maggie hadn't been able to reach for ages. Boot polish sat next to a tin of sardines, custard powder was squashed between bars of scented soap and bandages were rolled in rubber bands. Packets of bird seed lodged tightly against cat food. The bathroom gleamed, the furniture shone and Ellie had vacated her bedroom in favour of the sofa. She had expected an appreciative word but none came.

There was now a mingling scent of lavender and beeswax. Ellie hoped that Maggie would have forgotten about the bats. Somehow Celeste thought of Ellie as a maid (servant would perhaps be too strong a description) and within hours had begun to give orders. Ellie might not choose to answer back but she was adamant not to be submissive. 'Celeste isn't the name I gave her, love, it's one she thought up for herself. It's because of him, he's some big cheese in the city.' As Ellie put out the cat food for the hedgehog she watched the Castile daughter through the window plumping up cushions, straightening the tablecloth and sipping strong, black coffee. Maggie needed support and sympathy; it would seem she was unlikely to have either. The drudgery of being housebound must weigh heavily on her. Maybe her daughter would arrange a treat. As it was she was getting on Maggie's nerves. Meanwhile Ellie was looking forward to the Doncaster gig.

'It's not nonsense at all,' Rev was protesting. 'I need some more cymbals, rock and ride, and that's that. We're in the town anyway so we may as well kill two birds with one stone.'

'There goes my chance of extra cash then,' moaned Boo, 'especially if we have to go early.'

'You don't have to come at all,' snapped Bas. 'Do you realize Cheddar can always step in?'

They were overflowing in Tiz and Boo's flat. It was raining hard and no one was willing to wait outside until the girls had gathered their belongings and made a few 'phone calls. 'I've had to cancel clients; it's not easy you know,' Boo appealed to Ellie. 'I only have one chair now; it's a bit awkward.' A picture hung in the entrance hall. It was of lovers entwined and seated on a carpet of rose petals.

'Did you do this?' Gary inspected it.

'Yes, only recently, do you like it?' Tiz hovered. 'It's schmaltz,' uttered Bas.

'Oh and you would know about interpretation and sentimentality, would you?' hissed Boo.

'My birds would want more than a few grapes to keep them sweet, I'll tell you,' he snapped.

'Why is it that every time he confronts something he doesn't understand he calls it ridiculous?' Tiz faced Boo.

'Because he's a numbskull,' she replied.

There was no basis for enmity in these outbursts, concluded Ellie; it was a series of catcalls which happened when boredom was creeping in. Bas seemed to be completely detached from insults; he often turned away smiling. The pub beckoned in Doncaster for him and Cheddar. Rev and Gary spent time in the music store and the girls in the market. The clouds had passed and among the colourful stalls Ellie was particularly drawn to the bright Kanga cotton cloth from Africa. She purchased a length of fabric in preparation for a brighter future.

'Don't lug that stuff in here,' cautioned Rev. 'Watch the drums.'

'OK!' agreed Cheddar. 'I don't mind helping as long as I'm not hassled.'

The girls appeared. 'I would not have hesitated to have her thrown out,' commented Tiz.

'What's this then?' queried Rev.

'A shoplifter. Grabbed a handful of blouses from a stall, out the door and into a car.'

'Then,' continued Boo, 'to top it all her mate started yelling and shouting, raising the roof, hitting out at the poor Asian girl.'

Gary slammed the back door of the van. 'I bet you shut her up.'

'Damn right I did,' said Boo, straightening her skirt, 'right between the eyes.'

'Let's get out of here,' beseeched Bas. 'Before a lynch mob comes tearing after us.'

Boo decided it was not worth the effort responding to his sarcasm especially as the instrument in the corner caught her interest. 'Hey, a keyboard!'

'More than that,' said Gary. 'A synthesiser, a Moog, who's interested?'

'I'm not,' ventured Bas.

'Nor me,' said Rev.

'Me neither,' sighed Cheddar.

'Up to you girls then,' suggested Gary.

Cheddar was introverted, nervous on stage and at his most relaxed when he had all but disappeared from the eyes of the crowd. He also had an overt hostility to keyboards. 'Singers sing, pianists play and drummers drum,' he groaned. 'Not altogether absent on one instrument.'

The weather was changing. A slight drizzle quickly turned to heavier showers and through the window at the back of the van Ellie relaxed as she watched the leaves rustle and shake themselves in the ribbon of rain. They parked in the square behind the venue, in a bike-littered courtyard overlooked by student accommodation. There was a great deal of confusion out front. Several musicians were crouched around instruments on the pavement and others were crowded on the steps seeking cover under a leaking roof. The black entrance doors were firmly barred. Quarrelling broke out as the musicians increased in number and the crowd became hostile.

'Apparently,' explained Gary who had acted as chief

scout, 'the caretaker hasn't arrived and no one knows where he is.'

Rev stood rooted to the spot in amazement. 'Why, if they can't get access, have they unloaded?'

Cheddar nodded rather wryly. 'See what you mean.' A police car drove slowly by. Many people don't trust the police, Bas had pointed out to Ellie. Indeed it seemed to her that he was in a furious temper about a remark he had made in the presence of an officer at one time and no one understood why he had been cautioned. His defence of obiter dictum (said by the way) an incidental remark got him off the hook thanks to his solicitor. Even now the mere mention of Police made him shudder.

As the crowd grew bigger they spilled onto the road and dozens crammed into a nearby bus shelter out of the rain. As some clambered onto buses more came to take their place. No one had managed to track down the caretaker; the police sensed that there could be a problem and Bas was becoming agitated. 'Look, by the time we get in, get set up and, remember we're headlining, it will be too late. I suggest we go home.'

'Go home? Are you joking?' screamed Boo. Her eyes flashed, her chin was thrust forward with an air of fierce hostility. 'I have already lost pounds coming here. Surely somebody knows where he is.'

'The whole world seems to be crowding in,' moaned Tiz. She wasn't feeling very well. 'I think we should call it a day.'

'I've told the lads they can put their gear in the van,' offered Rev.

'That's very admirable of you Rev, but we're not staying,' Gary replied. He was suddenly very tired, he could only operate within the sheltered hours the dosage permitted and his drugs were well overdue.

The band which Rev had befriended had travelled from Portsmouth with another from Bristol who had planned to play in Newcastle. 'They are picking us up tomorrow night on their way back,' Roxy explained. 'We planned to kip in the gig.' Most people schooled in good manners would not have hesitated in helping the youngsters. Roxy could not have been older than 18, fresh-faced and confident. His three companions were a little older and at least one had dared to attempt a tattoo. Roxy's lead singer, Badger, had an abundance of spots and a slice cut out of his hair.

It was Roxy who organised the arrangements at Bas and Rev's and it wasn't long before they came to behave as though the place belonged to them. Roxy had sympathised at great length with Boo on the journey back to Sheffield even to the point of sitting with his arm around her, emphasizing that there was much more to life than making money. He suggested that she should take stock of her life. Bas sniggered in the corner.

The journey was uncomfortable. Wet bodies squeezed between instruments and lank hair dripped onto bean bags. It was a pathetic group that sped towards Bas's pad and Gary was desperate for sleep. Ellie was becoming more aware of the class culture – ask, plead, demand, then take. An unusual approach but which ultimately led to a gratifying conclusion. The language was coarse and vulgar; she had to ignore it. It accompanied a general air of self-assurance and seemed to be a form of defiance. The girls swore, usually in anger or frustration, and a good deal when on tour.

It was Gary who suggested she practised on the synthesiser. 'There wouldn't be a great deal of difference in playing this and the piano, would there?' Well, why not? In a few days she would start work at the Quays and Celeste would take charge of Maggie. Taking charge, but at what price to Maggie? Ellie felt the pangs of culpability.

She sat on the edge of the bed and wrote a long letter to Gran. She moved nearer to the bedside lamp, it was getting dark and the bulb in the ceiling was very dim. Gran always preferred a muted light, much more homely she would smile. Just as she liked her toast the proper way, toasted on a long metal fork in front of a Yorkshire Range and that is how Ellie remembered her childhood. A childhood which ended at eight years old when she left to live with her mother.

"It is considerate of Celeste to let me have my bedroom back," she wrote. "I think she must have heard the flutterings and the squeaks in the roof. Maybe Maggie prefers her company to mine in the night. Who understands bats, anyway Gran?"

Gary showed her where to board the Supertram. From the stop it was a short walk to the Quays and the cafe. Ellie had dressed neatly in a black skirt and white short-sleeved blouse. She was early, it was 8.45; she was to start at nine. Through the tunnel she paused to read the forthcoming attractions, a list of cruises and cruise menus, and to breathe in the fragrancy of late August. It was quiet and then there was a flurry of movement on the water and the chink of crockery and laughter. 'You let your tongue run away with you,' she heard June remark. Hardly appropriate in her case, she smiled. The staff greeted her warmly.

By mid-morning she was buttering bagels and croissants, by lunchtime she was plating broccoli bake with salad and serving cakes and pastries for tea. Whilst June took her break in a large comfortable room the girls slipped out in pairs to sit on the bench overlooking the canal. From the noise of traffic and crowded streets here was an anchorage of peace and somnolent sounds. At cruise time the canal came alive with shouts of excited children and the antics of a clown sent one small girl into fits of wild giggling. Ellie realized that it would take time for the girls to familiarize themselves with her lack of speech and they tended to shout at her, assuming she was deaf. June assured them that she had all her wits about her; they could talk normally.

Arriving home, Ellie could see instantly that something had happened to Maggie. Her tiny wrinkled face was grey. She was in a state of confusion and, as she waited to speak, she turned her hands over and over in a circular movement. It was almost a croak. 'She wants to put me in a home, lass. I don't want to go. I can manage; we can manage between us can't we? He's been onto her, you see.' Maggie continued to bite her lips. 'I know it's him. She would never have thought of it.' Ellie bent over the chair and held her close. She could feel the damaged knees bony and twisted beneath the knitted blanket and cradled her head. The smell of lavender clung to her hair and Ellie ran her fingers down Maggie's cheek. She needs reassurance, comfort, someone to speak up for her, she needs love, thought Ellie. Yet she dare not speak. Is this what this visit was all about? Not that the truth had been easily recognised by her. She looked around. 'She is in the bathroom,' Maggie whispered. 'I wish Mustard was here, he would know what to do.'

As obstinate as she was and a fighter what could she do against a daughter who was determined to disagree with her mother's wishes? Ellie understood that as her Gran grew older she showed a tendency to fault-finding, it was a natural process of ageing; surely we can all live with that? Maggie gave a deep, rasping cough at the precise moment when Celeste swept through the door, clutching her yellow bathrobe. With one swift movement she pulled Ellie away and lifted up Maggie's face. 'Now come on, Mother, let's have none of that; we can't have people thinking we are putting you away.'

Ellie was left standing in the middle of the entrance hall, her eyes brimming with tears. Soft words were what Maggie needed to hear; soft words that say 'Thank you' for years of dedication, soft words that speak of nights of caring and a lifetime of sacrifice. When we are young, strong and resilient we can often cope, but age and illness are merciless, decided Ellie. The latter she was to find almost unbearable when later she fell in love.

It was the tone of Celeste's voice that set Ellie on edge; an intonation of ruthlessness, of bullying and Maggie needed time. Time to adjust to her stroke and the incapacity it brought with it, however slight. Couldn't her daughter grasp the feeling of anxiety or was she the only one who genuinely could understand her? Perhaps Maggie saw herself in a single room divided by thin walls, intimate details typed neatly on pieces of plastic hanging behind a door with bells constantly ringing and unstable commodes. Perhaps she imagined a regimented existence of early mornings and early nights and staff with little time to talk. The rasping cough continued. 'Help me get her to bed will you?' Celeste directed and between them they lifted her firmly and slid her under the duvet.

****

'Looking after an old man is a bore,' June was heard to say. 'I wouldn't mind if he could help himself a bit more. Everything is left to me.' It was halfway through the morning and the cafe was busy. Ellie was preparing a cold buffet for the Cruise menu and June kept bobbing from the kitchen into the stillroom with suggestions. 'He doesn't annoy me, he's never rude or gets in my way or anything, it's just that he's teetotal and boring,' she continued.

'But he's wealthy,' exclaimed plump and amiable Sue, smiling at Ellie.

'Yes, you're right,' sighed June. 'I bet you will marry a rich man, Ellie. He will have nothing to complain about, you can't answer him back.'

It was not a scornful or mocking remark; she had learned to differentiate between spitefulness and observation. Although her lack of speech interested people with whom she came into contact no one had actually asked her the reason. In the early days living with Jan she had overheard Tiz discussing her and Fab had suggested that perhaps she had aphasia, dumbness due to a disease of the brain. 'I don't think there is anything wrong with Ellie's brain,' was Gary's short reply.

Much later in Ireland Fab queried a condition called selective mutism but this was discounted as it was evident that Ellie chose not to speak to anyone. 'It is perhaps simply an illness affecting the vocal chords so why don't we just leave it at that?' dismissed Gary. It continued to be speculation and she found it amusing that speech was so closely associated with hearing that almost everyone shouted at her and at first the sound of raised voices had alarmed her. Not now!

It was the band from Plymouth, including Roxy and Badger, who accompanied Dark Horse at the local gig. There was open animosity between Bas and Roxy. 'He thinks he's a bloody rock star,' Bas growled. His aggressive manner concealed a certain disquiet. 'More than you'll ever be,' sneered Boo.

Cheddar was overcome with enthusiasm about his flat and after the gig they descended on his two-roomed accommodation, taking with them pizzas and cartons of chips. Gary had advised and assisted him through the Foyer and with the Housing Support team behind him he was enjoying a freedom and independence he had never experienced before. The flat was in a pleasant area; it was on the second floor with smatterings of stencils on the pale green walls. Furniture was sparse but the bedroom was reasonably large with two bedsteads, as Cheddar preferred to call them. He was feeling strong, he told Rev, mostly because he had a job with the local milkman, and felt that he had at last achieved something.

'God, he must have hurt himself badly,' Boo whispered to Tiz. Badger's wrists were puckered and scarred; he had removed his sweat bands, taken off his boots and loosened his collar.

'What do you think?'

'The unwritten law of the punk scene is to let sleeping dogs lie,' Fab soothed. So they did and left Cheddar to revel in his new-found freedom.

****

Sometimes silence is the worst kind of news. Gary was uncommunicative about Jan. He had visited her regularly in the burns unit at the hospital but his only comment was, 'Oh she's improving, she's getting along fine.' The girls wanted to see her. 'Better wait,' argued Gary. 'She is not ready to receive visitors yet.'

'Do you think we'll be shocked?' hinted Tiz. 'Is she that bad?'

'We want to go; we have as much right as you,' insisted Fab.

They were back in Cheddar's flat after a long practice, lounging on huge beanbags, chewing pistachio nuts and shouting over the CD player. 'We won't disturb her, honestly,' pleaded Boo. His head shook in indecision.

After a while he relented. 'OK, we can go between eight and nine in the evening tomorrow.' An imperceptible movement of Gary's shoulders and elbows revealed to Ellie his disapproval. Yet words were healers and it might mean a lot to Jan to see her old friends again.

Sickness had never been a part of Ellie's life, not serious illness, only the usual childhood ailments like measles and chickenpox. That is until her mother had an alarming few weeks when she thought she had cancer. 'Why me, how could it happen to me?' She was unbearable to live with and no amount of sympathy or stimulation helped to lessen the stress. Phil meanwhile seemed to have a perverse desire to appear callous. When the results were negative Ellie had never seen such a radical change; her mother's generosity reached extremes and she felt so happy and triumphant that she would burst into tears or laughter for no apparent reason.

A hospital reminded Ellie of Gran. Not that she had ever visited her there but Gran used to say that, as a young woman, she used to walk through the grounds of the Infirmary just to inhale the heady smell of ether. 'Hospitals don't have that clinical feel anymore,' Gran complained. 'Or a notice requesting "Silence Please". They are more like public buildings now, walk-through structures; they even put in shops.'

If such shops existed in the burns unit they were behind wooden shutters. It had taken some time to find the ward and Gary was parking the van. They caught the sharp words of rebuke from Sister. 'Are you relatives? Only two at a time. No sitting on the bed.'

Bas shrugged his shoulders. 'I don't want to go in anyway. I only came for the ride.'

'You always had a kindly turn of speech,' chided Boo.

'The hardest part was knowing what to say,' Tiz sighed. She and Boo had been replaced by Gary and Fab while the rest had taken refuge in the coffee lounge. It had been a long night.

Gary laid his hand on Boo's shoulder later in a fatherly fashion; she was crying quietly, unable to comprehend the changes behind the face mask. 'It doesn't look like Jan, Ellie,' she sobbed. 'I shouldn't have come.' A bell rang. In the sudden rush of people heading for the exit struggled a group of friends unable to comprehend the pain and anguish which the fire had put them through.

The city was settling down to sleep. Ellie was tired and upset and didn't feel ready to leave her friends and face the sadness in Maggie's eyes. It was obvious that Celeste was keen to lay the foundations for Maggie's seclusion. She would be placed in a home and the independent old lady could see nothing but the loss of her liberty. She cried. There was something clammy and lifeless about Maggie's hands as Ellie held them and kissed her cheek gently. She propped up the three pillows and pulled the sheet up to her chin. 'I'll miss you lass,' the thin lips quivered. She was too tired to open her eyes. 'I am as weak as a kitten, I can't stand upright any more.' How she has changed, deplored Ellie, from dragging her feet around the room, careful to manoeuvre round the furniture with her zimmer. 'When you are old you don't have to be a burden to your children,' she had stated proudly. The stroke had changed all those sentiments.

****

'What rumour?' June challenged Sue, squeezing her way between the oven and the freezer.

'That your Mark is buying a long boat.' June straightened her back, continuing to turn the fish with an expert turn of the wrist.

'It's no rumour, duck, he's planning on joining the fleet,

doing the Victoria-Carbrook cruise.' She turned to Ellie who was busy plating chips and juggling with cartons of mushy peas. 'Right, tell you what, why don't you take tomorrow off and go with him? I'm sure you will enjoy it. It does somewhat resemble a converted barge but it's a pretty one at that.'

This was when the act of speechlessness was at its most awkward; she needed to contact her friends. Perhaps a Sunday spent on the canal would interest them. She scribbled a postcard to Tiz and Boo and decided to purchase a mobile phone. "Like to take a trip on the canal, Sunday pm?"

The Heritage Cruise took approximately a little under two hours with a full on-board commentary. Cheddar arrived with a surprising knowledge about Sheffield's East End. The grimy, industrial canal had been transformed into a pleasant and valuable resource for leisure and for Ellie, Mark made it all the more intriguing.

On first sight he was running as fast as he could along the bank followed by a sheepdog. He looked athletic, muscular and up to now Ellie had never given a thought to other men; she had neither the advantage of speech nor experience but her first reflections were clear-cut and simple; here was someone she was keen to know.

Around her, as they moved gently past the bridges, were the new additions to the canal – the Arena and the Stadium, both tall and splendid against the blue sky. She reached out to the water lilies as the hot August sun kissed the spray, nudging the trailing buddleia, and marvelled at the dandelions which reached up to the sun through the spoil heaps.

Words came easily to Mark. His voice was soothing as he described the architecture and history of what had been a neglected and derelict canal. Ellie removed her gilet; the boat was full and she was hemmed in between Cheddar and a pushchair. She wished she had worn shorts rather than jeans. She studied Mark at length, from his cropped black hair and his crisp white shirt to his black jeans and trainers. It was a sideways scrutiny as he engineered his craft through traffic and under bridges. The clouds were spreading and threatened to obscure the sun but the vibrant colours of the potted geraniums adorning the decks of passing boats and the moving paths of yellow lilies added their iridescent charm, forming a colourful display.

It was customary to assist people off the boat as it returned to the quay and Mark did this with a slight nervousness which Ellie found amusing. Holding his hand she smiled up into his face, could this be the promise of an escapade? The advantage of not speaking was that there was more time to think and observe, but Mark was unaware of the impression he had made. 'Mark said we should go back to the café,' informed Tiz. As they ate at the water's edge they watched the ducks squabbling between the boats. They did their tricks and their twiddles and their quivers and their quacks and yet the kingfisher was the one on parade on the canal corridor. "It doesn't seem fair," thought Ellie.

Her eyes lit up as she saw the figure of Mark approaching. She hadn't learnt about diplomacy; she had no need. Discretion had been the landmark in her closeness to Gary and some internal spirit had kept their friendship on an even keel. Love is too strong an emotion for some people. Yet if love talk enhances acts of love it was all her fault that some sort of relationship hadn't developed with Gary. She missed him, but absence was not making her heart grow fonder, and Mark's presence was causing her throat to ache.

He joined them, carrying a huge plateful of chicken and chips, and they talked canals. Cheddar admitted to being a Gongoozler, a non-boater who spends time watching boats and lazily collecting thousands of sticklebacks, dragonflies, damselflies and flatworms, as a child in the Sheffield basin. 'Pond dipping we used to call it,' he sniffed. 'We used to store them in big jars nicked from the vinegar factory and line them up in a row in the classroom. Nature study it was called.'

'You're joking about Gongoozler though, you must be,' tittered Boo.

'No, he's right,' agreed Mark. 'We used to rely on you

people for support when the canal first opened in 1987, although I don't know much about it; I was only six at the time.'

The flirting began when the girls took a stroll to the parade of shops. Cheddar went in search of a terrapin. 'My mother says you have lost your voice.' Mark leaned forward. His eyes were a deep blue. 'I have been given my orders not to shout, gesticulate or intimidate.' Ellie thanked him with a nod and a smile. She could tell him nothing about herself and if she could what would she say? That she chose not to speak? It was a decision made as a result of abuse? No! Gary was the one who deserved to know the true Ellie; he was the one person she trusted, the only person who could teach her how to survive.

Mark talked incessantly about his time at university, his lifestyle, his family. Would she have been given so much information if she could reply? They were now holding hands across the table and she wondered how far she could allow things to progress. In the rest room she studied her reflection. She was very flushed; she experienced an outpouring of restlessness, a quivering of excitement, an awakening of something tangible inside. Infatuation, perhaps? How would she know, lacking experience as she did?

She was in this mood when she found him leaning over the rails and talking on his mobile. He pointed out a huddle of hidden ducklings.

The girls linked arms as they boarded the supertram together. Ellie felt that the precious journey had been cut short, that something invisible that she had tried to hold onto had been breathed into time and space. She felt cheated. How long would she be affected by her vow of silence? Was there room for interlopers? Mark had managed a wave. 'See you tomorrow.'

Celeste was colouring her hair, more blonde on blonde. Ellie watched the pain move across Maggie's face, from her eyes to her pinched nose and her clenched teeth. "Cocoa?" she mouthed. 'Yes, love. Make it sweet, and a piece of parkin, if there's any left.' Had she been out of bed today?

Probably not. The room lacked fresh air. Celeste insisted that she would not have the smell of the cemetery in the room, it was unhealthy and she would prefer Ellie not to feed the animals.

'Death written all over them,' she ranted.

Although she couldn't answer back she could still rebel and whose home was it anyway? Leave philosophising until you are old, wasn't this Gary's proclamation? Ellie sat by the coffee table holding warm cocoa, thinking of his smile. She couldn't account for her feelings, she recognised that her lack of freedom and strict upbringing had formed a pattern for her life but she was on her own now and it was time to take chances.

****

'It's for charity and I think we should do it.' Gary was adamant.

'Dunno,' Bas responded. 'Weather unpredictable, outdoor venue, dodgy.'

'For goodness sake, we've done lots of concerts here; they've always been great,' Boo added.

'Yes, and we've raised loads of money.'

'What is it with you?'

'That's OK,' smiled Fab. 'I'll front, it's the principle of the thing.'

'Huh,' scoffed Bas, 'there is all the difference between principles and actions.'

'Get you,' mocked Boo.

Cheddar had made a huge pan of lentil soup and noodles and plonked a plate of bread cut into doorsteps onto the hearth. He rattled as he walked as numerous chains hung from several pockets. Ellie wondered if he ever changed his clothes. The practice over they were in a relaxed mood though the news that they might lose the church hall was upsetting. 'Not to worry, we'll find somewhere,' was Gary's reply. Bas was almost asleep, a scaffolder by day and when available a doorman by night. Rev was his usual vigorous self and the girls were drinking heavily. Ellie drank only juice and concentrated on Gary. How could she compare him with anyone? He was sitting quietly in tee shirt and torn jeans, his guitar at his feet, hair a little longer these days and glancing occasionally over to her.

It had been four days since her meeting with Mark. She hadn't seen him either on the boat or in the cafe. No one had mentioned him. She rose and helped herself to more bread, then placed herself at Gary's feet. Why? It was a bold move, she thought. 'Can you play the keyboard yet?' he asked. She shook her head. 'Would you like me to show you?' She nodded. 'Do you mind if we bring it next time, Cheddar?'

'Fine.'

She was the last to be dropped off and Gary had been discussing Maggie and the hateful, bitter and cold attitude of her daughter. She did not want to be reminded of the odious Celeste. 'You know, Ellie, relationships need gentle nurturing and attention and unselfish care if they are to survive.' Was he referring to Maggie? Ellie thought not; his eyes betrayed him. He helped her from the van as always but this time kissed her gently on the forehead. 'See you Saturday. We are playing at Hillsborough Park.'

The tender and respectful way in which Gary treated her was on her mind as she wrote a brief note to Gran. In some respects he was difficult to fathom, in others he could be described as a man who would give all and never ask for repayment. How could she not be fond of him?

The park was much bigger than Ellie had expected and at 10.30 in the morning was exceptionally noisy and full of young men with long, greasy hair and torn jeans and girls with short skirts and multi-clique tattoos. This recreational area was where people took advantage of greenery lying on their doorstep and where it was still possible to find peace and quiet. But not today, not in the middle of a charity gig, not with seven live bands, a disco and a mini fairground for the children. Each person in the group had managed some time off work.

A slight breeze was wafting over the water on the boating lake but the warm air filtered through the trees and preparations were progressing well. 'I would imagine,' snorted Bas struggling with amps and cymbals, 'that the club bands think they have precedence; well they are sadly mistaken!'

Fab's reply: 'What's with the mood?' was quickly followed by:

'There is a lot of difference between imagination and accusation, in my opinion.' Bas scowled.

'That is well over his head,' Boo pouted.

Bas stacked the equipment under the awning and returned to the van. There was a slight feeling of unease, of dubiousness between the performers. Rev chatted amiably whilst Cheddar sat on a dusty old box gulping down a bottle of beer. Tiz and Boo wandered off to confront the Park Rangers. Ellie was content to sit and watch an endless stream of vans and musicians make their way through the park along with children pushing and squealing towards the icecream van. Gary gave an irritable sigh. Fab looked up from her lyrics convinced that Bas had altered them deliberately. 'Boo is getting feisty.'

Gary stared at the group of four standing close to the water. His face puckered in a frown. 'If she loses it she plays lousy. It's important that we prove ourselves today.' Gary moved slowly towards the lake. A couple of young boys busy fishing put down their rods to listen to the argument which was close to boiling point between a brown-shirted Ranger and Boo. 'I'm hearing what you are saying,' he shouted. He flattened himself against a tree. Tiz grabbed at Boo's plait but she shoved her away forcefully. She wriggled her body. This was one of her darkest moods and she was determined to let it run its course.

Ellie ran after Gary; he was stumbling. He looked to be in pain. In one angry thrust, one massive shove, Boo pushed the Ranger into the water. The effort of walking had weakened Gary. Ellie helped him to a bench and sat close to him, holding his hand to stop it from shaking. She had seen this before in Ireland. Gary had dismissed it then; it was impossible to hide it now. Easing herself closer to him, she clasped his arm until the spasmodic movement stopped. What was it that he was fighting, was he ignorant of his illness or in denial? He was too intelligent a man to ignore the changes in his body, too sensible to dismiss the strange feverish activity which took his speech and left him vulnerable. Yet Ellie could do little but offer him her silent devotion. She felt like a bird in midair flying between a delicate situation and a meticulously timed explosion. They sat in silence.

Although the water was shallow the incident caused concern. There was a great deal of amusement and some onlookers were convulsed with mirth. Bas was livid at having missed it and retorted, 'When Boo is enraged she's a reckless fighter, she needs somebody like me to take her in hand.'

'What was all that about?' mumbled Cheddar in between bites of bread and swallows of beer.

'About the concerns of youngsters playing near the water,' answered Tiz. 'The Rangers were more taken up with their image than doing their job.' Sunlight streamed through the trees and caught the sheen of Boo's blue/black hair as Tiz knelt beside her and calmed her until she smiled. She stroked her hand and Bas laughed aloud as the Ranger squelched his way towards the big house.

Gary, reconciled to Ellie's concern, recovered as the bands took their places and the shouting and the jumping and the joy of music filled the park and obliterated the pain. Dark Horse gave an exciting and exhausting performance. Boo was glowing with success, Tiz was alive with passion, Fab unbearably competitive, Rev on form with hands full of fire and Bas was loud and immovable. Gary, close by, managed a smile.

In the early evening as the sun reached out through a haze of blue Gary led Ellie through the Walled Garden. The scent was pure and calming and rare flowers and plants gave out a mixture of forest and herb. In the shadow of the hall they sat close together on a rustic bench and the complexity of his illness seemed a long distance away. Now the possibility of simply touching him was teasing her mixed emotions. The stiffness in his body had eased; whereas before he had dug in his heels in the long grass and positioned himself rigidly against the back of the seat, now his head was forward and his shoulders hunched. The overwhelming feeling she felt for him was of pity and tenderness and what he saw in her eyes brought him out of his reverie and what Ellie saw in his eyes was a flash of humiliation.

'It isn't what it seems,' he smiled wanly. 'It passes. My bones get a bit stiff and I lose coordination but I'm in control. I easily get tired; there's always something on my mind, plans to make, places to go!' He squeezed her hand. 'This is nothing new. I'm used to it. Bodies don't keep silent, Ellie, they speak to you, tell you when something's amiss. The important thing is that you don't worry.' The colour had returned to his face and his eyes had lost the strained look. He patted her cheek. They moved silently around the paths and back into the park. This would be the last word on the subject. She was dismissed. Yet the hunger to understand his pain, to be aware of how debilitating this condition could be, continued to nag at her. It had been a day of conflicting emotions. She loved him and he accepted her the way she was. As the band boarded the van for home his words were comforting. 'Come on now, Ellie, confess that all things considered it was a nice place to be.'

CHAPTER TEN

"He that is silent gathers stones." (Proverbial.)

Bas was outraged. The hatred and resentment boiled inside him and he was incensed to the point of despair. It was the bad dream that had materialised, Rev's worst nightmare and out there in the street were even more dogs with weapons, snarling and cussing, waiting for signs of screaming.

Where there had been a window was a gaping hole. The walls were scorched and grey lumps of plaster hung precariously, their jagged edges pointing towards the charred floorboards. Somebody was handing out punishments, someone was settling scores somewhere lurking in the dark, directing their hatred towards Bas. Yet there were no onlookers, no police, no passers-by, no one.

The fire had not taken hold but still damage had been done. Rev turned his attention to his records, some of which were irreplaceable. His tapes, his reference books and notebooks which were on a stand in tottering stacks in the passage were charred and shrivelled. He sat cross-legged on the filthy floor in the middle of the debris, staring ahead.

The screeching of the sirens increased the sense of panic. Gary and Ellie were the only two witnesses; the others had been taken home but in any case what was there to tell the police? That they were lucky not to be hurt? That it was an act of retribution?

Bas dealt with the questioning and the probing with a

colourful spate of his usual obscenities, pacing up and down the room clenching his fists. Whilst the sergeant took notes his companion walked slowly upstairs and paused, carefully inching the bedroom door open. There was no one, nothing was disturbed and he breathed a sigh of relief.

Rev had not moved from where he had slumped. In his hand he held broken pieces of vinyl and blood dripped slowly from his pierced hands onto his torn jeans. Nothing around him made sense. Noises were falling on deaf ears. Gary interjected in an effort to calm Bas but it was Ellie who knelt before Rev, carefully removing the breakages, and wrapped his lacerated fingers in tea towels. 'Best get him to a hospital.' The young officer was concerned. 'Probably need a few stitches. Come on, lad, up on your feet.'

Rev was recovering sufficiently to turn on Bas. 'This is all your fault. Looking after your own pitch, were you? Sorting out the druggies? A one-man army? Well, look what's happened. It's taken years to build up a collection like this.' He swallowed hard. 'The ones that aren't broken are unplayable.'

Bas made a move towards him, reaching out to touch his shoulder. Rev stepped backwards, his heels crunching in the rubble. Bas spoke, a sickly grin slackened his mouth 'Oh come on mate, we're in one piece, you know, I mean, well, somebody has to make a stand.'

'It's nothing to laugh about though, is it?' Rev dismissed his gesture, 'and it looks as if I won't be drumming for a while.' He vomited. Ellie could share his mood of hatred; she had kept her resentments locked up since childhood, only to bring them to mind now and again as a gentle reminder. There would be no apology from Bas. He would be staying behind to attend to the window whilst Gary and Ellie prepared to take Rev to Casualty.

It was with a great deal of concern that Ellie returned to work. Rev had raised his shoulders sharply in a shrug when he was told that the wounds were minor but he was not ready to forgive Bas and had moved in with Cheddar.

****

'I refuse to get mixed up with beggars,' moaned June, dipping the plump pieces of fish in batter. 'I'll give to charity; mind you it's difficult to know who is genuine nowadays, and I'll sell raffle tickets, but no, I'm telling you, I avoid street beggars like the plague!' Ellie was slowly being introduced to Flute. Young and slight, a boy with haunted eyes and sunken cheeks who occupied the patch of dry cobbles underneath the bridge. She studied him from the large window opening on to the river.

His clothing was well-worn with added layers of woollen jumpers and multicoloured scarves. If he had hair it was well hidden under a black hat shaped to a cone. It brought back memories to Ellie of Puck in "A Midsummer Night's Dream". A dark grey blanket was tucked neatly around his legs and he played the flute. He played it well. 'They are everywhere,' continued June. 'In and around the underground, under your feet in the paths, stretched out in the sun and in doorways in the rain. Faceless individuals grunting and holding out their hands for a freebie. I can't be doing with their utterances. By the way, Ellie,' June teased. 'Mark has been asking for you. He'll be around later.'

The excitement which Mark had aroused in her and the deep desire which had caused her to catch her breath had seemed so intense. Now it was vanishing. She hadn't thought about him, there had been other things on her mind. Perhaps she was a naturally fickle person, not disloyal but in a capricious kind of way quite unpredictable.

Yet when he put in an appearance at the end of her shift she knew that the effort she had made in combing her hair into a neat coil and adding a little colour to her face had lifted her spirits a little. They walked towards the Hilton. It towered above the Quays. She had never stayed in a hotel; her holidays had been spent with Gran, usually in a guest house and occasionally in a caravan. Nor would she get a glimpse inside today. Instead they walked towards the Wicker and into a badly lit alley. Ellie held her breath. What now? Reluctantly she followed him. However she was pleasantly surprised to find herself in a neat cul-de-sac, where behind a security gate and a sturdy oak door was a small, compact flat. Mark had chatted all the way, swinging his arms, demanding space on the pavement. He offered her something to eat but she declined. Mark was very generous with his conversation, his compliments and his energy. 'Don't pay too much attention to compliments,' Gran would warn her. 'It's the same as a kiss through a veil, something to be wary of.'

She had neglected Gran of late. What would she tell her about Mark? They sat close together on the small futon. He had lit four scented candles and plumped the cushions behind her head. He jumped up suddenly. 'I'll put on a video, shall I? See how we get on?' It was blatantly offensive to her, not what she expected. He left her sitting there and from the kitchen came the clinking of glasses.

She watched the twisting, contorting naked bodies on the screen and grimaced as she heard the moans and the squeals of excitement and pleasure. Ellie reached for the remote and turned it off. She was not about to sit down again, she could hear her own breathing. Ellie was sickened by Mark's intentions and distressed to see the darker side of him and reached for her coat. He stood before her, a glass in each hand. 'Oh, come on Ellie. You've seen it all before. Surely. And you with a rock band. Don't kid me you don't know what it's all about?' He was smiling; a look of appeal spread across his boyish features as he handed her the glass. 'It's only orange, nothing more.' She didn't believe him but she was not going to be pressed into panic. Instead, she moved over to the fireplace and placed the glass on the surround. Mark helped himself to a handful of crisps. 'I was going to propose a toast to the flush on your cheeks and the success of this evening. What do you think?' Ellie trembled. She did not have a reputation for saintliness but she would be the one to choose the time and the one man she would love above all others, the place was incidental. As he moved towards her she grabbed the wine glass and took a sip. It was not orange and she flinched at what it might be. 'If you could somehow say something, do something just to let me know how I stand, it would be a help.' Now he was being cruel, heartless. For her protection, for her own good it was necessary to leave. Ellie put down the glass, grabbed her bag and with her coat over her shoulder walked swiftly towards the door. Mark ignored her protests; he was clearly annoyed by her reticence. Was this the turning point? A time of new resolutions? The temptation to hit him was almost overwhelming. The world in which she had no need to ask for anything could deny her nothing but she knew where true humiliation lay.

The temperature in the room had risen. She felt dizzy but she faced him calmly. Exasperated, he ran his hand through his hair. She reached up and held both his hands in hers. Carefully she selected her brief exchange. "No," she mouthed firmly. It was almost a pout. "Not tonight. Do you understand?" Ellie, who believed in facing problems straight on immediately, played for time. His expression changed; he wasn't looking to be deceived, for points of delay, but Ellie was learning how to be a woman, learning to achieve finesse, cunning with which to meet the moods of men.

The dizziness passed. Mark called for a taxi to take her home and whilst they were waiting he showed her his selection of CDs. "It's a brave man who trifles with me." Ellie smiled to herself. But it was little comfort, simply a case of lady beware.

Celeste eased Maggie's wasting legs over the pillows, balancing a bottle of oil in one hand and impatiently lifting up Maggie's nightdress, enabling her to massage her legs whilst not embarrassing her mother unduly. She straightened her back as Ellie entered. 'What a day I've had,' she moaned. Leaving Maggie stretched out on the bed, half-clothed and hardly able to move, she placed the bottle on the table and began to shout. 'You would think that moving someone into a Nursing Home would be a simple matter, wouldn't you? You would assume that the caring profession would help, wouldn't you? You would think that there would be simple guidelines to help people like me who only want the best for their relatives? It doesn't work like that. Oh, no! Questions, stupid, unnecessary, unconnected with health or finance are thrown at you. And who do they send? Some jumped-up, officious, intimidating bureaucrat who did nothing but fill in numerous forms and who continually wiped his beard with a paper handkerchief.'

A whimpering sound, a moan and a sob appeared to travel across the sudden silence. Maggie's body trembled. Ellie covered her with a sheet and a warm blanket and kissed her gently on the cheek. Maggie was carrying an internal sorrow which she could not express and anger twisted Ellie's heart. She confronted Celeste with a look of disgust. Where was the support, materially and emotionally, that her mother needed? Maggie was a good mother; she had looked after her daughter, not like her own. What was it Gran had said. 'The mother should always come first in every child's life. It should always be the mother.' Should be. But what if they were contemptuous towards their children or refused to speak to them or chose deliberately to harm them or even to hate them? But Maggie wasn't like that and Ellie wanted to make Celeste understand. Fair words and empty promises were no good to Maggie now.

Ellie wiped the tears from the wrinkled cheeks, smoothed the wet hair from her brow and tucked her in. Then turning to a startled Celeste she took her by the shoulders and shook her so hard that she collapsed in a chair. Ellie roughly raised her face and mouthed, "Look after her. I am watching everything you do." Celeste rose to her feet and moved towards the bed and Ellie triumphantly climbed the stairs.

****

Boo had arrived with Tiz at the cafe in an excited, carefree mood eager to show off her red mini. 'It's great,' she bubbled. School parties meant that the cafe was extra busy. The days were drawing in and the air carried a hint of autumn. Ellie scrutinized the schoolgirls in their short skirts, hair coloured and braided, pushing and giggling as they boarded the boat. She felt like a naughty schoolgirl sometimes, keeping secrets from her elders, unwilling to tell, not only what she had done, but what her thoughts were at the time. Her thoughts at the moment were on Mark.

From the cafe window she watched him. He sat on the cabin roof twisting rope between his fingers. Well aware that she could see him, he looked up occasionally. She was attracted by the dark looks and had decided to see him again. He would be permitted to take her only where she felt safe for if he came too close she could snatch herself away gently. Was it necessary for all lovers to be articulate? Is verbal seduction the surest road to love? She intended to find out.

A misty, autumn Sunday with little to do and no friends to break the silence. Ellie had hardly slept. She had been kept awake by scufflings and squeaks, probably the bats, and distracting sounds from downstairs. As the light cast its shadows on the stark walls the muffled birdsong brought her little comfort. She could not explain the sadness. Perhaps it was not knowing how Gran was coping.

She decided to spend some time in the chapel down the road, and the rest of the day writing to Gran. The chapel was tiny, lovingly cared for and smelling of beeswax. Between the neat houses in the row it was set back a little with glossy black railings supporting straggling roses with only half their petals remaining. Among the lively young children was the Boys Brigade, well turned out in their uniforms, occupying the front pews and mischievously pushing and pulling at each other. A plump, red-faced jolly looking lady played the organ and was committed to playing the opening bars of each hymn and hummed loudly.

As the minister faced his congregation a hush descended, almost as if a record was being faded out until there was a silence, He was elderly, tall and bearded, his arms were folded and he stared straight ahead. Ellie had seated herself next to the radiator halfway down the aisle. She smoothed her long, grey skirt and unzipped her fleece whilst the congregation prepared to settle down.

There were two types of churchgoers, she observed. Some

who were completely at home in God's House and others who were visiting, unsure, in a no man's land and unwilling to cross the border, considering whether it had been worth turning out on this miserable morning. They fidgeted. Chapels somehow survive where parish churches are often described as the Cinderellas of tourism, she had been told

The sermon was uplifting, the hymns were sound and powerful and Ellie knew in her heart that although she had promised herself not to speak she could sing. She smiled as she recalled the rules for Methodist singers.

1. Learn the tunes. (Oh yes she had done that.)
2. Sing modestly, do not bawl. (As if she would.)
3. Sing in time, do not run before or stay behind. (Noted.)

And, as always, if a hymn moved her she would feel the tears sting. "Love with everlasting love" she sang and for the first time in ages she heard her own voice strong and clear.

After the service she left without speaking to anyone but she had what she needed, a spiritual heartening. In her letter to Gran she overspilled the good news – her job, her friendships, her ambitions but not a word about Maggie or Mark. She expected criticism from a lady who was also quick to praise. What a pity that any reply would go unread. Ellie was not yet prepared to divulge her whereabouts.

There was a red glow severing the darkness as Ellie stared towards the city lights from her bedroom window. The mist hovered, skimming the grey buildings and winding its way upwards. Earlier she had bathed Maggie and washed her hair. Maggie held the flannel to her eyes like a young child and blew bubbles as the shampoo ran down her face. Celeste stood by. Ellie judged her guilty but persuasion is preferable to pressure and it was for her own good. Wearing a pretty pink bed jacket and with her hair brushed into a neat bob, Maggie drank her cocoa from a beaker, she was improving.

On her way to work Ellie posted a long letter to Jan. It was a combination of Get well and Thank You. It was a relief

for Ellie to write, there was so much to say. Silence is not
the same as reticence. Jan had taught her to cook and given
her a home; she had fed her innocence with a streetwise
knowledge and treated her like a sister. Ellie knew that Jan's
life, which had so cruelly been interrupted, would need a
new direction and friends to lead her there.

Bas felt that his ill-judged and precarious involvement
with the underworld was becoming increasingly dangerous.
Rev had agreed to move back in with him providing he
could offer some sort of protection but this seemed unlikely.
What could he do? 'It's only a minor incident,' he lied.

Rev almost choked. 'A what? It's cost me money having
time off work and stress and having to come to terms
with having to face other attacks. And for what? For doing
the job of the Bill, that's what and poking your nose into
something that doesn't concern you.' Bas scratched the top
of his head. He was stretched out on the sofa, his black tee
shirt barely covering the bulge he called a stomach, drinking
Asti spumante, a gift from his cousin.

'It's bloody awful this,' he spat. He had nothing to say
about the thick pads protecting Rev's fingers; he wasn't yet
ready for practice. In any event their room was no longer
available, it had been put up for sale.

Gary called a meeting. He knew of a studio with recording
facilities and he was anxious that they had a look. 'Hey, I
know this place,' divulged Bas as they climbed out of the
van. 'It's a night run for working girls.'

'I'm surprised you put it quite so politely,' scorned Tiz.

'All the same he seems to know all about it,' derided
Boo.

'Anyway,' chimed Cheddar, 'there's nobody here now.
Maybe it's too early.' He marched off ahead leaving Gary
shaking his head; they would return later when Rev's hands
had healed.

****

'I do not like the way he is lingering about, or the way

he watches me.' Sue was suspicious of Flute. 'What if he's a stalker?'

'How can he be a stalker when he sits in the tunnel all the time?' asked June. 'He's harmless enough. We never see a bottle, do we? Or dubious characters hanging about? Leave him alone to play his flute.' Later June was to regret her charitable approach.

Sue was not convinced. She whispered to Ellie, 'I would not trust him as far as I could throw him.' She wrapped her chubby hands around the mixer. 'I mean, where do you suppose he lives?'

'Sue, stop chattering, we have a Blues cruise at 7.30 and it is all to do before you go home,' June swept through the cafe.

Mark had invited Ellie to join him but she declined. In any case he would be busy with passengers, he told her. Looking deep into his blue eyes she suspected that there were worse things than the breath holding force of anticipation and far too much at stake. 'Work to live and live to work,' she heard Sue complain as she pulled the steaming pies out of the oven.

It was Tiz who suggested Hope Valley. 'Let me know when you have a day off and I'll get in touch with Fab and we will have a day out.' October arrived with its vermilions and mustards and the changing light on the leaves. The gentleness of the settling season, the lazy descent of the first dying leaves and the nip in the air, heralded the season of autumn. The cemetery seemed to be more at peace, the ground was softer with its brown carpet and the stillness was comforting.

They left Sheffield a little after nine. It was warm in Boo's recently acquired red mini and the sun was determined to shine despite the few clouds. 'We would like to show you the caverns,' smiled Tiz, 'but we can't do them all today.' Nature's palette of colours, ablaze with coppers and russets, was displayed in a gallery of trees as they passed through Derbyshire. Ellie wanted to express the emotion she felt but could not. The girls' chatter was about hair and clothes, the band and unscrupulous landlords. It would have been unkind to assume that they did not appreciate the beauty of nature and probably untrue. They stopped overlooking a stretch of water, a sheet of foil without a ripple reflecting the blue sky.

Castleton was enjoying one of its mild, wind free days and it was glorious. The Blue John cavern was their first port of call and the stalactites and the stalagmites were a magnet for Tiz who darted between them taking photographs. Ellie realized how very fortunate she was to have friends who made no demands; they were neither selfish nor critical for criticism meant disapproval and harboured grudges. Tiz now had blue hair but it was still quite short. In contrast Fab's curly hair was scarlet and Boo's long black hair flashed in the sunlight. From the rocks the water appeared to speak as it eroded the stones and pebbles on its descent, smothering them with glistening shades of colour.

It was difficult not to linger but Tiz spotted an antique shop, a Grannie's Attic tucked untidily in a passage. Two elderly women were opening packing cases, sacks and boxes, holding their backs as they stood unsteadily focussing on the ground. The shop was a junk haven, a collection of misshapen, shoddy clothing and chipped, tired bric-a brac. For Tiz it was Aladdin's Cave and she greeted the women with a broad smile as she dived into drawers and searched behind an Indian Purdah type screen.

Fab saw the boots first. Thigh length, red laced-up boots with a four-inch slender heel, sedately poised on a shelf surrounded by swathes of taffeta and silk. She asked to see them and the taller woman obliged by grudgingly dragging over a pair of unsafe stepladders and heaving herself onto the top step. 'Oh they're gorgeous,' Fab could hardly contain herself. It was not a case of wanting them but of hanging onto them as Tiz suddenly, in an outburst of fury, shouted. 'They're not your size, they are far too big.'

'Nonsense,' Fab retorted and grabbed one boot and forced her foot with a quick thrust into it and pulled up the zip. Snatching the other boot, Tiz began removing her jeans in full view of the window and was hastily directed behind the screen by the harassed assistant.

Reappearing in just her underwear she lifted up her booted leg, declaring, 'There you see, perfect. I bet you couldn't get a better fit than that.'

'They're mine,' insisted Fab. 'You will never be able to walk in them, you've been too long in Doc Martens.'

'Is that right?' sneered Tiz. 'We'll see.'

Boo had her head buried in a selection of tapes in the corner whilst Ellie giggled. The ladies looked on in bewilderment. 'You do realize,' began Fab, 'that they are Vivienne Westwood. There's a tag here.' Suitably impressed they asked the price. Ten Pounds. It was a mistake to have mentioned the top designer. Tiz looked appealingly at Fab, each had a delicate burden of choice.

'A fiver each; we could take turns in wearing them.'

'Course we could,' agreed Fab and they hurried towards the car, arms around each others' shoulders, to a chorus of "These boots were made for walking". Ellie, now convinced that they did indeed understand each other, relaxed in the warm mood of friendship.

Boo had the last word. 'You should never put a pair of shoes on a table, you know. It invites dire misfortune and is likely to lead to an argument.' Tiz cupped her hands round her eyes as Boo attempted a complicated manoeuvre on the approach to the motorway. 'Well we've done it arse about then, haven't we? Argument first, table later.'

Tiz had lost none of her eagerness for her venture into design and the anarchic covers which she had sketched for the Independent library in Bradford were now ready to put on display. It was arranged that they would travel on the Saturday and despite last minute provision to arrange cover for their various jobs everyone managed to pile into the van in time.

Ellie was tired. She settled back on a beanbag and plumped two oversize cushions around her head. Last evening had been spent with Mark on his boat at the Quays along with a couple of mates and their girl friends. It had

been a fun evening. The men had their share of drink but
they had played a game of Pictionary which required very
little movement and a minimum of drawing skills. Ellie
wrote down her answers. There were no romantic overtures,
just the gentle stretch of a hand towards hers and a kiss on
the cheek as she boarded the tram to go home. The shared
activity, the physical closeness, was tempting but the rules
were now tacitly hers.

The Women's' Rights Movement straggled across the busy
approach road to Bradford in a colourful and vocal display
of solidarity. 'How come we didn't know about this?' queried
Fab, always anxious to fight for human rights.

'Dunno,' murmured Tiz, 'but we can't do much about it
now,' as she relaxed against Boo's knees. The Muslim chador
garment brushed alongside the sari worn by the Hindu, the
sarong from Malaya shone bright against the Kanga draped
around the body of the women of East Africa. A multiracial
display of harmony, but how hard it must be to cultivate
and educate so many contrasting beliefs, mused Ellie.

A bustling city. 'A bit like an octopus,' Rev exclaimed.
'A central body with tentacled streets.' The bright colours
contrasted unfavourably with grey buildings, brick dust
and chunks of cement mingled with clumps of grass and
fragments of moss. Yet the cosmopolitan citizens chatted
and smiled.

The popular One in Twelve was begging for a revamp,
and was much bigger than Ellie expected. It was here where
friends caught up with one another, where lines of gossip
passed from one seasoned band to the amateur musician.
Where everyone talked and no one appeared to listen.
Tiz was anxious to meet her sponsor and visit the gallery
but first they must eat and it was an experience not to be
missed.

It had become obvious to Ellie that vegetarians ate well.
The meal was excellent, cheap, fulfilling and hot. There were
books on shelves and in cupboards around the dining area
and patrons were encouraged to read at the table. Bas chose
to read "The Idiot Proof Guide to Booking Bands at the 1

in 12 Club" while tackling three helpings of sticky toffee pudding. He ate prodigiously. Later when Tiz left for the gallery the rest decided on a jam session.

The gallery, described as "An innovation in the modern art for rising stars" was a tuberous building, ugly and ingrained with years of pollution. For Tiz, who saw well within the exterior, it was her platform and she sailed confidently through the large doors, straightened her back and advanced to the centre of a wide circle of spectators. There were other exhibitors with contemporary craft and design but her visual concept of artistic anarchy was exceptionally well received.

That is until a tall, overbearing gent in a herringbone suit and a rose sitting in a stiff lapel approached the group of young enthusiasts. He coughed, raising his little finger to stroke his upper lip. 'Is this about posterity and what you like to call Europe's destiny? It seems to me to contain the truth of your arrogant error in government. I call it anarchical vulgarity.' Tiz could not believe she was listening and remaining still. The moment was isolated. She turned, smiled and told him to leave, only it was said in a way that there would be no misunderstanding about the significance of her remarks.

Tiz was not expecting compliments from the likes of him, nor did she want any, but even without propriety he continued with his barrage of insults. 'I want to say this about the language that you spat out so unbecomingly. If any of you were just a little in touch with major political events you would realize how outrageous and futile your protests are.'

Tiz paused in her striding in the middle of the room. A faint flush rose in her cheeks. She grabbed the rose from his lapel and thrust it into his mouth. 'You arsehole!' she shrieked and watched him gasping and choking as he staggered down the stairs and into the street. The group of young people applauded.

'We don't mean to start any rough stuff,' moaned Rev when the incident was discussed at length on the journey home.

'It just seems to happen. It's not as if we are political extremists, we don't advocate destruction of all existing and social and political institutions. I mean we're ...'

'Idealistic,' interrupted Boo.

'Anyway,' yawned Fab, 'snobbery is repugnant and Tiz did a truly marvellous job of bringing him down!'

'Who was he?' enquired Gary, driving through the rush hour traffic.

'Dunno,' replied Tiz. 'Who cares? I happen to have received a great response from the exhibit.'

****

Bas looked around the bar and perched himself on a stool half hidden by a screen, but which allowed him a clear view of the street. He leaned his elbows on the table and cracked his knuckles. He felt ill at ease, his local had an uncivilised feel about it. It was his darts night; it was rowdy but there was an underlying impression of retribution, or was it his imagination? He wasn't afraid, of course he wasn't – nervous perhaps. He took a long swig of lager and smacked his lips. Violence was on his doorstep, a couple of streets away; he had read it in the paper. Brutality and bloodshed at the hand of a gun, the victim a sitting target in a car. Gang warfare maybe, nothing to do with him. Short days and long nights for drug dealers, he imagined. Disconcerted he looked around and then climbed the stairs to the lounge.

Snapping his fingers, he ordered another lager. His anxieties were gradually disappearing. The dart teams were a little overrated but friendly and dispersed in a cheery manner. Halfway down the stairs he saw the shadows on the wall. Three men. A frightening, chilly premonition crept over him. They moved towards him swiftly and barred his way. 'We want a word.' The voice revealed cold determination. 'Empty your pockets.' Bas felt the clout on his face and the stench of bad breath as the hooded figure leaned over. His house keys, wallet and loose change fell to the floor. 'Take off your boots.' This could take a while, he thought, struggling with his laces and his fear. 'Now the socks.' He knew that his brawn and muscle were no match for three and black eyes gaped through deep slanting grooves from under heavy overhanging brows. Voices inside his head were screaming. This was no time for heroism; nearby a body had been filled with bullets. The screech of tyres and excited yells filled the air; the thugs retreated but the respite was short-lived. Bas received a blow to the head and the thuds of many feet echoed in his subconscious.

Gary called a meeting. Together maybe they could do something to change the situation that Bas found himself in. 'Somebody seems to think that you know more than you do,' sighed Rev. 'I tell you what, you got away with it this time but who knows who will be chasing you next time?'

'Thanks a bunch.' Bas was nursing a badly lacerated head which required stitches. 'Look, I've a mind to clear off, leave you to sort it all out.' Bas refused to argue; the short drive from the hospital had been uncomfortable.

CHAPTER ELEVEN

"A wise head makes a close mouth." (Proverbial French.)

This was Gary's home. A large Victorian house situated on the outskirts of Sheffield and divided into flats. Ellie had tried to imagine where he lived and how he lived but she was not prepared for the impact the surroundings had on her. The rest of the group had been before and settled in without ceremony in the spacious lounge. Boo and Tiz made herbal tea and Ellie was taken into the office.

One wall was completely filled with books. Most dealt with homelessness, social problems, legal procedures and community relations. The computer had pride of place. The flat was neat and papers and folders were categorised in uncluttered piles. 'I have a surprise for you,' he smiled. He looked pale and there were dark shadows around his eyes. Ellie wondered if he were under threat from some disease would he tell her? She would want him to.

He opened the doors into what appeared to be a small conservatory. 'This is special, Ellie, I promise you,' he teased and held her hand tightly. "The virtue of the mouth healeth all it toucheth." She remembered this proverb, beautifully embroidered and framed behind Gran's bed, pondering on Gary's words 'this is special'.

It wasn't a conservatory but a roof garden with a paned glass covering and white floor tiles. At sundown peace encircled the greenery and the moss-covered stones: the pebbled statue of an angel peered over miniature roses and

144

Ellie drew a deep, deep breath. A fountain gurgled and she drew Gary towards it. 'This is my sanctuary,' he whispered. 'As you can see there are parts of the roof missing, allowing access to birds and butterflies, to Oliver the owl, who waits until the starlings have completed their ballet, leaves Parliament and lords it over me. This keeps me sane.'

Leading her towards a small bench he slowly put his arm around her; he glanced down and then back into her eyes. 'You are very beautiful, Ellie, and very mysterious. I know very little about you but it isn't that important. What is, is that we discuss what is to be done about your future, which is why I have called this meeting. If there is anything you cannot agree with let me know. It is your life and you may have plans which don't include any of us. That's OK. Meanwhile I would rather you stayed with us. I can't imagine you not being here!'

Even if Ellie had chosen to speak at this time she would not have known what to say. She expected more in this 'special place' – emotional recollections, influences which had aroused her, sentimental reminders of the warmth and contentment she had felt being close to him. His hand burned against her shoulders. She turned to face him; why didn't he kiss her? Surely he could read the truth in her eyes.

Ellie lowered her eyes. It was OK was it to dismiss her? Was a frank explanation of her plans all he wanted? Clearly he no longer regarded her as his charge. She had no desire to be an intruder in his sanctuary. Dislodging herself from his arm she walked away and hid her tears.

Her friends hardly noticed Ellie at all. They were engrossed in a list of future gigs and a number of new songs which Gary had composed. Gary pulled up a chair and enquired after Bas and the state of his injury. 'I don't know why they singled me out,' he groaned. 'Yeh, I roughed somebody up but he asked for that. No explanation, no nothing, just an excuse for a beating.'

Boo was scathing. 'It's your extremely insolent attitude, that's what it is.' Bas shook his head dolefully; his head bore the hidden marks which Herculean fists had struck. He

moved to the back of the room and sat on the floor hunched
up against the wall.

'Right,' began Gary, sitting on the edge of the chesterfield
between Tiz and Boo. 'How do you feel about a squat?'
Cheddar had not been listening, nor Rev; they were deep
in conversation.

'Shut up,' bellowed Tiz. Turning slowly to Gary she
mused. 'Did I hear you say squat? You have to be joking!'

Everyone joined in the protest. 'No way.'

'All of us, together?'

'Bollocks.'

'You must be ******* mad.'

'Not after the last shambles.'

'We were evicted.'

'Too much hassle.'

'Bloody hard work!'

'Get lost Gary.'

The outburst came to a halt. Rev shuffled. Boo sighed.
Ellie remained detached. 'Pity.' Gary slid his fingers down
his polo neck jumper. 'I know just the place. I mean what
with Bas being on the hit list, Tiz and Boo faced with a
huge increase in rent, Fab soon to leave Uni and her student
accommodation, Ellie won't have a home when Maggie goes
into care and someone has to take care of Jan and all the
responsibility that goes with it.' Gary ran out of breath.

Ellie managed a smile. He had done his homework and
she at least had been half prepared. Bas moved forward.
'What do you mean, you know somewhere?'

Gary leaned forward. 'It's not far from the town centre,
in a cul-de-sac, has four bedrooms and has been empty for
a couple of years. There is a large garden at the back and
space for a vehicle.' He waited. "If nobody praises you then
you must praise yourself," thought Ellie.

'I suppose we could take a look.'

'It won't hurt to think about it.'

'After all it's not illegal, just unlawful!'

'Think what you will,' argued Rev, 'but I believe there is
safety in numbers. I say we give it a go, have a butcher's

anyway.' Cheddar was non-committal.

Bas looked derisively upwards as if he was about to send an arrow prayer straight to heaven. 'I daresay you will want me to break in. Anybody got any overalls?'

'We'll go during the day; people get a bit jumpy if they hear suspicious noises at night.' Boo shuffled uncomfortably on the sofa.

'Just be careful,' she directed, 'that we don't get caught red-handed breaking in or make any stupid statements.'

Ellie, perched on a bar stool near the window, could only manage a weak smile at Tiz. 'It's OK, Ellie, we've done it before, we'll take care of you.' Undoubtedly they would and she had always felt protected in their company. Yet a shift of extreme circumstances like this was out of her control. Now it seemed it was simply a matter of trust. No one seemed afraid of their own rash hopes. Ellie had visions of the squat where she had first met Jan and of the youth with whom she had shared a room, stretched out on the mattress on the floor, cap beside his shaven head and smelling of yesterday's garlic. Neither person knowing the other cooped up in one small world.

****

'We appear to be running short of mixed vegetables'. June was flushed. 'It's not the cooking, duck, it's middle age,' she puffed wiping her forehead with her apron.

'How do you fancy making pastry tomorrow, lass, do you good to get your hand in.' Through the side window of the cafe Ellie was watching Mark as he helped a school party onto his boat, teasing the girls. At a distance she thought of him as irresistible yet at close contact she was wary. He had invited her on board that evening along with his friends and the thought did appeal to her. 'I see that Flute fella is there again, looking thinner and more tormented than ever,' observed June. 'Goodness knows where he disappears to at night.' Maybe, thought Ellie, he is squatting in some hovel. What was it Rev had said. 'Only a small minority of

squatters ever get nicked and with good legal advice they
often get off.'

The sweetish sharp odour, an indefinable mixture of musk
and jasmine, greeted her and she was met with a kiss from
Mark as she stepped into the galley. 'Aromatherapy,' claimed
the tall blonde sporting a jewel in her navel and a stud in
her tongue. 'A small demo for friends.' Already a huge
amount of alcohol was being swilled down unceremoniously
by the four men and five women. Ellie had met them once
before on the autumnal equinox and they were drunk then.
It was hot, it almost felt as if the heat was seeping through
the walls. A small youth with a pebbled complexion made a
pass at her as the night owl replaced the call of the starlings
above the Quays. He called her his unpicked apple and
shoved her against the galley door. Ellie waited for Mark to
intervene but he found the situation amusing and appeared
undisturbed by the whole thing. She made a dash for the
door, grabbing her bag from the sink.

It was November yet the air held the warmth of late
autumn and the musk lingered with the dampness of the
earth on the towpath. She trod carefully away from the boat
and towards the gates. Only the light from the tunnel was
visible. Suddenly in front of her loomed a figure; silently,
a ghost-like, sombre shape, and it leapt at her. She turned
to run back to the boat but it quickened. And lurched. She
couldn't scream; hands tightened around her. Together they
slid on the bank; she fought. She remembered the fight in
the cafe, self-defence, and hit out, kick, bite, go for the eyes.
Twice she almost hit the ground; she was dragged along;
they reached the boat. She could see the party through the
window, hear their laughter.

She was being pushed still further down the path,
slipping and sliding. Strong arms pinned her down, stale
breath brushed her mouth, she was weakening, the effort
was unbalancing her. Ellie gave one violent shove and the
figure fell backwards into the water. As it came into contact
with the boat she heard a crack and then it disappeared into
the inky blackness.

There was no time for delay, no time to hang about with dumb explanations. The complex predicament of her nature could not disguise what she had done and she was not prepared to speak, not even now in those desperate moments when she could so easily have been killed. It was Philip's fault. He had touched her, threatened her, come to her like a thief in the night and what had he called her? His little berry because, he said, she had the flavour and the texture of a sweet fruit.

She ran all the way to the tram and once aboard hugged her elbows to her remembering that she had already put one man behind bars. Why? Why her? She had no desire to be different, she wanted life to open up opportunities, to enjoy it, to have fulfilment but not at the expense of others and none of the drama in the past was her fault. She felt infuriated and afraid. She was grateful and relieved that tomorrow was her day off.

Gary drew up outside the house and waited until the rest had clambered out of the van and sat tight. 'Hell, it's big enough,' Tiz exclaimed.

'It's shored up, it's falling down. Looks pretty dangerous to me,' Rev complained.

'Oh, come on, houses like these last for years,' Boo urged.

'How long has it been empty? Two years? I don't know. Seems like a big gamble to me,' Rev uttered.

'Look, it depends on what needs to be done and we ought not to be standing around out here looking conspicuous,' added Tiz. Bas said nothing. He stepped back into the road and made a general inspection of the building.

'It's not going to be easy getting in at the front,' he informed them. 'I'll reconnoitre round the back, have a bit of a survey.'

The light was fading as it began to rain. Tiz accompanied Bas to the rear of the building via a stretch of open ground fenced off at the top of a steep bank leading down to the railway. 'Ideal for the bus, unless it's a right of way?' queried Tiz. Ellie sat in the van with the rest. Squatting was the last thing on her mind. She watched Gary scribbling notes on official looking documents on a clipboard and noted his smart suit and shirt. Who was he intending to impress?

'I can gain access through the back by way of a window above the bathroom.' Bas pulled himself beside Gary. 'It's boarded but a crowbar should do it. Shall I have a go?' Everyone agreed. He struggled into an overall and armed with knives and a crowbar he swaggered up the wide lane but this time taking Rev with him.

Fab sniffed and adjusted her glasses nervously. 'I hope he doesn't get caught,' she sighed.

'With a crowbar? No. He'll say it's for unblocking a drain,' suggested Cheddar. 'He's done it before.'

As the banging grew louder Gary jumped out of the van. 'Won't be long, try not to draw attention to yourselves.' He looked very authoritative as he rang the bell of the house next door. Ellie moved into the front seat but was ousted by Tiz who was anxious to relay what was happening.

'They are shaking hands, that is always a good sign.'

'Who is at the door?'

'I think he's a Bangladeshi; there are a few round here; he's friendly. I don't think he is inviting Gary in though.' Tiz took note of the body language. The man passed one hand across his mouth, under his moustache, and took the piece of paper Gary handed to him. A buxom long-robed woman appeared in the hallway and after a few moments they closed the door.

'The people with the most to hide never have moustaches,' informed Fab.

'What did they say? Are they likely to cause trouble?'

'Stuff them,' protested Cheddar. 'We've dealt with the likes of them before.'

'Oh, yes,' scoffed Boo. 'It's got nothing to do with you, you're not invited anyway. Stay in your own gaff.' The banging ceased. All eyes scanned the front door.

Rev appeared round the corner. 'Look lively, he's in.'

'The neighbours are from Pakistan,' began Gary. 'His name is Sobuj Bhai. I think I convinced him although he studied my ID at some length. We'll see.'

Bas appeared triumphantly at the front door waving a torch. 'There are no services, no gas or electricity but there is a water supply,' reported Bas enthusiastically. The house was big enough for all of them – three large bedrooms, one small, and an attic with open stairs. Street lights provided shafts of silver in the upper rooms and cobwebs danced above years of dust and grime on the wooden floors. The bathroom was small and the bath stained; ugly pipes were lagged with dark brown felt.

The girls inspected the kitchen. A filthy electric cooker sat alongside a kitchen cabinet, tall with glass doors and a pull down front. One very similar was once Gran's pride possession, thought Ellie. She was beginning to nurture a spark of interest despite the state of the place. The sink was cracked and pitted and the taps were missing their heads. Adjoining the kitchen was a "walk in" pantry. Ellie had followed Gary into the living room. It had a huge fireplace with iron hobs, two windows, both boarded up, but with Tiz ready to move in and with remarks like, 'Wow, what potential' and 'we could really make something of this', the intent and enthusiasm was spreading.

There was a porch leading from the kitchen into the garden but Gary was reluctant to make any further noise. Bas described it. 'It's big but neglected like the rest of it. There is some sort of a building which looks as if it has blown down forcing a tree to the ground but I couldn't make it out all that well!' Was it her imagination or was the permanence of her life shifting too quickly, questioned Ellie. Would this circle of friends help to determine where the rehearsal would end and the true living start? It was as if she had been in limbo yet she had done so much and learned a great deal; she must never appear ungrateful.

Gary had one arm on the mantelpiece. 'This, Ellie, will make a great open fire; you can just imagine it, can't you? I almost wish I could move in myself.' She doubted it, his vested interest and intense obligation to the group did not stretch to giving up his lifestyle but she knew that his knowledge of the legal implications would be invaluable.

They discussed this at length after Bas had replaced the lock in the front door and secured the window at the back. 'We'll be back tomorrow,' he told Tiz. Among other minor injuries he was nursing a broken tooth but no sympathetic response was forthcoming. Cheddar invited them back to the flat and they compiled a Legal Warning Document which quoted Section 6 Criminal Law Act 1977 as amended by Criminal Justice and Public Order Act 1994. It began "Take notice that we live in this property, it is our home and we intend to stay here!" It continued in this confrontational vein for several paragraphs and concluded with a signature of occupiers.

'Remember,' Gary instructed them, 'this warning on its own will not stop you from being evicted. There must be someone in the place all the time to back it up. This is where Jan will be invaluable!' Ellie thought this a little harsh. What Jan wanted was fresh air, peaceful surroundings and sun, not being cooped up all day waiting for the police to come knocking with a warrant.

Boo placed a cup of herbal tea in Ellie's hand. 'Don't look so worried, Ellie, it won't mean a miserable winter without heat, and rain pouring through the ceiling. I've been in a London squat, in Brixton, and believe me squatters aren't a different race. Do you know that an empty house deteriorates by over £2000 per year? Just by taking over this house we are saving it from decaying even further. Why isn't the owner using this house? Why hasn't the council bought it on compulsory purchase to rehouse the homeless? All we know is that the owners are in New Zealand. Well, we are willing to put in the work to make this place habitable without even knowing how long we can stay here!' She patted her arm, leaving Ellie to her hot tea and comforting thoughts.

The atmosphere at home was cold. There was no sign of a thaw after Celeste's frosty approach to Ellie and Maggie was becoming more depressed each day. The arguments were one-sided. Maggie did not have the strength or the will and it was only a matter of time before she would be forced to move. In an effort to calm her nerves, Ellie retired early. She wrote two letters, one to Gran and the other to Mark. To Gran she filled five pages. She mentioned good friends and her job, her concern about Gary's health and Jan's homecoming, but omitted to mention the squat. It could be seen as a backward step. To Mark the message was much shorter. "Sorry I left early. See you soon. Ellie."

From her book of verse she read:

"I know that tomorrow, I shall see the sun rise. No ugly dream shall fright my mind, no ugly sight my eyes. But slumber hold me tightly till I waken in the dawn, And hear the thrushes singing in the lilacs round the lawn."

****

The officer began to pinpoint places and times and sat back in the cane chair near the cafe door. At a nearby table two more policemen were drinking coffee and comparing notes. 'They are taking up more room,' June grumbled. 'It's not at all good for business, they're not even buying lunch.' Ellie froze in the doorway. 'They want a word with you lass,' June beckoned to her.' I've told them you can't say anything but you know what they're like.' Ellie attempted to look puzzled; expression is evasive when not accompanied by speech. 'Oh, of course you won't know. They pulled what's his name out of the canal the other night. You know, Flute.' Ellie's astonishment was genuine; she had no idea. Taking a deep breath, she edged her way towards the officer. Diners were reluctant to leave. June refused to close the cafe.

Ellie sat opposite the fatherly figure with searching eyes, her hands neatly placed on the table before her. She was so afraid. He leaned forward and pushed a notebook and pencil towards her fingers. 'Now, Ellie,' he began. 'I understand that you are unable to talk. Is this a temporary condition? No? Well I suggest that you write it down, the information I need, that is, and we'll see how we go from there.' Ellie adopted an innocent, almost childlike expression. She remembered her dealings with the police; it didn't pay to be clever, it paid to be tractable, willing to help, to have the ability to memorise what had been said before. 'Right,' he brushed crumbs from his jacket. 'Can you tell me what time you left the party on the night in question, the night the young man was found in the water?'

"I'm not sure," she wrote. "I wasn't paying particular attention."

'How did you get home?'

"On the tram."

'Had you been drinking?'

"No, I don't drink." She guessed that he would know her age.

'Did you know the young man known locally as Flute?'

"I have never spoken to him," she scribbled. The answer was not meant to be facetious but he raised his eyebrows and stuck the pen between his teeth.

'Why do you suppose anyone would want to harm this man Flute? Has he upset anyone, caused anybody grief?'

Ellie shrugged her shoulders. "No idea," she wrote.

She was becoming increasingly uncomfortable. He put both hands on the table in front of him, straightening his back. 'Has he ever threatened you?' he pressed.

Ellie adopted an indifferent, casual manner. What, she thought is the reasoning behind this? This time she left the pencil on the table and shook her head. 'You see, young lady,' he said sternly 'the law is a profession of words but that doesn't mean to say that we can't have justice without them. Maybe I'll need to speak with you later.'

Ellie felt intimidated, fearful of the ghosts from the past. Lies that could come back to haunt her. Even knowing, way back then, who the offender was, she had perjured herself, but this time it was an apparition, like the rough sketch of a face without definite form. She had run away to begin again; were there yet more barriers she had to crash through?

Maggie had been restless and Ellie watched the pallid light of dawn beyond the windows and prayed. Suppose these suspicions continued? She knew that her footprints would be on the path and she had every reason to be there, but there was the struggle which had left fragments of broken willow as she had fought to hold onto him. She lay on the bed unsure of what to do next. How magical the canal had been when the leaves furled and lilies floated on the water but the magic ended when the greenery turned to slime and she had slithered on the towpath caked in mud.

There was not one word of kindness from Celeste. A bowl of oats and a mug of tea presented on a plastic tray were left to balance precariously on a wobbly table spread across Maggie's knees. She could not possibly manage unaided. Ellie remembered her when she had been inquisitive and clumsy but now her fingers refused to grasp and hold and she looked so miserable, her uncombed hair dangling over her eyes. Ellie fed her; she was in no rush to go to the cafe. There had been rumours of a mugging, an attempted break-in at the wine bar but nothing definite, June had reported.

****

Outside the cafe June lit a cigarette and inhaled deeply. The cafe was quiet. Ellie threw yesterday's crusts to the ducks and searched the canal for Mark. June studied the slim, long legs and the straight back and the blonde hair neatly tied back with a black velvet ribbon and reflected on what Mark had said. 'I'd really like to spend more time with her, Ma, but it is just so frustrating. There is no two-way conversation, no feedback. It is like having a pet. No dialogue, no discussion, no response. I like a bit of confrontation; I feel mortified sometimes at the looks I get from her and even if we share something we both enjoy it isn't as if we can discuss it afterwards. She's a bit of a mystery, I can tell you.'

June let the smoke drift into rings above her head. She turned to Ellie. 'Of course we shall get the full story when he comes round, Flute that is.' It seemed to Ellie that she held her breath for a surprisingly long time. Come round! Revive Flute? No one had mentioned that he had survived. She had imagined him still deep down in the water surrounded by pitch blackness. She had not mistaken the impact of the fall, the crack, and yet he had endured all of that? Fear, they say, lends wings. Not for her. Not at this moment. She turned and walked quickly into the kitchen, and drank a whole glass of water. Her skin felt cold and clammy; would he admit to what he had done? Perhaps because of a deep-rooted objection to conformity Flute would remain silent. Perhaps he proposed to explore other means of reprisal? Her mind zigzagged and she spoiled a whole batch of mushrooms and ruined the walnut tagliatelle. June reorganised the menu and told her to sit down quietly with a cup of coffee and strutted away shaking her head.

CHAPTER TWELVE

"Beware of a man who doesn't talk, and a dog that doesn't bark." (Proverbial Spanish.)

On a fine day No. 68 didn't look too bad. The windows which had been boarded and wired to protect them from intruders were letting in pale sunlight, transforming the bare, austere rooms into a home in waiting. Gary had contacted a local squat group and borrowed a number of cleaning utensils and contacted the local Electricity Board by telephone. He said he was working in the area and about to move in. When the application form had been filled in and returned then, in Boo's words, 'We'll soon have the leccy on.'

In the great gathering of such enthusiasm it was hard not to show the same exuberance and Ellie threw herself into the work and tried to forget Flute. Only a stone's throw away she could hear the train on its way to London. She could lose herself there. But beyond that, what? Running away again into the heart of a big city with no friends, that was no solution.

'Start at the top,' Tiz yelled up the stairs. 'In the attic and top two bedrooms.' The specific object in view was to disinfect, dust and discard. It was hardly surprising that everyone was covered in a film of grey powder.

'We should have had the chimney swept,' grumbled Fab.

'Sorted,' croaked Rev, removing small stones and earth

and the remains of a bird's nest from the grate. 'He's coming tomorrow.'

'Who's paying for all this?' asked Bas.

'I don't know,' muttered Boo miserably. 'I daresay Gary has it all in hand.'

It was almost midday when Gary appeared. One by one they emerged from different parts of the house. It amused him to see them so organised. Sobuj Bhai followed closely behind him. He bowed his head as each one was introduced. He had very white even teeth and smiled hesitantly. The entrance was filled with large black bags containing letters, catalogues, newspapers, withered house plants and falling plaster. Sobuj offered to put them with his rubbish; it was the beginning of a long and valued friendship. Because Gary was back in his torn jeans and tee shirt he was perhaps less intimidating and in any case the Alsatian, which was being held on a tight lead by Sobuj, had become increasingly interested in Gary's knees. They ate standing up in the living room, which had yet to be cleaned. The takeaway pizzas, bottles of Spring water and cans of lager for Bas and Rev were soon gone. Bas ate a large pizza to himself. 'You fat pig,' rebuked Boo. Ellie wanted to say "Not in front of Sobuj, it might offend him," but couldn't and the conversation moved on.

In this dirty room it felt almost as if she was being kept in order, thought Ellie. She was being asked to take on as much as she could and having to cope with stained tops and filthy jeans and hair clogged with domestic grime. This was not what she was used to. At home Mrs Abbott had done the cleaning. On spring days Ellie had sat out in the garden reading poetry or weeding the rockery with her cat curled up among the geraniums. First her Gran and then her Mother had spoiled her. Her Mother had never loved her but she gave her everything. That is why she did what she did. To Phil.

In loosening the U bend under the sink Bas caused a flood of water to gush out all over the kitchen floor. Rev wedged a cloth tightly around the hole and the girls stood around cursing and blaming with language more fitting to a drunken lout. The result was an army of mops and buckets and an extremely clean kitchen floor. Ellie was exhausted. It was time to go home. In the van she let her hair fall untidily on either side of her face. She closed her eyes. Perhaps this grave situation which had developed with Flute was yet another time of testing, and she should now look to her friends. Did they have a rare sense of the real values in life?

She slept until the van stopped at the cemetery gates. 'It has been left to us to tell Jan,' Tiz commented. 'We are going to the hospital tomorrow night, want to come?' Ellie wasn't sure. They assured her that Jan was improving and that she should be encouraged in preparing herself for her discharge. Ellie was more than shocked, she was distressed. Suddenly Jan's anxiety was more pronounced, her breathing was laboured and she spoke in brief sentences. Gently Tiz held the scarred hands in hers. The chair positioned by the window was hardly visible for the number of pillows and cushions which propped up her head and arms. A white silk scarf covered her lower face and neck and a deep red flush crept onto her cheek and across one ear.

Boo suggested that they should think again about Jan's living arrangements; a squat was hardly the place to recuperate, she required somewhere warm and germ free; it could hardly be that. Jan agreed that it could be an uncomfortable period for a while but added 'I don't want to be on my own, I'm not able to see beyond the next few months.' Her eyes betrayed her pain; she shuffled until her elbows were well bedded in the pillows. 'I have skin grafts on the agenda and I can't face that by myself. Before coming here I spent three winters in a crummy bed sit, hauling myself out of bed each morning to the smell of damp washing. I couldn't go through that again. Gary says that you will see me OK until I've regained my strength.'

Ellie smiled, unwrapping the teddy with a "Get Well" slogan tied around its neck. Jan cradled it thoughtfully. 'How are you, Ellie? It's good that you came.' They made their way home relieved. Boo manoeuvred the mini through the busy traffic.

'It seems an excellent suggestion of Gary's and we should encourage her to come to us. We shall just have to sit back and wait, see what happens.'

****

Fab may have momentarily entertained the notion that she could stand, walk and even dance in the Vivienne Westwood shoes she was so taken up with. In the run-up to their performance she was excited. Up to then the bands had been average, tired travel-stained musicians who had hopes of a breath of stardom. It was a very long time in coming. Ellie watched Fab from a table near the bar. Gone were the days when she rubber-stamped hands at the door and counted the takings nor did she anticipate doing so again. Moreover she did not intend getting involved in pogo gymnastics in the pit.

Dark Horse had an enthusiastic following, some excessive, a few frenzied but mostly loyal and appreciative of Fab's punk image. The long, red boots complemented her red hair and the black cropped top and short black skirt completed the outfit. Add to it long, lace fingerless gloves and she looked stunning. Bas was not impressed. He was angry, he hated being upstaged and it was beginning to show. 'There's too much feedback,' he complained after the third number.

'Rubbish,' yelled Rev. 'Get on with it.' Halfway through the song, struggling to control his temper, he grabbed the microphone from Fab. She tried gamely to hang on, lowering her hands to get a firmer grip but Bas had made a loop with the wire large enough to pass over his head. He continued to sing. Fab felt the heel of her right foot slipping beneath her; she tried to increase her weight onto the other foot. She was toppling over and she wrapped her arms around his stomach and his tee shirt parted from his jeans revealing his paunch. They fell backwards and stumbled across the stage. The crowd, roaring with laughter, sang 'Who ate all the pies?' Tiz stepped over the knot of wires searching for Fab's hand to pull her free and got caught up in the mass of debris. And then the worst happened, all three fell backwards onto Rev, toppling the cymbals and bringing the drums crashing down.

He keeled over as the stool collapsed.

In spite of this appalling predicament no one left the stage. The microphone was still attached to Bas and he disentangled himself as Rev hauled up his drums and inspected them, cursing loudly. One heel of the boots had broken off and they were slung across to Cheddar who was sniggering. Boo had escaped injury but turned on Bas with such ferocity that it silenced the crowd. 'This, you arsehole is all because of your megalomania. You have to have power, don't you, have to be Number One? Well, you're not, you are nothing without us. Just try, try and go it alone. You won't be able to hack it!'

The situation looked grim but Bas remained astonishingly cheerful. 'I didn't mean nothin', her and me, well we understand each other.'

There were mumblings from the audience as Tiz led Fab to the front, minus shoes but unharmed. Her blue lipsticked mouth puckered. 'Do you get the gist of what she said? You had better watch out.'

Bas, with great deliberation, placed the mike in front of her. 'Good words cost naught,' he hissed and bowed to the crowd. They roared in appreciation.

Gary stood at the entrance, amazed at the applause the band were acknowledging. It was undoubtedly the result of a successful night and he had missed it. He had been in the van for over three hours and still felt as if he needed more. His mind seemed to be wandering; he couldn't get to grips with the noise and as Ellie moved towards him from the bar he stared, not at her but into space. The crowd was dispersing, pushing past them, knocking aside chairs and kicking empty bottles. Ellie grabbed his arm and shoved him into a corner. 'What's up with Gary?' Tiz lowered him into a chair. 'I'll get some cold water; it's stifling in here.

Stay with him, Ellie.' Ellie held his head against her chest and felt the tremors of his body and longed to comfort him. She stroked his hair. In a short while he recovered but this incident was yet another to add to her list of concerns about his health.

The only hopeful element in the comically disastrous situation was that the band would have earned a reputation for unselfish commitment, decided Tiz. Everybody was shouting, swearing, blaming Bas whilst Gary, fully recovered, drove them home. Fab was shaking with resentment and embarrassment; she hated being the object of ridicule. Rev was angry that the damage to his reputation could be extensive; he was cool; drummers didn't end up on stage arse over tip. Tiz was lecturing on gender discrimination in the punk scene, a woman's appearance being a reflection of independence and the decision not to be subservient to men.

She did this whilst standing, balancing on a beanbag with one hand holding on to Boo and one finger raised like a schoolmistress. Bas clenched his teeth. Cheddar giggled uncontrollably. Ellie put both hands to her mouth, the situation was getting more hilarious. Suddenly Bas rose, stumbled over to Fab and removed her glasses. She froze. 'What did you really think?' he began, 'when the crowd broke into a shout of wild approval? Make you feel good, did it? Remember the squat we played in two years ago, unreliable electricity supply, high ceiling and no heating? Cold food and foul expensive beer? Is that what you want? Look, tonight was great, it was fun, nobody got hurt and we got paid. What more could you ask for?'

Tiz was about to make an acid reply but instead sat down. Blame and incrimination had gone in a few unburdened minutes. Here was a Bas they had never seen before.

Among the first to turn up at the house was Cheddar. All in all, he had decided, life was good. He made no bones about it – he wouldn't mind sharing the squat but there was a hell of a lot of work to do and he wasn't that eager to give up his spare time. He had reported for duty today just to take a look at the garden. He thought he might be of some use; he was aware that his character had become slightly soured after his stepfather threw him out but Gary had sorted him out and he was drug free.

The farthest end of the street led onto a busy road but No. 68 was secluded with the occasional train rattling by at intervals. Cheddar straddled the fence with his back to the line and looked down the row of terraced houses. Not a blade of grass, not even the odd weed clinging bristly to a brick wall, only raised broken pavements and cellar grates held down by concrete blocks.

Ellie was the first person to alight from the van. She mouthed at him through the window, pulling childish faces and grinning and putting out her tongue. He was fond of Ellie. He thought at one time he loved her but during the tour of Ireland Gary had taken him to one side. 'Love does not come to order,' he explained. 'Give it time. She is only a slip of a girl.' Incredible though it might seem those days were gone; now she was more woman than girl but there was still nothing but the silence between them. His place would be taken, he was sure, by someone with far more to offer than a bed-sit and moderate income. She wasn't the sort you could feed with an empty spoon, he imagined.

Hope of moving in before Christmas was a certainty. After ten days the whole house had been scoured. The squalid, unkempt appearance had been replaced by clean windows and the paintwork had been uncovered revealing a somewhat faded shade of cream. An SOS had been despatched for unwanted furniture, carpets and utensils and once again "skipping" became operational. 'The leccy's on,' cried an excited Boo, exuberant at the prospect of moving in, but it was Bas and Rev who had first footing; they planned to take advantage of an advanced housewarming.

'What the devil is she doing?' queried Bas as Boo carried from room to room a loaf of bread and a bowl of salt.

'It is to quiet any existing presences,' Boo replied in a whisper.

'You what?' Bas followed her up the stairs, everyone else

tagging along in single file.

'It is essential to make one's peace with any spirits already residing in the house,' Boo continued.

'If you ask me it's a load of old cod's wallop,' Bas snapped but pushed open the door to the bathroom anyway.

'And also to safeguard the house from invasion by evil spirits,' Boo claimed.

With every room protected they returned to the living quarters. 'Anything else?' Rev enquired sarcastically.

'Only horseshoes over the doors and iron nails to scratch chalk patterns on the doorstep,' she innocently responded.

Tiz put her arms around her. "Bless you,' she said.

It was not time for hard arguments, it was a time for compromise. Jan was to be given the bedroom at the back of the house overlooking the garden. From there beyond the small hedge separating the garden from common land could be seen a small copse and through this the lights of the city. Ellie pondered. If sometimes she felt secretly tempted to indulge in self-pity then perhaps, when the trees were in leaf and the garden came to life, nature would help to heal. Moonlight and water light, as vital for healthy living as the air we breathe, prescribed Fab.

To Ellie it was irrelevant where she slept. She would be rid of the antagonist, Celeste, the daily distressing scene of having to watch Maggie being bullied, and the inadequate way she had handled the situation and dealt with the enmity. For a while the sleeping quarters here would provide a little privacy until Fab joined her. Whilst Boo was intending to scratch out the chalk patterns Ellie was soon to scratch out the shapes which had been haunting her. Phil who had squirmed his way faster than most into her mother's affections had been dealt with but only temporarily.

Flute's account of the evening by the canal was crucial to her future and she dreaded most the possible investigation into her past.

It wasn't long before Sobuj Bhai appeared at the door. He was followed by his wife and between them they dragged in a large tapestry carpet, red with gold stripes. He offered his apologies for the threadbare appearance but hoped it would be of some use. 'It's lovely. Cheers,' enthused Tiz and arranged it in front of the fire.

Cheddar had actually succeeded in clearing most of the garden and bulky objects were waiting to be taken away by Gary. Ellie suspected that the situation in which Gary found himself was not easy. It seemed to her that all the energy had been drained from him. He needed care in which tenderness would play a part. Maybe in time she could be more involved when the future looked more optimistic.

Enclosed behind a high fence Sobuj Bhai's garden was neat and orderly, with leaves piled high, stirring in the gust of an autumn wind, rotting into next year's mulch. It was a practical garden, proficient in vegetable growing, lacking in flowers. The girls were the only ones showing interest, peering over whilst standing on a worm-eaten bench. 'Nothing stands still in nature,' Sobuj claimed.

'You have a lot to do.' His wife smiled.

'I hope this isn't going to become a habit, him dropping in when he feels like it,' Bas moaned. 'He's irritating.'

'Interfering,' added Rev.

'He's interested in us,' Tiz suggested.

'And what is the first rule of squatting?'

'Make friends with the neighbours,' they chorused sarcastically.

****

Ellie saw the police car as she stepped off the bus. The rain was coming down in sheets and she pulled the hood of her jacket over her head and ran across the road, through the arch and onto the waterfront. Her heavy breathing, she hoped, would disguise her panic and she pushed open the cafe door. She gathered her thoughts. Two policemen were drinking coffee and only one looked directly at her as she swept through into the kitchen, dripping as she went. 'Oh what a chuffin' morning,' June grumbled. 'We are not going to do much today'. Ellie looked up from buttering scones to

take a sly look through the glass. The older policeman rose
and walked towards the kitchen. Ellie stared in his direction;
she couldn't ignore him. He had an unusual appearance; his
neck was long. Folds of skin hung from his throat, giving
him a lizard look, almost menacing. 'Thanks, love. Cheers,'
and they were gone.

It was the icy silence that came on cold days, a shock
to the system and had she chosen to speak, still she would
have been stunned into soundlessness; not in words but
deep inside her head. Memories kicked into place – his body
shoving, pushing at her, the hardness of him sliding and
slipping in the mud, diving through the blue-black water,
cracking against the barge. 'Well, that explains it, doesn't it,
duck? You know Flute. Says he can't remember a thing.'

June bent down to arrange the shelves in the oven. 'Pass
me the sausage rolls. Apparently he'd been drinking, walked
along the towpath and fell in. Serve him right, he shouldn't
be around here anyway. I've told Mark to have a word. He
pulled him out, you know. Bloody lucky, if you ask me.'

Lucky, yes, agreed Ellie but shrewd and streetwise and
she had no choice but to go along with it. June straightened.
'Are you alright, love? Soon be moving into your new home,
I hear. I might have some bits and pieces which might prove
useful.'

The Legal Warning notice was given pride of place in the
top drawer of a sideboard which had been rescued from
a skip. It had been easier this time. Ellie simply rolled up
her sleeves and pitched in without a second thought. She
searched and stretched up to the armpits to expose half tins
of paint and clambered in and around piles of household
goods at the tip. Gary was at hand with the van which was
a definite improvement on last time when they hauled every
item by hand.

Charity shops gave them first choice of unsaleable goods
and they were gathering a stack of wood ready for the open
fire. 'Well, this is no sweat lodge,' Bas said, gobbling down
his curry and chips in front of a roaring fire.

'Mind your feet; remember we haven't got a fireguard

yet,' Boo reminded him. He was relieved not to have been rooted out and set upon; he felt reasonably safe. There were mates he missed and that hit him where it hurt, he admitted – no more darts or away matches – but there was sure to be a decent pub near here, he thought.

****

'I'll have another bash,' laboured Cheddar. 'I can't see the fault, must be the circuit.'

'You can sort it out, surely. You're brilliant with electrics,' Tiz simpered. Cheddar sniffed.

Boo grabbed the clump of wires under the sink. 'Can't do without a washing machine,' she appealed.

'Leave me to get on with it then,' he snapped.

It was Saturday evening. Everyone apart from Cheddar and Fab had moved in. For Ellie it had been a painful experience, heartrending to leave Maggie, and she had hugged her and kissed her wrinkled, pale face and felt her thin body heave beneath the blanket. Celeste stood by unmoved. 'She's not going far,' she said. 'Quite near, in fact. She'll like it; it's a very reputable home.' Maggie attempted to raise herself from the pillow but sank back with a deep sigh.

'Yours is the only touch of love I've had, lass. God bless you.' Ellie grabbed the address from Celeste's outstretched hand. It took some restraint not to smack her. She walked slowly down the path towards the cemetery gates, carrying the two holdalls containing all her possessions. The cat bounded towards her, rubbing against her jeans. What will happen to it? she wondered, and the hedgehog and the stoat? Perhaps she could return for the cat? Boo helped her into the mini, her dark eyes apprehensive and sad. Taking hold of Ellie's hand, she pressed it. 'She'll be OK, you'll see.'

The three chums in the kitchen were very drunk. The twin-tub washing machine which had been donated by June had not been a success. It had broken down in the middle of the first wash and had to be emptied by hand.

It mattered then; it didn't matter a fig now. All three sat on the floor, drinking vodka and separating earth from live. Bas swaggered in and intervened. He dislodged Cheddar from the wires and Boo from Cheddar. He lifted her and carried her into the living room, depositing her on the sofa. She giggled. Tiz stumbled after them and threw herself on top of Boo. Bas tidied the wires and shoved the washer under the sink. Then he returned to his lager; there was a sound at the door.

Ellie's soft fingers continued to massage Gary's neck and shoulders; she hadn't had the time or the opportunity since the Irish tour. She suspected that he was downplaying his illness and knew that there was a pain threshold that concerned him. With her thumbs she located the tension spots and massaged gently until he relaxed. Another sound at the door, this time a loud tapping. Bas grunted and let Sobuj in. The white teeth glinted in the firelight. 'I have come to play for you, to welcome you.' In his khurta and tight trousers he bowed slightly towards the ladies sprawled on the sofa but the response of muffled laughter did nothing to deter him. Perched on the edge of a kitchen chair he began to play. Bas helped himself to another lager. He played the sitar well and Rev soon responded with a drum accompaniment although it wasn't easy. Ellie continued her massage and Cheddar slept in the kitchen. It was midnight before they all retired and Gary left for home. 'Thanks, Ellie,' he said and kissed her on the cheek.

Incredibly, Cheddar had remained on the cold slabs of the kitchen floor all night. Ellie, dressed and washed, knelt beside him professing to sympathise with his drunken misbehaviour and prodded him with her boot. He was too exhausted, too hung over to find words and she stepped over him, reaching for the muesli, and watched him sleep. She held the spoon near his mouth and let the milk trickle over his tongue and smiled. The chains holding his jacket together clattered on the stone floor as he raised one arm and promptly went back to sleep.

They had had moments of intimacy in Ireland, she

recalled, when they had walked in silence, holding hands and blinking in the strong sunlight. Then she had been enthusiastic, eager for friendship, but he was just a boy and it had been hard work persuading him that they both needed to grow up.

No one stirred at the squat on Sundays. Not until noon at least. Since this was an ideal opportunity to have time to herself, Ellie caught the bus at the corner of the street and from there to the chapel. Ellie had never intended to hide her faith but without speech it would not be easy to explain. The small congregation sang "So let our lips and lives express" and Ellie chorused the words and shook hands with the minister. She bought a Sunday paper with the largest number of supplements, just in case anyone queried where she had been. There was no movement anywhere in the house.

It was a step back into the past, a glimpse of her early life with Gran when she cleaned out the grate where the fire had glowed well into the night. She rolled up her sleeves, coaxed the shale and cinders away from the boiler shelf, and cleaned the hob. This was the last of the coal. She wondered if Rev would continue to keep them supplied with fuel. On tour he would rise early to collect great armfuls of wood for the campfire.

Wearing a huge pair of rabbit slippers and a well-worn maroon dressing-gown, Tiz crept downstairs. 'Hi, Ellie. There's a heap of clothing in the kitchen, prostrate, inert and covered in puke. Any ideas?' Ellie shrugged her shoulders. 'You too, eh? I got exactly the same response from Boo, who turned her face to the wall and covered her head with a blanket.' Deep guttural sounds came from Cheddar, grunts and groans as he tried to free his arm from his straps. 'What an idiot,' Tiz sighed, dragging him to the wall and sitting him upright. He wiped his face with the back of his hand and belched loudly. Tiz unbolted the door to the garden and shoved Cheddar in the direction of the coal house. 'A bit of fresh air will do you good,' she urged and slammed the door shut.

Bitterly disappointed but accepting his decision, Jan made arrangements for a further stay in hospital. The doctor was right of course, she didn't feel ready to face the world. A further two weeks was suggested. 'Well, it gives us time to prepare your room and get a few more bits and pieces together,' Boo enthused.

Three beds, a few chairs, two mattresses, a sofa and beanbags, an Indian rug, a table and a kitchen cabinet would hardly suffice, thought Ellie. It would take more than a few bits and pieces to warrant calling the place a home. As someone on the edge of danger from infection, Jan needed a place of safety. Could Gary be fabricating a haven? Would he regret his decision? Were the friends ready for responsibility? Jan had experienced a grief none of them would understand; she was disfigured and most likely would require a lot of attention. Yet by her own admission she was afraid to live alone. To Ellie it seemed obvious; it was only to herself in silence that she admitted the truth; she was nervous about long-term illness and the heartache it brought.

At midday on the Saturday the group of musicians entered the recording studio. Cheddar stood guard at the entrance to the yard until all the instruments had been dragged up the stairs. Fab was late. She arrived flustered and apologetic, to infuriated stares from Bas and relief from Gary. She had, she announced, had a couple of sessions with morbid-minded drama seekers who were studying paranoia, looking for macabre settings to act out their melodramas! 'Fatalism at its worst,' she expounded. 'Everybody was either stoned or inbred.' No one responded. Bas held the mike to his chest and stared at her wide eyes behind narrow glasses, then at her feet.

'University is a stumbling block, mark my words. The only thing in life worth having is pleasure,' smiled Bas and slapped her backside with his fat hand.

'It doesn't have to be elaborate, but it does have to be clean and warm,' suggested Gary. It had been established that the fire at the restaurant had been started by a cigarette in the lounge and once it had spread to the kitchen then it flared out of control. Jan had been drinking. She was semi-conscious before the flames reached her. He handed Tiz an envelope. 'Buy what you need; it's part of the insurance. You don't mind, do you?'

This, thought Ellie, was the Gary she remembered. She could picture varied shades of green on the valley floor and the clouds coasting over the Irish hills and hear the appeal in his voice when he needed silence to keep the world at bay. He arrived at No. 68 with a Calor gas fire and a spark guard both purchased cheaply through an ad in the newspaper. In the corner Boo and Tiz were sorting out remnants purchased from the market stall run by Sobuj and his wife. Ellie worked an old treadle machine, making curtains. It had a sporadic action occasionally making no movement at all but a quick thump at the treadle and it jerked into life. It was borrowed from the local Tenants' Association, who were firm believers in spreading skills and resources.

Rev described Gary as an alternative Estate Agent. 'He uses his imagination and intelligence and applies them realistically to the local situation,' he explained to Ellie. Bas had piled wood onto the fire then settled back with Rev to listen to music. Fab was fast asleep on the sofa. Gary, cross-legged on the floor, was surrounded by papers sorted into neat piles, marked with highlighters. Ellie suspected that these were the itinerary for Europe. He was always the centre of everything, always out to succeed, and she didn't know what she would do without him. Life rarely played out the way we anticipated, but that was the joy of expectancy. She watched for a moment as he straightened his legs, rubbing them and retracting them. He had difficulty in walking sometimes; there was an element of stooping in his posture but he would most likely put it down to tiredness.

****

There was an ugly expression on Bas's face. 'In summer it might be possible, if the weather was dry, yes, but no way am I climbing on the roof to mend that skylight and replace the slates.'

'But you are a builder, you do things like this all the time,' pleaded Boo.

'I am not a builder. I erect scaffolds; without a roof ladder I don't do nothing.'

'It's started to leak, there's a bucket underneath to catch the rainwater. I had plans to use the attic to paint,' appealed Tiz. 'You know, for the exhibitions.' She was recalling how the water ran from the edges of the roof in tiny rivulets. Tiz and Ellie had provided a mouth-watering meal of vegetable lasagne and Bas's favourite sticky toffee pudding. What, he wondered, were they after? He pushed his chair away from the table.

'It's impossible. The wood is rotten, we have no slates and the whole window needs replacing. Anyway it's freezing up there, you can't paint if it's cold.'

He slumped on the sofa, rubbing his stomach. Tiz nudged Boo. 'You try.' Boo shook her head. Tiz approached the sofa and sank into a beanbag. 'I remember, she began, 'on our tour of Germany you said that nothing was impossible. Do you remember? When we were in the flood and faced with crossing the ford? You said it could be difficult and daunting and dangerous but not impossible. Still,' she sighed. 'That was then. In any case I plan to paint in the early morning; it is always the nicest part of the day.'

'No way,' he exhaled.

The following Saturday Tiz awoke to the sound of scuffling and rose to find Bas climbing through the skylight, supported by Rev, who was grabbing his legs with force significant enough to warrant a 'Watch it' and a string of abuse. With preparation and determination he had removed the rotting timber. It had been a tight squeeze and he had struggled to hold his ground. He replaced the slates which he had appropriated from work and the sun came out and sparkled on the roof top. Although autumn had slid suddenly into winter there was a little warmth in its rays, only to be shut out as the window was boarded up in readiness for the glass. 'Wangling that would be no problem,' he grinned. Tiz bought him a packet of six.

CHAPTER THIRTEEN

"He who preserves a wise silence speaks well." (Proverbial Serbian.)

'It was touch and go, believe me,' Mark explained to Ellie.

June nodded emphatically. 'It has been known for patients to be unconscious for months in his condition.' His conversation went on at length about Flute and his narrow escape. Ellie, busy making vol-au-vents for the wine-tasting evening later, pretended not to hear. The radio almost completely shut out his words. There was a strange look of mingled astonishment on his face. 'Aren't you interested, Ellie?' called June.

In spite of the deepening dusk there were no lights in the cafe and from the kitchen the silhouettes of Mark and his mother were barely visible. She shook her head. She didn't want to appear rude or shocked or surprised but the less she had to do with Flute the better. Ellie did appreciate that they had both got off lightly; she wanted to put the whole incident out of her mind. Mark came up behind her, putting his arm on her shoulder. 'I've decided on one good deed,' he whispered. 'I'm going to offer Flute a job.'

Beneath his air of benevolence somehow Ellie suspected a hint of mischief. After all what was it June had said. 'They are faceless individuals holding out their hands for a freebie.' Would she block his act of compassion? Yes, the answer was definite. 'Not in my cafe, you're not. I know I defended him when Sue slagged him off but it was only to make her feel better. Anyway, clear off, if you want food for your party tonight.'

Mark ran along the quay, grabbing two girls carrying wine onto the boat, and raised his arm in salute. Ellie shivered. She felt a tightness in her chest, saw again the lurking figure in the gloom, the smell of his breath, remembering how her heart raced with fear pushing her nerves to the limit. The obvious thing to do was to make sure the experience was never repeated; she would stay well clear of the towpath.

****

'Can't you do something about this plaster?' Boo pleaded.

Instinctively Bas manifested his seniority. 'Yes,' he barked. 'I can if you move and let the hounds see the fox.' Tiz held aloft a framed photograph of clothing spiked on hawthorn bushes, taken on tour and intended for Jan's bedroom. 'That's rubbish. What you want is a picture of a pair of dolphins or a vase of sunflowers' He loosened the plaster on the ceiling with a long brush.

'Oh, and you would know, would you?' sneered Boo. She glared at the beefy skinhead sweeping away the rubbish, who shrugged and slowly made his way downstairs. Boo wasn't one to give away unqualified praise, Bas wasn't the type to accept criticism.

'You're messing up the flowers,' Tiz chimed up the stairs. 'Why can't you look where you're going? You're not often here but when you are you don't half get in the way, Cheddar.' He swore. Dumping the large stoneware vase on the bedside table, he arranged the flowers carefully and sat on the edge of the bed.

'I'll go, then,' he said to himself; no one else could be bothered to speak to him.

In making the decision to have Jan with them Tiz knew there would be adjustments to make, a cool courage on the part of Jan that would be hard in any sphere of human relationships. They were all on trial. If they succeeded in creating a peaceful atmosphere then Jan might recover but if they failed it would be a disaster. She needed to be back to a safe life with friends and support.

There was a narrow ledge below the window in Jan's room and on it miniatures of elephants. 'Make sure they face the door,' insisted Boo. 'They are naturally curious animals and like to know of any comings and goings.' Tiz heaved a pile of winter clothes onto the bed. The pale blue fitted carpet was new, along with the double bed. Cheddar had installed an electric wall heater but the wardrobe, cabinets and a rocking chair were seconds. It did not spoil the lilac-purple haze of the walls or the purple border that tickled the bumps near the ceiling.

The railway which could be seen through the scant trees and bushes ran onto the wooded area beyond. White net curtains and floral blinds provided Jan with the choice of withdrawing into her private world or of opening her arms to experiences which beckoned. 'It's womanlike to want these things,' informed Rev. 'I mean, we have two mattresses, two sleeping bags and half a dozen nails knocked in the walls for our gear. What more do we want?' He and Bas moved nearer to the open fire, their hands outstretched like giant antennae, and wiggled their toes on the threadbare carpet.

****

Gary picked up a pebble and threw it into the water. Immediately there was a scurry of birds and intermittent calls and screeches. Only one week to Christmas. Ellie watched him walk away from the bank, slipping in the mud, partly pushing himself forward with one foot. She held out her hand, reaching for him. An overwhelming feeling of wanting to hold onto him came over her. She was suddenly weakened by her own lack of self-control. It was cold and she shivered. When he put his arm around her she held up her face to his but he was looking across the pond and away from her. He was, she knew, sometimes shy and rather secretive but he had asked her here today, to Endcliffe Park, where they could be alone. But for what reason?

He complimented her on her cream fleece and her hat with bobbles which fell about her face when she moved her head. She walked tall and straight and he was aware of the scent of her and the flush of her cheeks. He had grown used to the way she smiled. He led her past the statue of Queen Victoria, along the banks of the River Porter and towards the cafe. Few people were about in the mid afternoon but the sun shone and the air was fresh. They sat by the window and ordered hot chocolate and a mince pie. In a voice half apologetic, half resigned, he announced that he was going away. 'To Bradford,' he smiled. 'I applied for a post as one of three dynamic co-ordinators as part of the Sure Start programme and I was lucky.' Ellie saw enthusiasm in the earnest grey eyes and nodded her approval. Inwardly she felt sick. She was going to lose him without ever having the opportunity to know him. Then a reprieve. 'It is only for a three-month trial period. Starting January, then we do the European tour. I haven't told the others yet.'

He was conscious that each was assessing the other's feelings. Her eyes were anxious but suddenly she was glad for him; he must surely feel well enough to take it on. Fortune, they say, favours the brave. She wrote it down on a paper napkin and he laughed and put it in his pocket. 'There is just one little thing,' he pleaded. 'Will you write to me?' Her face lit up, she threw back her head and the bobbles bounced around her ears. She could send him words, unveil her feelings, choose carefully what she wanted to say and there was so much she needed to express. Gary felt that perhaps he had not said enough about his awareness and commitments to the community but she appeared happy and to him that was all important.

On the way home there was yet another surprise in store for her. As she alighted from the van he handed her the keys to his flat. 'Stay as often as you like, whenever you want a bit of peace and quiet.' He kissed her gently on the cheek. In the swiftly gathering dusk she watched him drive away.

Having Rule No. 1 – making friends with the neighbours safely established, life at the squat was comfortable. There was some vague moral law of obedience and loyalty and they drew strength from each other. There were moments of calm and over exuberance; there were no set tasks but each one accepted responsibility in some form. Each day brought new overtures of friendship from neighbours, which began on Bonfire Night.

After sitting at the back of the house for over a week, clumps of wood and broken furniture had been neatly stacked into a pyramid. Jan had a keen interest in the steady build-up of the fire; she was afraid. Tiz, whilst appreciating the problem of Jan's foreboding, did not want to upset the neighbours. Maybe they were the wrong sort of neighbours, quizzed Rev, who could easily get upset. Boo suggested a bonfire spread, held indoors which would tempt Jan out of her room and away from the flames and heat. It worked.

For Ellie they were exciting and fulfilling days. Bas was proving popular with a couple of rockers down the street but not with Sobuj or his wife, Golnar. 'Did you hear the commotion?' he spat. 'That Alsatian wants putting down, yapping and growling every time he sees me. Haven't done a thing to upset it. Not yet.'

'Thought you supported animal rights?' derided Boo. 'Some campaigner you are.'

Tiz was installed in the attic with her paintings and Boo had a weekly hairdressing arrangement with the ladies from the OAP group. Cheddar, wearing a smile of accomplishment, had tidied up the garden and painted the front door a shade of damson. Impressed by this, Tiz dyed her hair the same colour.

It was the sight of the winged sofa that urged Bas to drag Rev out of his slumber. It was being held aloft by two men and carried towards the bonfire. Black, thick smoke blew around the onlookers and the flames crackled, spat and curled upwards. In his bare feet, wearing only his shorts, he sped up the garden, jumped over the fence and bellowed 'Hang on mate, that's not for burning.' There was no argument, the men were pleased to lower their load. A tall, sprightly youth thrust his way through.

'Who says? It's a cheap piece of stuff, it cost right nowt. I brought it. Kids are looking forward to it; Guy Fawkes on top and all that.'

Bas scratched his head, this could develop into something quite nasty. 'Look, it's just that we're short of a sofa right now; how about I offer you a couple of pounds?'

The youth drew hard on his cigarette. 'Dunno.' They watched the fireworks for a couple of minutes.

'It just seems a shame when our lass can do it up and all you were going to do was burn it.'

'You just moved in 'ere then, have you?' He threw down his cigarette. 'I tell you what ...' His sentence was cut short. Boo, Tiz and Ellie appeared with trays of toffee apples, jacket potatoes, sausages and burgers.

'No need to tell anybody they are meat-free,' Boo declared. 'It's seldom we get to save Bas from an altercation.' By the time toffee apples had been handed round the sofa was in the house.

'I see that you have taken to sarcasm and two-pronged sentences. Who is your lass, anyway?' probed Tiz.

Bas had stretched himself like a fat cat on the newly acquired sofa and licking his fingers quipped, 'That would be telling.'

Now with Christmas just a week away this was a marvellous sight, Ellie agreed. An artificial tree which Sobuj had given them stood proudly in the corner covered in tinsel and baubles and angels. There were curtains at every window and a wood-burning fire. Every day piles of wood appeared at the side of the house, gifts from the neighbours, and Cheddar spent hours cutting it.

He had treated the rusting iron shed in the garden with creosote and stored the timber on the cement floor. 'It was as cold as a crypt and infested with tiny flies,' he shuddered. Most nights he returned to his flat but it was only a matter of time, and it would seem perfectly natural that he moved in with them. The presents had been bought and wrapped, the cards posted and the meals organised.

The girls had mingled with bargain-hunters at car boot sales, church bazaars and scout fairs. Christmas was not a time for monetary motivation; they would never become casualties of the capitalist society, according to Rev, nor succumb to a commercialised culture. 'He's not religious,' Boo explained to Ellie, 'just Bolshie.'

'Cultural complacency, that's what it is.'

For a long time Jan sat in silence in her room. It was warm and she was able to discard the scarf she wore to hide the redness of her lean face and scrawny neck. She loved to see the stars, to watch the silver-edged clouds glide past the moon and then she would shut her eyes; try to forget the shattering of glass, the acrid smoke, the searing pain. The nightmares and the headaches would wake her and she would curl into a pillow in the rocking chair and watch the overnight frost dissolve on the rooftops and the naked branches of the old oak.

It was Fab who suggested that she kept a journal. Of what? She didn't go anywhere, do anything, talk to anyone. 'Maybe not, but you have thoughts, memories, experiences. It's not a diary, Jan, it is an expression of you, of your past and your development. Please give it a try,' Fab pleaded. Meanwhile Jan concentrated on compiling a photograph album for Ellie, to send to Gran, she said.

She watched the garden undergo a vast change from a jungle of coarse grass, thistles and scrap nuts and bolts, compounds of plastic and stones, to a space almost resembling a lawn. She had marvelled at the energy Cheddar had put into it at the weekends and was surprised to hear Ellie's irrepressible infectious laughter at his antics with the scythe. How is it she cannot speak, she wondered?

Gary had always had a photographic memory for anything musical – new compositions, symbols and melodies. His eyes were in his fingertips, Rev concluded, and he caressed his guitar as he propped himself against the sofa. Ellie listened as she prepared the meal of broth and tofu. Tiz and Boo were chattering, excited about the gigs over Christmas and the street concert. Bas gave a sharp, agonised groan. 'Oh hell, you have to be joking. Look, we shall have done enough when we have covered both Bradford and Leeds, but to expect us to do the charity gig and the street concert, well I don't think so. Count me out!'

Tiz popped her head around the door into the lounge. 'Hey, Christmas isn't all about booze, bingeing and blackouts. Spare a thought for others.' From the kitchen came the appetizing sizzle as the tofu and mushrooms fried in the wok.

'Three days, three nights, that's all it is really,' Gary proposed. 'It would be infinitely expensive not to do it and not too good for our reputation.'

Bas breathed in deeply. 'Fair enough,' he conceded.

Gary's luck was holding. Ellie smiled. She thought him to be the most understanding and wisest of men and handed him his meal on a tray with an extra helping of garlic bread.

****

Tiz emerged from the clean, cold air from a room barely aired by the smouldering ashes. She had worked solidly for an hour until her fingers had become firmly rooted to the brush and the paint no longer ran freely. It was far too early for Boo so it meant a bus ride on a morning tinted with frost. She sucked in air which caused her nostrils to quiver with the cold, pulled her collar high to cover her ears and held the portfolio tightly under her arm. What a stroke of luck; she had been invited to present her photographs to the Gallery and not knowing which to choose had brought all of them.

In the warmth of the bus she recalled rural France and the band's visit to Saumur and the River Loire; the campsite and tents and the guy ropes that were always festooned with their laundry. With the chateau as a backdrop it made an enchanting black and white picture. These are the things worth remembering, Tiz reminded herself.

The bright pink scarf caught the wind and whipped around Golnar's face as she led her daughter by the hand and out of the Asian Centre. The cold air made her wheeze and she was incapable of catching her breath. Tiz followed them up the street and heard her choking cough as she turned into their house. It had been troublesome for most of the night. Tiz had heard the light switch being turned on and off and the muffled tones of Sobuj. Later Tiz suggested, 'Maybe we should offer the eucalyptus oil and the burner? You don't suppose she would object, do you?' Ellie opted to stay with Jan and practise her form of complementary healing, merely to listen.

Downstairs a card game was in progress. and Bas had invited bikers, much to the annoyance of Boo. 'They could become a pain in the neck. Remember what Gary says. Just because we are squatting doesn't mean that we have no control over who we invite.'

'You are wrong there, Boo,' Rev argued. 'What he means is that we exercise strict control over who else we live with.'

Bas played his hand. 'We've got nothing worth stealing anyway.'

When Tiz returned from the neighbours she offered servings of vegetable biriani from a huge casserole dish. 'Want some?' Tiz placed the food on a tray in front of Jan.

'What is it?' she sounded tired.

Tiz responded with a smile. 'It's vegetables mixed with rice and coloured with turmeric, from Golnar.' She found the stairs a bother at this time of night. 'Shall I bring some for you, Ellie?' Ellie wanted only her bed. She had listened long enough to poor Jan.

Ellie's bedroom proved to be much more uncomfortable than Jan's despite a covering of white emulsion on the walls and bargain rate carpeting on the floor. Instead of being smooth, the door had jagged wedges of wood protruding at the bottom long and sharp enough at the corners to puncture a tiny wound on her ankle. Bas was approached and although bruised and smarting from a blow by a length of guttering at work, he offered to smooth it down when he had a minute.

There was a keen frost and the room was cold. In the hall the Calor gas fire had been turned off and draughts found their way through any available crack and crevice. The fireplace was covered with plasterboard and the window frames treacherous, loose and flaking. Wet and shivering in her bathrobe, swinging a colourful towel, Ellie made for the bathroom from where Boo was emerging. "Such coldness is dispiriting and exhausting", grumbled Ellie to herself as she filled her hot water bottle. The tiles sparkled behind the basin but the toilet still lacked a seat. 'Spend as little as possible; you may be evicted tomorrow and the incorrect perception that whoever does it will respect your property encourages people to invest. Be warned.' Gary had advised. 'Leave nothing of value in the house.' Surely, Ellie sighed, a toilet seat wouldn't come amiss!

On waking they felt they had been dealt a cruel blow. An unnatural silence filled the rooms. A heavy fall of snow covered a thin layer of ice and the roads shone like glass. 'It will be a hell of a rough trip and Bradford is a long way in weather like this,' challenged Bas, gulping down a mug of tea. They sat in a gloomy circle round the table.

'Maybe Gary will cancel,' said Boo hopefully.

'Maybe the gig will be called off,' sighed Tiz.

'It could have disappeared by tonight,' chimed in Rev. 'You know what British weather is like.'

'Yes,' they chorused with a strong hint of sarcasm.

'That's me off work, anyway.' and Bas settled down on the sofa.

Ellie immersed her hands in the hot water; it was almost a pleasure to wash up. The morning chores had been designated to her; she had no recollection of volunteering. Once the fire had been cleaned and relaid and the breakfast prepared for Jan there was just time for the quick sprint to the bus stop. The bitter wind whipped round her legs and twisted the wool scarf around her neck. Head down, she trod carefully, her hands deep in her pockets. At the road end the traffic had come to a standstill, impatient drivers were tooting, edging their way forward. It helped to confirm Ellie's theory that the British have yet to acknowledge their diverse weather conditions or have the comprehension to deal with them.

The frosty bite of morning was like a smarting blow across her face and she shivered. A lorry loaded with coal was holding up the traffic. It had veered into a garden spreading cobbles on the pavement and in the way of a school bus. Children draped themselves over the fence, wrapping snow around the coal ready for use as missiles. Along the road the trees lowered their branches in a forest of frost under a snow-laden sky.

The barges were in harness, there had been no attempt to free them from the pockets of ice. They were snowbound. There would be no serving at the long trestle tables today, no pre Christmas cruises. Mark greeted her at the door to the cafe. His cold lips briefly touched her cheek and he sighed. 'Nothing doing today, Ellie, I may as well go back to bed.' She closed the door gently behind him.

A short, burly man was in conversation with an elderly gentleman and at the same table sat Flute. Why did she feel this darkness whenever she saw him? Why did she feel this hidden well of doubt? It was almost as if any moment she could plummet into deep water. June pulled her into the kitchen and slammed the serving hatch shut. 'I had to literally drag him in,' June exploded, pointing to Flute.' He's been there all night, so he says. When I nearly fell over him in the passage he managed to get to his feet, then he stood there stiff as a board almost motionless.'

Ellie was empty of feeling. She had no sympathy for him. She accepted that her emotions jumped in leaps and bounds but there was something about Flute which unnerved her. June continued on about him whilst poaching fish until she had to take a breath and coughed. 'It's self destruction, that what it is. Anyway Mark is letting him stay for a while and later find him something to do on the Quay.' When Sue began her shift in the afternoon Ellie had it all to listen to again. Mark and Flute together? Perhaps her name wouldn't be mentioned. She hoped not.

Bradford was on. It was not a decision taken lightly. Cheddar was unavailable because of pressure of work (he had orders to supervise and an early start) and Ellie was to take care of Jan. 'Have you got a minute?' Bas always yelled when speaking to Ellie, He was still under the impression that she was hard of hearing. She followed him through the kitchen and out of the back door.

The wind howled, blowing flakes of snow onto the stone floor. 'Look. I've grabbed half a sackful from an overturned lorry. Just in time for Christmas.' He grinned and kicked at the coal which was stacked alongside the logs in the shed. 'Little Sobuj told me, saw it on his way to school.' How easy in the pantomime season it would have been for her to have taken the role of Cinders, except that her sisters were neither ugly nor jealous. Instead she smiled in appreciation.

'It's for him to take decisions as seem best,' Tiz told Rev. 'He's driving. What's your problem?'

'My problem is we're on double time at the warehouse, it's three days before Christmas and it's bloody shit deep in snow. That's all. We'll be alright,' simpered Boo.

'We'll take blankets and hot flasks of tea, warm clothes and hot water bottles,' Rev sneered. 'And shovels and hazard lights,' he continued.

Fab lit the festive candles in the window. 'Tell you what, Rev, you stay at home. We can always get another drummer to stand in for you.' Even the icicles clinging to the window could not match the cold, homicidal glare pitched at Fab.

But it was Bas who replied. 'God, you're a pain.' He rose from his seat by the fire. Fab watched him cross the floor towards her, tossed her head and the huge hooped earrings brushed against her red hair. She turned away from him and he was reduced to thrusting forward in a sideways position. He grabbed her wrist. 'You and your bloody super ego. You have a displacement somewhere, a real false impression of yourself. You are nobody. All you think about is taking centre stage and to hell with anyone else.'

She pulled her arm free. 'Is that so?' she croaked.

Maeve Crawford

'Yes.' Bas was angry. 'No one can replace Rev, not in a month of Sundays. Don't you forget it.'

There was a long silence, an embarrassing silence and then, hesitating for a moment, Fab turned to face Bas. 'You know, Bas.'

'I could stand in the shadows and observe, I could be non-aggressive, keep a low profile, not speak my mind, but we are all different and this is the punk scene. I understand it to be a progressive scene where we are judged equal but different. I won't apologise. The remark was meant to be funny.' 'At least you didn't come to blows,' quipped Tiz and Ellie shook her head. Had she been in a position to speak she would have been at a loss for words. She recalled Gary's remarks on taking the band on tour. 'Everyone must be contented and happy on the road or there is trouble.' Tonight they would be sorely stretched.

Golnar knocked on the door as Ellie was putting away the dishes. Could she visit Jan, she had heard that she was housebound? This was unexpected and Ellie was not afraid to envisage the possibility that Jan might refuse. But it pleased her, perhaps the thought that soundlessness for yet another evening was too depressing.

Listening to Jan over the weeks everyone had concluded that suicidal thoughts which had been festering had passed. Her nightmares were of dead people melting into giant cauldrons and she had very little sleep. She stayed within her room, only occasionally sitting downstairs for a little while. Her consultant had said, by way of encouragement, 'What you think today and say in truth you may contradict tomorrow. You must devote all your strength and determination into getting better.' Jan had discovered something infinitely more important than dwelling on the past and that was to work towards the future. She was to compile a selection of vegetarian recipes and introduce them to the Asian Women's Centre. When faced with depression the only weapon to use was optimism, concluded Ellie.

Ellie added the pasta and beanfeast to the vegetables swirling round in the saucepan of hot soup. No doubt they would be cold and hungry when they returned from Bradford. She stoked up the fire with logs and a small shovelful of pilfered coal, straightened the throws and plumped up the cushions. In her bedroom she drew the curtains and tucked a hot water bottle underneath the duvet; at least the bed was warm despite the wind howling down the chimney and the windows rattling to the clatter of the trains. Somehow the meaning of home was here. She felt safer than when sharing a house with her mother and Phil.

In all their years together there had never been a touch of tenderness from her mother; she had felt detached almost as if fate had put her there for spite and left her to fight for living space and to be moulded into shape. Where was the father, who in her insecure imagination could perhaps be dozing over his papers in his easy chair with his feet towards the fire? Instead the small child in the big bed in the grand house saw only a black gap in both time and distance.

It was the jingle of the milk float and Sobuj's Alsatian that roused Ellie. Together they managed to wake little Sobuj and Golnar who protested by entering into a paroxysm of coughing. Ellie unravelled herself from the blankets on the sofa and peered through the window. It was a sorry sight. The van drew to a halt and Bas and Rev emerged with Gary between them dragging his feet on the snow and tripping over the kerb. Ellie threw more wood on the fire and warmed up the soup. Automatically she covered him up and rubbed his shoulders as he collapsed on the sofa. No one could express what they had experienced, they were too cold, too tired. Afterwards Tiz berated, 'There are much safer ways to have fun.'

Boo, red-eyed and exhausted, had driven from Bradford in a blinding snowstorm, in a van she had never driven before and with heaters that had given up the ghost. Gary was curled up with one hand held tightly to his stomach. 'I warned him something like this could happen,' Bas swore.

'He's been awfully sick,' Boo whispered tearfully. Ellie

stroked his forehead and intimated that he should sleep in her bed.

'I doubt we'll get him upstairs,' sighed Fab.

'We will,' assured Bas.

Gary was not responding and the weakness in his legs was draining all his energy; he was unable to hang on to Bas and Rev as they hauled him upstairs. Once they almost toppled back-wards but the girls were holding up the rear. 'Shall we call a doctor?' Boo was distressed.

'Give him an hour or two. Will you keep an eye on him, Ellie, we're knackered?' pleaded Rev.

They could sling plenty of insults at each other, enough in fact to sink a battleship, thought Ellie, but they dealt with situations such as this with a caring and unselfish approach. Once he was in bed they left her alone with him to have their supper. It was an effort almost to lift the spoon to their mouths.

Bas had removed Gary's shoes and jeans. Ellie folded them and placed them neatly on a chair. Gary was breathing heavily, his chest tight against his shirt and his legs pulled high. He was in pain. Then, as if a minor earthquake was about to erupt, his body began to shake. It started with his foot, a sudden jerk, then his leg, followed by his other foot until within minutes all of his body went into spasms. Ellie jumped into bed beside him. She put her arms around his waist and pulled him as hard as she could towards her; she wrapped her legs around his and buried her head in the small of his back. As he cried out Ellie cried inwardly. Was this an inevitable progression from his lack of balance, his fatigue, his cramps? Those involuntary movements which he tried to hide? Intolerable thoughts entered her head, and passionate loving thoughts entered her heart. She loved this man. He needed her. The shaking stopped and she loosened her grip. The trembling that followed was less severe and Gary moved position. She moved away slightly but kept hold of his hand; it was a hand reaching out on the worst night imaginable.

Ellie had no idea what these symptoms meant, how could

she? She would find out more in due course from the others, maybe. She would stay awake for the rest of the night, if need be, to help fight this condition whatever it was.

She had barely snatched two hours of sleep when the alarm shrilled at 7.30. Gary was lying flat on his stomach and Ellie had to wriggle like a lizard to release her arm; he was still sleeping. He had the greyness of a sick man. She dressed quietly, listening to his heavy breathing, and crept downstairs.

Bas dropped the paper onto the hearth and rolled it into spirals, placing it under the sticks. 'What a bloody night,' he groaned. 'I'll tell you what, lass, I don't relish another night like that. Twice we got stuck, clambering around abandoned cars, pushing until you felt your lungs were bursting. Sliding all over the place, freezing cold right through to your bones. Some things of this world are unbelievable. And Gary, well he was out for the count, poor sod. Don't know what happened to bring that on.' The fire burst into life. As a final confirmation of his concern he asked, 'How is he now?' Ellie shrugged her shoulders, they headed for the kitchen. She had hardly dared to hope for a fuller explanation; perhaps the girls would be more forthcoming.

She was aware that this could be the most dangerous part of any relationship as little by little habits, concerns, fears and secrets were all stripped away to reveal shortcomings and doubts.

But she loved him and it would all fall into place. He awoke shortly before noon to find Ellie standing near the window, arms folded, watching little Sobuj in the garden next door with a spade and tiny bucket forming lumps of snow into something resembling a snowman. Gary sighed deeply. The bed was soaked in perspiration. He was embarrassed but the relief on Ellie's face dispelled all thoughts of an apology. 'I've had some peculiar dreams,' he ventured. 'A sea of white sheep swaying and moving like waves and at some point I planted a whole row of trees and shrubs in the desert. It's amazing what a dose of flu can do.' She held his hand, hot and wet against the coldness of his palm, and sat

on the bed shaking her head; she was not prepared to listen
to excuses, she was not secure enough to listen to lies. Only
truth would keep her anxiety at bay; she might be in for a
long wait.

'Why don't you make me a cup of tea, please?' It was
almost an order, he wanted space to gather his thoughts.
A few hours ago he was unable to express himself, now
with luck he could be the same as always, in quiet control.
Downstairs Bas was in the middle of a strip and show
procedure, he was happy to disclose his bruises on his
thighs and chest and the grazes on his arms.

The gig had been great, he enthused, well up to
expectations, but he still had a nagging ache in his side
where he had been in collision with a Ford Escort. Rev gave
a warning cough as Gary limped slowly down the stairs.
If he believed that he would be allowed to forget how ill
he was on the night he was mistaken. Bas was raking up
everything that had occurred from Gary losing the way, his
slurred speech and his blackout.

Rev interrupted, 'And the pay, remember. You forgot to
pick up the earnings.'

Gary took a long drink of tea, wrapping his hands round
the mug and closing his eyes. Ellie could see that the
words were hitting him hard and she had an overwhelming
feeling of sympathy and wanted dearly to hold him and
console him. 'I didn't quite know what was happening,' he
acknowledged. She presented him with a plateful of beans
on toast with the hope that deeds are better than words. But
there was still more to come.

'I gather you cancelled the Leeds gig?' Bas urged him to
reconsider. 'We could do it, you know, Boo could drive.'

'No.' There was no hesitancy in his reply. 'After all we
have been through? It's not fair on the girls and anyway
I doubt whether it will go ahead. Too risky.' Rev almost
believed he could discern frustration in his voice when Gary
added. 'In any case, I think I've caught a fever.' He glanced
back at Ellie and waved as he drove away.

After a short time with Jan Ellie busied herself with the

evening meal. The stained carpets and hideous appliances had gone. This kitchen could easily be contained in one quarter of her mother's in-vogue, stainless steel emporium in which very little cooking took place. When she and Phil entertained, Dorothy did the preparation whilst Ellie kept out of the way. Dorothy was a person of variable talents, an excellent mimic, a member of a dramatic society and a mobile caterer. She described Moira as a smug snob personified, forgetting how well she was paid. Ellie no longer felt bad about leaving home. She did not miss her mother, not one bit. She missed Gran but her letters to her had become very sporadic. By now she would have received the photograph album full of Tiz's pictures of Ireland. She missed her wisdom, common sense, the many concepts of life, the full figure, the white hair and the smell of talcum powder.

Ellie stirred the quorn, quietly humming to the radio in Jan's room. It was good to have space, to feel it expand inside her. The men had found a pub round the corner and she was given leave from the cafe until January 7th. Celebrations would begin tomorrow, Christmas Eve, when the girls finished work and made their way to Crystal Peaks. Would it be as fascinating as she imagined?

Bas very soon discovered that there was no escape from the drug scene. 'You know nobody takes any heed, it's rife in the pub. It is a microcosm of mainstream society,' he informed his audience as he gulped down his food. 'I read it in a punk zine. People are people,' he continued, 'and what you see is that all the people are from different areas, different backgrounds and life experiences.'

'So?' Rev reached for the garlic bread.

'Well, there is no specific factor in addiction and it's no good blaming anybody else.' This speech was unusually complex for Bas.

'That's the lager talking,' sniffed Boo, clearing the plates away.

'So you won't be going again?' Tiz asked.

'Oh, yea. The music is great, loud, aggressive and there's

a civil darts team.'

'What he has failed to mention,' interrupted Rev, 'are the wide boys operating the cheap, stolen goods' scam and the couple of football shirts costing a tenner.'

'You don't like football,' chimed in Boo.

'What's that got to do with the price of beer?' snapped Bas.

The girls decided on an early start. It did not materialize. Outside the house the road was still packed with ice although the main roads were clear of snow. Boo's mini was reluctant to start. Bas swaggered towards them with a bucketful of ash from the fire and like a farmer sowing seeds scattered the residue around the tyres and carried on up the street until the bucket was empty. 'Perhaps we should have taken the bus?' Tiz bit her lip. It took a surprisingly long time to persuade the engine to start.

'No problem,' dismissed Boo as they clambered inside. 'If I can drive that clapped out van all the way home in shit weather I can drive this little beauty.'

They sat with Maggie's presents on their knees. Ellie had sent notelets and didn't really worry that she hadn't replied. Perhaps Maggie was ill? How difficult when most of our lives we rely on muscular strength, to find that we reach a point when it is cruelly taken away from us. A picture of Gary, weak and strained, appeared before her.

Tiz wore combat trousers and a blouse with epaulettes and a cap over her damson-tinted hair. Bas had been saluting her all morning. Fab, on the other hand, chose tartan trousers with zips down each side and a black jacket. In comparison Boo looked quite conservative with a sparkly top and long black skirt. Her thick black hair hung in two plaits almost to her waist. Ellie had developed a great acuteness of observation since refusing to speak.

Women are a decorative sex, they never have anything to say but say it charmingly. Was this Oscar Wilde, she couldn't remember? She caught her reflection in the driving mirror; the combs sparkled when she turned her head, holding in place her shoulder length fair hair. The blue jumper complemented her blue eyes and clear skin. Her skirt was loose and comfortable. She was no longer being told what to wear, no longer being tested, she had been released from criticism and disapproval. She felt gratified.

They hadn't time to linger at Crystal Peaks. They gulped down cappuccinos, kissed Santa Claus and headed for the Rest Home. The Grange was impressive, in an elevated position with extensive views over the hills. The snow had blown into drifts against the stone walls and the wind had patterned the fields, perming the snow until it branched away from the frozen lake. The tree-lined avenue gave the impression that here was a vast wilderness and the sun formed a yellow pool of light in the melted snow.

It was a maze of corridors and bends, of wheelchairs stacked in line like supermarket trolleys. Of uniformed staff busy with concentrated awareness and doors in uniformity, same colour, same brass handle, same italic hand giving the patient an identity. The friends breezed into the lounge, bringing with them a breath of youth and vitality into a room of yawning old age. Maggie's delight was uplifting. In the room there were over a dozen people, sitting in an arc, facing the centre. All except Maggie. Her high-backed chair was facing the garden and she had her feet on a pouffe and a box of chocolates on a table beside her. There was little conversation in the room and all eyes turned towards the visitors. 'You look wonderful, Maggie. So well.' Tiz rounded up some chairs. The presents were distributed but Maggie wanted to save them for Christmas Day.

'I want to open them in my room,' she whispered. 'Not everyone will have presents, you see. Some don't even have relatives. I'm very lucky to have you as friends.'

Ellie could hardly estimate the depth of relief she felt at the difference in Maggie. She was sitting straight in her chair, her skin was clear, her hair was neat, and her eyes had lost their dullness. She was quick and she was sharp. Time had passed since Ellie was blinded by her tears and deafened by her cries. 'Some in here are like children, you know. I tell them growing old is compulsory but maturing is

optional. They haven't a clue what I mean, poor dears.' The
chocolates were handed round.

'Celeste hasn't been near for days,' she chatted. 'Although
I must admit (she waved her arm around the room) this is
one of her best ideas so far.'

'Have you noticed,' asked Boo, turning her head towards
the window, 'that old people never look and turn away?
They stare openly for ever.'

'Is she in the army?' The voice was directed at Maggie
and belonged to a frail, small woman curled like a cat in an
oversized basket. It was not easy for her to remain upright.
'Her there!' she pointed at Tiz. 'Is she in the army?'

'Yes.'

Maggie munched through a chocolate. 'She's left her tank
in the car park.'

'That was rather unkind,' tittered Boo.

'Well,' laughed Maggie, 'she's simple, poor old dear.'
What must it be like to be old and feeble? At least, thought
Ellie, Maggie had a sense of humour and a logical mind; for
some such attributes would be lost for ever. Words can sting
but surely it is silence that breaks the heart?

The river coiled like a snake, wide and twisting. It
welcomed the walker, the rambler and the hill-climber in all
seasons and invited them to share in the rich greenery of the
countryside. Within a stone's throw of the sunlit water they
stopped the car, and visible between the snow clad hills
were changes of texture, scars and the wrinkles of ploughed
fields and coarse grasses.

They drank their hot tea and coffee in the bleakness of
the countryside. Then from a branch came a rustle of wings,
a pretty show of colour, a swoop and a musical note which
brought a precious moment of brightness into their lives – a
robin. On the way home they discussed Maggie and her lack
of pretence and Ellie was concerned that she still treated her
as a poor girl to be pitied.

The curtains were open, the Christmas tree a blaze of
colour as they rounded the corner and the wheels slid on
the approach to the lane. Tiz carried in a couple of blankets

from the car to curl up in by the fire, and cursed as she fell over Bas's boots left lying in the hall. Boo could hardly conceal her annoyance as she struggled to step over and around crates of beer stacked against the wall. 'It's obvious that they are making sure they have sufficient booze to see them over Christmas.'

Pizza cartons and chip papers littered the kitchen table and unwashed mugs and plates were piled up in the sink. 'Look at this stinking mess. We shouldn't have to clean up after them.' Boo stormed into the living room. She had hardly taken more than half a dozen paces when she exploded. It was the sight of Bas and Rev laid out on the two sofas with Cheddar fast asleep on the beanbag, half a bottle of Navy Rum beside him, that aroused her anger. She flung obscenities at all of them. Rev remained unmoved. Bas swung his legs over the arm of the sofa and raised his eyes to the ceiling.

Then he turned to face her. There was a faint look of gratified amusement in the stare he gave her. Tiz appeared in the doorway. 'Oh, yes,' she smiled. 'Look, Boo, up there.' It was an extraordinary moment for Boo, a mixture of delight, surprise, of suppressed tears of regret at her outburst to friends who had found her chandelier and installed it as a gift for Christmas. Bas's sense of timing, developed over years of practice, now stood him in good stead. He would be guaranteed a conciliatory Yuletide.

No one thought it incongruous that amidst fraying carpets, soot ingrained mats, second-hand sofas and soiled beanbags a chandelier could hang in such lustrous splendour. The fuse on Boo's line of smouldering anger had blown itself out. Tiz had painted a mural on the far wall of the sitting room – of trees, a river and a fish. Underneath were the words "Only when the last tree has died and the last river has been poisoned and the last fish has been caught, will we realize that we cannot eat money". 'A quote from an anonymous 19th century Cree Indian,' confirmed Tiz.

From the kitchen Ellie recognised the noise of the van. The mess had been cleared and Ellie hurried out to meet

Gary.

He had his head under the hood peering at the engine like a cat watching a mouse. His colour had returned to his face and he had regained sufficient energy to scramble up into the van and reappear with a television. 'I thought you deserved some pleasure during the holiday, especially after the chaotic time in Bradford and the madness on the motorway and having to cancel the concert at Leeds.'

'Yea, well,' said Bas grudgingly. 'I think it was a disgrace.' Nobody was influenced by his ratty temper.

'It's the law of the jungle, the struggle for life,' Fab mused. They were thankful for Gary's forethought.

Ellie instinctively knew that she could make no demands on him, that she would have to let him go for three months at least. She had experienced his confusion, irritation, was there perhaps a hint of depression too? She would pray that he would stay with them for Christmas.

Tiz and Boo were discussing Jan at great length. She had taken to roaming in the middle of the night, peering into bedrooms, making strange, ominous noises and waving a torch. They were concerned but the greatest fear was that she would fall. The stairs were uncarpeted and uneven in places. Tiz nodded deferentially. 'It's early days yet.' She likes to know where everything and everybody is at night. She'll be better when the nights are short and summer's here, although whether she will step outside, that's something else.'

'The television may cheer her up a bit,' sighed Boo.

They were deciding what to eat when Golnar appeared in a striking dress of orange and yellow. She beamed from ear to ear. 'Ah, here!' She handed over two buckets of traditional Indian cuisine and smiled. 'For Christmas Day.'

'That's our veggies sorted,' thanked Tiz, accepting the cauliflower bhajee, sag paneer with spinach and cheese, and dahl masala with spice and pink lentils. They were kept with all other provisions in the "fridge", the walk-in pantry which contained a marble slab and an air vent which was superior to any air-conditioner.

This would never be a slum world of squatting, it was a practical means of surviving cheaply, of looking out for each other, of a self exile. Ellie did not deny that it lacked many home comforts but she felt protected in her life of silence.

Rev was on one of his many long walks. Despite the chilling wind he chose to leave the house on an evening and walk for miles. Always alone. He felt suffocated, he said, when the curtains were drawn and night fell. Ellie found his sensitive nature appealing. He was usually happy between gigs but when performing on stage his true rhythm was revealed, everything synchronized, his music, his mood, his personality.

Bas, on the other hand, had shot out to the pub. It was Christmas, what else would he do, he asked? 'The noise level in that pub is an assault on the ears,' Boo stated.

At this hour of the evening Ellie would normally be at the Carol Service. Perhaps she could suggest they look for one? It was her sole link with her Gran at this special time of year. From under her bed she dragged the synthesizer downstairs, meeting Cheddar on his way in. 'Is that you, Cheddar, we have a job for you. Come and fix the TV will you?' Boo shouted. He did not exactly jump at the invitation; he had been at the depot most of the night and delivering orders most of the day. As swearers go he was not the most accomplished in the group but at times he could do his share. The outburst over, he disappeared behind the television. Boo smiled. 'You go ahead,' she said consolingly.

Ellie was determined to have her moment of carols. It had not been planned, she simply wanted to create the mood of Christmas and hymns and carols were the only tunes she could play. Cross- legged on the floor, she plugged in the instrument and the tune of "Hark the Herald Angels Sing" echoed across the room. Collectively heads turned towards her. She finished the first verse and stopped. 'We don't know the words,' said Boo.

'Well, we know some.' said Tiz. 'We know the chorus and the tune.'

'Write it down for us,' Boo pleaded. They spent some time

copying the words in triplicate, along with "Oh Come All Ye Faithful", "Once in Royal David's City", "Silent Night" and "The First Noel".

Gary had been quietly working in the corner with Cheddar. The same thought had suddenly occurred to both of them. Gary coughed. 'Why don't we take it outside, have a street concert, instead of punk we'll do praise?'

'We could do it for the kids,' suggested Cheddar. 'I'll get the extension lead.'

'Hang on,' Tiz was hesitant. 'Not a good idea. We haven't practised. And what's this "we" anyway, you're not singing.'

'What's with the practice?' Cheddar sneered. 'It's not the Royal Albert Hall, for cripe's sake.'

'Let us run through one verse of each carol, see how we do,' cajoled Boo. Halfway through "Silent Night" Rev appeared; Ellie thought he would explode with incredulity.

'I've heard everything now,' he exclaimed. 'I suppose you could thrash it up a bit, give it a fun mix of grind and punk.'

'We're not heathens,' responded Tiz. 'You could bring the snare.' He stood with his back to the fire looking detached and uninterested.

'It's cold out there.' They had reached an unwilling agreement, Ellie thought, but still they decided to go ahead and curiously enough attached some importance to being neighbour-friendly.

They wrapped up well; comfort mattered and their street credibility was on trial. Gary, astute and perceptive, realised that this show of musicianship could be skilfully turned to their use. In a few months the bus would be a focal point in the street; making provision for this could begin now. They huddled outside the front door clutching their sheets of paper like primary school children in their first nativity play. Seating herself on the pouffe with a cushion to her back, Ellie leaned against the brick wall and balanced the synthesizer on her knees. It was a shaky start but after the initial realisation that they could stand as one and that they had nothing to prove (as Tiz remarked afterwards), they began to enjoy it.

Rev had allowed time to acclimatise and then decided to join them. One by one neighbours began to gather. They appeared at their doors only to be grasped by children and pulled towards the group. Through the night air the carols cut with a sharp anticipation of hope. Their voices gathered strength, Rev complied with a gentle beat and gradually the onlookers joined in. They ran out of carols. Ellie, who made no parade of her growing self-confidence, decided on this occasion to show a little initiative. She began to play "Away in a Manger" and the children, without hesitation, sang all three verses. Every note magnified the truth – a choir of every colour, heedless of status, the blueprint for a better world. Gary counted over 40 people who had come to listen. He could have kicked himself; he could have been better prepared.

No one retired until after 1.00am. Golnar and Jan had watched the performance from the sitting room and Jan had stayed up to party and watch television. She could expect to be on her own all day when the holiday was over but the frantic activity of getting drunk was not something she was planning on doing.

Ellie found it hard to hide her disappointment when Gary left. He was always bemused by her but when, without any warning, she followed him out to the van and hugged him he felt that her energies were at their height whilst his were waning. Her vitality, her genuine concern for him meant that he could be dealing with all sorts of challenges in the future and that he could not bear to think about.

He rejoined them for Christmas dinner. Bas had to be coaxed out of his sleeping bag and pushed into the bathroom by Tiz before he was allowed at the table. Fab appeared in a most striking dress of animal print and velvet. 'I didn't realize we were dressing up,' muttered Boo sarcastically.

'Ellie has,' Fab retorted.

'No she hasn't, not purposely. She always looks classic,' replied Boo.

'You either have it or you haven't,' Bas grinned. Across the table Gary and Ellie faced each other. He marvelled at the expression in her eyes, the loveliness of her. For a few seconds he was lost in confusion.

He changed the subject. 'This is the best bread I have ever tasted.'

'Golnar brought it along with the vegetables,' replied Tiz. Arguments about and around Ellie were rare. They caused mixed emotions. She could neither agree nor deny but in this instant it brought a smile to her face and lifted her spirits and she gave Gary a mock sophisticated glance. He looked less tired and his cheekbones were less prominent, she thought.

The snow had melted although it still lay on the slope of land leading from the house to the railway. It was quiet. Jan, who had joined them for dinner, had stayed to watch television with the girls and Bas had returned to bed. When Gary suggested a walk it was treated as an affront. Not by Ellie. 'We will ride part of the way if you don't mind,' he said. They drove past the Botanical Gardens; he was delighted how well the carol singing had gone and how impressed he was with her. He smiled. Why did she feel he was being condescending? She was a well-educated, well-spoken, well-mannered young lady. But then he wouldn't know that, would he? He knew nothing about her and if he did would he like what he saw? Would he condone what she had done? A deliberate, premeditated act of revenge?

It was a short walk to the cottage from the main road. There were no street lights and Gary held her arm as they struggled over the broken flagstones and deep ruts in the pavement. 'I want you to meet Cassie,' he chatted. 'I used to live with her when I was younger. You will love her; everyone does.' Ellie didn't understand. She felt an icy shiver down her spine. What did he mean, 'Live with her'? Were they lovers? Was he preparing her for something?

Cassie had long, dark hair tied back neatly with ornate combs and wore a tee shirt displaying the yin yang motif. It was difficult to define her age; she was probably around

40, Ellie surmised. She wore a long, colourful patchwork skirt and boots. Her face lit up at the sight of Gary and after kissing him on the cheek she hugged Ellie so hard she could hardly breathe. 'Gary has told me so much about you.' Her voice was quiet, composed. 'We will have some cake and green tea and then I will introduce you to Nanny.' Whilst Ellie took in her surroundings they talked and Cassie watched the young girl who had captured Gary's interest.

Dotted around the room were scented candles and a healing arch with crystals and gemstones sparkled in the corner. 'They are the tools of healing, Ellie. You see the blue.' She stood by her and put her hand lightly on her shoulder. 'The turquoise, sapphire and aquamarine, they are the throat chakra. Now come and meet Nanny. Her goat kept the lawn trimmed and provided hair for her angora and mohair sweaters. Ellie nuzzled her face against its beard and hugged it. 'I'm having risotto for supper with paprika if you want to stay,' smiled Cassie.

Ellie felt she was with a sympathetic, wise person, a healer, and suddenly became aware that this visit was more to do with her than any courtesy call. She did not want to be drawn into a dragon's den but did not want to force a wedge between her and Gary.

The wintry darkness had enveloped them as they returned through the city streets. The headlights shone on a group of homeless people lying close to a rear entrance to a hotel. 'They are waiting for left overs,' sighed Gary. 'The chef is pretty generous to them but he would be dismissed if he was found out. I'll have a quick word.' Ellie watched them move silently away. 'They'll be back as soon as we are out of sight,' he said.

He brought up the subject of Cassie on the approach to home. 'We were brought up together and she is almost like a sister. She gave me this for you. It's an aquamarine. If you keep it in the velvet pouch it will protect it, and you probably.' Was she a wild, awkward child needing protection, she thought? 'Oh yes, and this is from me. Happy Christmas.' She fastened the gold chain round her

neck and kissed him politely as he pulled up outside the
house. Ellie recalled Tiz's resolution about presents for the
men. ('We don't bother, they only get embarrassed and feel
guilty.') This applied to birthdays and yet when they were
celebrated no one contemplated what lay ahead or discussed
their past. Their lives swung like a pendulum, free-swaying,
moving between music and alternative lifestyles, nursing a
desire to be the speaker and the spoken of but never to be
spoken down.

Gary drove to his flat. It was not an inviting prospect
leaving Ellie for three months. Up to now he had been able
to protect her yet despite having her friends to support
her he felt a nagging doubt. She was not one for fretting
or fuming or for throwing tantrums but he felt that if he
searched for a deeper Ellie he could be wrong. Now it was
a matter of containing himself, of hiding the demands and
desires until he was clear of the obscurity that was dogging
him. This would be the longest wait and whilst he had the
energy he would continue to take care of her whilst not
letting her come too close. It was not a dream, as often
dreams ended too soon. They had shared the same bed, he
had felt her presence, the warmth of her body and the scent
of her and sensed her unspoken love. But they were never
lovers. Loving her was his secret and there was still a lot to
learn about Ellie and a lot to discover about himself.

Her letter to Gran was enthusiastic and full of the heart
of Christmas. Boxing Day morning was cold and bright. The
house was still and Ellie had cleaned out and lit the fire,
brought in a supply of wood, put on a pink wool jumper
and jeans, and settled on the sofa. Her main contribution to
the house was a new toilet seat (which had yet to be fixed
properly) and a clotheshorse for drying clothes in front of
the fire. There were stares of amazement when she insisted
on airing her clothes overnight ready for the next day.
She explained all this to Gran and how she had managed
to start an account with a building society, adding to the
considerable amount which Gran had saved for her over
the years. How unlike her mother who had to have the best

of everything and in no time at all had squandered large amounts of money.

Ellie described the carol singing and the Christmas cards which Tiz designed and delivered to all the neighbours, and the kindness of Golnar and Sobuj. On the other hand she omitted to mention Cassie. Introducing Gran to alternative or complementary therapies would be like describing a spider on a thread, dangling and swaying, blowing in the air with nothing of substance to hold onto.

Words came easily, flowed over the paper, and she could imagine the small room in which she and Gran had last talked, filled with life's treasures and the comforting smiles on photographs around her. Of Ellie as a baby, a toddler and a growing child. There is a limit to all times of sheer happiness but Ellie loved those early years with Gran who provided security and protection when there was every chance of abandonment. In her letter her main objective was to assure her Gran of her continued respect both for herself and other people. She would not lie to her but perhaps would be economical with the truth.

It was almost midday before Tiz and Boo appeared. They were relieved to see the fire blazing and the table laid. Everything closely resembling a vegetable was thrown into the wok and the vegeburgers were slipped under the grill. It must have been the smell of food that coerced the men out of bed; it wasn't long before they were all round the table planning their next move. 'I could murder a pint right now,' Bas hollered.

'There's still plenty in the pantry.' Rev gulped down his burger. 'Naw, better wait.' He fell back into the chair.

'He's a hopeless boozer,' moaned Boo. 'Better make sure we avoid him tonight. You know what he's like when he's had a skinful.' It wasn't as if Bas had no command over his life, thought Ellie, it was almost an essential part of it.

'Aren't you coming with us then?'

'You must be joking,' Ellie flinched at the foulness that followed.

It appeared that she would be left to her own devices.

Should Gary decide to stay away she would spend time with Jan and assist her in collating her recipes. Poor Jan. She was still conscious of her scars, still afraid to show her face; she had shown no desire to exercise or take part in any activity with her friends apart from an occasional meal. Was that important thought Ellie? Such a devastating incident would take time to come to terms with. She could not imagine having to face the future with such an appalling disfigurement. What was important was that Jan had the support and understanding of her friends.

In the late afternoon Ellie and Jan watched a musical on television. They ate a whole box of Brazil nuts between them and lounged on the sofas. Jan was becoming more perceptive. 'I have watched the moon through every phase,' she sighed. 'I've watched it through the trees, the chimneys, the clouds and when I can't sleep I've watched it wane. It is so beautiful. Beauty should never be allowed to be spoilt by progress. Why do men want to go to the moon anyway?' She chewed carefully through the nut. 'Boo has a lot to say about the moon, no doubt a pet superstition of hers. A full moon that falls on Christmas Day, she tells me, is lamented by farmers as a prophecy of a poor harvest in the year ahead.' Ellie had fallen asleep.

Nothing had been established as to Jan's future, and yet nothing was left to chance. Golnar would be her safety net when the band were on tour in Europe but the friendship had to be proven first. Little Sobuj was in awe of Jan. He had seen her once wearing her mask, the filmy veil which covered her lower face and neck. The white face appeared uncanny to him and he clung to his mother's skirts and hid behind her. Jan was genuinely distressed and turned away.

Jan rose from the sofa, leaving Ellie stretched out and her face turned towards the glowing fire. The lights from the Christmas tree cast weird shadows around her and the shapes became monstrously distorted in the silent room. Jan hurried up the stairs and to bed.

They came in late and Bas took it upon himself to be the custodian for Boo. Their conversation was developing into a full scale row; she had been literally dragged away from the party and he had many reasons, he said, for taking matters in hand. Only a cursory nod towards Ellie interrupted their dispute. Boo was staggering and red in the face. 'You see, you've had a skinful, you don't know these people, you could easily get into a bottleneck with fellas like that before you know what's hit you!' He followed her as she swayed into the kitchen.

'Shift!' She pushed him away. 'Shift, I'm perfectly capable of looking after myself. Look, I don't need you to hold my hand. I'm going back to Tiz.'

Bas poured a glass of water and thrust it into her hand. 'I want a proper drink,' she hiccoughed. She turned round and tried to negotiate the space between the table and the cabinet.

'I've just about reached my limit,' Bas raged. 'She's gone off with a bloke.' Boo gulped down the liquid, spilling most of it down her tee shirt.

'She wouldn't leave me.'

'Yea, well, some women get a sudden blockage in the brains when it comes to fellas,' stated Bas, 'and this is a prime example.

She swallowed hard.' I want to go back.'

'I don't think so.' He pushed her into the kitchen chair, firmly but gently. It would prove impossible to estimate the danger she may have been in, he told her. 'They were high on drugs, Boo, four of 'em, out of their bloody minds, full of shit and just you. It's just not on.'

Boo contemplated. The signals were kicking in through the fog of liquor. 'How come you were there?' She looked up at him through half-closed eyes.

He sighed deeply. 'I followed you from the pub. Waited till I saw Tiz leave. OK?' Ellie, listening, was aware that relationships moved from stage to stage, characters move towards and away from each other, and speak for and against. Conversation isn't just crossfire where you shoot and get shot at. Words are not bombs and bullets – they are little gifts containing meanings. Would Boo remember in the cold light of day? Bas peered round the door. 'Trouble?' he said blandly, pointing at Boo sprawling over the kitchen chair. 'Can you make sure she gets to bed, Ellie?'

On still nights Ellie had no difficulty in falling asleep. The days of the enquiries, the doubts, the trial and the recriminations no longer veered back and forth in her mind. She was no longer maddened by the heavy notion of guilt or by the gravity of her perjury. Phil deserved all he got. Had she been clever? She had thought so at the time. She certainly had not done it out of love for her mother. Only for herself. Time had forced a gap between guilt and justification and only occasionally did she think back to the spring day and the body in the ditch.

Tiz had sold one of her paintings for a considerable amount, she confided in Boo. 'For crying out loud,' Rev echoed as they sat down to their evening meal. 'Don't be shy about it, how much?'

Bas interrupted sarcastically, 'At least a fiver. Which one was it, anyway?'

Rev probed. 'Not the one with fairies flying around toadstools and drinking syrup from daffodils?'

'No,' spat Tiz. Life had returned to normal, everyone was back at work, Cheddar had returned to his flat and Gary had taken up his new post in Bradford.

'Well, go on then, tell us,' Rev insisted.

'It is called "Subterranean"; it represents the accumulation of shells and myriads of creatures whose skeletons have been compressed into rock. It sold for £350.'

A silence was followed by a list of expletives. Ellie remembered the blank canvas building up to the beautiful colours of yellow and blue and here and there diagonal bands of pink and a smattering of red. Now it had been moved from the cold attic to the warmth of an elegant, warm gallery and adorned with a simple signature, "TIZ".

CHAPTER FOURTEEN

"Silence was never written down." (Proverbial Spanish.)

Work was being carried out at the designer furniture store in the refurbished riverside arches. Ellie loved the relaxed feel of it despite it being contemporary. The noise was deafening at times and the peaceful days on the canal were on temporary hold. Dogs from the nearby kennels barked madly to add to the din. 'After a few waves of the pneumatic drill you accept the certainty of fewer customers and less profit. Still needs must if we want to improve the canal,' June soothed! 'So at least we don't have to listen to Flute for a while.' Ellie was relieved; she still did not trust him.

During the first week Ellie had written to Gary. She had purchased a pen with which to practise italic handwriting and show a little of her penmanship with calligraphy. She thought it might amuse him and show him that she had taken time instead of scribbling a few "keeping in touch" notes.

She had a suggestion to make, she wrote. "Why don't you come home for the weekends? Bas apparently has a carefully laid-out plan of campaign with regard to the gigs, but if there is the slenderest chance of coming, please try." There was little in the letter about her personally. Before going any further she was preparing to use a sounding line and wait to see just how curious he was.

Bas and Boo were again having words. This time it was about an intended visit to the Speedway. 'Look,' Boo emptied the spin dryer and threw the clothes onto the table. 'Stu is arranging for us to meet the Star Tigers.' She tossed back her long plaits.

'Anything to say about that? I mean if there is I should know, so don't hesitate to tell me.' Her sarcasm escaped him. He leaned on the sink and stared as she moved quickly away from him.

'You will do as you have a mind anyway,' he agreed vociferously.

'Damn right I will.' Suddenly the wiring behind the washing machine sparked violently. There was a blinding flash and a strong smell of burning. 'Pull out the plug!' yelled Boo. 'Bas, on the wall, pull it out quick.' As he did there was a terrific bang and he recoiled, the plug still in his hand. There had been good reason for his sudden panic but for Boo came a great sense of relief that it had happened to her and not Jan. There could have been a fire and another disaster. She took a deep breath. 'You all right, lass?' Bas pulled her to him, his large hand resting on her shoulder, his ample frame leaning against hers.

'Course I am,' she replied weakly. 'Course I am.'

'She feels as if she has been given a life sentence,' Tiz ordered a glass of white wine and squashed in beside Boo and Ellie on the corner seat in the pub.

'Maybe when the weather improves and we can drive her out into the country,' suggested Boo 'she will be more able to cope, to respond more.'

'What did she say, the Health Visitor?' asked Boo.

'Not a lot. Jan's general health is good, her heart is strong, I think it is more psychological, she's really into the menu and recipe idea for the Asian Centre and Golnar is encouraging her a great deal,' replied Tiz.

The noise from the bar was raucous. Bas was holding court and he threw wide his arms in a burst of laughter. His red football shirt hardly covered his stomach which wobbled with each outburst. Rev, on the opposite side of the bar, quietly drank his pint and women stopped to talk to him and hemmed him in. It was early evening, the place was full, the music deafening. Unless you were very close to someone and your mouth was pressed against an ear it was impossible to be heard. It was one way of initiating a relationship, she supposed. Boo drank her beer, Ellie sipped her pineapple. She was never bored when there were people to observe. Groups of girls swept in from the street, short-skirted and fragrant, their arms linked for additional support, eyes searching for a glance of admiration. The effort to resist flirting demanded every ounce of integrity but Ellie had the feeling that this was not part of the strategy.

Tiz, Boo and Fab on the other hand appeared to have a more down to earth analysis of men. Their chosen environment with music where they could empower themselves meant that they belonged to society on equal terms with men. This Ellie recalled was Fab's view. Smoke was swirling in small pockets around the room. The fans had stopped working and Ellie's eyes were beginning to smart. She motioned that she was stepping outside for a breath of fresh air. There were almost as many people on the pavement and Ellie stood back in the shadows. Someone pushed against her, a strong hand grasped her shoulder and warm lips brushed her cheek. 'Hi. Don't I know you? You live with Bas, don't you? Are you on your own?' Ellie recognised the leathers, red and black with a Draconic emblem in silver across the back. Was he one of the men who had angered Bas? If so she did not want to encourage him into escorting her into the pub. His hand slid to her waist. 'Fancy a walk?' The cold January night seeped into her bones and she was beginning to feel vulnerable. She shook her head. He was not convinced. As he pulled her to him she brought up her knee and he cursed her as he let her go.

It was hot and stuffy inside and it was a struggle to reach her table. There was little room when she got there; she had to push and wriggle her way, squeezing her long limbs between the girls, who giggled and flattened themselves against the wall. Their companions, a local band, were even

more colourful with at least two Mohicans and a bondage
jacket. 'In my opinion,' Bondage began, 'Punk is more than
raunchy poses and subtle teasing, you know, an exposed
cleavage here, a bare thigh there. Sexy mini skirts and that.
Let's have ripped stockings and pink hair!'

'I like all of that, me,' added his mate.

'And vocals that cut through the music and ring out
above heavy backing.'

'Right,' chorused Tiz and Boo, totally blase.

When all the glasses had been collected and the lights
dimmed the girls left. They sang, their arms around each
other all the way, until they reached the ginnel and realized
that they were being followed. There was no going back,
yet ahead of them were unlit entrances and backs of houses.
Somebody was stalking them, pursuing them through the
alleyways. They broke into a run, knocking into each other
in their desperation to get away. They dragged each other
along, tumbling over cobbles, worse the wear after copious
amounts of booze. Out of breath they fell into the house
where all three collapsed on the sofa. Within minutes Bas
arrived and stood before them. He threw his arms wide, his
eyes narrow like slits in a money box. 'Gotcha,' he grinned.
It was too much.

It must have been the drink, concluded Ellie, but the
double-headed axe of the feminist could cut either way and
they held him down while he struggled and bellowed with
laughter whilst they stripped him naked. Ellie, well aware
of what was about to happen, did nothing. The sound of
his consenting laughter was almost a gift of approval and
she went into the kitchen to make tea and fill her hot water
bottle. His laughter subsided as Ellie closed her bedroom
door.

Ellie sensed, after the holidays, that Mark was tempted
to continue his friendship with her and he was behaving
in a particularly charming way. She quickly snubbed him,
hoping the idea was a delayed action; after all she could not
know whether there might be a follow-up after what had
happened to Flute. Nor did she want to be hypocritical and

use him as a substitute for Gary. 'I thought you might like to go bowling. To the Hollywood Bowl. It's computerised scoring,' Mark pleaded. Is it? She thought. Did he think she couldn't add up? "I'm busy," she mouthed. "Sorry." June was conscientiously and persistently opening up the cafe each morning despite the dust and noise from the builders. But adding to that was the presence of a tramp – there was no nicer way of describing him, moaned June.

'I mean, what can I do, duck? He sits in the window all day with just a bowl of soup and a roll. Nobody wants that, do they? It's bad enough drumming up trade as it is without him clogging up the works.' On the third day the old man began to cry. There was no stopping him. They were real tears, maudlin sentimental tears and something had to be done. It was a foolhardy move on Ellie's part to sit opposite him and take his hand. His pitiful eyes, tired with crying, searched her face for sympathy like those of a dog appealing for some kindness from its master.

The late afternoon sun picked out the variety of congealed matter on the worn jacket and trousers. His scarf was held together with ragged fibres of wool and the deep creases on his face were ingrained with dirt. He had very few teeth and those he had were yellow and broken. Sue remained at arm's length busying herself with a variety of tasks to escape the boredom of an empty cafe, but then work itself was appalling among all the debris, she grunted.

'The Salvation Army,' June said. 'They say that they will take him but we have to get him there. Run and get Mark will you, Sue? It has taken four telephone calls to get this far.'

It was Flute who stepped off the boat and hurried towards the cafe. Ellie breathed deeply half a dozen times. What could develop from this encounter, she wondered? The old man hung onto her arm so firmly that his long fingernails dug into her skin. She tried to understand how a human being could be so undignified. How must they live? By instinct? Neither needing nor able to think. To live a life without variety and where days drag interminably?

'You may as well go home when you have dropped him off,' June suggested to Ellie. 'Go with Flute, will you? We can't wait for Mark.' It took some effort to drag the old man from his seat and into the taxi and as they rushed towards the Citadel through the busy traffic she was aware that Flute was handling the situation with quite amazing resourcefulness. He was astride the mephitic man pinning him down and that must have been unpleasant.

The Captain welcomed their Prodigal Son with open arms. 'Nice to have you with us again, Godfrey. Been walkabouts, have we, for the last few days? Go with Tom, he'll fix you up before tea.' His reply was nothing more than a blurted sentence.

Ellie found it stiflingly overpowering in the kitchen and Flute's presence did nothing to cool her down. She was about to leave when she heard a voice, a sharp reminder of her deceit. 'Hello, there. How nice to see you again. How are you?' It was the minister from the chapel. Ellie froze; she was aware of Flute's curious stare. She pointed to her throat. 'Ah, laryngitis. Very painful. Pity to spoil that wonderful singing voice. Never mind, hope to see you again and thanks for returning Godfrey.' They shook hands.

"You and me have got to talk.' Flute pointed to a low stone wall and she sat nervously beside him. 'I know you can speak. If you can sing, you can speak. What sort of a game are you playing? You must be hiding something.' Ellie looked sideways at him. He was leaning forward, his forearms on his knees; he was only a boy, she thought, with his sideburns and his black hat pulled down over his fringe. Dare she maintain her innocence? With God's help she would never confirm his allegations. It was time to take control. The church bells chimed, and Flute sat up straight. He exclaimed accusingly, 'You've taken a vow of silence. That's it. I'm right, aren't I?' He rose to his feet. 'Come on, that's it, isn't it? You're religious. Mark said that you—' He stopped quickly. So she had been the subject of discussion but in all probability it had helped. It was cold now and she shivered, but she was no longer afraid of Flute. He was childlike, unworldly. 'Your secret's safe with me,' he verified and left her to find her own way home. It might be unkind but she could not imagine that anyone could be that naïve, so unsuspicious.

The bus left the last houses of the town behind and Ellie relaxed. Thin clouds snaked across the darkened sky and the moon appeared circled with frost. She opened the door to Gary's flat and felt a lump in her throat. Why, when she had his permission, did she feel like an intruder? Apart from a few scattered papers on the coffee table the flat was tidy; it mirrored his personality, neat and orderly. There were drawings on the bureau, sketches of animals and a painting of a horse by Tiz with a scrawled signature blazoned on its left flank. How the memories flooded back, of the bus, of the smooth grassy slopes of Ireland, of the stone cottages and timbered roofs and the castles that soar to the blue sky. But closer to her heart was the recollection that she had become part of a family and cherished the protection that they gave her. No one had ever made her feel like an object of charity and one day, maybe, she would be in a position to repay them.

Ellie removed her coat. It did not eradicate the smell of stale urine or sweat which had been passed on involuntarily by Godfrey. Goodness knows what germs she had been exposed to, she shuddered. She spent some time in the shower. It was a stark, masculine fortress. Man occupied this region; it lacked the niceties of bubble bath, scrunchies, body lotion and talc. Yet it bore the scent of Gary and she was missing him.

She dressed only in her underclothes and entered the bedroom. The central heating switched itself off and odd noises circulated around the room like a swarm of mosquitoes preparing to land. She smiled. Strange new noises, strange new emotions. Pulling back the duvet, she slid between white cotton sheets, burying her head in the pillow. She dimmed the lights; preparing to meet the welcoming blaze of a clear blue sky in the morning. It was difficult to lie still; she couldn't stop trembling. Ellie wanted Gary more than

ever. Well, she could dream but it might be a better idea to
return home to friends who would miss her. Friends who
threw words like stones and yet none caused permanent
injury even when they hit the mark.

From the drawer she chose a tee shirt and a pair of jeans
and bundled her smelly clothes into a plastic bag. Why was
there this strong desire to rummage? She was curious about
his lifestyle but it could only satisfy her inquisitiveness and
not really add to anything which she had learned about
him.

On the bedside table sat an alarm clock. There were no
photographs, no diary, but in the drawer was a dishevelled
and dog-eared poetry book. Here was an opportunity
to speak out loud, to voice her thoughts, to release her
innermost feelings, to liberate the words that had been
locked inside and that were meant for Gary if only she had
chosen a different path. Over the months the sound of her
voice had developed a richer tone, more sensitive and she
had deposited a vocabulary of thoughts in her memory
bank which one day she hoped to share with him. She read
a poem by Jeni Couzyn.

"The way towards each other is through our bodies.
Words are the longest distance you can travel,
so complex and hazardous you
lose your direction."
She replaced the bookmark.

****

Most times when anyone visited Jan she would be gazing
wistfully out of the window. Beyond the garden and the
clumps of trees a forsythia somehow had found root in the
stony soil. Perhaps someone had planted it and lost interest.
Surrounding it were a number of stunted trees and young
children found it an excellent place for playing games.
Occasionally it was a rendezvous for dog- walkers. All this
and more was noted and written down in Jan's journal.
Despite having television, there were few programmes

which held her interest. Travel documentaries were once a favourite but travel was out of the question. 'Too late for such thoughts now,' she grieved. Nowadays she could only reflect on the past.

In the night she continued to roam around the house, creeping into the girls' bedroom. Tiz would rise out of her warm bed, bite her lip and escort Jan, shivering with cold, along the landing and into her room. When it came to Jan she portrayed an angelic patience.

Snow had fallen on the eve of Valentine's Day, a gentle covering of white awaiting spring's green yawning shiver. In the early hours Tiz was suddenly uprooted from her dreams. She was blinded by a yellow light and a metal object being pushed into her face. An all-white figure carrying a torch, crying and pushing at her arm demanded her attention. Tiz spluttered. 'Not again. What is it this time? This can't go on you know. Some of us have to work.' Tiz tried reasoning with Jan. 'Go back to bed for goodness sake, it's too cold to be wandering about in the middle of the night.'

'No,' Jan whispered. 'You don't understand. There's a noise. It's been going on for some time. Horrible, it is.' Tiz was fully awake now and Boo was stirring.

'Where? In the house? Downstairs?' Tiz sat up in bed. Should they be in fear for their lives? Had someone broken in?

'No.' Jan lowered the torch and sat on the edge of the bed. 'Listen, it's outside. By the side of the house. Can't you hear it? A cry, a whimper then a howl. Listen.'

'What's the matter?' Boo rubbed her eyes.

'Shush, we're listening.'

'What for?'

'Goodness knows.' Tiz was losing patience. 'You are sitting on my feet, Jan.' After putting on her slippers and her dressing-gown she grabbed Jan's arm more tightly than she intended.

'I heard something,' Boo breathed. 'Definitely, from the rail track.'

Jan was escorted back to her room, Boo in pursuit. 'Well

that's it, then. There is nothing we can do about that,' responded Tiz. 'It will have to wait until morning.'

'Please,' implored Jan. Boo switched on the light and in the brightness Jan flinched and turned away from them, pulling the hood of her white robe over her head. Tiz felt ashamed of her abruptness and impatience; Jan had certainly aged and as she stumbled against the furniture Boo held out her hand. 'What if I ask Bas to take a look?' she smiled.

'You, ask Bas? Now, are you sure?' Tiz was astounded, Boo cautiously optimistic.

Normally no woman would set one foot in Bas and Rev's bedroom.

It was not the sort of place anyone would wish to linger. It was the coldest room in the house, bare and devoid of comfort. The sleeping arrangements were a sleeping bag apiece on a mattress on the floor. It housed a drum kit, an ancient record player, records and a tea chest crammed with magazines. Plus two crates of beer for emergencies. It would be unwise to creep up on Bas; that would be dangerous; tactics would have to be direct with a tough strategic approach. Boo took a deep breath. 'Bas,' she almost shouted. 'Bas, are you awake?' She studied the shapes on the floor in the light of the landing and crept away from the dark head of Rev and walked towards the window. She pushed hard at his shoulders. 'Bas,' she urged 'Are you awake?'

He belched loudly.' I bloody well am now. What's up?' She told him. 'Shove off. Can't a fella get a bit of peace around here?' He pulled the sleeping bag over his head. Why, thought Boo, was there this fierce stubbornness in the face of every obstacle? She pretended not to have noticed the gesture.

'What if someone is fighting for their life? What if someone has been beaten up and left to die? What if it had been one of us, Bas?' Her voice was soft. He lifted up his head. In the semi-darkness he could see only the outline of her body and the silhouette of her face. Ordinarily he would have found some derisive comment to inflame her but at that moment he found her presence appealing and waited.

She tried again. 'It shouldn't take long, it's only a matter of pacifying Jan, you know what she's like.'

The result was instant. Bas jumped out of bed, unravelling himself from his sleeping bag, and Boo hurriedly withdrew. All men, Boo decided, conduct their conversations in between grunts and groans if the situation is not to their liking and Rev was unceremoniously shoved out of bed to help.

It was a bitterly cold night with a sharp wind curling the snow around the fence between the house and the track. With a torch apiece Bas and Rev searched for a hole and a way down the steep bank. They stumbled along in the dark then in front of them appeared a low fence of twisted branches. They slipped and scrambled down the slope, digging into the clumps of grass with their boots and cursing. At the bottom ran the railway lines and beyond them a long slope of rubble and loose stones. The cries were louder and sickeningly pitiable. They had to clear a passage between the matted foliage and nettles. They stopped, caught their breath and spoke in whispers, unsure of what lay ahead. They discussed what they should do. The cries became a shriek and they lunged forwards in the direction of the sound. It was instinct that took them to a patch of brambles covered in a shimmer of snow and a brutal sickening sight awaited them. Tied to a slender tree, gasping for air and yelping with pain, was a tiny mongrel puppy.

The harsh light of the torch shone on the bleeding foreleg and the cut above the rope around its neck. It cowered. 'The bastards.' The words echoed in the night air as they knelt before the puppy in an effort to comfort it whilst releasing the rope and extricating it from the thorns. 'It's badly injured,' uttered Rev. 'Its leg is almost torn in half.' Bas remained silent.

They dug their toes in hard as they climbed up the bank. The thought occurred to Rev that this was probably a Christmas present which some moron had tired of. It happens. He went on hurriedly ahead. The girls were mortified, Boo inconsolable. Jan, waiting downstairs by the rekindled fire, knelt down and carefully held the puppy in her arms, wrapping a towel gently around him. 'I'll look after him,' she wept.

He was unable to stand. He drank bread and milk from a lying position and bled all over the carpet. Jan remained calm and bathed the paw despite his wild protests and wrapped it in a face cloth and he fell into an exhausted sleep. Tiz was heard to remark as she escorted a distressed Jan and the puppy to bed, 'Animals have the same rights as humans; there is nothing inherent about the human race. We'll take him to the vet tomorrow.'

Sobuj provided meat, advice and the name of a vet when Boo called before 7am at his front door and it was left to her and Tiz to arrange an early appointment. Bas and Rev had to work despite the weather and it was Jan who described the dramatic events of the evening to Ellie who had slept through it all. 'What shall we call him, Ellie? I thought Valentine. He is a gift, somewhat battered and bruised but adorable. I'm pretty sure his leg is broken.'

Boo refused to touch him. She kept going on about a preparation called Powder of Sympathy that incorporated powdered worms or something similar. 'I think she has become a victim of an almost superstitious fear. Poor girl,' muttered Tiz. Ellie prepared breakfast and marvelled at the change in Jan as she stroked the brown fur on Valentine's back.

'Do you know I had forgotten my pain when I saw him?' Jan soothed. 'I feel different.'

Boo drove her mini into the large car park and sat quietly for a few minutes in the shadow of a high wall. She had a busy day ahead and the news about the puppy had not been optimistic. 'Leave him with me. Luckily, it seems, he had spent only one night out there otherwise the cold may have killed him. On the down side we may have to amputate!' The vet laid a hand on her shoulder. 'Call me later in the day.' She couldn't bring herself to ask questions. There was always this inward fight to gain composure. She was the victim of sentimentality and tried desperately to harden herself when injustice raised its head.

She heaved the holdall out of the boot and waved to Jason who was always ready to assist her in the small booth they called the salon. The house was red brick; twice as long as it was in height and tucked in behind a high stone wall. Melting snow dripped from the rambling rose clinging to the trellis surrounding the carved, oak door at the side of which was a brass nameplate "The Retreat". It was curiosity which tempted Boo to answer the advertisement in the paper for she had no idea what a retreat was, but her monthly visits were a joy. It was simply a quiet place which provided tranquillity and harmony in the midst of a busy life. There had been a marked lowering of vitality after last night but when the ladies were seated at the washbasins she became quite confident. She sank her fingers into the Willow Bark and Fennel shampoo, massaged, cleansed and chatted. There was something wholesome about clean hair. She remembered her first tour with the band and her first shower after almost a week on the road. How it threatened to open the floodgates of her phobia against dirt.

Believing that colour communicates information about the person she was convinced that red- haired people have irascible tempers and that fair-haired people are pretentious, whereas she was sure her own black hair suggested strength and vitality and was also lucky. She and Jason discussed this over lunch. He scoffed at the whole idea. 'What does my hair tell you about me?' he laughed, and rubbed his bald patch.

She yawned, stifling it as best she could. 'I've been awake for most of the night,' she explained, 'with a sick dog. We think he may lose a leg.' He's only tiny. Fortunately we have someone at home who can care for him.' Jason drew in his breath.

'I hope you have insurance. Could cost a bomb.'

'No, we haven't and yes, I know,' Boo groaned.

Jason offered her a £20 note. 'Here, this will help; let me know how he goes on.'

Darkness closed in as Boo made her way through the busy city. The world of beauty, the quiet atmosphere and creative activity had changed into something ugly and disordered when the news of the puppy came through. Her gratuities were generous and would help to pay for the vet's bill; she had wanted so much to give her friends good news. 'The little chap will be OK,' forecasted Rev. 'He'll manage with three legs; there's many a one that does.' The five of them were sitting around the fire, wood piled high, halfway up the chimney, loose splinters cascading on to the hearth. They hardly noticed the heat. They were remembering the shivering, soaked body and the trust in the large brown eyes, and Jan who was more aware of the world than she was before and who had once vanished under an avalanche of sickness. Now she remained upstairs trembling with indignation and exasperation.

Valentine was brought home after two nights. He had survived the surgery and was happily installed in the padded basket which Tiz had purchased from the PSDA charity shop. It was left to Jan and her newly acquired nursing skills to care for him and in the warmth and comfort of her room he settled down.

Breathing with difficulty and red in the face Bas cradled the logs, balancing them under his chin from the shed to the pantry. 'That's a stupid name for a dog. Whose idea was it to call him that? If anybody should have the choice it should be me. Personally I think he suits Tripod.' The logs scattered in a heap on the stone floor.

Tiz rose from the table and made a gesture of disgust. 'That is a gruesome, revolting thing to say.' Trembling with indignation, she turned to him. 'You rescue him, go to all that trouble and then sour mouth.' She licked her lips. 'You are your own worst enemy.'

'Me?' he blustered. 'Naw. I'm a complex character, ask Boo, that's her opinion anyway.'

Rev laughed loudly, moving his skinny frame into the pantry, kicking the logs into a neat pile. 'Come on, time for practice.'

So far they had said nothing about the discovery to anyone. It seemed unlikely that anyone would claim the puppy and he was heaven-sent for someone who needed a lifeline. Bas, who took all reproaches in good part, agreed that the forthcoming gig would be in aid of animal welfare and in particular for raising money for the pup's care. Tiz, always ready with her camera, had taken numerous before and after photographs of Valentine and she and Ellie were on their way to have the copies enlarged. 'We can display them at the venue. I shall make a poster – "Humanity holding its wounded at the spectacle of the just".' Ellie nodded.

The bus inched its way slowly into the city. Tiz prattled on. Instead of grey mottled buildings Ellie saw blue sky and wet sand, felt the warm sun on her bare shoulders and the taste of salt on her tongue. Gary had written to her and he had made it clear how important her letters were to him and how he looked forward to her filling in the blank chapters which had been a mystery to him. She wondered if he had perhaps considered her a potential embarrassment but for now she was happy. The thought of him always conjured up a memory of a time past but she looked forward now, more than ever, to a closer understanding of their relationship.

The tempo of the music increased and the band were fired up to the point of exhilaration. Fab was late and missed two numbers and the crowd were crunching over pockets of dancers whose cries were obliterated by the shouts of 'Shame'. Bas had made a fiercely opinionated introduction. 'All lyrics will be about animal rights, animal testing, fox hunting and badger baiting!'

Ellie seated herself directly under an open window at the back of a packed room. It was heavy with smoke and perspiration.

Conversation was limited to just a few who had somehow managed to crack the code or had pieced together words that were dangling on a uni-lingual hook. All the rest simply yelled at one another. It was a canvas of music and movement and belly laughs, of colours and youth. Conversation had no place here, she ought to feel at home, but Gary's letter had unsettled her and she missed him.

It was the clatter of boots on the steps outside the

window that startled her. There appeared to be more than one person and they were climbing up towards the roof. It was taking them some time. Ellie climbed onto a chair and peered through the window. She pulled back quickly. Had she been mistaken? Two figures certainly wrapped around each other, unaware of anything other than their sexuality, lying on the hard platform of the fire escape. She scanned the room furtively before taking another look. There was no mistake, it was Fab. Ellie was unable to see who the man was but she watched as he straightened up with some difficulty and stood for a moment fastening his belt. There were a few hushed words between them and they descended the steps.

The interval was over, the lights were now in position and the stage was being marked off. Tiz and Boo were at the bar; they offered Ellie a pineapple. Tonight, she thought, I can really taste the spirit of love. I am shaking, hanging on like an autumn leaf but I cannot hang on forever.

'We have weighed it up,' divulged Boo, spreading notes and coins on a towel in front of the fire. 'We have enough for the vet's bills with a considerable amount left over.' He considered himself in charge although self-appointed. Gary, on the other hand, trusted him and knew that Tiz would step in if needed.

****

It was a delight to see daffodils and tulips appear in the sparse grass at the farthest end of the strip of garden. 'You will find there are more in summer,' claimed Sobuj. 'Nasturtiums and petunias, very colourful.' Valentine had discovered a humped clump of earth near the shed where he rooted and scraped. He was clumsy and unbalanced with a lop-sided walk and still heavily bandaged. Jan had ventured out and had him securely controlled by a lead; she had without question taken on full responsibility for his daily needs.

The journal was on hold although Golnar's frequent visits meant that she was still involved with the collection of recipes. Jan was looking less strained. Her hair had grown over her ears and covered the red area on her neck. She had replaced the heavy veil with a thin covering of silk and on a sunny day when she knew there were no neighbours around she had been sitting out in the shelter of the shed.

Boo had spent some time in the bathroom and emerged after tea in a pink top with pink tasselled blue jeans. She wore her hair drawn back from her forehead and caught up in a neat chignon in the nape of her neck. Bas, spread-eagled on the sofa, looked up from his paper. He swore, so cuttingly that the rest fell silent. It was not meant as an insult but as a compliment. 'Why don't we all use that language?' Tiz spat. 'You have a very restricted vocabulary. You think you can brazen it out with obscenities; well, it doesn't wash.' A team of experts would be unable to explain why Boo chose to do what she did. She was never given to exaggeration or impulsiveness but Bas was caught off guard. She was pink and angry. She walked over to him quickly, placed her hands on either side of his face, bent over and whispered in his ear. Lifting up his tee shirt she rubbed her hand over his bare midriff. She grabbed her coat and strode out of the door. 'What did she say?' mocked Rev. Tiz giggled. Ellie smirked. 'None of your bloody business,' he raged.

At his place at the bar in the local and after many pints, he relayed the incident to his mates. Entirely blown out of all proportion and slightly one-sided nevertheless as his audience increased his confidence grew. As he let himself into the house he was his old self. Until, that is, Jason arrived at the front door, his arm around Boo's shoulders, and followed her inside. 'He wants to see Valentine,' she explained and ran upstairs to fetch him.

Jason was left to stand in the middle of the room and four pairs of eyes focused on the tall, balding man who smiled self consciously. Bas's words always betrayed what he felt. 'So you are the reason she's all tarted up then? Scrubs up well. Don't you think?' Jason nodded his head in silent approval. Bas wagged his finger and laughed. 'Only joshing. Want a beer?'

When Boo returned with Valentine Jason was balanced precariously on the arms of the sofa discussing darts whilst the others watched in curiosity and relief. 'He came snarling at me like a beast of prey,' Jason stammered to Boo as he left. 'Aren't you going to tell him?'

'What?' Boo pressed.

'That I'm gay.'

She sighed. 'I didn't know you were.'

CHAPTER FIFTEEN

"With silence one irritates the devil." (Proverbial Hungarian.)

Most Sundays for Ellie were such a joy. It was the most satisfying day of the week. Chapel provided a ready answer to spiritual needs and the afternoon and evening gave her the gratification of closeness to Gary when she visited his flat. She would sit at his desk and write long letters both to him and Gran. It would have been easier to email but if he had wanted it that way he would have suggested it, she decided. She had concluded from the categorized filing system that he had launched into a number of commercial undertakings and reflected that perhaps he was wealthy. If he was it didn't show.

The birds had appreciated the seed and fat cakes she had provided over the cold spell and she had been well within range of the thrush and the robin in the roof garden. The squirrels had left peanuts in the tubs among the tulip and daffodil bulbs and the vine was producing tiny tendrils.

It was unlikely she had been observed; the house seemed unusually quiet at all times. This was the peace that Gary undoubtedly needed and she reflected that, taking all in all, she had not come off too badly and that she was blessed with quiet moments, too.

The vocal exercise which was becoming more of a minor mental display was important to her. It was strange to read out loud, to hear the inflections in her voice and to be able to do it without fear of being overheard. She chose to read from "The Picture of Dorian Gray", a well-worn copy from his large selection of books. She read, "As we were sitting together, suddenly there came into her eyes a look that I have never seen before. My lips moved towards hers. We kissed each other. I can't describe to you what I felt at that moment. It seemed to me that all my life had been narrowed to one perfect point of rose-coloured joy. She trembled all over and shook like a white narcissus." Was love so rapturous, so ecstatic? If so, how long could she wait? Or could this inner debate within her hold firm?

Jazz Club on the Canal was a special feature evening held in mid March and Ellie had drawn the short straw, a disclosure she made to Tiz. She placed the flyer on the table as they were ready to eat. 'Don't you like jazz? You're not a hep cat then?' asked Rev. She shook her head. 'I rather like the New Orleans style, you know Dixieland, but not your no melody type without a proper beat,' stated Rev.

'I don't take a shine to it at all,' groaned Bas.

'You in charge of the buffet?' queried Boo. 'We'll come then, give you some support.' It was one way of showing their appreciation.

Conversation at mealtimes was usually about music, of tape and CD sales and profit and loss but there had been moments of dissent on who should feed the dog. Without griping they found enough dry wood to light the fire, they cleaned the toilet, sorted the laundry and trekked round the open market for basics, yet giving meat to Valentine stuck in their craw. So Ellie was the one to fill his bowl in the morning from a plastic container kept on the windowsill outside. She had no problem handling meat, she did so everyday in the cafe, she simply didn't eat it. It was all new to her being a vegetarian but she hadn't allowed it to take over her life. 'What if we feed him veggie food?' Bas had suggested.

Jan disagreed. 'I don't think so, not all the time.'

There were over 40 passengers on the private charter and

the music was lively and the dancing boisterous. Gently and graciously the boat slid beneath the bridges and onto the basin, cruising through Sheffield's industrial heartland where the banks were preparing for spring. 'In the early eighties,' June had told Ellie. 'These long boats were churning the mud on the canal bed and shifting it from one place to another. Then we were awash with silt and muck and yet, look now, duck, the banks are licked clean with the filtered water.'

Ellie was to be well rewarded for her evening "Jam with Jazz" promised June and it was difficult to ignore Mark or be angry with him despite being brushed aside for a chubby schoolgirl with frizzy hair. Perhaps it was a condition of wear and tear, she thought. Did Mark have an odd, nagging curiosity still about what sort of girl she was?

On the other hand, Flute had been keen to express his impression of her and this evening her estimation of him had jumped in leaps and bounds. Dressed in a maroon paisley waistcoat and pin striped trousers he played the clarinet with such enthusiasm even Fab remarked, 'Isn't he the one who plays the flute under the bridge? The one who was pushed into the canal?' Ellie nodded. She would have preferred "fallen into the canal" but the result was the same. He had not lost his former sharpness of vision and his playing was fantastic.

There was so much food left over; open rolls, cheese flans, pork pies, cakes and pastries. It was left to Ellie to dispose of it. She remembered the homeless, the small group of people outside the staff entrance of the hotel on the night she and Gary had visited Cassie. She proposed to Boo the idea of distributing the food. There was an impatient look on her face. 'Do we have to, Ellie? I'm knackered.'

'Come on, I know you would help your sisters if you felt they were hungry,' Tiz said benevolently. Together they packed the food into foil, stacked the few remaining dirty glasses in the galley sink and placed the food in the boot of the mini. For the first part of the journey Boo remained silent. She became very argumentative when Ellie could not remember the hotel where the group of itinerants hung out, and really angry when she spotted the warning light on her petrol gauge. It was a journey where there was more attacking than containment on Boo's part but Tiz reminded her that for some, life is harsh and unrelenting. 'Come on, Boo, think back. We have had to turn in some nights with just a crust between us. How grateful we would have been for someone to bless us with decent food.'

Gary had not exaggerated about the beggars. They were a banal band of society's misfits hanging around, emitting sounds of whining and whingeing. Boo pulled up a short distance away. They unloaded the food. Without warning a stampede lurched at them and they dived into the car and sped away. 'Don't you ever, ever put me in that situation again,' Boo raged. Ellie knew that the reprimand was directed at her but Boo was looking directly ahead, driving fast and muttering.

'That is one unforgettable experience I wish I could forget,' berated Fab, who had been unusually calm.

When she was dropped off at her flat she pressed a note into Boo's palm. 'Towards the petrol,' she smiled and walked quickly up the path. The street lights brought out the red in her hair and as she threw back her head her long hooped earrings shone in the glare of the headlights. Without looking back, she held up her hand and waved. "Oh, Fab," Ellie thought and repeated the words that Flute had said with such assurance "Your secret is safe with me."

March was moving into April as gentle as a lamb. The ice cold nights had given way to rising temperatures and the sun found its way into every room. The house had a cheerful, bright look and everyone took pleasure in seeing the sunlight sparkle on puddles in the garden left by the winter rain. Small birds shook off their winter grime and fluttered and squabbled in the pools.

Soon, thought Ellie with a smile of optimism, Gary would be home. In Bradford he had fulfilled his promise to Tiz, helping to promote her paintings, and had been rewarded by a sale or two. The glittering lure of success was a stimulant for Tiz who could hardly hide her excitement. It was encouraging for them all. She had worked throughout the frosty mornings in the chilly attic, clutching her jacket about her to stave off the cold. Ellie had a theory that Tiz held a romantic belief that a disadvantaged artist would later be renowned.

'I'll swing for that dog one day. Snapping and barking, baring its teeth every time it sees me. Another daft name for a dog, Ralph.' Bas turned the chair around and sat down. Tiz and Ellie were adding boiled potatoes to the beanfeast in the casserole. 'Make us a potato butty, Ellie, with salt and ketchup.'

'Make one yourself,' glowered Tiz, 'and the dog is called Rolf.'

'Get away, well Sobuj wants to learn to talk proper and control that Alsatian!' Ellie smiled and ladled a few potatoes onto a dish and drained them. She chopped them into small pieces and piled them high between two slices of thick sliced bread. 'Thanks, Ellie. How about a mug of hot tea?'

It was an early start that evening, a gig in Doncaster. Ellie would stay behind; there was an emptiness without Gary and there would be room in the van for Jason who was new to the scene. In any case, she intended to visit the flat for the last time on her own. Had Gary told her friends she had been given a key? Did they understand that being on her own was important to her? No one had mentioned it.

She found herself wishing she could move in. She sat on the edge of the bed and spoke out loud as if he was somewhere out of reach yet could at any moment appear. There was little tidying to do but she dusted and sprayed a little polish on the dining table and replenished the fruit bowl. Stretched out on the bed, she read more of Oscar Wilde, aware of the softness of the duvet and the scent of Gary around her. She stayed there motionless until her eyes had accustomed themselves to the change of approaching night, realizing that her daydreams might just be pipe dreams but she intended that they should be an aspiration. On returning home she said goodnight to Jan with a kiss on the cheek, stroked Valentine and went to bed.

Gary arrived looking refreshed and enthusiastic, dressed in a blue and white checked shirt and jeans. Everyone had something to say and it was as if he had been away for years. Too much agreement kills a chat, thought Ellie, but she was content to look and listen. She was spared from questioning for the time being. Meantime she behaved with pleasing cordiality, providing eats and drinks and stacking more wood on the fire. In the far corner Jan sat quietly, scribbling down thoughts for her journal, and Valentine stretched himself and moved to join her.

After a lively celebration at the pub they took a short cut through the waste ground, a grassland mound of earth and dirt and a tip for household rubbish. Bas, always curious and astute, spied a garden bench with both feet missing. 'That'll do nicely,' he boomed. 'Two new legs and it's as good as new.'

'You are joking,' trashed Boo. 'Who is going to sit on that?'

'Jan will, in summer. All she has is a kitchen chair when she sits out and that can't be very comfy.'

'It's only suitable for firewood, and it's filthy,' Tiz complained.

'Oh, come on, where's your sense of restoration?' moaned Bas. 'Grab the other end, Rev.'

'You only restore antiques, anyway, not rotten wood,' Boo smirked. Bas, close to bursting point, swore non-stop to the house, carrying the bench, puffing and panting, with Rev a few steps behind at the other end. Gary walked in front, his arm around Ellie's shoulder. 'He's like a bull at a gate but he means well. You watch, he's determined to make something of it. There's no escaping him when he is in this frame of mind.'

To Ellie the evening was pleasant but she had the feeling she was being put on hold, ascending a gentle slope but to descend would be more difficult still. Yet it was obvious she was more than just a passing interest. It was a sensation of ups and downs. She had decided that whatever came her way tonight she would accept for now. 'Show me where you found the puppy.' She led Gary to the crown of the hill and pointed. 'Well, Bas certainly showed some courage, and it was snowing.' He held her hand and they walked through the short grass towards the woods. 'Thank you for your letters, Ellie. I liked your sort of enjoyable gossip. I know you a lot better now but I still have a lot to learn, don't I?' His grey eyes were clear and sparkling. 'I think of you now as safe. You are as streetwise now as any of the girls and I can see you coping with anything!'

He pressed his hand in hers. 'What I would like you to do is to continue to write to me. Tell me if you have given any thought to the future; if you have any plans or would like to try something new. I will give you all the help I can and I will never lose touch.' Why at this beautiful moment was her heart full of sorrow? It made her feel weak when he thought of her as being strong. She would fret over this evening. She felt drained as if she had been dragged through a car-wash. The flippancy of the thought made her smile. 'I like it when you smile,' he said. She withdrew her hand as they approached the house. Had she chosen to speak she would have asked him about his plans. Was she a part of them? Words unspoken didn't mean things unsaid but Gary never wasted words.

Ellie lay awake for most of the night. She had said her prayers as she always did but they were selfish and entreating and she childishly asked them to be cancelled out. She cried softly into the pillow. This was part of the price she had to pay for her deceit; she understood that. She would continue to write to him and let him know how much she appreciated his friendship. That is all she could do for now. When the sun was well up she closed her eyes.

Jason was now a frequent visitor to the house and his introduction to Jan was quite revealing. 'I'm doing a pioneer survey of sanatoriums,' he told her. 'Convalescent homes for people recovering from illness.'

'I know what they are,' snapped Jan. 'I hope you are not thinking of studying me; I don't want to be a guinea pig.'

'Heaven forbid, I wouldn't dream of it.'

The two of them and Valentine were sharing the sofa and the evening sun formed patterns on Tiz's mural. It was practice night and they were alone in the house. Jan was dressed neatly in an embroidered long-sleeved blouse and loose cotton trousers. The tee shirt and braces had long gone. 'Why are you doing this then?' asked Jan

'Sorry?'

'What is the survey for?'

'Oh, for more qualifications. I am not interested in sickness, only in helping sick people get better. There are so many ways in which people like you can be helped. But of course it has to come from the patient.' There was a long pause. 'Why do you cover up your face?'

Jan grunted. 'You know why. I'm disfigured.'

'Why don't you show me?'

Jan shook her head. 'No, and don't ask me again.'

He flinched. 'I won't, I promise.'

While he made a sandwich and tea Jan looked about her. She was comfortable in a room devoid of luxury, cared for in a house lacking supervision and free in a building that offered no secure tenancy. What did that say about her and her journey on the road to convalescence she wondered?

'I've made peanut butter.'

'Thank you.' 'How many people do you need to take part in your study?' Jan asked.

Jason chewed and swallowed hard. 'A minimum of three and a maximum of six.'

'And how many do you have?'

'None; you are the first I have come across.'

'You need some help then, don't you? Oh, come on then what do you want to know?'

His face lit up. 'I'll bring the questionnaire round tomorrow.'

Cheddar arrived on the Saturday afternoon to tidy up the garden. Also he was well aware that arrangements would soon be set in motion for the European Tour and he did not want to be excluded. Sobuj lent him a rake and fork. 'Don't you put any weed killer anywhere,' Jan rebuked, 'and watch out for Valentine.' The little dog hobbled around after him, around him and under him. The garden seat was placed prominently against the fence in the half shade with two new legs, inelegantly made from blocks of recycled wood and painted with creosote. The smell lingered for days. Ellie had made colourful foam cushions and Jan graced the seat, wearing a wide-brimmed hat and sunglasses. Chimes tinkled below an engraving to Helios, God of the Sun, provided for luck by Boo.

There was an emptiness in everything Ellie did for the few days following her time with Gary. To be secretive was not part of his nature, nor did he make mistakes when talking to her, she believed this. She was aware that he would take note of the expression on her face before he spoke. Why then would he act like her guardian? All six friends lived together in a state of mutual tolerance, perhaps a little hostility but much cordiality and on equal terms. She was reading too much into this; she supposed that life was a vast ocean of knowledge in which she hadn't even dipped her toe. She was 17, was now the time to bury her childhood and face the world?

Easter brought sunshine, warm weather and a holiday spirit. Yet there was work to be done in the garden. 'It calls for skills and stamina.'

'What does?'

'To be a scaffolder,' Bas hammered the stoop into the ground. 'You need a head for heights and nerves of steel.'

Cheddar grinned. 'That's a bit over the top. Now steeplejacks, that's a job and a half.'

'Yea, well. We have to put up with bad-tempered fellas and stupid women who draw the curtains as soon as the van draws up outside. We've more to do than gawp at them.'

Jan had reported a gap in the fence between Sobuj and their land. 'I think the Alsatian did it,' she moaned, 'trying to make friends with Valentine!'

'More likely trying to bury him, I would think,' sniffed Cheddar.

'Any more jobs lined up for us?' Bas appreciated that

Jan was left with as little to do as possible whilst they were away and that she had nothing to concern her or slow down her recovery.

Mustard had arrived in Dover and Gary broke the news to them the minute he came through the door. 'He'll be here the day after tomorrow. The bus is in one piece and he is looking forward to seeing us.' He was attacked by a barrage of questions and everyone was talking and no one was listening. Gary hid his face in his hands then stood up thrusting his hands into the pockets of his jeans. 'Do you know, I would never have imagined that you would be ready to move back into those sweat-infested bunk beds!'

'Oh, we're not,' Boo challenged. 'Bas is staying behind.' The air became thick with obscenities as Boo made a hasty retreat.

Reluctantly, or perhaps not entirely with reluctance, Jan offered to come downstairs to prepare the meal. Her moods differed from hour to hour and too often proved an implement of play. Maybe, thought Ellie, it had something to do with Jason coming to supper and set an extra place at the table. Ellie cut the potatoes into cubes and chopped the garlic; she halved the button mushrooms and chopped the coriander, jobs which Jan still found difficult. She was careful to wear cotton-lined gloves as she heated the oil in the saucepan and fried the onion, garlic, ginger and curry paste. 'What time do we eat?' Bas poked his head round the door

'Half an hour.'

'Right.' Great drops of sweat stood on his forehead and he flopped into a chair.

'What have you been doing?' Jan asked. Potatoes and tomatoes were brought to the boil.

'Clearing builders' rubble from next door but one,' he coughed. 'They aren't likely to want to get rid of us in a hurry, we're far too obliging.' He counted the place settings absent-mindedly. 'Who's coming?' and glanced at Jan. 'Oh, not that ponce, can't he keep away?' Although irritated with his question both girls ignored it. So he might as well have kept quiet, he thought.

****

'It's not a good night for it. Not at all.' Boo burst into the kitchen with Tiz at her heels. Ellie spooned mushrooms, peas and ground almonds into the pan. 'No one should travel on the evening of April 30th unless it is absolutely essential.'

'Says who?' Bas was ignored. 'Oh, why on earth not?'

Tiz fell into the chair. 'Because it is Walpurgis Night, that's why not.' There was laughter followed by a long silence. Finally Tiz pursed her lips and half smiling asked, 'What precisely does that mean?'

Boo sat beside her. 'It is one of the most auspicious times of the year for casting spells. Mustard should postpone his journey.'

Bas shifted and menacingly leaned forward. 'Let's have a shot at being normal, shall we, instead of having distorted spirits all over the place?' It was the appearance of the bowl of basmati rice that altered the mood and the huge servings of vegetable curry and, right on time, Jason.

It was the familiar sound they were used to, the recognisable throb of the engine and the vibrating sound of the chassis. The bus was back and with it an exhausted Mustard carrying the drowsy strain of travel. It was almost 11pm; he was too tired to speak so he settled on the sofa with a bowl of lentil soup and the promise of a good night's sleep. Ellie fondled his beard and remembered his pain, how he had staggered and moaned and dragged his leg and how she had massaged it better. She offered him her bed but he raised his hand in protest. 'No, Ellie, I must admit it's tempting but I'll take the sofa in front of the fire,' noting, no doubt, the good, dry wood which Cheddar had already sawed and stacked high.

They ventured out to the bus next morning. Bas and Rev were the first and they could not hide their fury. This had been their home which they had thriftily put together; more

than a touch of hard graft, an effort which had taken time
and exertion and pride, and it had been wrecked. It was
filthy, harbouring months of grime, dented and scratched.
Tiz and Boo stopped short in the door of the house and
stared, the hurt visible on their pale faces. The tender
memories were buried under squalor and the celebrations
marred by dirt. Once inside there was more evidence of
neglect and rough usage. Dirty crockery and cutlery were
piled unwashed in drawers and cupboards. The carpet
around the sink squelched with stagnant water and two of
the bunks were broken. On the lockers telephone numbers
had been scrawled in lipstick and a pair of curtains had
been torn in half. Had weeks of work been in vain? Could
it possibly be made ready for early June? Fury and defiance
put harsh words into Bas's mouth; there was no doubt about
it, if the band members had been there he would probably
have killed at least one.

It was possible that Mustard could have prevented such
loutish behaviour. Bas said not. Driving the bus would in
itself be enough to worry about. When Mustard finally
awoke he directed at himself a number of vintage insults
and was full of apologies and shamefaced. 'It got completely
out of hand, they were having all-night parties and inviting
all sorts of yobs. Most of the time they were out of their
heads and didn't care a sod about me. Must admit it is the
last time I'll have anything to do with them. Sorry.' If it
was merely a question of building on existing trust then for
Mustard it had been a failure. Boo scowled. The four sat
disconsolately round the fire. All were justifiably furious but
this could not have been predicted and it was better to wait
and see what Gary had to say.

Ellie and Jan had yet to be told but there was no way
round, it the bus had been vandalised by people they
had counted as friends. Mustard parked the bus at the
side of the house; it was well away from prying eyes and
somewhat sheltered. Rev believed that there was little point
in complaining about it and set out for one of his long walks.
For a brief moment Boo weakened and began to sob.

Mustard solemnly dabbed at his moustache. 'I'll pay for the damage, you know. Let me get it through the MOT and then we can think of putting it right.'

Bas, who refused to listen to any such suggestion, began, 'We are all responsible in a way. But they haven't got away with it, no fear.'

A cheerful feminine voice added, 'Say no more about it,' and Tiz added wood to the fire and bit hard into a ripe pear.

Sobuj had developed his own versions of what is right and wrong and his friends had been badly let down. He said as much to the neighbours who stood around the bus in twos and threes until Bas obliged and allowed them to look inside. 'You know, Ellie,' chortled Jan as they looked down on them from the bedroom window, 'Sobuj has his mysterious deals with the neighbours. I think he allows them credit on goods from his stall. I've often seen callers at his home when you have all been out. It wouldn't surprise me if he hasn't got something up his sleeve.'

When suddenly the rain came down in sheets and swept the mud and leaves from the roof of the bus and streaked brown channels down the side, forming puddles, the neighbours dispersed. The news was broken to Gary by Tiz. 'He's dealing with it,' she informed them. 'You know he won't go over the top. He'll be here about eight.' When he did he appeared to be in that peculiar state of mind which was neither angry nor concerned. He had invited Bas to accompany him to Leeds, where the band were playing, to demand compensation.

'In that case,' challenged Bas, 'We'll take a couple of bouncers with us, just for the ride. You never know.'

'At all costs just stay together,' instilled Boo whose emotional climate changed constantly. Tomorrow she might be insufferable.

Over in the copse the May blossom was bursting into flower. The greenery appeared, weaving its way between brown hedges, and birds flew upwards from the trees away from the grey squirrel. The winter rot had gone and spring had taken over. All the spare time was now concentrated on preparing the bus for the tour. It had to fit in with work and other commitments and often it was tiring and hard but it was taking shape. It was revealed that there were joiners and glaziers among the neighbours willing to lend a hand. Sobuj had supplied a new carpet and his neighbour the use of his skip to house the rubbish. The children were eager to wash the bus and armed with cloths and brushes and wax they had earned a trip on the canal, which Ellie paid for. Gary had constructed a plan and had returned from Leeds with £300 and a very satisfied Bas. He gloried in the fact that when a threatening presence replaced confrontational dialogue, the former usually won.

****

Gary was restless. He lay on his side, his head propped by three pillows, gazing out of the window. He had added another wool blanket and despite his warm bed and the central heating full on he was shivering. Today had brought problems. He had found it almost impossible to concentrate and was having difficulty swallowing. Macaroni cheese was all he could stomach and that was hours ago. Closing his eyes he stretched out his legs; the shivers developed into erratic movements. At times it seemed that his hands, his legs and his head felt as if they were being consumed by millions of insects.

He had never slept well and needed to move constantly. He knew at the back of his mind that he needed to return to his GP for more medication. The occurrences were too frequent to ignore. He thought of Ellie with her bright eyes and proud smile. In her world nothing was mean or bad, nothing needed unravelling; whilst he felt like a fugitive, an escapee who would never be free. He helped himself to a glass of soda water; he preferred his quinine this way; he wouldn't give in to this, never. It was now the most silent phase of the night, a time of reflection and concern but even this was too draining and he closed his eyes and waited for sleep.

'Would you say you were serene and peaceful, Ellie?' Boo looked across. Ellie smoothed the material across her knee. 'I have just given Bas a piece of my mind, all the swearing and cursing he does, it's not necessary, especially with kids around although I don't know where they all come from. Don't blaspheme, I told him, only bad luck will follow. Anyway, Jason says it's because you can't talk that you are so placid.' Ellie continued sewing, repairing the torn curtain from the bus, and shrugged her shoulders. So she had been the subject of discussion again! This thought brought her a sense of relief; at least she wasn't being ignored or taken for granted. Did they imagine that her dumbness made her evasive and solitary?

The fire crackled and spat. The chandelier sparkled, casting coloured patterns onto the painted ceiling. Tiz balanced the sketch pad on her knee, Fab was learning lyrics and Boo was changing channels on the television. 'He's staying here to look after Jan, you know.'

Tiz looked up. 'Who?'

Boo switched off the set. 'Nothing but repeats. Um, Jason. He's sleeping over while we're on tour. He's sorted it with Gary. I think it's a great idea!' Ellie concluded that a whisper is unknown among the girls, it is usually a muttered conversation that results in important bits of news.

Since it was obviously impracticable to refurbish the bus until it had been thoroughly cleaned, they were taking time off. The mattresses had been thrown into the skip and the paintwork scrubbed. The new carpet stood propped up in the hallway waiting for the floor to dry out. Liberal amounts of disinfectant had been used, a reminder to Ellie of her time with Bella and the household soap and the smell of San Izal.

A year had passed since then. A year in which she had shaped her own personality, moulded her character to suit those around her. Her friends would say only what was uppermost in their minds; she said nothing and would strive to hide anything that would arouse suspicion.

Bas gave vent to what amounted to a yell. The bunk had

slipped and landed on his head. 'This amounts to criminal neglect; I tell you if ever I set eyes on that scum again they are for the high jump, make no mistake about it.' Rev buttoned up his jacket and held the pieces of wood together whilst Bas hammered nails into the joints. The wind howled through the open windows of the bus; they were still wet with paint.

'Screw it and glue it, that's what Tiz always says,' retorted Rev.

'Well she can come and bloody do it, then.'

It was not accidental that the two sexes avoided each other whilst all repairs and fittings were being undertaken. For almost six weeks they would be living in close proximity; they needed a little privacy for now. Each one had given a month's notice and all but one employer had agreed to have them back. June was full of apologies but she would need help during the busiest time of the year; she hoped Ellie would understand. She did.

A few days before they were due to leave Fab decided on an open day. Everything was in its place, from the newly-washed and ironed curtains to the cutlery which had been steeped in boiling water and soda. New mattresses had been purchased at cost from Sobuj and the bus sparkled inside and out. Papers were laid on the floor and children walked single file from the driver's cab through to the emergency door. Mustard whispered. 'If you promise to be quiet I will take you for a ride. Strictly speaking I think it's illegal but we'll keep it private and confidential. Must admit you have earned it.'

They returned to a veggie buffet laid out on the kitchen table outside the front door, and Ellie experienced a moment of poignancy. It was as if she was being seized by sentimentality for the squat which had seemed to offer her more than a place to spend the night and a hideaway to say her prayers.

The sun dipped gracefully on the late May evening and the people dispersed. Valentine had been nursed and fed and spoiled and clumsily mounted the stairs to his mistress.

Whether Gary had succeeded through indomitable willpower or chance it didn't matter, he felt such relief that he was for the moment free of pain. There had been only one bad incident when muscles in his legs had begun to stiffen but the latest medication appeared to help. He sat on the sofa, a portfolio on his knee and at a small table covered in maps and papers surrounded by the group. He reminded them to refer to their checklist, passport, Euros, credit cards, E111. He gave a short speech and Ellie found herself comparing him with an American Indian tribal chief and imagined him with a headdress with feathered plumage. She bit her lip. It wasn't fair someone had to take responsibility. Maybe she could lighten him up a little once they started their tour? Maybe he would relax among the quiet fields and the curve of the river? Maybe it would be the point of no return for her?

The girls' conversation was going round in circles. It happened, Ellie noticed, when they were overexcited. 'It's only a tent, for goodness sake, anybody would think you had a great marquee,' teased Bas.

'Look,' responded Boo. 'Be as sarcastic as you like but it will give us more privacy and a bit more space. We have experience of the European tour, remember, it can get very hot in that bus.'

'Yea, well,' Bas continued. 'If you need help with the gear, ask. Don't be so obstinate next time.' Rev raised his eyebrows. Anarchic, unpredictable, living within his own code of conduct, Bas was a crazy friend to have around.

The packing was almost complete, the bus stocked with packet and tinned food and the smell of paint had almost disappeared. One day to go. Ellie was aware that she and her friends had been together long enough to establish the fact that from this point onwards she was equipped for anything that lay ahead.

It may have seemed incredible to her friends that Ellie had never crossed the Straits of Dover or the English Channel. They must assume, she thought, that her family were

impoverished when in fact it was their choice not to take
her with them. Nor had she had any desire to go.

The sea was calm and the wind merely ruffled the waves
as they stood on deck as the white chalk cliffs slowly
disappeared. Everyone relaxed. Cheddar had decided against
travel pills and Fab was the only one feeling a little queasy.
Bas especially was on form, losing his usual peremptory
manner. For Ellie, settling on a comfy seat facing the wind,
there was little to be seen but the sea and the foam and the
sunlit water under a cloudless sky.

'They don't like us, the French, they never have!' Bas
squashed himself into the front seat.

'Why do you say that?' asked Mustard, manoeuvring the
bus to the right lane.

'Couldn't you see the Customs bloke? There was a state
of increasing irritability in his attitude!'

'You were rubbing him up the wrong way, anyone would
think he was responsible for the Channel tunnel and built it
all by himself.'

'They should learn to understand our sense of humour,'
Bas snapped. One thought buoyed him up; they had
three more days in France, the fire had returned to his
belly.

Tiz stuck the photograph of Valentine above her bunk
with blue tack. She had a great talent for making anywhere
she lay her head her permanent property. It was after eleven
in the evening. Conversation was stilted and the lay-by
secluded; the travellers were weary and getting ready for
bed. Mustard was asleep almost as soon as his head touched
the pillow. It happened after a long drive.

Not a breeze was stirring, not a quiver among the
leaves on the trees, not a beating of wings and Ellie was
full of expectations as all of France lay ahead. Suppose, she
thought, snuggling into her sleeping bag, suppose there was
a slender chance of strengthening her fragile bond with Gary.
Surely Paris would be the city? The city of lovers. Then in
the corner of her eye she saw a note pinned to the curtain
– "PARIS, LE SQUATT DE LE 13". She closed her eyes,

her illusions shattered. Here she felt able to allow herself some self-control; a squat and sensual sensitivity do not go together in her experience.

It was a while before she fell asleep. She drew back the curtain above her bunk and opened the window quietly and just a little. Her prayers were for Gran, as always, and Jan and Jason and especially Gary. She could hear his deep breathing and the stertorous snorts of Bas, in company with the sound of the river.

The rota was simple, fair and workable. Well-organized groups are never out of touch with each other's needs, Fab declared. She had been responsible for the colour code and Ellie was orange on the list which was stuck behind the pan rack. Women cooked and laundered, men maintained and cleared up any mess, so she said, and were responsible for all the gear and musical instruments.

It was estimated that no fewer than eight bands would be performing at their first Parisian gig in an air force base. It was not as successful as they had hoped and there appeared to be a large number of children, over whom the parents had little control. The noise from the hangar reverberated about the whole camp. Children invaded the stage and each successive onslaught was unnerving. No one was admitting responsibility. Bas interrupted a number. 'Look, somebody had better do something about these kids. Somebody is going to get hurt. You can't afford to be lax when it comes to youngsters. We don't want to mount stage posts but we will.' It was the man in goggles and a leather hat who went berserk. Ellie thought of Biggles; he looked preposterous but dangerous and Tiz and Boo, on stage, stepped back, grabbing Fab's arm. The man leapt towards them, tripping over wires, and lunged at Bas. They grappled and rolled against the backcloth; the man pulled it down as he fell against the speakers and Bas hit him hard on his chin and then even harder in his stomach.

As he struggled to breathe Bas rolled him, with his foot, over the edge of the stage and into the pit. Eventually the man was untwisted and unravelled from the cloth but not before a free-for-all had raised the temperature even further in the baking hangar.

It was not the best of gigs; there seemed little point in carrying on and the girls, Rev and Bas made a hasty retreat down the fire escape. Cheddar made a valiant attempt to flee to the bar but the crowd pressed him back until he could hardly breathe. Ellie swung her long legs over the bar and hauled him over the counter. They caught up with Gary, shocked and anxious, waving to them from the nearby gates. From the dim interior of the hut suddenly the luminescent sky of arc lamps blinded them and they groped their way like a potholer through a tortuous passage. Mustard started the engine, they fell into the bus just in time to see the hangar doors open and the fight spill out onto the field. 'It's not my fault, bloody French git.' Bas was fuming.

'Nobody said it was,' Rev replied.

'At least you separated him from his hat,' laughed Tiz and threw it across to Bas.

'And we were paid up front,' grinned Gary, placing a pile of Euros on the bunk. The sentimental picture of them all being together was evocative of Bas's exploits where to conquer and survive was paramount and defeat wasn't even to be considered. Perhaps the greatest success of the night was the confidence they had built up in each other, Ellie suspected.

Mustard had the route well-planned; he wanted to be as close to the capital as he could. Night driving, he swore, was no big deal and he would veer from the main roads. 'Not a mark on me,' boasted Bas, pulling off his shirt.

'For goodness sake cover yourself up,' sniffed Boo. There was little sign of tiredness in any of them. Even Gary responded amiably to the criticism that Bas was too loud and too violent by replying, 'Compared to whom?'

They shared a cocktail of vodka and rum and words became incoherent. Street lights had disappeared and the road narrowed. The track began to descend steeply and the bus rocked dangerously as it jumped between the ruts, so deeply pitted it was like driving on a river bed,

Mustard grumbled. Fab was looking increasingly hot and uncomfortable. Ellie remembered Gary's description of her. "An intellectual female who reads philosophy but requires only the simple things in life to make her happy." On this rollercoaster ride she was far from happy, she was pale and looked almost delicate.

The lights of Paris shone below them as they pulled into a large park. Brilliant and sparkling, the beguiling city welcomed them. Were there any competitors for the incomparable combination of stunning views and romantic images? Or was it simply that Ellie had fallen in love? She stepped out onto the pebbles and the soft grass, holding tight onto Gary's hand as he pointed to the unmissable Eiffel Tower and longing for him to hold her. They stayed for a while shutting out the outside world, soaking in the warmth of the summer evening until gradually the stars were veiled and the night blackened. There was so much he wanted to say to her but instead he uttered, 'Everyone should visit at least once.'

Fab had been sick in the pail and was tucked up in her bunk. 'Women,' grunted Bas. 'Never could take their ale.'

Rev was an extremely observant man and a devotee of equal rights and had never been known to show disrespect towards the girls. He had confided in Ellie that he had regarded his first tour abroad as a magnetic experiment wondering if they would be drawn together in pairs but they fell out most of the time.

After a breakfast of grapefruit, cornflakes and peanut butter sandwiches, the bus was driven into the heart of the city. Rev unexpectedly invited Ellie to walk with him; he didn't mind showing her the sights, he said, even though he had done it all before. Where was Gary? Why had he not planned to spend time with her? Ellie drew a deep breath as he poked his head round the door. 'I'm off to the squat to arrange the next gig. Why don't you go with Rev? he knows Paris like the back of his hand.'

Rev was an expert guide and remarkably good company. He was content with what he had already achieved, he

pointed out, and his music had taken him all over the
continent. Ellie was beginning to warm to him. They stopped
to listen to the birdsong in the park and strolled along the
banks of the Seine in the sun, and the slight breeze on the
June morning ruffled her long fair hair. 'It's a matter of you
standing on your own two feet in this changing world,' he
told her. 'To try to bring some sort of order out of chaos.'
They came across a picnic party and they relaxed alongside
them, taking pleasure in being on that particular stretch of
the Seine.

Ellie adjusted her short skirt and sat on the grass. Rev
pulled at his spiked hair and her attention was drawn to his
polo necked sleeveless top which covered his scar, and the
studded belt which held up his black jeans, fastened with a
large silver buckle. He treated her to a lunch of vegetable
soup with garlic bread and a dish of strawberries and cream
which she managed to spill down her top. 'Take it off,' he
grinned and they spent a few hysterical moments grappling
beneath the trees.

In a long, wide, quiet street they came across a record
store. Rev searched through the latest releases intently whilst
Ellie became increasingly hot and irritated. She wandered
out through the side entrance and froze. From a run-down
hostel a large man shot out, dragging a young semi- clothed
girl with him. He wore only a pair of trunks and plimsolls.

Spitting and cursing, he thumped her about the head,
pushing her slight body against the wall. Her cries were loud
and harrowing, and Ellie could almost feel the wave of pain,
listening to the pleas in a language she couldn't understand
and a voice in her head willing her to do something. Rev had
heard and was quick to act. His belt came off in one swift
pull and twisting it, he whipped it around the assailant's
waist, embedding the studs in his back. The man was
brought to the ground. The girl staggered into the hostel
and bolted the door.

Ellie and Rev fled. They were breathless as they boarded
the Metro and Ellie had been grateful for the steady grip of
Rev's hand as they sped away from the scene. 'Promise me

you won't say a word about this to anyone,' he pleaded. She smiled. 'Well, you know what I mean,' he grinned.

The girls had been surprised but not particularly impressed by the squat. It was clean; the French were friendly, supportive of local talent. 'Secrets of a happy life,' taunted Boo sarcastically.

'I'll tell you the secret of a happy life,' responded Fab, who had fully recovered from her sickness.

'Oh. here we go,' moaned Bas, 'more psychological claptrap.'

'It is,' continued Fab, 'never contradict, never explain and never apologise.'

'Rubbish,' disagreed Bas.

'Not according to John Fisher,' she explained.

'Never heard of him,' sniffed Cheddar.

'Nor me,' teased Rev.

'Was he a shrink?' mocked Tiz. Mustard started the bus and the conversation came to an abrupt end. It didn't matter where the journey ended, the journey alone was an education in navigation, thought Ellie. A pause or insult in the wrong place by her companions and the whole topic would be re-routed.

Ellie settled down to write her postcards on the route to Grenoble. Here, she was told, they were to stay on a makeshift campsite and meet with a Spanish band. It was rough terrain and the approach to the camp was pitted and steep and perched high overlooking Grenoble. Arriving in vans, bands brought with them tents and awnings and pitched them in small circles like American Indians. There was even a tepee.

There was little evidence of joie de vivre; the occasion was political and grim. On the sparse, dry grass the young Spaniard greeted his supporters. 'As you know,' he began, 'the government have orchestrated tactics to criminalize the squat movement in Spain and have started to beat hard in Barcelona.' There was a chorus of boos. 'The first to be evicted, without any legal order,' he continued, 'was the Casa de la Muntanya, the oldest squat in the city, and 18 people were arrested. Everything in the squat was destroyed including information and computers. People were arrested and face four years in prison.' There were sounds of dissent and support.

Boo, greatly impressed by the handsome Spaniard, whispered to Tiz. 'They are the only Spanish band here. The squatters are descending on Barcelona and re-squatting only to be deported. They are taking a big chance.'

Everyone had been taking it seriously but then the campfire sparked into life and pots and pans and food appeared and bodies bent over utensils and eyes screwed up in smoke. Then out came the guitars and the beer and tapes, and tee shirts were bartered and Ellie felt a sense of relief.

She was a stranger to politics; she didn't have any answers but she did share Gary's loathing of injustice. He remained quietly in the background, for a while lost in thought, whilst the girls circulated among old friends. The Spaniard's close attention to Boo brought colour to her cheeks and a new sparkle to her dark eyes.

They set out in the direction of Grenoble en masse with everyone in good spirits and ready for a successful gig. It was. The enthusiasm was infectious and hundreds of pounds were raised for the cause. Even those unable to get into the gig threw money onto blankets spread out on the ground. Ellie left early and joined Mustard in the bus shortly before l.00am. There was never any feeling of safety unless he could remain with the bus throughout. He slept, but with the doors locked and everything of value well-hidden.

It was Ellie who took him food and drink and massaged his leg and noted the slight grimace of pain around his mouth. Tonight, he told her, he was rested and tomorrow they would be in Italy.

Tiz, Boo and Fab were organized and trendily equipped for the fashion capital of Italy – Milan. They discussed this at length as they left France behind. 'Of course its origins were Celtic and then it was conquered by the Romans,' explained Fab.

Bas was quick to interrupt. 'I bet I flog some football shirts here. Italian men always wear shirts, hardly ever go bare-chested.'

'Listen,' Gary demanded attention. 'Before we enter Milan a few words of advice. Be wary of thieves, especially in the shopping areas; they are numerous and lightning fast. They use the same technique of waving cardboard or newspaper in your face to distract your attention whilst they head for your pockets or purse. Their major haunts are the Piazza and the Astazione Centrale. OK? Now I realize that you girls want to see the shops but be very careful. Today is free time. We meet up at 7.30 for a bite to eat and onto the stadium at 10pm. We are third in line for a sound check. We can't be late or we lose our slot.'

It was uncomfortably hot. Gary chose to stay in the cool of the Palazzo di Brera and the Art Gallery. Bas, Cheddar and Rev made for the buses and the football shirts went with them. The girls, wearing the very minimum of clothing, headed for the shops. 'Every item of clothing you have ever wanted to buy, but could never afford, is in Milan,' Tiz sighed to Ellie. 'We are going to take you behind the Duomo and around Corso Vittorio Emanuele 11 and you can window-shop to your heart's content.'

Ellie could hardly believe she was here surrounded by an extraordinary sight of clothing, footwear and accessories, in the heart of Milan with friends she could trust and yet with a background of deceit and maliciousness which had to remain hidden. They followed Fab through the glass doors and up the five gold-edged steps into the shop. Ellie clasped her hands in front of her, ignoring the curious stares of the assistants. Tiz and Boo discussed materials and cost and Fab tossed her red hair, moving delicately between the mannequins and sighing. In each shop they chose an outfit and came away empty-handed after a bold 'Quanto costa?'

At a sandwich bar they ate panzerotti, a savoury turnover made with pizza dough stuffed with tomatoes, garlic and mozzarella. Ellie refused a glass of wine, not because she was unsociable but because there was always the underlying fear

that too much would loosen her tongue and the consequence
of this would bring about absolute terror.

The sun-baked square was packed with people. The heat
was oppressive without the slightest trace of a breeze. The
temptation of the cooling waters of the fountain proved too
much and they removed their sandals and dipped their feet
into the cool water. They giggled and paddled and splashed
each other and Ellie raised her bronzed arms to the sun and
waved like a sail in the wind. A paparazzo on his way from
a society wedding at a church nearby snapped her at the
precise moment she turned her head in his direction, and
continued taking pictures. This was to be the turning point
of her life, the point of no return and she likened it later
to a string of beads; a few memories, some ill-fated, some
unorthodox, strung together on a cord called routine.

They sprawled out catching their breath after running
through the crowded streets, away from the paparazzo and
his shouts of 'Mi scusi, Mi scusi'. This life was to abandon
her but she knew little of this as she lay on the grass between
alabaster statues in a quiet park, and thought how lucky she
was.

It was not a good time for Cheddar; he had forgotten to
refill the water container and there was barely enough for
washing. 'It's a good job we don't drink the stuff,' moaned
Bas. 'The girls will give you earache, that's for sure.'

'Well, I forgot,' he muttered.

'That's what the list is all about,' Fab reminded him. It
was a rush to change and this was done en route by which
time everyone was getting involved in the water dispute.

Mustard, who constantly defended Cheddar, shouted from
his driving seat, 'Must admit it's an easy mistake to make.
I'll stop at a service station.' Discretion is more important
than eloquence, Ellie decided.

It was an hour's ride into the country surrounding the city
and there were dozens of people on foot heading towards
the venue and soon the fields were filled with enthusiasts.
Music blared from a sound system on a truck and the
party had begun long before any of the bands arrived. Bas

remarked on the number of police waiting on the periphery but Gary assured him it was normal when groups of foreign bands congregated at concerts. The bus was often a magnet for fans. The painted horse on the bus, looking artistic and burnished, still attracted a lot of attention and Tiz was always ready to take the credit. Effective scrutiny had taught Ellie how to understand her friends and their approach to relationships. It was not something that just happened, it was an activity, a kind of operation that was dealt with there and then. When the young man smiled at Tiz and she looked into dark brown eyes in a tanned smiling face she did not move, not by so much as an inch. 'You did this?' his voice drawled in admiration. He took hold of her arm and walked with her across the grass enthusiastically chatting. When would normal conversation resume for her, Ellie grieved. When would her speech be a two-way partnership with neither side dominating? She watched them walk towards the barn which lay in the hollow; the girls remained behind at a discreet distance. 'I don't trust him,' stated Boo. 'His eyebrows join in the middle.' The sun was setting as the tall Italian and the slender girl with an accumulation of body piercings and tattoos returned to the bus, her face transformed by lovemaking. Ellie was close to tears.

It seemed as if the town never slept. It occurred to Ellie that the group were becoming more interesting and inventive and playing off each other, throwing in little changes and influencing each others' moods. They often invented things and then believed in them. She could never fully share what they had, but she understood the mirror relationship they had with each other and envied it.

By 2.30am the party had moved to the top of the hill and the last note had been played. The noise of firecrackers rose above the shouts of revellers, making it impossible for Ellie, Mustard and Gary to sleep. The rest celebrated until dawn.

'More trouble is caused in the world by bloody Italians than anybody,' Bas complained at breakfast.

'I thought it was the French you disliked,' quipped Rev.

'And the Italians,' Bas continued. 'They drive like maniacs

and don't like work.' Tiz sat on the steps of the bus munching cereal, gazing across the field now strewn with cans, bottles and tents sagging loosely under the weight of accumulated water. It had rained heavily during the morning but most were too overhung to notice.

'Italians are passionate. They treat their women to a language of romance,' she said dreamily.

'Anyway what's your gripe? Somebody have a go at you?' asked Cheddar.

'Yes, and I bloody well sorted him.' He failed to mention who it was.

There was no rush to leave Italy, Mustard informed them. Boo cooked vegeburgers served with long, thin Italian breadsticks and spaghetti. Fab had spent some time retching over the pail again. 'This argument you had, Bas,' Rev began. 'What did you say it was all about?' Rev intended to keep pressing.

'I didn't. Some Eytie wanted his money back on the shirt I sold him. No way, I said. Genuine Man United shirts, nothing wrong with 'em.'

'Let's have a look,' Gary opened the cellophane removing the red and white shirt and stretched it over the mattress. 'Are they all like this?' he asked. 'Because if so there is a spelling mistake. The E is missing from Manchester. Look – MANCHSTER.' Uncontrollable with laughter, Boo and Tiz paused in the washing-up. Little did they know that they hadn't heard the end of it. 'If you are going to succeed in the world then you should be wise in who you deal with,' advised Gary.

Bas rose, thrusting his face at the girls. 'Shut up,' he bellowed. They collapsed in a heap.

Ellie chose to sit with Mustard, her favourite seat, on the journey to Austria. His route had been expertly planned and pinned above the dashboard and he appreciated her silence when he needed to concentrate. The girls were discussing food. 'Eating in Austria is a nightmare,' complained Tiz. 'Food is loaded with fat, salt and cholesterol but at least they have decent supermarkets. Last time we ended up with noodles and those tiny yellow mushrooms, do you remember?'

Graz, the second largest of Austria's cities, was alive with energetic nightlife when they arrived. Customs had not posed a problem and they made their way to a campsite where they had the use of a laundry, shower and even a pool. In the early morning they all explored the gently winding streets but it was cool and they were directed by Tiz to Mangolds where they rested in the cafe among the students. 'Bas made a pig of himself, as usual, this time with a rich chocolate cake layered with marmalade,' Boo relayed to Mustard. 'And we have brought some back for you.'

The intimacy that Ellie and Gary had shared on the first evening in Paris had petered out. She no longer felt that she had his protection, she was streetwise he had told her. There was little curiosity about her whereabouts or who she was with; it annoyed and upset her. It was almost as if he had lost interest. He had a lot on his mind and he was tired, perhaps. Why did he not express his admiration or concern for her anymore? Should she suggest a walk?

They headed out into the grassy slopes and soon reverted to the routine of his gentle approach and her undivided attention. They walked down the long, steep bank towards the river and he held her hand while they kept each other upright. She wanted to tell him that it had been over a year since they met, that she had grown fond of him, that she was trying to distance herself from him to give him space. Was it her imagination or were they closer in that first meeting in the squalid but riotous place filled with babble and exotic spices? She needed his warmth to envelop her again before her heart became cold.

His conversation centred on any subject other than her. 'We are here for a couple more nights; I'm not sure whether anyone is keeping you up to date. If you have time you should visit the park on the top of Schlosstiege up the zigzagging stone steps built by the Russian prisoners during World War 1!' He dragged it out reluctantly it seemed. She stared at the reflections of the trees in the water; she was hurting. Yet despite his aloofness Ellie was conscious of his kindness and his infinite amount of patience towards her, a human creature responding to him in silence.

His first steps up the bank were shaky; tucking his tee shirt into his torn jeans, he faltered. Behind the indication of fragility she knew was a steel-like strength.

CHAPTER SIXTEEN

"Silence is wisdom when speaking is folly." (Spanish.)

'Do you like it? How about I give you a Grad?' laughed Boo. Tiz was cropped; a sandy brown replaced the damson. The bus tilted on the uneven road. They had vacated the campsite which had proved too expensive.

'Quit whilst you are ahead,' prattled Tiz. 'Anyway I intend having more tattoos in Hungary and maybe another piercing in my eyebrow.' Boo brushed loose hairs from her shoulders. Ellie sat on the grass beside her.

'Why don't you have one, Ellie, a rose or a butterfly? It doesn't hurt.'

From the window came Fab's voice, 'Don't you believe her, Ellie, it does.'

'Worth it, though,' smiled Boo.

'Oh, come on, I'll treat you.' Tiz who could talk with equal vivacity on every subject was very convincing but Ellie wasn't so sure.

A succession of attempts had been waged with pertinacity to encourage Cheddar on stage. 'Have some sympathy, he hates performing and anyway he doesn't practise,' Boo argued.

'He won't do it. I'm telling you he's like a scared rabbit. Anyway banging your head against a brick wall only means that you end up with a headache,' Bas said. After several glasses of Gosser Bier and womanly guile Cheddar crawled on stage and gave his first performance before a wild audience in a large Austrian campus near the Hungarian border. The first step had been taken, he was a hero.

It was a long drive to Hungary's Northern Upland and Mustard was feeling tetchy. There had been little chance of sleep after the gig and his leg was playing up again. 'Can't wait to see Budapest,' said Tiz. 'To get my tattoo done.'

Mustard shouted above the noise of the engine. 'Sorry, we don't touch Budapest. We're heading for Eger.'

'Not going to Budapest? You are joking.' Tiz was furious.

She appealed to Gary. 'Why are we by-passing Budapest?'

Gary put down his book. 'Because we have two gigs close to Eger and the route is already mapped out.'

Bas rubbished the idea. 'Hang on, who's in charge of the line-up anyway? Since when has Mustard decided on anything?'

'He didn't make the decision. I did.' Gary remained calm but there was a defiant note in his voice. 'Listen, while the rest of you are brilliant at what you do on stage, give me credit for doing my homework. Budapest doesn't feel very Hungarian; it has neon-bedecked Western companies, Las Vegas lights and capitalist ideas and the streets are dirty.'

'You suck, Gary, do you know that?' Bas was challenging him but Gary had to retain control. To climb down now would have been disastrous but physically Bas could easily have won.

'Do I?' He pulled himself up from his seat and moved forward. The bus swayed and Mustard manoeuvred the roundabout. 'In that case here is the itinerary. I'll leave it all to you.' With as little ceremony as possible he passed over the briefcase to Tiz and nodded in the direction of Bas.

Tiz groaned. 'Him. In control? He couldn't organise a prayer meeting in the Vatican.' With a hefty shove she pushed Bas to the rear of the bus, where he all but collapsed on a bunk. There was a sigh of relief and the briefcase was returned to its owner.

Ellie was shaking; life with the band was a continual series of surprises sprinkled with crises. The rest had stayed silent and only Mustard was heard to mutter, 'Must admit that was a bit dodgy while it lasted.'

The sourness of Bas disappeared at the mention of The Valley of the Beautiful Women. These vibrant wine cellars where visitors and locals are seduced with infectious friendliness are at the heart of Eger. After an overnight stop they arrived shortly after 11am. They settled to lunch in a narrow clearing in the volcanic hillside in Hungary's red wine capital. But conversation was stilted and emotions still raw between Bas and Gary. Fab explained softly to Ellie, 'When people are shoehorned into a tight area like this it is never easy. It's best not to instigate trouble but arguments occur anyway!' Ellie sensed that Gary was becoming more nervous and less patient and during the night, listening to his shallow breathing and spasmodic movements, she wondered if this lifestyle was becoming a struggle. Why did she feel deeply moved to protect him?

'The valley is for people who are serious about buying wine,' explained Gary. 'But the smart thing to do is to enjoy all the samples and buy one or two bottles at the end.' Moving from one smoky cellar to another through tunnels filled with tipsy people, they settled on benches, clutching plastic cups of Medoc and Medina. The custom of pushing coins into the spongy fungus on the cellar walls was ignored whilst Boo reminded them that it is unlucky to pass a wine bottle in anything but a sunwise direction. 'What a load of old cod's wallop!' belched Bas. Ellie had sampled her first taste of real wine (the Communion was redcurrant usually) and longed for a breath of fresh air. Heady and blinking in the bright sun, they sauntered back to the bus, waving a bottle apiece and followed by Bas, who banged litter bins brazenly and staggered on.

Bas collapsed on the grass like a sack of potatoes. His mood had mellowed and he had forgiven Tiz for taking his photograph earlier when he was changing the gas cylinder while wearing only his Y fronts. She worked ambitiously at her photography. 'They are not just snaps, you know,' she told Fab. 'They are works of art.' Fab nodded.

She plumped her pillow and stretched out on the springy grass. She had limited her intake of wine as well as her food, continuing a weekly regime of a day's fasting and hoped that this would be a gentle restorative from feeling sick. It was the turn of Tiz and Boo to prepare the meal, she could rest for a while longer.

It was the Bull's Blood that almost killed Bas. Eight bands took part in the night's performance and the cellar under the food warehouse was packed with students. Dark Horse played well and Cheddar, perspiring with nervousness and coaxing chords from a borrowed guitar, cowered at the back. Fab, although feeling a little delicate, sang well and there was the usual spitting and jostling and cursing. There was distortion in the speakers and some electrical fault but Rev dismissed this as normal. Gary, on the other hand, took nothing for granted. He depended on no one. Apart from the stage lighting and a couple of lights above the bar the cellar was in darkness. He pushed and elbowed his way out of the narrow entrance and into the confined space of the corridors and navigated his way along a cobbled passage into the street. There was no fire escape.

'Bikaver is featured in Hungarian legend in giving the soldiers strength in their fight against the Turks in 1552,' stated Gary to Rev much later. 'They downed barrels of it; they call it Bull's Blood.'

'How much did Bas drink?' enquired Rev.

'The whole bottle that he brought from the Valley plus cans of beer from the bus and who knows what else?'

Rev sighed. 'He lost it completely, you know. OK, so the prat should not have thrown the bottle onto the stage, but we've dealt with these morons in the past. It was just unfortunate that Bas kicked it into the faulty circuit! He rubbed his head. 'I felt the flames before I saw them. Hell we were so lucky, Gary, thanks to you!'

Ellie watched the two of them in hushed conversation back on the bus. She recalled with fear the wall of flame at the rear of the stage and Gary's yell for her to get out of the door. She froze as she saw him stride across the room and jump onto the platform. Then he and Rev helped Bas through the cellar, dragging him by his trousers out of the entrance into the corridor and along the cobbled passage.

Suddenly she found herself face to face with people hemming her in and smoke began pouring into the doorway. She was short of breath which turned into a spasm of raucous coughing and her eyes were smarting. She felt strong hands pulling her and she pushed and booted anything that was in her way. They arrived at the bus in a state of exhaustion and Gary was still holding onto her, reassuring her. They were spared from any major injuries and the fire was quickly extinguished. However the incident healed all wounds and only Fab seemed to be affected by a little dizziness.

Bas had slipped comfortably into the unknown. He was not to surface till the afternoon by which time he would be at the mercy of a man he had maligned. It was not a happy position to be in but it was unlikely that Bas would give it much thought. As Fab had philosophised earlier to Jan in one of her cynical moods, 'Never explain – your friends do not need it and your enemies will not believe you anyway.'

Ellie awoke a little after 11am. Gary and Rev were already deep in conversation and around her she could hear the sound of regular breathing. Rev leapt from the bus, eager to begin his long walk; every movement was quick and purposeful. Gary, on the other hand, grabbed a cushion and spread his legs on the grass, his back against the step. Behind the curtain Ellie dressed quickly and quietly then washed in the bowl in an effort to eradicate the stench of smoke which clung to her clothes and the sleeping bag. She was hoping for a few moments alone with Gary just to say thank you. How she wished she could be herself and speak her mind. Instead she knelt behind him and put her arms around his neck; he placed a hand on hers and helped her down the steps. One word, one word of encouragement, of closeness, that was all Ellie wanted. Did he realize what sort of reassurance she was seeking?

'Let's see what you can do with a man who is prepared?' challenged Bas, leaning over Boo and pulling at her hair as she lay in bed. She lunged at his chest with her tiny fist.

'Shift, move, you great ape. What do you think you are playing at?' An outburst of aggressive laughter greeted her question and he breathed out stale wine into the warm air.

'I recommend we visit Eger Castle today, if you are all up to it,' Gary paused. Ellie and Cheddar finished the washing-up and Fab struggled to finish her grapefruit.

'I'm giving it the thumbs down,' Bas yawned.

'Naw, seen one castle seen them all.' Cheddar sniffed.

'I think we'll chill out,' Tiz stretched.

'OK, so you don't want to see the catacombs, the crypt, the art gallery and the wine cellar?' He had their attention. All but Mustard were persuaded and on the way became embroiled in wit, argument and discussion and applied sun cream in the heat of the day. The 15th century paintings in the gallery were an inspiration to Tiz and a collection of torture equipment in the dungeon exhibition was said to inspire sadists and masochists alike. The wine-tasting had not lost its attraction but the consumption was considerably less.

This ducking and diving of conditioning and training with alcohol was a serious part of being on tour, Rev declared. On the other hand it was possible simultaneously to enjoy all the pleasures of temperance, too, decided Ellie. "I think I am so fortunate," she wrote to Gran, "that I don't worry anymore. I know I can travel further afield with confidence among friends who look after me. I miss you but I am sure that this is what you would wish for me, the freedom to make my own decisions and to live without fear." Perhaps she needed to be more explicit but dare not. She wanted to say that she was not in fear of being seduced or of being led astray; not in fear of the unknown or in fear of change. She prayed that Gran would read between the lines. How the situation had changed since leaving home. She had replaced the breeding ground of jealousy and resentfulness with protective vigilance. Postcards were sent to Jan, Maggie,

June and Golnar; it was another task but not a chore.

'They are in cosmic alignment, you know, Paris and Presov, on the 49th parallel,' Gary explained. No one bothered to reply; there was never any show of pretence; if they weren't interested it was ignored. On one of his many walks Rev had chanced upon a football and last evening had been spent tackling and challenging. Men versus women and Gary and Fab in goal with Mustard the unwilling referee. There were rules, red cards and rude and sexist language and an eventual score of 10–2 to the men. The high score was partly due to the fact that Fab had little intention of being hit by the ball and swung her body the opposite way.

Today they were aiming for Presov and Slovakia and friends who had offered them a small farmhouse for three days in return for a donation for the orphans in neighbouring Romania. Their first task was to stock up with fresh food and on Legionarova they discovered a Tesco supermarket where Bas was rudely accosted by the Grocery Store Attendant for not having a trolley. 'I don't shop,' he shouted. 'I'm with them,' adding, 'where's the nearest Netto?'

'You are hardly a testimony for the Brits,' cried Boo. Yet, to Ellie, going ridiculously and delightfully out of control was what Bas was all about, it was him being excited.

They had been on the road about half an hour when the farmhouse came into view. The bus descended through open land without a trace of a hedge or fence, the road hardly visible through overgrown weeds and moss. It took some time before they recovered from the discomfort of their descent and then Mustard had to steer clear of the great open tracks in the mud. They shuddered to a halt. Through pebbles, gravel and grit they picked their way carefully towards the front of the house and into the entrance. It was overgrown and sadly neglected. Tentatively Gary pushed open the door. Without further ado Boo pushed past him and stepped inside. 'Come on, it's not too bad.' She disappeared, her footsteps echoing on the stone floor. 'The floorboards squeak and one of the beams is loose but it's OK.'

'Oh, well, that's alright then,' quipped Bas sarcastically.

'You've changed your tune, thought you hated old buildings.'

'Not with ivy growing on the walls,' she smiled. 'Ivy protects the occupants from evil.'

'I give up,' Bas grunted.

Someone had cleaned the four main rooms and provided benches and chairs. Logs were stacked under the back porch beside a rocking chair. Paraffin lamps provided light and there was a loft with an anchored ladder.

An ancient water heater hung precariously on the kitchen wall above a grey stone sink but the place was reasonably clean and free from bugs. 'We could all do with a bit of elbow room,' uttered Fab. Meals were prepared in the bus but they settled in front of the fire discussing the dis-commodious aspects of travelling and the choice of songs for the Romanian charity appeal. Here we are, decided Ellie, in different rooms, with similar resolutions – foreigners, yet completely at home. A murmur of birds gathered among the rustle of the trees and the sun moved behind the cloud shaping it as a symbol of change.

'If you are ever at a loss to liven up a flagging cause you produce a photograph,' suggested Tiz. 'We'll take a few pictures of crying babies and have them developed in time for the gig.'

'Anyone seen a loo?' Fab crossed her legs like an infant.

'Over there.' At least it was accessible, there were no bushes to climb over or ditches to straddle. The sensitiveness and embarrassment of nature's calling disappeared on the first night on the road.

The floor was strewn with fresh straw and the toilet was at the far end of what might have been a pen or sty. A large zinc bathtub hung on nails on the whitewashed wall and close by the snecked door was a free-standing tap and bucket. 'I gather that you fill the bucket, do your ablutions and then swill it away,' said Boo.

'Better than nothing,' decided Tiz. It was hard not to feel a sense of optimism. The men were arranging their beds in the farmhouse and the girls would have the bus to themselves.

'The Slovaks have got it sussed, you know. To have a national dish which is vegetarian is really great. It's a sort of dumpling-type pasta with a thick covering of goat's cheese, Ellie, you'll love it,' Tiz enthused.

'Except when they put bacon in it,' complained Boo. It was only 10am but they had everything prepared for the evening meal.

Rev tapped on the window. 'We have a problem.'

'What's that then?' Tiz was hardly paying attention.

'It's Gary; he's had a rotten night; he's falling all over the place.' First down the steps, pushing Rev aside, was Ellie who ran as fast as she could towards the house.

Bas stood like a sentry at the door to Gary's room. 'He's really sick. Worse than before. Should we get a doctor?'

The sun was shining directly on Gary's gaunt features and his eyes were closed. The bed was damp with perspiration and his legs were jerking spasmodically. Ellie closed the wooden shutters and laid the palm of her hand on his forehead. He was burning up. She glanced at Bas. If only she dare ask for help; was this to be the defining moment of her life? Bas stepped forward and she waved him back with an impatient gesture, ran down the stairs and filled a jug with cold water. She used a tea towel to bathe Gary's face and neck.

The movement in his muscles stopped and he gripped her hand; she felt a huge power of faith, of trust, of love and of sorrow. She knew Gary was showing signs of an impending illness; what if the symptoms raged on? His eyes remained closed and Ellie remained with him until he fell into a deep sleep.

Rev had discovered a side road leading to the main highway so all the bumps and jolts could have been avoided. He and Mustard were willing to take Gary to hospital and Tiz called for a meeting. 'I think we should talk about this. I remember Gary saying "I don't do sick, I can handle this". Remember when we came back from Bradford?'

'That was England. This is Slovakia,' said Bas seriously.

'Look,' Rev suggested. 'We don't have a gig till tomorrow

night. Why don't we see how things go? He got better pretty quick last time.'

'Meanwhile we'll take turns to sit with him,' decided Boo.

But it was Ellie and Mustard who sat as nursemaids in front of the wonderful old fireplace, listening to the logs crackling, eating baguettes and drinking cappuccino. Mustard perched uncomfortably on a cane chair reading fanzines while resting his head on the hard frame. Ellie offered him a pillow, he refused. He had no understanding of luxury, she decided. He chose not to sleep in a bunk on the bus, he preferred two seats shoved together.

She was reading one of her favourite books, "The Wind in the Willows", and smiled, putting their own situation in context as she read "Late in the evening, tired and happy and miles from home, they drew up on a remote common far from habitations, turned the horse loose to graze and ate their simple supper sitting on the grass by the side of the cart."

Mustard had fallen asleep; his lower lip trembled and his moustache quivered as he blew out each breath, disturbing the breadcrumbs that decorated his beard.

Earlier the friends had set out for Svatoplukova where they were to meet some happy locals at "The Thirsty Monk". Ellie crept quietly up the stairs to check on Gary. He was sleeping and his colour had returned. 'I don't do sick. I can handle this,' he had said. Ellie sent an arrow prayer to God. "Please help him."

By noon next day he had recovered sufficiently to eat a meagre lunch although his legs were weak and he was still experiencing a loss of balance. He apologised. 'There's no need,' Bas sighed. 'But you missed a great night out. If these people are oppressed it doesn't show.'

'They're not oppressed, they are coming to grips with progress, they have emerged as an independent country,' Gary replied.

'What I enjoy most about travelling,' declared Fab, 'is that you encounter so many different people with varied psychological levels.' She was applying make-up in front of a mirror propped up against a tree stump in the shade of the bus. 'Do you think I have the slightest resemblance to Siouxsie? They had incredible style, Billy Idol and Debbie, pity it's so long ago. She was such a neat, trim person.' Tiz brushed Boo's hair into a chignon and fastened it with clips.

'She shouldn't have worn the swastika, it didn't help the cause.'

'Yes, well, I have to agree there,' Boo echoed the sentiments. 'We wear bizarre clothes and live in squats, some of us are highly aggressive, like Bas for example, but we do not endorse violence.'

'Where are they going?'

Striding out across the field, Rev and Cheddar were deep in conversation, Bas a little way behind. Tiz yelled after them. 'Where are you going?'

'To catch the bus to the station. In ten minutes.' The air turned blue with abusive language with the odd word like selfish, ignorant, mindless and inconsiderate thrown in. There was a mad scramble to put together money bags, camera and timetables, a quick wave to Gary and a sprint across the grass. They chased after the bus which pulled up short after Rev flagged it down and all four girls sank exhausted onto the back seat.

It was not easy photographing babies, especially babies on the move. No one in the band had any idea how to speak Slovak and mothers with pushchairs were highly suspicious of their motives. Tiz was about to give up when Boo noticed, across the square, a young mother seated at a table with a lively baby in a pram. Pigeons were pecking and cooing under the table and mother was asleep, her head on her arm and her hand on the pram handle. Tiz concealed herself behind a wisteria-covered trellis and snapped whilst the girls stood guard. A bee was ready to land on the baby's chin and he/she (unaware of it) gurgled happily.

'Child homelessness continues to be a problem in Romania and I applaud you for what you are doing tonight. You will be OK without me.' Gary was sorting out photographs for

Tiz whilst rocking himself backwards and forwards in the cool shelter of the porch. 'How about this one?'

'We waited nearly three hours for these to be developed, but worth it don't you think?' Tiz blue-tacked them onto a piece of cardboard, a cute collection of a healthy, bonny baby, below which the caption read "WHOSE BABY"?

It was a heartwarming experience to have raised so much money with such little effort. The baby, looking down on the teeming mass of gyrating bodies, would never know the impact it had from its place on the backcloth. It would never know why Fab seemed to be on the verge of tears and why she ran off mid performance with head bowed. Nor would it ever know that the money raised would help provide food and medicine for babies in need. The memories of that evening would keep coming back to Ellie for it would be a baby that later in her life was to bring her both heartache and joy, and something that she was totally unprepared for.

Mustard had been told of a short-cut back to the farm and they passed rows of cottages, pastures and an urban meadow. They could not resist the temptation to gloat on their success even though it seemed that the Romanians had to beg on account of love. 'We all beg, we just dress it up, make it sound different like solicit, plead, humble ourselves,' sighed Boo.

'It's still begging.'

'Some people tonight had almost nothing to give,' added Tiz.

Only the lights from the glowing fire could be seen in the house. The men, relatively sober, left the girls to sleep. Ellie, concerned about the darkness and Gary, slipped a short jacket over her pyjamas before approaching the house. The wind whistled in the tall grass across the field and scooped up the dust in the tracks. It was as if every star was on a sleep out and Ellie wondered if somewhere there was a charmed birth taking place not far away. 'Gary is fine,' Cheddar told her. 'He's asleep. He's much better.'

Every word, every thought expressed on this hour before dawn would keep returning like a boomerang to Ellie. From the moment she heard the sobs and saw the tears to the hugs and the kisses and the promise, she shared Fab's pain. She was huddled on the bare boards of the porch, her hands grasping her knees, her make-up smeared across her face. 'Ellie,' it was a whisper. 'Sit down. I have something to tell you, only you!' Fab wiped away a tear. 'I'm pregnant!' Ellie hesitated, then held her close. This was foreign to her; she could soak up people's troubles by the bucketful, listen to problems, confident that nothing more was expected of her, but she had never had a close friend nor had an intimate relationship which involved tactile moments of affection. 'This is a shock but if we keep it between the two of us it will be fine.' Fab blew her nose. 'I'm upset mainly because I have wanted everything to be simple. Now it's complicated. It means letting go of the old life and preparing for a new one!' She kissed Ellie on the cheek. 'Tiz and Boo will say I am stupid and want to know who and when and where. It won't make any difference. Ignorance hasn't got me into this mess, carelessness has.' They stood up and Fab heaved a sigh of relief. 'Anyway all families need new blood and we are a sort of family, I suppose.' They walked towards the bus. 'Promise me, Ellie, you won't tell anyone. Not even Gary.' Ellie felt trapped. With secrets came responsibility. More secrets she could do without.

She had to admit that she hadn't reacted too well, she was only a sounding block after all and there was no mention of the baby's future, if indeed it had one. She pulled back the curtain, breathing in the smell of the grasses, stretching out her legs on the comfortable bunk, and prayed.

'I see a grand city whose glory will touch the stars,' Gary quoted from the travel brochure. They were on their way to Prague. Everyone was in good spirits despite the intense heat on the bus. It was on the left bank of the River Vitava where they planned to stay for a couple of days but first Gary was in search of an Internet cafe. 'They are incredibly fast and cheap,' he explained to Cheddar who was completely ignorant and innocent of all things technological but which Gary found spellbinding. This done it was leisure time and the labyrinthine medieval streets which straddled the river led them to Wenceslas Square and the umbrella following bands of tourists. Bas weaved his way until he heard the familiar English and they all followed, enjoying a freebie tour of the old town.

They rested in a rustic graveyard, bodies turning golden. Hot bodies but cool tempers. They bought tickets at the kiosk and boarded the Metro for the cafe Lotus, a restaurant recommended to them in Slovakia. With its unique organic menu and delicious Czech soups it was well worth the journey.

It is not enough for some people to share friendship. Fab was taking Ellie's sympathetic approach too seriously and closeness brought with it complications. 'As long as I can stick with you I won't be scared. I know these things.' What happened to the streetwise front, the stronger than thou attitude, the personal rebellion? Ellie pondered.

The evenings were cool and they settled amiably back in the bus. It had been exhausting wandering the alleyways of Josefov and exploring the maze of uphill streets but they could relax before the gig tomorrow. Rev and Mustard chose to take a walk by the river. Tiz went in search of wildlife to sketch and paint and Boo washed her smalls and hung them on a makeshift line between the trees. Gary and Bas were sorting out the currency and Fab, who complained of an aching back, climbed into her bunk.

Ellie sighed, sat cross-legged on the grass, and returned to Mr. Toad and "The Wind in the Willows". Cheddar gave no thought to Ellie's desire for peace and quiet and chatted on about youth being the voice of discontent. 'I inherited this way of thinking from my mother; she had nothing good to say about her generation. It's up to you, she used to say. What are you reading?' Ellie slipped in a bookmark and he read out loud: 'They set off up the road on their mission of mercy, Badger leading the way.' He stopped. 'It's not just for children, is it?' He sniffed. 'Can I borrow it when you've finished with it?'

****

It was along the route of one of his exercise walks that Rev saw Angelica. She was separating feuding chickens and feeding the calves. He was too far away to see her clearly, a white-clothed slim figure in a world of green acres surrounded by clucking hens. He sat astride the gate watching her move quickly and expertly, coaxing the lone cow away from the fence and driving it skilfully to be milked.

Her low voice carried in the slight breeze and the cow responded with moos of animal sympathy. These moments were important to Rev; a complete contrast to the deafening music and the yelling of Bas and Boo as they bludgeoned each other with profanities.

The sun was moving slowly across the fields and dipping gently behind the farm buildings. It was time to go but Rev was curious. His long strides carried him to the main building, difficult to distinguish from the rest of the outhouses, apart from a much wider door and huge overhanging porch. Before he raised his hand to knock she stood in front of him; large grey-green eyes studied him intently and she gave him a smile which would have improved even the darkest mood. It lit up her face. She huddled her arms around her and spoke in Czech and then in Russian, then she shrugged her shoulders. The phrase book was buried in the back pocket of his jeans. 'Dobry den,' he stammered. 'Mluvite anglicky? Nemiuvim cesky.'

She bit her lip. 'Very good,' she laughed. She translated. 'Hello. Do you speak English? I do not speak Czech.'

In the kitchen she offered him homemade biscuits and sweet pancakes washed down with Velvet beer. The sky darkened, they were alone and he had no desire to leave. He suspected that he had been subjected to a spell which comes and goes but which is never spent. He was determined to return the following day; she would be ready, she promised.

'Where the hell have you been?'

'We've been worried sick.'

'We have been imagining all sorts of things.'

'Bloody hell, Rev, you cut it fine this time.'

He pretended to be startled. Everyone except Ellie chorused their disapproval but she could see beyond the excuses, he had a look brought about by wine or desire, it could be either or both but it remained hidden behind a wall of silence and a wry smile.

They sank into a well of arguments about the amount of time it would take to get to the venue and what would happen if they were too late. Fab was irritated at the indolence of Cheddar in the middle of all the activity but a mischievous smile softened her face as he complimented her. She certainly had a bloom about her. Had the forthcoming event prompted a choice? Did she see it as a threat or a blessing? Ellie wondered if she would share her decision; it would have to be soon.

'I'm not overkeen on all the security here,' complained Bas. 'They're in yer face, breathing down yer neck. Too much officialdom.' Somehow he sensed that he had been put in his place by a pompous female bouncer when she removed the bottle of lager from him as he was about to perform. Later in the bar at Molly Malone's at Vezenska they challenged each other to a Guinness drinking bout after discovering that it was cheaper than in Ireland.

Overturned beds and sewing machines doubled as tables and Bas settled down in the cosy bar with his new girl on his knee and his shirt in a pool of Guinness at his feet. 'It's the double F, Ellie,' Cheddar grinned as they leaned against the bar. 'Foreign Fling, Tiz calls it. Everyone has one apparently. Well, nearly everyone.' It would be painful for Ellie to discover that Gary had succumbed but tonight he was on the bus with Mustard planning the next trip over the border.

The road swung between rifts and rocks until the bus shook and Mustard brought it almost to a crawl and into a field of poppies.' They are so beautiful,' Tiz whispered.

'Corn grows better with a few poppies in it,' Boo declared.

'How about we stop here for a bite to eat?' Gary suggested. They had to double back to reach Zakopane in Poland, he told them, but it would be worth it. He was careful to keep everyone informed; he studied the guide books, made notes and managed. Rev stretched out in a sea of red dreaming of Angelica.

Angelica was still smiling when Rev greeted her, the same warm glow which lifted the colour of her cheeks and lit up her eyes. She moved quickly and a little nervously in the large kitchen reaching up on open shelves for the bowl in which she served dumplings and goat cheese. She lived alone but an elderly man and his son helped on a regular basis, she told him. At college she had been taught English as her third language and laughingly admitted to listening to the BBC. What a blessing, Rev sighed with relief. It would have been frustrating not to be able to follow her conversation. She was comfortably dressed in a long, shapeless pinafore dress and no shoes, despite the stone flags and the draught sweeping under the floor.

'My mother left when I was very young,' she confided, 'and now lives in the heart of the Bohemian countryside. I am not angry or afraid but I do get lonely sometimes.' Time was what Rev needed; time to learn more about her; time for her to understand him; time to stir up love until it pleased her. She stared at him across the table, her hands folded in front of her and a tabby cat lapping cream from a saucer at her feet. Here was a country girl who had no knowledge of high fashion but had scrubbed and scented and cooked just for him. It was obvious, the anticipation of love was etched on her face and he wanted to share with her the valleys back home which were as wild and as wonderful as their desire for each other.

Zakopane is set in a valley surrounded by alpine meadows, and is the gateway to the Tatra Mountains. It had been raining for most of the morning and Ellie settled on her bunk with her book, listening to the water pounding on the roof and watching it dripping into pouches on the windows. Life after Molly Malone's was a great deal quieter. Bas and Rev did not appear until morning light; their life was drifting the way they wanted, Ellie sighed. Mustard handled the bus with dexterity. The rain was heavier now and the stalls selling garden ornaments which lined the roadside looked bedraggled and bogged down.

They had been on the road for less than an hour when Mustard pulled gently into the side. A couple of hitchhikers, a man and a woman, hailed him down and almost fell up the steps in their haste to escape the downpour. Her long, orange dreadlocks hung like melting icicles onto her jacket and her companion removed his hat, revealing a shock of green hair. Their English was sufficient only to thank him and they stood at the front of the bus shivering and dripping.

Suddenly Gary, who had been sleeping, did such a crazy thing. He lurched towards the couple with no regard for safety and yelled at Mustard. It was an outburst of inexplicable rage. 'What the hell do you think you are doing? Pull in, pull in now.' He clenched his fist, thrusting it into Mustard's arm. The bus drew to a halt. Mustard sat back, his face white and Gary's eyes, unflinchingly angry, stared into the quivering moustache. 'You never, ever pick up anybody, do you understand?' The couple were frightened and confused. Everyone else was shocked and nervous. Bas stepped forward but Tiz pulled him back. Gary unlocked the door and kicked it open. 'Out,' he repeated over and over. They stumbled down the steps and into the deluge. Through the rear window Ellie saw the two figures huddle together and her eyes filled with tears.

There was a long silence followed by mutterings and insinuations. It was a stranger who slumped in the seat next to Mustard. This inappropriate behaviour was foreign to them. Their Gary was kind, calm and in control. Ellie saw another face and recognised the seriousness of an illness she didn't understand, and one she couldn't name. Tiz offered him a drink of water, he almost choked.

It was a solemn group which left the bus whilst it was searched by the Polish Customs and a grim-faced group that surrendered their passports for over an hour. It was at this point that Gary offered an apology and an explanation.

'Don't you see, the idea was for us to transport them over the border? We do not know them, their nationality, their intentions or their objectives. They could be drug dealers or any kind of criminal. You thought you were being benevolent, I think you were being stupid.'

Their fury abated when the campsite came into view. Shadowed with forests full of trees it overlooked a mountain lake. 'This,' said Fab, with an exaggerated sweep of her hand, 'is Poland. Unspoilt and beautiful.' Gary appeared to be back to normal, the girls made light of the whole affair and he and Mustard were on speaking terms once more. Ellie meanwhile wondered if he had a firm grip of the ladder and ought to watch his step.

The tent was erected behind the bus and a vegetable curry was prepared in less than 45 minutes. Gas was replenished and fresh water refilled. It was decided to visit the northern part of Zakopane and take the cable car to the top of the mountain. The market was bustling and the weather was sunny and very hot. They piled into the cable car and rose above the forest and the highlander huts and the many sheep which populate the mountain slopes. The views from the top of Zakopane were breathtaking. Why, thought Ellie, had no one ever told her how picturesque Poland was?

Gary was leaning over the parapet looking sideways at her. 'If we had our way we could stay up here forever, what do you say?' She would have replied, "Yes, the thought had been going through my head," but instead she smiled and turned away. There would be no more games. Her dreams were in his voice and his murmurings had been all around her; she had been listening but his words had confused her and left merely an echo in her mind. The six friends opted to ride on the dry bobsleigh run leaving Fab holding court with Gary. Rumours about epilepsy and bizarre foreign virus diseases were discussed in whispers but rejected when his vitality returned.

Fab slipped her arm around Ellie as they walked through the square to the Pizzeria restaurant. 'We've been talking about you,' she began 'Gary and me.' Ellie felt the pressure of her hot hand on her bare arm and squirmed. Her aversion to close contact had not totally diminished. 'We're not blind, not by a long chalk. We both feel that you have been through an extreme episode in your life but come through with flying colours.' Gossip is within everyone's reach but Ellie resented the smug, intrusive approach of Fab and the presumption that all was well. Ellie was not about to exchange secrets. She pulled away to join the others and caught up with them in the shade of the trees.

The tent was cool and after spending over three hours in the sun, a welcome respite. The setting sun gave way to dusk and the lights from the camp flickered, throwing glimmering silhouettes on the canvas. They had showered and the sweet smell of jasmine and talc hung in the air. Not one scent of masculinity and they giggled and stretched, imagining summers yet to come. Ellie prayed and pondered as Fab rubbed the palms of her hands over her precious bump, and closed her eyes.

It was a fair distance to Lodz but no one appeared to want to rush. They ate a breakfast of grapefruit, raisins and peanut butter sandwiches and fresh orange, packed up the tent and prepared to move. Bas was suffering from sunburn on his head and shoulders and Boo applied cream without sympathy. Ellie sat beside Mustard.

Poland's second largest city had a good reputation for musical appreciation and they had two gigs lined up. Internet access was the first priority for Gary and afterwards a decent site near the gig. At Presto Pizza, a quiet, informal, inexpensive restaurant, they sampled a "San Francisco" pizza topped with peaches and bananas and Bas, having had two large helpings, promptly dozed off at the table. 'Pig,' snarled Boo.

There was a diversion leading to the Jewish Cemetery and Synagogues and Tiz, who had paid it a visit on her last tour, quietly described it to Ellie. 'It is a place that rends the heartstrings; there are hundreds of thousands of graves all wonderfully engraved. The cemetery sprawls for miles and the poor Jews who died in the ghetto are buried in small marked graves. Lodz should be very proud of their people and what they have overcome. We just can't imagine what they have been through.' The occupants of the bus maintained a respectful silence as they drove slowly by. Ellie would have said "I suppose religious experience of faith is what people in times like these hold onto, Catholicism or whatever, who knows?"

Klub Fabryka had enormous steel doors and a warehouse atmosphere. The cultural aspects of Lodz had not gone unnoticed and there were students sipping, smoking and dancing to the loud, grinding music which had been gradually reaching momentum. Their fans approached the bus as it drew into the waste ground behind the club and Bas and company were almost dragged into the factory theme bar to sample the draught beer. Poland bathes in vodka but Boo was the only one to sample it; she proved to be the most popular member of them all. After a successful gig they partied until dawn and the following day planned to do it all over again.

It was Tiz who rose early and accompanied by Ellie, Boo and Gary, visited the Lodz Fine Arts Museum, home to works by the artist Max Ernst. It was quiet and cool in the galleries and although not all of the pictures appealed to her Tiz was impressed and wandered off by herself. Boo sat very still on the floor, drinking iced water and nursing her sore head.

Gary watched Ellie cross the room from his seat on the bench. Her long, fair hair, bleached almost white by the sun, fell into waves against the golden brown skin and her shorts clung to her long legs. She is so beautiful, he thought. He felt that he was falling back into the well of adolescence, dreaming of the depths in her blue eyes and craving for affection. Dare he place his faith in miracles? He could only be as strong as his body allowed. Ellie was shrewd and perceptive; he felt that she was weighing up the situation as his incapacity progressed.

As a youth entered the gallery she turned her head. He

walked over to a canvas covered in silvery reflections, a landscape with a moonlit sky and a lake. Slowly, deliberately she sidled towards him. They stared at the picture together, then he spoke to her in Polish. Ellie smiled that rare smile when she appeared to have a sudden revelation yet she could not have understood what he said. He was tall and he stooped to kiss her on both cheeks and then on her hand, continuing the conversation still holding her hand and pointing to the painting.

It was the first time that Gary had seen her attempt to describe her lack of speech with intimate signs but it was very effective. The young man sighed and fell silent, and smiled as he captured the mischief in her eyes. Her gaze lingered as he turned and left the room. And now jealousy was another emotion to add to Gary's dilemma. Gracefully she moved towards him, pulling comic, derisive little faces at him and sat on his knee. His mind was raided by images of her; he was no expert on the wiles of the opposite sex and Ellie was a mixture of innocence and awareness; he was beginning to feel uncomfortably warm. Boo moaned in the corner, 'Can we go now?'

'The best way of sobering up is to drink as much again,' was Bas's advice to Boo.

'Would you like me to play instead?' Cheddar was gaining in confidence.

'I'll be alright.' she groaned.

'Where to this time?'

'To Sopot.'

'What's there then?' asked Rev.

Gary took a deep breath. 'Well, there's the beach for starters.'

'Well, that's alright then,' smiled Tiz.

Ellie had lost track of the days. It was easy to forget which country she was in, secluded as they were in the bus, and in between the gigs and sightseeing came hunger and tiredness. Dates and places, itineraries and currencies were left in Gary's capable hands. Individually they paid only for drinks and personal items; all meals and travel were paid for by the income from the gigs. Monies left over would be divided at the end of the tour. 'It's the best way,' Bas explained 'I can't be bothered with this euro network and zlotys and forints and crowns. Much too complicated. I like things simple, me.'

They said goodbye to the 15th century city, bustling by day and raucous by night, and drove over a beautiful bridge which arched over a lazy river flanked by flower-covered hedgerows. Ellie felt that her life had been brought out of the shadows and into the sun, from loneliness to kindliness, with hardly any effort at all.

The tent was erected on a flat area of grass close to a field where half a dozen or so horses grazed in the setting sun. Mustard parked the bus in front of a billboard secured to a large fence. 'What's it say?' enquired Rev.

'Haven't a clue,' replied Gary. 'We are alright though, we're not trespassing.' Tiz and Boo served pierogi (dumplings with potato and cheese) and a mushroom sauce and tomatoes as big as apples. It was a hot night despite the breeze but they were spared the onslaught of mosquitoes which had been troublesome earlier. The girls were argumentatively washing and drying dishes. Social relations were to commit to the verbal, sighed Ellie, but listened instead with one ear to what was being said by Gary. 'Four more gigs and we turn around for home.' Where would her home be? No. 68 she guessed.

The four girls awoke to the sound of knocking and a chorus of Polish voices; a series of hammer blows to the side of the bus and loud protestations from three angry men. Tiz poked her head out of the tent in time to see Bas, almost naked, pull himself to his full height after stepping from the bus and point his finger. The man in the brown jodhpurs and carrying a whip looked menacingly at Bas, who stepped back, eyed him coldly and asked cautiously, 'What do you want?' The men were distracted. Four young scantily-clad young women appeared bleary eyed through the tent flap and blinked in the early morning sun.

'It's only seven o clock,' Fab whispered.

'English?' ventured the whip handler. 'Just the people we need.'

'Friend or Foe?' asked Bas sarcastically. They ignored him, they weren't paying attention, not until the girls slipped back into the tent amid giggles of laughter. The jodhpur-clad man explained a sports event was to be held later in the day in the field behind them and they were blocking the way. A gymkhana, especially for underprivileged children, but it was a first and they understood that the English were good at this sort of thing. It was decided that they would stay for a while although Bas admitted, 'I don't know a thing about horses, can't tell a forelock from a fetlock.' It didn't matter. Ellie and Tiz in borrowed jodhpurs led the horses round the field and helped the children mount and dismount. Boo related to Fab that horse brasses, charms and amulets were a defence against witches, which led the five men to take refuge in the beer tent.

It had been two years since Ellie had ridden but at the invitation of the groomsman she chose a black horse with white stockings and rode at a trot around the field. It was one memory of her childhood she did not mind recalling and Gary, glass in hand, watched with approval.

'We're only here for the pier,' chortled Rev as the bus pulled into Sopot. The longest pier on the Baltic, Gary told them. However it was hedonism not sightseeing which was uppermost in their minds, to relax in the sun and the sea and feel the salty bite of the spray on their faces and drink in the sense of well-being and fun. Too many bodies and not enough fresh air, too many restrictions and not enough space. Now behind them.

Life in the crowded bus was testing tempers. Boo had protested about Bas's unwashed clothes stuffed in plastic bags and beer-stained towels hanging from the curtains. Mustard too was under strain; it was a hard driving schedule and his leg was swollen and painful. Some people have instincts on how far to go before being pushed over the edge and with common sense and perhaps a knack of past memories Gary had timed it perfectly.

The campsite was pre-booked but there was a dispute about the size of the bus (they could not accommodate it) so a compromise was reached. They could use the facilities but had to park further along the road. 'No problem,' declared Mustard.

'At least there is a billiard hall,' claimed Bas.

They pitched the tent and Ellie's reputation as Jack-of-all-trades was confirmed. No one had consulted a memorandum on how she should be treated; no one delved too deeply into her past; no one had asked her to do anything. It had been a natural progression from the 16-year old with the slightly distant look to the self-assured young lady who secured the guy ropes with determination.

As he leaned against the bus Gary knew that he would miss these half moments just looking at her, feeling deep down how good it was to begin the day together.

'Water to gaze on or swim through, water underfoot, the air is laden with water.' Gary was in the mood for quoting poetry; he dug his feet into the hot, white sand and settled back into the deckchair. A lone gull rose and fell on the crest of a wave and voiced its disapproval at the mass of swimmers. Cheddar was beside him in boxer shorts doubling as trunks, surrounded by beach bags and towels. 'We are awarding the BA to you Cheddar,' Tiz smiled sarcastically. 'Beach Attendant.' Wit in Tiz's comments usually meant that she was happy; today everyone was in good spirits.

Gary could pick out the red of Fab's hair, the black plaits of Boo and the blonde tresses of Ellie as their heads bobbed in and out of the water. He had swum with them for a while but found it taxing, deciding instead to relax on the beach whilst they commandeered the water slide.

Before the first morning had passed in Sopot he felt a faint hope of optimism about his health. He was aware that the incident with the hitch-hikers had unsettled the group and was down to him, and that words like disgrace, scandal and shame had crackled round the bus like electrical disturbances. How could he expect them to understand? Yet with the cloudless sky, the vibrant sea, the heat of the sun

and the energy of summer he could allow time for himself
and to regenerate. Ellie turned heads in her black and white
bikini as she moved towards him like a dewy gazelle only
to find him fast asleep under the shade of the umbrella.

Sopot was a dream come true. After the beach there
were colourful shops to explore and street musicians played
outside the numerous bars. In the evening they visited the
trendy discos and drank copious amounts of Guinness and
cider. They ate from the many inexpensive food stands and
were impressed with their favourite Happy Meals Vegetarian
Kitchen with its bright yellow walls.

On the third day they stocked up with groceries at Monte
Cassino grocery store, did the laundry and prepared for the
road. Replenished, there was time for one last stroll and in
the little square in which they finally found themselves they
made a promise. Some day they would return.

'No answer is also an answer,' Rev announced. 'Well I
think so anyway.' He was muttering to himself, he often
did. No one apparently wanted to stir. Inside a stout wall
of an old construction by the riverside they flopped in the
shade. Rev, always fond of long walks and outdoor pursuits,
wanted to visit the huge medieval Harbour Crane, part of
the Central Maritime Museum, but the short ride to Gdansk
had tired them out and they were noticeably unenthusiastic.
Ellie raised her bronzed arms and Rev helped her up; her
face was tilted towards him, her sunglasses balancing on the
edge of her nose. As they walked he drank; each sentence was
truncated as he took a swig at regular intervals. It seemed
that Rev was worrying about the future. He introduced
Angelica into the conversation and his words were uttered
slowly. 'I think I might ask her to join me in England,' he
sighed. 'I dare say it could be a long process.'

Mustard had parked the bus by the river and they used
local buses to the Green Way Veggy Bar where they ate
pastas and salads washed down with beer. Then Tiz stopped
short as if she had been jerked back with a sudden force.
'It's time for another tattoo,' she exclaimed.

'Obviously not a bugle call or military display but body

art,' sniffed Cheddar sarcastically, spotting the studio across the street.

'Which one are you having, Ellie?' Tiz had chosen a Gothic design and pointed to a Japanese emblem. 'Just you, that is, a distinctive picture on your skin.' Ellie shook her head. 'Look,' Tiz suggested, shoving a catalogue under her nose. 'How about this then? Come on, it's about being unique, personal empowerment.' Ellie stood her ground. 'Or something archaic to symbolize power.' Tiz was pushed away forcibly. Ellie was becoming angry.

'Leave her alone.' Boo smiled with embarrassment. If ever there was a desire to speak it was now. Ellie felt vulnerable, sensing that this was some sort of induction ceremony and she was ready to rebel.

'You will never reach agreement,' appealed Fab. 'Anyway perhaps she is afraid of needles. Lots of people are.'

Gary then appeared in the doorway. 'Do you think that Ellie would have got this far by being afraid? Can't you understand that when she says no she means no. Stop bullying her.' Gently he asked. 'Are you alright?' She drew a deep breath and followed him outside. Normally he did not take these feminine confrontations very seriously but it was serious where Ellie was concerned. Gary knew that beyond discoveries of theories in dealing with Ellie he needed to be worldly-wise. She was complex, a mystery and a woman.

By the time the group was ready to play at the Jazz Club in Gdansk the incident had been forgotten. Gary viewed them from the balcony. It seemed that his life had been reduced to an interminable cycle of planning and touring, touring and planning. When he wasn't suppressing arguments he was causing them; he knew it was time to call a halt. They were willing, eager and daring but he was running out of steam. He would call a meeting when they arrived back at the squat; he would be brief but honest.

Boo clipped the ginger beard and trimmed the moustache and Ellie massaged Mustard's leg, which was swollen and burning. It was 2am but too hot to settle down to sleep. 'This is the heat wave to top all heat waves,' moaned

Cheddar. They sat on smooth, polished pebbles in the cold river whilst Ellie and Boo tucked Mustard into Ellie's bunk.

'I'm not sure he will be fit to drive tomorrow,' Gary hinted. 'We'll see how he is in the morning, we're going to Hel.'

They drove slowly into the sleepy village of Hel and marvelled at the heavenly wide, clean beaches. At midday they were not planning to eat. Tiz and Boo had prepared a substantial breakfast and they needed to relax, take photographs and write home. There was a special sense of piracy and history about the place. Tiz was in her element snapping the fishermen's hut, over 200 years old, she remarked, and the octagonal red lighthouse.

Ellie sat alone on the sand watching the swimmers and the sea which the mellow sunlight touched with iridescent colours. She sang softly; just to hear her own voice above the swish of the waves and the cries of the tourists. It was still there but for her ears only. She uttered words only when she dare, when she was sure of privacy. It was becoming more difficult not to speak. Losing her temper was more likely to cause her to falter, speaking her mind was something she had never been afraid of. What sort of madness had led her to make such a momentous decision?

Bas was in a rowdy, tormenting mood, hoisting Boo onto his shoulders despite her protests and heaving her into the water. Ellie stopped singing as Fab strode slowly across the sand towards her. She had merged into something ethereal and beautiful and smiled often when there was little to smile about. She looked pregnant and it suited her. How long before it became common knowledge?

It was the red brick of the Church of St Peter and Paul that stirred her memory of the chapel back home. Tiz wanted a picture, the last one of Hel, before turning in for the night. Ellie remembered her Sunday School teacher explaining to her class of six-year olds how someone had painted the walls and the door red because they were bad. The teacher spoke softly when she placed her hands on the table where the hymn books were piled neatly but her body was shaking and her eyes were filled with tears. She turned and entered the vestry and the little door squeaked shut in the darkness. Ellie was living with Gran then. Not until she moved in with her mother did she realize the consequences of what being bad meant.

Gary insisted that Mustard had ample rest before the long journey back to Lodz and later they followed the river for a couple of hours. It had broken its banks after a flood and the brooks, which should have purled and sparkled in their pebbly courses, crept thick and sluggish over slimy beds.

Ellie sat with Mustard on the homeward journey, happy that she had caressed Poland and seen the face of a country with such a turbulent past yet with a peaceful presence. Occasionally Mustard would wince; his leg was still troublesome, the road was uneven and he cursed. 'It's the journey from Hel,' he grimaced. 'Like climbing a ladder, you get a grip and then there's a dirty great gap.'

'Hi Ellie,' Cheddar called from the back of the bus. 'Come here a minute.'

'What do you want?' Bas was curious. Ellie leaned over the bunk.

Cheddar pointed to a page in "The Wind in the Willows". 'Who does this remind you of?' He read slowly, licking his lips at each comma '– on a cold winter's night, and his bedclothes had got up, grumbling and protesting they couldn't stand the cold any longer, and had run downstairs to the kitchen fire to warm themselves; and he had followed, on bare feet, along miles and miles of icy stone-paved passages, arguing and beseeching them to be reasonable.'

Bas slung a shoe at him. 'Idiot. Who but an idiot would read a kid's book?'

'It's Ellie's,' Cheddar sulked. 'That's alright then,' Bas sighed. Perhaps conversation on a journey does not sound as disparaging because of the many distractions but Ellie felt snubbed and sat poker-faced beside Mustard.

It was late evening when the tent was erected and the girls ready to settle down. But sleep would not come for Ellie. Her night seemed endless; she tried praying but her thoughts would break in with worries too small to define but large enough to keep her awake. She heard thunder in the distance and waited in anticipation for the lightning and claps of thunder but they faded away. Tapping noises came from the bus and Ellie shook a little and held her breath. It stopped. There was a creak as the door of the bus opened and closed. It would not be polite to intrude at this point, she decided, but she wasn't likely to sleep anyway.

There was a break in the cloud as she stepped out of the tent. The figure was stooped on the grassy ridge and he looked sleepy and confused. It was now about 4am and chilly. Gary was shivering, running his fingers through his tousled hair and his agitation increased when he saw Ellie. He made an effort to rise and meet her but fell back. Kneeling in front of him she saw dejection and pain in his eyes and held his hands. There was no smell of drink yet he looked intoxicated. This was, without doubt, a night of delirium, of an impossible love and an uncertain future. Bas helped put him to bed, quietly and with surprising gentleness, whilst the others slept. Are we ever prepared for what we expect from illness, Ellie wondered?

They returned to the Czech Republic with heavy hearts. 'Gary is weak, his hands are wet and clammy,' Tiz groaned. 'He's out of it.'

'Has he eaten anything?' enquired Boo.

'Food is the last thing he needs, I would imagine,' murmured Rev. They sat quietly on the bus staring at him as he lay motionless on the bunk. Mustard shook his head dolefully.

'Must admit he looks pretty rough! I suggest we move on, we don't have to do this gig, perhaps getting home is more important,' Fab suggested. They gave this some thought.

'Do you have all the details, do you know the itinerary, Mustard?' Bas enquired. He did. 'Right then, we'll do the gig tonight and move off tomorrow.'

Every detail of the countryside found an echo in Rev's heart, especially the smell of scented soap and homemade dumplings. To be out of reach of someone you love doesn't bear thinking about and he intended that his goodbye would be lengthy and heartfelt. He would not leave until he had seen Angelica.

'This is no time for flinching,' said Fab. 'Shall I stay with Gary?'

Bas, in the middle of tying his bootlaces, swore. 'You! Not do a gig? No preening and strutting? You must be sickening for something.' Ellie insisted that she stayed alone. Bas grumbled. Fab consented. Ellie smiled; pregnancy was beginning to take hold.

The savour of foreign lands, its food and its people abides. Yet the thought of returning home, of having someone take the responsibility for Gary, was to Ellie almost as if she had been relieved of a heavy burden. On the steps of the bus she gazed at the clouds moving without effort and occasionally the stars would break through the warm darkness.

There was movement within the bus. Gary was crouched over the bunk, his hand stretched out to her and he smiled, a smile which acknowledged her understanding and her support. Ellie's mind was spinning, this chameleon-like existence was unnerving but he sat confidently, his hands folded whilst she prepared lentil soup flavoured with garlic and the juice of lemons.

Loving her, he wondered if this was the right time, thinking how badly he needed someone to care for him. But the moment came and went.

They did not return to the farmhouse in Slovakia; they moved closer to Hungary where they met up with other bands. Gossip and drinking, music and zines took up most of the night. Never had Ellie known better wit among friends and as they sprawled on the grass verge they were joined by untethered gipsy horses grazing beside the road. Moths invaded the candles which Fab had lit for effect but Boo treated them with some mistrust even though she was careful not to harm the insects; they were reincarnations of lost souls, she proffered.

Gary had settled into a self-induced convalescence and Hungary did not have the same effect as before. There were fewer arguments and more time to wind down. A railway carriage was home to a group of squatters and the girls rather enjoyed the limelight when bands from further afield set up a stage in the clearing. They were invited to stay and Tiz could not conceal her astonishment when Bas intervened. 'No, they drink, get giddy and spew up all over the place. Best we get back ready for rolling.'

'Oh, is that so?' hollered Tiz. 'Would you do me a favour and drop dead?'

Boo, behind a haughty tone of voice added, 'We will do exactly what we want,' and thumped his stomach so hard that he recoiled.

'Must admit we do have a fairly early start tomorrow.' It was Mustard's turn to calm the situation.

'No one is born with arrogance, they cultivate it along the way,' Fab spat as they piled back into the bus.

'Somebody has to look after you girls,' Bas crowed.

Peace seemed to turn in a more generous circle as Graz approached. Perhaps it was time to bring to a halt the niggles that bit at their good nature. The campsite brought out the best in them, they almost behaved like brothers and sisters. It was the turn of Rev to carry on boosting everyone else's spirits when Gary's appetite and ability to swallow decreased. 'I'm terrified, me,' groaned Bas. 'We're a hell of a way from home.' Ellie tried hard to cope with a grief, deep as a pit, inside her. Voices were turning around in her head, voices she was unable to convert into words. She couldn't reach Gary through her silence and she hated herself. She was on automatic pilot now, greeting each day with an uneasy sense of foreboding. She was irritated that he had kept information from her; didn't she deserve some explanation?

Suddenly it seemed that there were things which Gary could not tolerate. He disliked being in the dark and insisted that the curtains were left open, ignoring the girls' requests for privacy and the need for security. The energy and motivation had been scaled down and he was nervous of traffic. Mustard became more responsible whilst Gary became more fearful and gullible. It was tearing Ellie apart. Tasks were shared out just as before but there was always someone on hand to check his impulsiveness. Balance and instability were sometimes obvious. At other times he appeared to walk normally. His fondness for going barefoot in the long grass and forgetfulness were added worries for them all.

On the whole the last day in Graz had been almost normal. It was a time of respite after days of upheaval and Fab remarked, 'I feel as if we have all taken a beating and need time to nurse our bruises and lick our wounds.'

Bas sneered. 'Thank you for your profound analysis.' Gary had taken more medication and responded well; he had quietly skimmed through the accounts with Tiz and settled down to a meal of vegetable curry and wild strawberries. The group now took the initiative on all measures relating to getting home, whereas before Gary was the one who carried the burden of responsibility.

In her prayer time Ellie cursed the devil for his relentless attack on the man who had shown her respect, consideration and given her self-esteem and confidence more than anyone else. And through the blaze of light which followed her devotions there came a sharp sense of foreboding. It stayed in her mind whilst she slept.

'It's not every question that deserves an answer,' remarked Boo.

'All I said was, how long are we going to spend in this poncy place?' quizzed Bas.

Mustard dropped the paper in front of him, one eye on the road ahead. 'One gig, that's all,' he muttered. 'That's what it says here.'

'Open air?' queried Fab.

'No, but does it matter?'

'Yes,' she snapped saucily. 'It does.'

Fab was blooming and bilious. She had a craving for banana, peanut butter and hummus and decided that it was pointless hiding her bump any longer. 'I like fresh air. Smoke and the smell of sweat and drink make me puke and it's

not good for the baby.' The announcement had the desired
effect. Mustard pulled the bus to a halt. Tiz and Boo were
rendered speechless.

Rev uttered, 'Wow!' Cheddar grinned from ear to ear.

Gary jumped from the bunk and tapped her on the
shoulder. 'Congratulations!' whilst Bas swore loudly, followed
by 'Don't look at me' and peals of laughter.

Milan was very hot around midday and a boating lake
looked the ideal spot to laze and talk about the baby and
its future. Rev, Bas and Cheddar chose to hire a paddle boat
and weaved their way around expert boatmen who were
swarthy and smug with little regard for others. There was
no doubt that the act was deliberate. Two boats, one on
either side, propelled Bas and his crew towards the island.
Sprouting from the bank and trailing into the lake were
clumps of coarse grass and Bas leaned forward to grab and
secure his hold whilst Cheddar and Rev fought to keep the
assailants at bay. Alarm had now mounted to panic. They
were well-hidden, cries for help were ignored. A paddle was
driven into the small of Bas's back and he fell into the soft,
warm ooze. He swam and crawled out of the lake and onto
the island and the two boats retired to a safe distance.

When the Italians waved their arms and shouted 'We
want our money' it all fell into place. These were the men
who had purchased the dud football shirts.

'You mean the ones with the E missing?' Cheddar was
shivering with apprehension, holding the paddle aloft in
defence. Bas ignored him, groped into his money pouch
and waved a wad of notes in the air. Rev sighed with relief
when he produced the money; one boat eased forward and
the notes were snatched out of his hand. Cheddar, usually
calm and often dilatory, took umbrage at this assault on his
friend and whacked the Italian round the shoulders with his
paddle. It was hard to tell how they found the energy to
drag Bas back into the boat and paddle out of harm's reach
but they did. And it provided entertainment for the girls
as they watched him disrobe and dry out in the sweltering
sun.

There was no contradicting the fact that the Milan gig was rated among the best. Perhaps subconsciously it was for Gary that such effort was put into it. Maybe it was because everyone was making a tremendous fuss of them or was it that they had in their midst a new life? A human being worthy of their causes; opposing cruelty to animals; homelessness; gender discrimination; and wars. Without exception everyone applauded them. Ellie concluded that walking the trail of punk was an adventure; it was a jungle out there and not all the natives were friendly. Yet there are other unseen pastures, untrodden and maybe the greenest one of all is just round the corner.

Paris welcomed them with a colourful patchwork of camping mats and sleeping bags. A regular stream of foreigners with their belongings arrived at the leafy park for the three-day festival. Dark Horse were resting; it was time to chill out and enjoy the bands and drink in the atmosphere. 'Playing burns up so much energy,' Rev stated. 'We deserve a rest and a pat on the back.' Mustard was reluctant to park the bus in the nearby field so he opted to leave it in a quiet street in an area close to the city centre. Music could be heard until well into the night and although the weather was fine and warm small bonfires were lit and potatoes and sausages were on the menu. From the fireside stories were exchanged and memories rekindled.

At first glance nothing appeared unusual. Ellie had never claimed that she had sixth sense, intuition or the like but there had been an undercurrent, a feeling of unrest on the second day of the festival. She couldn't explain it. There were murmurings and mutterings, devious activity within small groups but as she wasn't able to understand the language it posed no threat.

It was billed as a carnival and protest march and started off peacefully and in an orderly fashion with marchers in line, banners held aloft and slogans shouted with controlled enthusiasm. 'That's great,' grumbled Bas. 'A day of action and Gary failed to tell us about it.' The park resounded with the beating of drums, chants and whistles, and colourful banners decried vivisection and transnational corporations. Hundreds of bicycles invaded the packed roads whilst the marchers regrouped and gathered more people and momentum as they passed through the tree-lined streets.

Many remained in the park but the bands had stopped playing and many fires were left unattended. Stragglers, their curiosity satisfied, returned but it was obvious that the festival spirit had been dampened. 'I think we should call it a day' suggested Gary. 'We have seen most of the bands.'

'Yes,' sighed Fab, heaving herself from a sitting position. 'Let's go back to the bus.'

They scrambled down the bank towards the crossroads, joining the tail end of the main column. The noise blasted and pierced the air; the confused sounds of whistles and mayhem added to the bedlam. Then at the crossroads, from either side of them, two separate processions merged with such precision a general would have been proud. Then the nightmare of noise increased as the mob approached the barriers. Beyond the barricades were shops, banks and offices protected by the police in their body armour and helmets. A group of young men carrying a banner stating "Kill Capitalism, Not Animals" with bravado moved towards them and truncheons were raised. The police pulled handkerchieves over their faces and waited. Ellie froze in fear. They were a tight group in the middle now, forced by hundreds of determined protestors, and she could almost taste the terror as she felt for Gary's hand. Then came confrontation. The mob broke through the cordon and with sticks battered down the windows. Molotov cocktails and missiles flew through the air from all directions. Glass and debris were strewn across the road. Lines of police struggled with people and young women pulled at their uniforms and screamed. Cameras flashed and Boo clung onto Tiz as a water main burst and drove them into the wall. Ahead of them small fires were burning and Fab was yelling. There was a surge behind Ellie and Gary; they hadn't heard the rush above the screaming and crashing of glass. They were upon them before they could move. Bas was hit with a blow to the head. He was bleeding, blood running into his eyes and down his face. Boo was hit in the face and Fab was pushed with such force that she fell at Rev's feet and he lifted her up into his arms. They couldn't escape, they were carried away with the stream of men and women who came from nowhere.

Ellie was grabbed and flung into the hole which had once been a window and in her dazed condition saw Tiz waving her arms in the air and disappearing into the crowd. Ellie sobbed. Where was Gary? All her friends had gone. She half pushed, half stumbled across the road strewn with debris and the injured. And in the middle a half-naked man knelt and prayed. All around were burning torches and she felt her palm hot and sticky with blood as it ran in rivulets down her arm.

She had to find the bus. She tried to remember where it was.

Nothing was clear; she thought she might pass out. The mob divided. Cars were now the target, parked in neat rows outside meticulously kept houses and smashed to pieces. Ellie half ran, half hobbled in the direction of the bus. The hooligans were taking the same route. The bus came into view, there was no one else around, it could be wrecked. They would fire it. It was the first time it had been left unattended. Mustard was vigilant and wary; he had shown Ellie where the spare keys were kept, secured in a pouch near the rear wheels.

She felt above the tyre; she couldn't feel anything. "Please God, let them be here." She breathed a sigh of relief as she felt the leather brush against her hand. Shaking, she climbed nervously into the bus. Could she do it? Could she drive? She had no choice, the crowd was almost upon her. Her first attempt failed, the engine stalled. Praying, she tried again, it sprang into life and she drove at speed up a steep hill.

In determination she bit her lip until it bled and tried to remember what to do next. A long lane veered to the left and ignoring road signs she carried on, pulling up suddenly outside two ornate iron gates.

The engine stopped and for the first time Ellie noticed blood on the steering wheel and after washing her hands helped herself to bandages from the first aid box. On the steps of the bus she drank bottled water and breathed in the quiet and the peace of the sun-baked fields. From the distance came the faint hum of traffic and the barely perceptible sound of sirens. She would wait until the coast was clear and retrace her route. She had to find her friends.

CHAPTER SEVENTEEN

"The best word is the word that remains to be spoken."
(Proverbial Spanish.)

Madame Povall had been watching Ellie for some time from the lucarne window at the very top of the house. From here she had watched the despicable destruction of the city and was thankful when the riot had stopped short of her land. It had seemed that the bus was out of control as it approached the bend to the house and it changed course several times as it swerved towards the gates. Madame had picked up the telephone to call for help until she saw Ellie, alone and hurt. She hardly posed a threat, she decided.

Ellie was a believer in miracles, and as desperate as she was, a miracle was all she hoped for. It came in the guise of a young man in a smart grey suit who pushed open the wide gates and walked towards her. He spoke in French. It was difficult to control her emotions. Was he being friendly? She raised her hand to her mouth and shrugged her shoulders. 'You do not speak French? No matter, come in anyway.'

It took some time to explain that she didn't speak at all but after freshening up she was offered tea and scones served on a trolley in front of a bay window overlooking an immaculately-kept lawn. Madame Povall seemed mesmerised, and in broken English insisted on asking questions even though she was aware that no answer would be forthcoming. A nod or a shake of the head sufficed.

Ellie was not aware that she had been staring out of the window at the patch of sunshine wedged between the summerhouse and the gazebo. She was listening for the bus. Andre, Madame's son, had taken it to bring back the others. Ellie had drawn a diagram of where it was parked. Madame insisted that Ellie needed to rest and poured out more tea with well-manicured hands and adjusted a diamond ring which had twisted round her finger. She held herself very straight in the tall-backed chair and plumped up her silver hair. A jewelled cross rested on her navy dress and Ellie curled her fingers around the small gold cross given to her by Gary. She prayed that he was safe, that they all were, especially Fab after her fall.

Madame continued to stare. Ellie fidgeted, then jumped up as the familiar engine spluttered and juddered to a halt. Fate is unyielding and humans are so frail and weak, Ellie had been led to believe. She threw herself at Gary as soon as he came through the door. He looked ashen but he smiled and hugged her and kissed the top of her head. 'You clever girl. What have you done to your hand?'

Mustard cupped her face in his hands. 'Must admit you saved the day, girl.' Fab had been examined by the medic, all was well and Tiz and Boo were fine. Rev and Cheddar had escaped injury but Bas had seven stitches in his head and remained in the bus.

The grand room was buzzing with questions and answers. Madame was happy at last. They were served soup and garlic bread and wine and Tiz and Boo entertained each other on an 'S' shaped sofa where they could face each other when seated. 'It's called a tête-à-tête,' said Andre, speaking directly to Boo, and the response he received was a coquettish smile and a flirtatious look from the dark brown eyes.

The pain in her hand was causing Ellie some discomfort, but when Madame appeared in a state of agitation and excitement from her study waving a newspaper, she demanded their attention. Grabbing Ellie by the arm she almost exploded, 'This is you, is it not? You are wanted, your photograph has been in all the papers. Look.' She turned to the others for verification. 'It is you, isn't it?' She thrust the paper in Ellie's face. 'Take a look. You can see it for yourself.' Gary put an arm around her shoulders.

'It's in French.'

'I'll translate,' offered Andre.

Ellie sank into the velvet cushions on the large padded sofa and retched. The police must have discovered the truth, the deceit, the lies, the tampering with evidence, the perjury. She had no defence, any suggestion of a murky, sinful past was the truth and she was terrified. In her heart maybe she had known that it wouldn't be long before the past caught up with her.

Gary held her hand and through the sound of buzzing in her ears she tried to concentrate on what Andre was saying. Why, suddenly, was Gary kissing her? Why was everyone smiling and celebrating and folding their arms around her? Why had the darkness lifted and when is daybreak?

She studied the photograph. A picture of a smiling, slim girl enjoying the cool spray from the fountain in the square in Milan, and children paddling and splashing at her feet. The photographer had sent it to a fashion magazine and Ellie had been chosen from thousands of entrants to grace the cover. Only she couldn't be found. Her picture was publicised in the Italian and French press; Andre continued his narration, and Madame's curiosity was half satisfied. Rev threw up both his arms in grand theatrical style. 'Isn't this wonderful?' Ellie had little time to ponder. Why should she change this life when she had just won a reprieve?

In the half-light of the summer evening there were plans to be made. Newspapers and magazines had to be contacted by fax, telephone calls were made in a flurry of enthusiasm. The dialogue switched between English and French and champagne corks popped as each successful contact was reached. There seemed to be no suggestion of anyone leaving. Bas joined them and his somewhat ugly view of life, which at times was stark, sceptical and suspicious, took on a different perspective as he saw everyone's reaction to Ellie's good fortune.

The house lights shut out the shimmer on the leaves
and the gleam on the grass, and the late flowers closed
their petals as Ellie watched the sun go down while her
aspirations rose. Now she was calm. But in a moment of
sheer panic it had come flooding back, suddenly as if the
gates of that dreadful night had been thrown open before
her and the sullied side of Phil's act had washed over her.
The memories of the accident, the cut flowers in the ditch,
the damaged BMW and the blood flashed for a horrifying
moment before her. Would her story hold firm until another
was told?

Ellie sat on the edge of the bed tearfully waiting to say
goodbye. The cheval glass mirrored her reflection; a slim,
bronzed, blue-eyed beauty with high cheekbones and
long blonde hair. How would she cope without a voice?
There was still time to turn around. The guest bedroom in
Madame Pavall's home was comfortable but more Spartan
than luxurious, and she had slept well after a visit from
Madame's physician, who treated her hand. Earlier she had
packed her bags and left her sleeping partners with light
banter but a heavy heart.

At noon the magazine "Giselle" was sending a car for
her and she would be escorted all the way to Milan. Gary
had spent time with her and she knew, given the use of a
computer, she could always keep in touch. She could hold
her tongue and her promise. Why now did the picture of the
two of them come to mind as they had walked in the wood
behind the squat in the snowy moonlight? She could just as
easily refuse the offer of a new beginning; get back in the
bus and wallow in the friendship of people she knew and
trusted. Yet relationships can be marred by dependency and
she needed to prove to Gary that although she was speechless
she was self-assured. In any event, had she been attaching
too much significance to their friendship? She recognised his
faltering steps as he approached the door, and he knocked
gently. It was the flash of her eyes and the curl of her mouth
as she smiled that he would remember and they held each
other close and he stroked her hair. 'A little advice, Ellie. Be

good, be happy, be yourself. Remember I am here for you.' She tried not to look too deeply into his eyes as he walked her to the car but held onto his hand until the very last minute before waving goodbye.

On the plane Isabella was able to observe Ellie more closely. She was aware that she had been given an enormous responsibility as her chaperone, spokesperson, instructor and friend. On the other hand it would be easy to mould such a gentle, good-natured girl into the photographic and fashion model which "Giselle" was aiming for. Ellie spoke through her eyes, with her hands and the twirl of her head and her smile was genuine. Ellie was given copies of the agenda and left alone to digest and underline anything that she thought could pose a problem. She pointed out a few.

On arrival they checked into the Hotel Milano and after making sure she didn't lack for anything, Ellie was left in peace. She was to dress for dinner wearing the pink and cream silk evening gown provided for her. Alone on the sumptuous bed she stretched out, reading aloud the instructions and the timetable of her press conference and laughed loudly. Of course it was all a dream, she had been missing prayers and playing with the devil. How could it be true? It wasn't anything she had ever wanted, longed for. Her mother had. Moira had wanted her to be fashionable, to be chic, sophisticated like herself. Ellie drew up the sheet over her body. Gran had likened life to a compass; stay in the right direction and you know instantly when you are off course. At this moment she would beg to differ; it simply meant that she had deviated a little.

'I find it remarkable, don't you, that we have managed to track you down at last?' Ellie adjusted the napkin on her knee. She was especially reserved with the two Italian gentlemen who were to guide her through the pitfalls of her new life but had no qualms in refusing osso bucco in favour of a vegetarian meal; she hated veal anyway.

Isabella sat beside her at the oval table by the window and the impeccable waiter hovered like a moth round a glowing candle. It was explained to her, in detail, what was expected of her and she scribbled questions and answers on a notelet provided by Isabella. It seemed to Ellie that the men were used to unquestionable authority and were taken aback by her composure.

She wiggled her feet on the thick carpet under the table; her shoes had high heels and thin soles, her feet had yet to adjust from Doc Martens and bulky sandals.

They had reached the sweet course and Ellie was relaxed and comfortable. She studied the dining room with its onyx marble fireplace and the green-streaked marble columns at the base of the winding staircase. Oil paintings of birds decorated the walls; she was able to recognise some – kittiwakes, puffins and gannets, reminders of home – and memories soared through her mind like the flutter of innumerable wings. Now, as she was kissed politely on her cheek and escorted upstairs to her room she prepared herself for all eventualities and prayed aloud in the silence of her room. "Today, Lord, a new day, laid open. And here am I waiting to step into it, and yet there is a feeling of uncertainty of what it holds. Have I the resources, Lord, to meet this day? Can I enter it with joy and certainty and contentment? Yes I will accept it gladly, dance into it. Revel in it, absorb it. For it is today, new, just for me."

Ellie was too sleepy to wake up. The luxury of a deep, soft mattress was too enticing but with a cloud of questions buzzing around her head she shuffled into the bathroom. It was 7.30am.

It was with a tingling current of excitement and anticipation that she entered the photographic studio. Isabella introduced her. It was a relief not to have to make small talk; no one knew whether she was ignorant or knowledgeable, experienced or incompetent. She was a rarity without words. The German photographer came towards her with long, elastic strides. He walked around her, noting each curve of her body and the near perfect features. His lined, rugged face overhung a scraggy neck and at intervals he ran his long, bony fingers through his thinning hair.

Isabella explained. 'He maintains that youth is not a

period in life but a state of mind. He must be eighty at least.' He never took his eyes from Ellie, not even when the cameras stopped rolling. 'He does it with everyone,' Isabella whispered. Ellie felt a certain affinity towards this father figure and smiled broadly. He was hooked.

'I am never roused by passion,' he confided to Ellie. 'I can never find the right words to say. With you I make an exception.' He bowed and they had lunch in the trattoria. Isabella found him fascinating and tossed back her head and laughed at his jokes and his accent. She had nourished ambitions to be either an artist or a photographer, she told him, which brought Tiz to mind and opened the gate in Ellie's dividing world.

Contrary to her pessimistic predictions, the Press conference was anything but a problem.

It was a cocktail party, invitations strictly limited, during which the fever of questions and answers rose and fell and "La Stampa" stabilized the interviews. Here was the tabloid with a fashion reporter who could make or break a designer with her reviews and who had an appetite for fault-finding. Isabella handled her with tact and tasteful compliments.

Ellie, sleek in a short, black dress, mingled easily, using the pretext of studying the delicacies offered to her. There was a certain freedom in being speechless; the obligation to speak had been removed and in its place there was time for reflection.

She sauntered over to the wide windows and raised her face to the afternoon sunlight. It was hot in the hotel, it was hot everywhere in Milan it seemed. In the cool of last evening she had written a long letter to Gran, along with postcards to Maggie, Jan and the girls. She missed them and especially Gary. She explained to Gran that she was eager to please and to be appreciated in return, but that she would lay down rules and not abandon the code of self-respect and fragments of dignity which she had instilled in her.

Chatty and entertaining, Isabella relayed the evening's decisions in the comfort of the bedroom. 'They have agreed to call you Elise; after all, that is your name. Actually, it does sound more sophisticated although I'm not sure what they are aiming for!' She sighed, sipping her third glass of wine. Ellie raised her eyebrows and formed "Who?" with her mouth. 'The Morazzoni brothers; they are the ones with all the influence and capital. I wouldn't make too big a thing about it. What's in a name?'

It became clearer to Ellie as the days went by that she was becoming jittery. Back home the newspapers were buzzing with news of her success, of the plight of the girl who left home at 16, and tales of mischief rustled up by attention-seekers. It was no longer a question of her mother's spitefulness or revenge. To be fair, Moira had kept a low profile and revealed nothing of her early childhood to the press.

Isabella consoled Ellie as they enjoyed cold drinks in the hotel lounge. 'It is a nine days' wonder; you have everyone's sympathy. After all, several physicians have come forward with a probable cause of your speech defect; they all agree it is due to the trauma of the trial. It must have been horrendous for you. You must have had incredible self-control.' There was almost a hint of affection in her tone but how many more people would be deluded by her and how long could such a perverted act go undetected?

****

'In the end life is crazy, it takes many unexpected knocks.' Tony Morazzoni was impatient, he kept his finger firmly on the button and the lift bumped to a stop. They entered, Isabella trailing behind. 'There aren't any embarrassing questions,' he continued. 'Just embarrassing answers.' On the third floor they had to skip to keep up with him.

The whole scene was chaotic. Half-clad females were being treated to exotic hair extensions and made up in vibrant colours, each one chattering through clenched teeth and desperately gripping slides and hairpins. Thin models practically forbidden to laugh on the catwalk were now enjoying a joke although still suffering from the strain of late nights and travel. Tony clapped his hands and issued instructions in Italian. 'They have the gift of the gab,' he grinned.

The visit was designed to establish whether Ellie was catwalk material; whether photo shoots alone were her forte or whether she had the style and ability to do both. Her fees, Isabella told her, would almost double, but it did not depend solely on Tony; her mentor would be one Athol Picora.

Whoever interrupted the conversation of Athol Picora was cut short with a glare of rebuke. He was a man in control, loud and lacking finesse and all around him had learned to take insolence without protest. Ellie stood before him looking down on his bald head and turned her face slightly as the smoke from his cigar blew her way. She had been summoned and Tony and Isabella stood discreetly on either side of the large mahogany desk whilst he sat facing her, his palms flat on the table as if he was trying to force space between it and his stomach. He spoke in Italian and whilst his conversation was addressed to Tony he was staring at Ellie.

From his office on the third floor she could hear the early morning activity from the piazza and longed to be down there once again with her friends, especially Gary. She was aware suddenly that the conversation had stopped, she had lost the thread of what was being said. Tony shook his head blindly. Athol pushed his way from the table. Ellie stifled a smile as his fat, round body ambled towards the door. He was a little over five feet in height and about as wide. To his friends he was known as the cognoscente, the connoisseur of fashion; his enemies called him the barrel, but never to his face.

The desire to remain independent and carefree was a characteristic Ellie didn't want to lose but contracts had now been sealed and she was to remain with "Giselle" and Athol for a period of one year. Her flat within a secluded complex was one of six and a number of models shared. Ellie was spared this; no one would relish having no one to talk to.

She purchased a computer and at last her contact with Gary was resumed. It was important to him; she recalled how he had searched for an easy internet cafe. Without words she relied on intuition; now discretion was the answer but she shared the complexities of contracts and business meetings and asked his advice on her finances.

Then came the busiest time of Ellie's life. Early mornings and early nights, seven days a week. Visits from Parisian couturiers and tips on how to be chic and soigné. "Some take to it like birds to the sky," she wrote "but I find it very comical even though I feel a little proud of my capabilities."

There was a widely-felt suspicion that Ellie's kind of silence was counterproductive. Athol had been blunt. 'We cannot introduce her socially when she lacks communication skills. It would be unfair to her and hard on the client,' he explained to Isabella. So instead of dinner dates and promotional venues she was confined to the salon and the studio, or so he thought. Isabella accompanied her to a few parties; content to sit on the boundary line and not play the field. It was enjoyable, she told Gary, not to have to make conversation. She learned a lot.

On her 18th birthday she took her first steps on the catwalk, and it seemed as if all of Milan was there. Rehearsals had gone without a hitch and little notice was taken of tantrums and swearing and lost shoes. Athol, with the Morazzoni brothers either side, stood at the back of the Grand Hall puffing hard on his cigar, and leaning on his walking stick. He caressed the ebony handle with a small podgy hand and gesticulated with the other.

When Ellie's turn came she stepped out with some trepidation in a short, white boucle suit but then, like a snapped spring, she bounced across the dais. But then the tape began playing a heart-stopping guitar riff and the music released locked-up emotions which tempered her smile. Her future demanded a sacrifice, she realized that; she would have to take one day at a time and grab every opportunity that came her way.

The celebrations continued well into the night. Isabella sank down beside her on the chesterfield in the hotel bar. 'A good night, a full order book, dozens of enquiries, Athol is puffed up with his own importance, full of his ambition and his struggle for power.' Ellie sipped her champagne. 'He has no time for small talk, no preliminaries, a useless salesman yet he owns an empire,' Isabella yawned.

It was after 3am when Ellie returned to her flat. She slumped onto the cream sofa and pulled down the blinds between the flounced drapes, kicked off her shoes and rubbed her feet on the sheepskin rug. It was a comfortable lounge. The writing table displayed her precious snapshots and the table in front of the window housed her computer. As yet there were only eight books on the shelf in the corner. She hummed softly. By herself she could sing, talk out loud, remonstrate and pray. The simple words of comfort lifted all her doubts.

She knew when she opened the door to the kitchen that Frankie was waiting to be let in. His persistent scratching at the glass and clawing at the woodwork and the faint cries told her he was hungry. The yellow eyes in the black face looked beseechingly at her through the pane. Ellie scrutinized him closely. The back windows lacked an attractive view; there were no roof gardens, no green foliage of trees, only the iron step of a fire escape and a tall brick building which shut out all the light. Frankie climbed in, was fed and watered and dozed in Ellie's arms as she curled up in bed. Frankie had adopted her; she had no idea where he came from but he was her listening cat and she was his friend.

Words leapt and danced between computers regularly and at length and Ellie was kept informed of all events relating to Gary and her friends. Over the months that followed their separation Tiz had taken a full-time course in Fashion and Design at Loxley College and aiming for a Higher National Diploma. "I know it sounds very grand," she wrote, "but honestly you are responsible, Ellie, you have given me an incentive." Fab assured her she was well. "I have never wanted anything so much in my life. I know I shall be a good mother." Jan was a regular visitor to the Asian Centre and had undergone a skin graft. Gary wrote, "We all miss you but we try to keep up with the news and we have learned a lot about you since you left us. I have secured a post in Bradford and am feeling much better." Perhaps circumstances were improving for him, Ellie hoped.

'The best thing I can do is sleep,' sighed Sophie. 'I have not had a good night's sleep for weeks.' She flung herself across the bed and lay there motionless. Ellie was bursting with energy despite spending all day shopping and preparing the meal for her eight modelling friends who shared the flats. It was a birthday treat. They too had heard about her past; it would have been a miracle if they hadn't and each one had made an effort to draw her into their circle. They draped around the room, groomed and glamorous, Italian interrupted by English, sipping Asti spumante and Chianti. No one was allowed near the kitchen, there was only room for Ellie and Frankie.

She served pasta and vegetarian pizza, garlic bread and grissini breadsticks, quiches and meatless sausages. A fruit cocktail of kiwi, lychee and Sharon fruits followed. 'Where did you learn to cook?' Sophie was impressed.

'You've done it now,' smiled Isabella. 'Next time there is a party guess who the caterer will be?'

'You would have thought we would have been given more notice.' Isabella was peeved. Ellie had answered the door to frantic knocking, rubbing her eyes and checking the time. Isabella put the kettle on, Ellie opened the window and the sound of birds came bursting in and with it a gentle breeze. 'We are going to Paris, tonight, no warning just a phone call and all the gowns and accessories to pack. It's not good enough.' "Why must you dramatize everything?" Ellie thought! 'Surely you have been pushed for time in the past?' Isabella asked as she helped with the suitcase. Yes, thought Ellie, but Tiz and the others would have taken it in their stride.

The sun was drying the grass after the morning mist as they left for the airport. The flashy cars, in a hurry as always, repeatedly sounded their horns and Ellie was amazed to learn that she was the only model from "Giselle" and Milan.

'I have more than once taken Athol to task on this.' Isabella was pretty fed-up with everybody one way or another. 'I mean you photograph like an angel and yet here we are succumbing to the whim of a pop star. A private showing is all very well but there is very little publicity in it.' Music had brought the young, vivacious singer called Reeve fame and wealth and in the privacy of her riverside home Ellie was thrilled to pose and twirl and smile. In the heat of the late August sun she paraded in front of the whitewashed stone walls, among the tubs of geraniums and onto the small lawn with peacocks and ornamental pheasants. And, to her delight, the old, charming German photographer was there to capture her on camera. 'It is time you called me Walter,' he said.

Ellie did not find the endless succession of changes wearying.

Reeve was appreciative – a star, friendly and intelligent who could speak English, Italian and Spanish, and who was unable to sit still even for a moment. Her slim, agile body was shoehorned into a skimpy skirt and a top decorated with a tree motif, and she talked incessantly as she skipped between them, her long blonde hair flowing freely.

Before leaving, after a lunch of fresh trout and salad, they were all given tickets for her November concert. 'What a delightful girl!' sighed Walter. 'A diva with a heart.'

'There is a price to pay for fame,' Tony reminded her. Ellie thought him presumptuous; she would hardly consider herself famous. Celebrities had so much to say about themselves and others, and as Ellie had little to say the gossip had no real bite to it. Anyway, she thought, the crowds of people who gathered at every fashion show looked past the skinny models, spurred on by necessity to make money. 'Men don't realize that women can be all things at different levels,' Ellie was reminded of Fab propping up the feminine trail one day. 'We live in pigeonholes and can fly from one to the other without ruffling a feather!' How Ellie missed Fab's simple approach to psychology.

That seemed all of a thousand miles away. Two weeks to Christmas and Ellie was tired and travel weary. Now she was planning a month's holiday and heading for England and home. She made a reservation at the Hilton, on Victoria Quays, only because her old room had been converted to a nursery for Fab and the baby. She didn't doubt that she would be made welcome at the squat.

The sky was cloudy and heavy with snow as the train left London but when the countryside came into view there was a smattering of pale sunshine. This journey was so very different from her first visit to Sheffield. She felt rather more frightened, if that were possible, than before. Certainly she had gained in confidence but shyness can be a godsend when there is nothing to say. At the hotel she unpacked, folding her few clothes neatly in the wardrobe; casual, unpretentious trousers and sweaters and a suitcase filled with presents chosen with care.

All the deep affection she had for anyone centred around this city. Only Gran shared the love she felt as a child and it was from her that she had learned how to love and trust others. It was as if she had never been away. She took the tram from the Quays then walked the length of the street, wheeling her case over the uneven slabs. The Christmas tree lit up the whole window and smoke billowed from the chimney. It was Fab who opened the door, heavily pregnant with chubby cheeks and hair that matched the clementines in the fruit bowl. They hugged each other. 'You look wonderful, Ellie.' There was nothing gloomy or grimy about the squat; it was warm and welcoming. They prepared the evening meal together – thick leek and lentil soup, jacket potatoes with cheese and mushrooms, and chocolate pudding and custard. Ellie was home, Elise was miles away.

They came in dribs and drabs from work, Jan from the Asian Centre where she was the cook; Rev arrived and gave an appreciative whistle; the red mini with bursts of exhaust fumes dropped off Tiz and Boo, and Bas, sifting through a pile of DIY HARDcore Punk Zines, almost fell over Valentine on his way in. 'Get out of the way, you stupid mutt,' he yelled. Valentine did not appear to miss his leg at all.

On the third day when Gary arrived, Ellie was alone. Fab was walking the dog and Ellie was washing the kitchen floor with a mop which had seen better days. It was plain to see that he was ill. She tried to imagine what it must have been like for him on the journey home, and gently she put her head on his shoulders and held him close. There was a boyishness about him and her whole body began to tingle. She couldn't ask questions and if she could would he provide the answers? He began to shake as he pulled her towards the sofa. 'You look terrific. You did the right thing you know, even though we were all very concerned about you. I really appreciate the emails. I haven't got round to sorting out your finances yet, I've been a bit pushed.' There was a slight drawl in his speech as if he was choosing his words carefully. 'I am home now until mid January so I will have it sorted by then.'

He lay back against the cushion and closed his eyes. Ellie stroked the brown hair falling across his forehead and kissed him gently. She wanted something solid and real from their relationship but she suspected that she would have a long wait. He slept.

Sadness was evident on her face. It was Tiz who suggested a walk after tea and wrapped up against the cold wind they crossed the recreation ground towards the swings. They sat on the roundabout and Tiz searched for an easy way to explain. 'I know how you feel about Gary, Ellie, but it seems he is a man with a burden of some sort. It's in his eyes, his voice, his movements, everything he does comes with an effort. This illness, whatever it is, has got much worse. We know he is on medication but he won't talk about it. He is very forgetful, he doesn't organise gigs anymore, that's left to Bas and Rev.'

Tiz smoothed her close-cropped hair and swung her legs over the bars and held onto Ellie's arm as they crossed over the graffiti-encrusted bridge. 'Most times he behaves normally,' she continued. 'But I am sure when he is really bad he stays away.'

Ellie knew that after a life of relative freedom he faced a difficult adjustment. If he found life too hard who could make it easier for him? When in danger ponder, brood. Would this be his reaction? They stepped carefully on the Rec, there was a great deal of rubble everywhere. 'They are building another supermarket,' Tiz groaned. 'Decent low cost housing would be more sensible. Gary wrote to the paper about it.'

Ellie's photograph cut out of the newspaper was pinned on the wall at the squat with blue tack. The heading, "Elise comes home" was followed by a brief description of what she was wearing. She remembered the cameras and shouts of 'Elise, over here, give us a smile,' grateful that no one saw the point of asking questions. Her friends' reaction to her new life was rational, cool; for the most part they agreed it was no more than she deserved and Rev's attitude, 'I can see Ellie coping OK, she'll go her own road anyway,' summed it all up.

The next morning was fresh with a pale blue sky and swiftly fleeting clouds. She pulled on her boots, gathered up the spray of chrysanthemums and left the hotel. Across the canal a cold wind stirred the water and as she approached the cafe the smell of newly baked bread and coffee brought to mind good food and good company.

June was delighted to see her and introduced her to the staff and customers as 'my friend, Ellie, the model from Italy.' June looked older; there were dark shadows under her eyes and she had lost weight. Well, Ellie sensed in some way that Mark was responsible. June sighed. 'I was right about Flute.' Ellie gripped her hands together under the table. What now? she wondered.

Water rippled under the long boats and from the cafe window the reflections of the street lights danced on the waves. A steam hammer thumped on the nearby site and sounded prodigiously loud in the surrounding silence. June sat with her sleeveless arms folded and occasionally rubbed her elbows in turn. 'They were in the flat, you see, Mark's flat. I've always been emphatic about drink and drugs, always, but I did trust him with girls. I mean, he was alright with you, duck, wasn't he?' No he wasn't, Ellie recalled but it was too late for disclosures now. June lowered her voice as a customer entered. 'Anyway they were caught, him and Flute with underage girls. Well, you know, in the act, so to speak.' Her voice broke. 'They are due to appear in court this coming March.'

Ellie held June's hand and pursed her lips, and thought of all the misery that people shovel into their lives. The steam hammer thudded continuously. 'I don't know what to do. You think you are making headway and kids throw you right off the track.' Pushing back her chair, she kissed Ellie warmly. 'Got to get back to work; thank you for the flowers. Keep in touch.'

****

With blankets in the mini the four girls set off to visit Maggie. It was a relief to see her full of life and equally full of mischief. It was a day of laughter and for Maggie one of respite. 'They have no idea, you know how to enjoy themselves.' She nodded towards her aged companions. 'Their clothes are washed, they enjoy good meals, plenty of rest. What more do they want? And her...' pointing to a podgy woman in the corner whose lisle stockings hung in folds around her ankles, Maggie laughed. 'She says she is getting married again.' The girls giggled. 'Well, I don't mind telling you I find it all positively disgusting and repulsive at her age. Who would have her, eh?'

Fab lounged in a recliner near the window. Boo had been banned from any talk of superstition about pregnancy and birth. 'I wouldn't dream of it,' she snapped. Maggie neatly stacked the Christmas presents by the side of her chair. The long, tough years she had endured had brought order and discipline into her life and later comfort and she was happy at last to be rid of the enmity of Celeste.

The darkness set in and the open fire crackled and spat as the logs took hold. Jan sat on the sofa surrounded by menu cards and a bright yellow boardroom file. She had improved beyond all measure and adorned her neck with pretty muslin scarves whilst making chapatti and nan bread for the centre. During their tour Jason had been her strength and given her confidence and boldness to face the outside world. 'We all have a way of planning and searching for a solution, and thank goodness Jason seems to have the answer,' Fab acknowledged. 'She no longer stays in her room alone and copes very well, even with Bas when he becomes shamelessly obstinate and loud- mouthed.'

Unlike last Christmas, there would be no carol singing in the street; there were so many other jobs to attend to. It was imperative that Boo's ladies were shampooed and permed, that Tiz's art work was displayed in the Gallery and that Jan's Indian Cookery course was properly organized. Ellie caught the bus to the Chapel on the Sunday before Christmas. A thin boy with a dark mass of hair sang "It Came upon the Midnight Clear" to a hushed congregation. God was absent to many yet Ellie was witness to His love and had held onto her faith and a belief that was something special and personal.

'Try to remember everything,' Tiz bellowed, pushing the trolley down the supermarket aisle.

'We're booze, you're food,' shouted Bas, shoving unceremoniously past unruly and overexcited children. He loaded the trolley with cans of lager and an assortment of beers. 'We don't want swipes.'

'Swipes?' queried Rev.

'Poor quality beers,' claimed Bas and with an angry gesture steered an abandoned trolley against the wall. It was no surprise to Ellie that a dispute arose at the cash desk. The convoy of three trolley loads queued behind a line of five, a wheelchair and a child carrying a life size model of Hulk. Bas, whose schedule was overrunning his drinking time, was far from happy but it was Ellie who managed to upset everyone. As Tiz and Boo were packing and Fab loading and Bas disappearing out of the door towards the van, she produced her credit card. It would have been easy had she chosen to speak to exercise her right to pay but instead there was a commotion. Everyone, it appeared, was refusing to take her seriously. Suddenly she grabbed the next customer divider and banged it as hard as she could on the counter. A large bottle of lemonade toppled over onto a carton of eggs. The customers whispered among themselves. Gingerly the assistant took the card from Ellie, handed over the receipt and pen and when the transaction was complete wished her 'A Merry Christmas' to which Ellie mouthed "Thank you".

'What a palaver,' Bas remarked later. 'It isn't as if she can't afford it. She must be loaded by now. Anyway she's been bloody well looked after.'

Boo looked at him with contempt. 'Isn't mercy and loving kindness part of your language?'

'Naw,' he spat. 'It's action that counts,' and he swiped sleepy Valentine off the sofa and sat on the cushion covered in dog hairs.

The punk telegraph informed them of the party at the pub on Christmas Eve. It coincided with the Dinner Dance at the Hilton but without a partner Ellie knew the evening would be an embarrassment.

Over a cup of steaming coffee she pushed the invitation card towards Gary. He had arrived with crates of bottled water for Sobuj and looked frozen. His teeth were chattering as though with intense cold. His meal had been keeping warm in the oven and Ellie served it on a tray in front of a roaring fire. In the background she could hear Fab singing from her bedroom; the room in which once Ellie had dreamed of a life of freedom, freedom from guilt and remorse. Now the walls were stencilled with pictures of animals and nursery rhymes; the floors were nicely carpeted and there was an electric fire in the stone fireplace. Ellie was moved by her singing and smiled as she saw Gary's amused look and thought what a kind, peaceful man he was.

From her hotel window the following morning the quay looked dead and desolate. The trees and bushes drooped over the grey water and the ducks scattered noisily on the banks. The colours of the long boats, the crimsons and the dark blues, shone through the weak rays of the sun and lit up the twisted shapes of the new structures built along the towpath. The complex of lochs and pools would be a faded memory of another life. She knew that she was being talked about. She had breakfast brought to her room. Some staff invaded her silence with chatter, others shouted at her (she found this highly amusing), whilst her chambermaid treated her like an invalid, giving her sympathetic looks with every turn of her head.

Ellie shopped at a small boutique near the Botanical Gardens. She chose an ice blue, sleeveless embroidered dress in crepe voile with a matching scarf for her dinner with Gary. 'I don't have a dinner jacket,' he smiled. 'I don't suppose it will matter, will it?' The memories of moments spent together were a reminder of how much she had missed him.

It occurred to her that although she hadn't exactly planned their evening together it was meant to be. At least she was prepared for a lot more pertinent questions and she felt it her duty to be as honest as she dare.

All in all he looked rather well, Gary decided. It came as a shock, this illness which crept up on him, this disease which made decisions about his capabilities, that took away his energy and limited his endurance. It had made him physically weak and mentally fatigued and he needed time to understand what was expected of him. The medication which was constantly being changed and updated sometimes took a while to kick in.

In the bathroom mirror he adjusted his bow tie. Everything appeared to be a struggle, to get up in the morning, to maintain a career, to handle finances. Now he was struggling to hide his changing moods but one thing he did well, he thought, was to deny that he was ill at all. He was not exactly an optimist but he had convinced himself that he and Ellie would continue to enjoy the affection they had for each other for a while yet.

He waited in the plush, crowded bar among the fashionable well-groomed diners at the Hilton. He was early and nervous. Ellie swept in with a vitality and freshness that turned men's heads and tightened women's lips. Her profession had taught her little; she was by nature captivating, and again Gary whispered 'How many men would change places with me?' On occasions like this it would have been marvellous to speak but sharing a table with five other couples it was pleasant simply to enjoy the excellent food and to listen. She did feel a twinge of resentment and jealousy as the woman on his left shared gossip with Gary whilst he in turn offered her a taste of his vegetarian dish. 'I might become a vegetarian,' she simpered, biting inelegantly into a sliver of duck and gulping down a half glass of wine. It was really something to see Ellie communicate with people despite having no conversation. Her eyes relayed her thoughts and her expressions her voice. She helped a little with finger talk and body language but left a lot deliberately unsaid.

He watched her, holding his breath, as she danced, and envied her partner. His balance refused to allow him to reverse anywhere; even moving forwards could cause him problems. On the days making camp on tour he remembered how Ellie had left her tent to tend him and how comforting it had been. It was hard to imagine life without her. Perhaps later tonight they could move a step closer.

Towards midnight the medication was wearing thin. Gary was tired and beginning to slur his words. Neither high nor drunk, this however was the impression he was giving. Ellie knew the signs; she took his arm, not as a sign of frailty but of affection, and walked him to the lift. He caught the sweetness of her perfume and felt the smooth touch of her skin and love was swirling on the surface of his floating thoughts.

He had known love but had never had the urge to want to possess a lover. 'It's as clear as day, isn't it?' Cassie had remarked after her meeting with Ellie, 'that there is a magnetism about her which you are finding hard to resist?' And no one knew him as well as Cassie.

The heat and stuffiness in the hotel room was stifling. Ellie turned up the air-conditioning as high as it would go and removed Gary's jacket. Nothing we say, nothing we do can describe the feeling of being in love, thought Ellie; it is a feeling no one would want to lose. Quietly and shyly Gary began to undress.

The wild, exciting world of passion was theirs for the taking when suddenly the seizures began: he fell heavily onto the bed and covered his face with his hands. 'Oh, God. Ellie, I'm so sorry.' As his head touched the pillow he turned away from her. There were so many questions she wanted to ask but instead she had to stand by and watch the spasms attack his limbs, unable to stem the pain. She felt his frustration and sobs rose in her chest. It was more than she could bear to see a young man trying to cope with such a crippling disease.

He had curled into a foetal position with his arms wrapped around his legs and as Ellie bent over her tears fell onto his face. She whispered "Doctor?" but there was no response. She walked towards the door and he called her back. 'My medication. In my pocket. Please.' The tablets worked quickly and it may have been her imagination playing tricks but he seemed to have fallen into a deep yet relaxed sleep. All the same she would be on her guard.

She undressed and lay beside him listening to the rhythm of his heartbeat and became conscious that memories of the past were beginning to disturb her, that her lies, her guilt were gnawing at her conscience. When would it be time to tell the truth? The moon, ringed with frost, shone on his face and then the clouds came like a thick, grey veil only to move on to reveal its radiance. She stared at the ceiling, wanting to move away from the past, but it was still there, haunting her. At odd times the bad memories would flicker on and off like an old film projector and always Phil would emerge as the villain.

Resting beside him she knew she loved him. He accepted her the way she was; to tell him the truth about her past risked scaring him away. She had lied to him from the very beginning; there was little honesty in her present actions. Was there a need to confide any more of her shortcomings? Did he need to know what a scheming, revengeful woman she really was? And to what lengths she had dared to go? If so what would she say in her defence? She would begin with Phil, mull over the words in her head and pray that sleep would come and blot out all her contemplations.

CHAPTER EIGHTEEN

"Tuck your shirt in between your legs, and your tongue behind your teeth." (Proverbial Polish.)

Phil was the second of her mother's live-in-lovers, and had put in an appearance when Ellie was eleven. She remembered the sullen, olive looks, the black hair and the dark eyes, as he met her in the hall, and the dismissive glance as she was introduced. The next few weeks were charged with complaints and confrontations but, he warned her, he was here to stay. He planned to make changes in her life. He converted her bedroom into an office and suggested she moved her toiletries out of the bathroom. There were times when she hated him; when his conversation became discourteous, his vulgarity only too obvious and his manner offensive and when he ordered her about and told her that she was nothing but a liability.

She witnessed the way he controlled the business that her mother had built up over the years and was suspicious of the way he disappeared for hours on an evening. But Moira was infatuated with the younger man and if Ellie complained she would be reprimanded. 'What do you know about anything? Just shut up and mind your own business.'

Ellie tried to convince herself that she was happy in this impressive house with its columns of tall trees and a large pond which rested in the hollow at the bottom of the garden. She was friendly but not gregarious and the proud owner of a black horse called Milton. Despite constant pressure she could not be persuaded to follow her Mother's love of clothes although she gave up her Saturdays to work in the sewing room.

She would alter garments but refused to think of it as a future career. Sundays were the days she enjoyed most of all, being with Gran and her young friends from the chapel. Phil, always ready to pour scorn on her faith, described religion as tedious morality. 'All this self denial and piety based on a star which supposedly shone somewhere in the East. You must be mad, girl.' Ellie would give him a contemptuous look but remain cool and reserved and formally polite.

There was no jostling for Moira's attention but if there was an area of jealousy it centred on Ellie's ability to talk non-stop to Moira, following her around the house and garden and never listening to anything Phil had to say. Here was a man who had little respect for women. He strode about the house when sober but was bad-tempered and unpredictable when drunk. After four years Ellie knew all his moods and avoided him whenever she could.

There were endless squabbles but the turning point in their lives was Moira's impending visit to London. The row began before dinner, continued through it and reached its peak when Moira stacked the crockery in the dishwasher. 'Hang on.' Phil followed her into the kitchen. 'What you're saying is that you will be away overnight with some buyer in London, again. Why can't I come?'

Moira sighed. 'It's business and a small matter of expenses. Plus the fact that it is only one night for goodness sake.'

'Business,' he repeated sarcastically. 'Well, now, no doubt I shall find something to do with my time.'

Ellie, watching from the dining room and knowing Phil very well, suspected that he had plans to visit the village, and Tracy in particular, and that the whole act of protest was a charade. It was impossible to keep anything secret in such a small village. Tracy, whose chestnut hair reached almost to her waist and who had piercing blue eyes, worked as a part-time barmaid at "The Huntsman". She had a reputation for being sociable but had little social tact and Phil was just one of her many admirers. Riding Milton along the bridlepath one late summer's evening, Ellie heard scuffling in the bushes and recognised the two of them. It wasn't easy to hide from a rider on a horse, Ellie conceded.

Moira left for London on a bright September morning, on the first day of the school term. Ellie cycled the two miles to school curious as to why the BMW was still parked in the drive with no sign of Phil. She waved to the cleaning lady as she turned her mini into the cul-de-sac and Gran's saying came to mind, "Show me a clean house and I will show you an angry woman". Moira was certainly that as she left for London.

There had been a great show of histrionics from the bedroom the night before and no one had the quickness of a querulous tongue like Moira; she was an expert. A cold breeze rustled through the trees as Ellie arrived home after 4pm and the house was quiet. She helped herself to a roast beef salad from the fridge, washed up and settled in front of her computer in the boxroom she called her bedroom. A little after seven she spent time with her friends at the stables and returned just as Phil pulled away in his car in the direction of the village. Couldn't he be more discreet about his affair? Not that Ellie could do anything about it. He was obsessed with the belief that he was attractive to women.

As the sun set rabbits popped out, one by one, out of the low hedges forming a line like a reception committee and Ellie drew the blinds and prepared for bed. She had barely fallen asleep when she felt a sudden move beside her. It was the smell of whisky and the rough growth of beard that shocked her out of sleep. She cried out. Phil, stripped to the waist and greasy with sweat, forced her under him. She screamed and kicked out, clenched her fists and screamed again. He pinned her down, ripping her top and she brought up her knees. He was cursing her, demanding, commanding but she struggled and bit his arm, dragged her hand free and grasped the nearest thing on the bedside table. The paperweight was triangular with a sharp, pointed end. With a powerful thrust she aimed it at his head; it pierced his temple and he yelled with pain. He recoiled, releasing his grip on her, and she fell out of bed and stumbled down the stairs.

In the hall she grabbed a coat and ran out into the night. An owl screeched and a lone wood pigeon flew past her head. Barefoot she ran across the field to the stables and hid in the barn. A pitchfork was at hand; if he touched her again she would kill him. Not once did she close her eyes. It was an effort to remain calm, to breathe normally. Her heart had stopped racing but she battled to take in air; she had to keep taking deep, long breaths. Why, she cried, could he not be civilized? What happens to some men when drink takes hold? Ellie was 15 and had never experienced a loving, tender embrace from a man let alone the brutal assault which had left her broken and in tears. She was lost, she had no idea what to do.

Daybreak. The sun rose, spreading light on the wet grass, and Ellie moved cautiously towards the house. The car had gone. Maybe he had, too; maybe he was drowning his sorrows. The kitchen door was ajar. On the table was an empty bottle of Jack Daniels and a glass. She listened for any sound. Nothing. She drank bottled water from the fridge and crept upstairs. There was blood on the carpet in her bedroom and on the towels in the bathroom but no sign of Phil. Peering through the window, scanning the lawn now sparkling in the sun, she thanked God she had not been harmed. Her pride had been dented and her dignity assaulted, she had been attacked with profanities and had been fearful for her safety, but she had fought her way out of a petrifying situation and won. All that was left was contempt for him and the need to cleanse herself.

The water soothed her and she let the shower run until every part of her body tingled and she felt free from the clammy imprints of his hands.

She flung the blood-stained towels into the bath and dressed for school. He could sort out the mess, he could explain to her mother. There was no way he could sweet-talk his way out of this.

It was difficult to behave normally at school; she was excused games because she feigned a headache, aware of the bruises and scratches yet unwilling to explain them. At break she shared sandwiches with friends on the grass, little clusters of human life ready to take on the world. But on the way home she felt less confident. Tired and bewildered, dirty and ashamed, the problem seemed immense; how could she tell Moira the truth? 'You are expected to tell the truth however hard,' Gran would say. But her Gran was upright and honest and Ellie didn't have the courage. There had to be another way to get rid of Phil.

After a long drive from London Moira was short-tempered and weary. Ellie was scared and desperate to know what Phil had said. His half-empty plate was still on the dining table so they must have spent time together. Did he have such an insensitive perspective on what had happened? Surely not. It had been the worst night of her life.

Moira was not one for asking questions. She had no interest in anything that didn't directly concern her. All she asked was that her world ran sweetly. The subject of Phil would never be introduced; she knew how much he and Ellie hated each other. After tea came the ritual of recounting the first day at school but she was dismissed with a gesture from a well-manicured hand. 'I'm going to take a nap.'

Later, as Ellie coaxed Milton along the path and past the spinney, she felt strangely alone. Sometimes loneliness is every bit as deadly as a disease, she thought. They climbed the gradual slope to the hills and rested as sounds from the village carried on the slight breeze. Police sirens wailed and faded and closer still a Land Rover sounded its horn and Milton pulled back.

The night was gently closing in and there was a lot for Ellie to think through. She rode on the trail behind the farm where two police cars were parked and police were preparing to cordon off part of the wood. A word or two of instruction was passed around and a man in a white coat emerged from the thicket. Ellie was moved on. It was no more than an utterance, but she heard the words 'hit and run'.

The dampness of the mist had spread over the pond and Ellie closed the curtains and climbed between clean sheets and said her prayers. Having decided that she had no longer the slightest intention of being a target, she switched off the light. She had yet to face Phil.

It was a busy scene in and around the village hall. Inquisitive pupils on their way to school were shepherded away by officious police and quickly the news spread. Someone had been killed. 'The post mistress found her whilst walking her dog. In the wood, just off the road to the deserted farmhouse. Blood and guts all over the place!' Ellie stared in disgust at the spotty youth. 'Go on,' he was elbowed. 'It's whatsher-name from the pub, Tracy, you know she served us drinks in the beer garden.' The news was not received well. Ellie had a sudden vision of the two of them together, Tracy and Phil. Niggles rolled around in her brain. Could he be capable of murder? If she was questioned what should she say? She felt numb but there was no escaping the fact that the rebellious voice within her was hankering to get out.

The village was alive with speculation; words of scandal and suspicion were expressed and repeated in the press but there were expressions of sympathy too. Ellie remained silent, for now. During the following days the investigation continued. It was a hit and run but then the body had been dragged some way off the road and rolled off the verge and into a ditch. The ground had been dry and clean and there was some semblance of shade. This was said to help the enquiry but still there appeared to be no suspects.

Life at home was very tense; there were no niceties between the three of them and a hidden sense of contempt between Phil and Ellie. There was also a deep feeling of awareness on his part; she hadn't turned her back on retribution. Moira appeared oblivious to it all.

Trying to keep pace with events was no easy task. The police were looking for a car which had been seen in the vicinity, a red car. There were rumours of Tracy being pregnant. 'She was killed at approximately 11.15pm,' confirmed the post mistress. 'She doesn't normally walk that way home. Maybe someone gave her a lift and threw her out of the car.'

There was a great deal of activity once Tracy's body had been removed; men prodding the ground with sticks and sweeping the undergrowth. It seemed also that they were being weighed down with suggestions but nothing concrete. It gave new life to the village. Science gained a foothold and the cordon was removed.

Phil had returned from the hospital after having the stitches removed from his temple. He must have sought treatment some time after she had hit him, Ellie concluded. But what was the time lapse? Tracy died on the same night he had tried to rape her, this she knew for certain, but he was with her at the time. He couldn't have been in two places at once, could he? His comments to Moira were unnerving. 'The place is crawling, the police are sticking around, maybe they think there will be another. Maybe it's not a one-off.'

When the track across the fields was reopened Ellie rode Milton and kept him close to the main road. There was little traffic and ahead a small clump of woodland led to the stream. Suddenly a gust of wind rattled through the branches and Milton stopped. Ellie gasped but it was nothing more than a tree and not a man with outstretched arms as she imagined.

All through the night she remained anxious. Phil wasn't being punished for what he had done. Because she was ignorant there were no accusations from Moira and he still remained a threat. There had to be a way of making him suffer. Unexpected sunshine flooded through the window. Ellie figured that she had a solution. It was simply a matter of directing suspicion.

The next day she cycled to where Tracy's body was found and added her small bunch of flowers to the sea of blossoms which decorated the grass. They glowed where the sun touched them and the dead blooms had been tossed into the ditch. From the stone wall Ellie picked out two pieces of rock and concealed them in her bag. She scooped up a handful of gravel from the road and put it in a plastic envelope. Then she cycled home, aware that the game of cat and mouse was about to begin.

There were generalizations about who may have killed Tracy; it had to be a man, obviously drunk, married of course and a regular visitor to the pub. All theories were explained earnestly to the hirsute landlord. Takings had understandably increased. Tracy, meanwhile, was buried quietly in the local churchyard with most of the villagers present. It appeared that the trail had gone cold.

For a few days Ellie struggled with herself. Was this really the right thing to do? Why not? She only wanted to scare him. And the disgusting way he had behaved had fired her imagination. The most difficult step was the first step.

Kenwood Park was where Phil played golf every weekend and a mini bus collected him early on a Saturday morning. Moira was at work, Ellie would join her later. This was the opportunity she had waited for. The red BMW, shiny and almost new, was left in the drive. From her bag she removed the sharp pieces of rock and slowly, deliberately, gouged three lines along the paintwork on the passenger side of the car. She could not be seen, residents could come and go in virtual privacy here. Next she sprinkled the gravel over the nearside tyre and pressed it in firmly. She took her time, there was no rush.

In the hall cupboard she found Phil's spare golf clubs thrown in the corner. She chose one with a very wide-angled face. It looked the stronger; she hoped it would do the trick. She whacked the iron against the apron of the car directly beneath the lights. Twice. It buckled. One more for luck. This car certainly showed signs of being in an accident.

Ellie swept up around the car clearing the debris and tidied the drive, placing the rocks among the plants in the rockery. After wiping the golf club clean she replaced it in his bag. On her way to the boutique she made a telephone call from the kiosk in the village.

Moira's business was run efficiently and sensibly; she knew her market and her clients. Once a year she organised a fashion show for charity and she would mobilize models from members of the public. Last year it was held down by the river, a colourful display of copper and russet blending in with autumn and so successful it was about to be repeated. There was a lot for Ellie to do and to think about. She stared out of the window for long stretches. What was happening at the house? The sewing machine hummed as she tackled the crisp material expertly and her thoughts returned to Tracy and the knowledge that mankind could be so evil.

There seemed to be a great many policemen milling about the house. Ellie's heart sank; what had she done? Moira was first out of the car. 'Something must have happened to Phil. What's the matter? Has there been an accident? Where is he?' The tall, burly constable calmed her. They entered the lounge. Was this pursuit of reprisal going too far? Ellie felt cold. As a young child she could remember looking up at her mother waiting for words of love that never came. She would never hear them now.

The confusion that followed was indescribable. It was plain that there was a feeling of optimism, that this was the break the police had been waiting for. An anonymous call, Moira was told. Whilst this in itself was a shock to her, it got worse. The car was removed for examination and Moira was in tears. Ellie made coffee and retired to her room.

Phil was in no state to listen to anyone; he fell into a chair, his golf cap stretched tight against his forehead, and attacked the police with a malicious stroke of drunkenness. Because of his delicate state the interview was postponed until the following morning.

The inexorable programme of questioning caught up with him but he denied categorically any involvement in Tracy's death. There was nothing to suggest he was lying and no one saw his car during that crucial period. On the back seat a number of Tracy's hairs had been found and he did admit to giving her a lift on a number of occasions but not on that evening. Perhaps someone had borrowed the car?

Questions probed into their relationship. 'I haven't touched the woman,' he insisted. 'My only contact was across the bar!' And the injury to his head? Nobody else was involved, he argued; he walked into a cupboard door.

The interview room was hot and airless. Phil took several sips of water. After two hours he was allowed home; he was fit for nothing but sleep. Ellie had her first sight for a long time of the compassionate side of Moira. Her voice shook with emotion. Her understanding manifested itself in the way she cared about what was said to him and about him. She believed him. Ellie had a certain amount of sympathy for her and prayed that the ache of bitterness and revenge would go away.

Ellie listened to the drama of events which followed the return of the car. Phil was shaking and swearing with rage and indignation. 'Who in their right mind would do this? To steal it and return it? It doesn't make sense.' Apparently the police were remaining tight-lipped; the absence of sexual activity within the car was adding to the mystery. The rest of the village were making up their own minds whilst Ellie was lying low. She made a point of not being directly involved in any discussions; most evenings were spent with Milton and on a few occasions she wondered whatever had possessed her. Was it time to let go of the heavy burden?

It was lifted from her shoulders. Investigations came to a halt. Phil returned to his job in the Estate Agents, the car was repaired and villagers deprived of a nationwide scandal. It was over or so she thought. Ellie spent Christmas with her Gran. Her tiny flat was just a bus ride away from Moira but a world away from parties and late nights. Ellie took it upon herself to prepare everything from the presents to the food, and she needed to attend chapel and take communion. Did she still believe in forgiveness? she sighed. Moira and Phil were at the point of unquestioning devotion; Ellie might as well not have existed. It was deliberately contrived and suited her.

In March whilst they were away on a cruise Ellie took a call from the Police, a courtesy call. Gavin Marshall had confessed to the murder of Tracy Frank. Everyone threw themselves into the whirlwind of press photographers and once more the village came alive. It was a village surrounded by beautiful parks and gardens but soon became a hive of unwelcome sightseers. Ellie was alone in the house and in a mood of tense anxiety, but at least she was off the hook. On reflection Ellie regarded this view as probably sinful; Gavin was just 17. One week later she was idly watching the clouds float over the moon and listening to the north wind as it howled in the branches when news came over the television. The ache turned her stomach. It would appear that Gavin was mentally ill and confessed to every murder that ever was.

April sprung into May and Ellie contented herself with rejuvenating the neglected garden. She moved from the rockery to the pond with the agility of a lively sparrow, planting and pruning. She discovered a track through the wood close by which had been hidden for years behind huge yew and box hedges. Shuddering, she paused; she could imagine when the wind shrieked dismally what a menacing place this could be. Now it was a tangled mass of weeds and dead branches. Never one to give in, Ellie armed herself with a pair of long-handled secateurs, donned her shorts and prepared to tackle the undergrowth. Struggling to separate the burrs from the wild roses, she ventured further into the maze of hedgerows.

A sudden noise caused her to hold her breath. If she kept very still and quiet it would go away; it was a rabbit or a squirrel maybe. 'Are you OK?' Phil's voice carried low in the stillness. 'What do you want?' she snapped.

His dark eyes scanned her face. 'Wondered where you were disappearing to.' He stationed himself between her and the opening, peering over her shoulder. 'What's through there then?'

She stood her ground. 'Look I'm trying to fettle these vines, I'd like to get on.'

'Now there's an interesting turn of phrase, here let me help you.'

Ellie felt at once there was something sinister about his intentions. She raised the secateurs, pointing them at his stomach. For a second the brooding eyes flashed and narrowed. He fingered the scar on his temple, and moved towards her. 'If I had really wanted to, I could have you know. I was simply testing the water.' Ellie rallied herself and faced him. He was referring to his assault on her and she responded quickly.

'And risk being charged with statutory rape? I don't think so.'

He swung round. 'My, we have been busy. Don't delude yourself. Your holier-than-thou attitude is a right turn-off. Now, Tracy, she was something else.'

He paused; it appeared that he wanted to say more but retreated and then, stepping out into the sunlight added, 'I had nothing to do with her death and anyway you are my alibi.' On his own conviction he had admitted the assault on her. He walked away. She wanted to scream. Instead she smashed down the overhanging branches, shredding the leaves where she imagined his body to be.

It was when Moira had returned from a routine appointment with the Well Woman Clinic that she abandoned her social evening and burst into tears. Ellie ran downstairs in time to see her help herself to a glass of brandy, her hands shaking and her eyes red with weeping. 'I've got cancer, I know I have. They said it might be nothing, these lumps I have in my breasts, but I know different!' She swallowed hard and threw herself on the leather sofa. 'I don't want to be disfigured, I want to be normal. I hate sympathy. How can it happen to me? Tell me what have I done to deserve this?' Her blonde hair had slipped from the chignon and hung in strands round her velvet collar. Without showing sympathy Ellie did not know what to say and knelt in front of her. 'Oh, go away. I don't know how I will cope, we have enough to put up with without all this.'

It took less than an hour to finish the brandy and by the time Phil entered the house she was raging and waving her arms and screaming about the unfairness of life and the insensitive approach to women and the casual procedures of hospitals. He calmed her, disliking the feeling of helplessness whilst struggling against his desire for peace and quiet. Ellie retired.

During her stay in hospital Moira was peevish and complaining. The rubber mattress was uncomfortable, the pillows were hard and the fan by her bed too noisy, and Phil was giving the impression that he would rather be somewhere else. Meanwhile Ellie was snuggling down in a duvet on a worn moquette settee with a mug of drinking chocolate and a chunk of malt loaf, listening to Gran singing softly, unable to accept the oncoming of a dreary old age.

There was a vast change in Moira when she returned home. She did not have cancer but she did have a greater appreciation of what life had to offer her. A small annexe was hastily constructed at the rear of the shop to house the new range of clothes and she took on an extra member of staff. The days of anxiety had passed.

At the end of June a television crew arrived to reconstruct the murder of Tracy. Crowds gathered around the scene in the failing light to watch the young actress in the chestnut wig walk past the woods, the red car behind her picking up speed. Such was the fascination of murder; did it spring from an unearthly preoccupation with death or a recognition of the good gift of life? Ellie wondered and whether this going over old territory would heal her qualms.

There was no other choice but to reopen the case against Phil. A witness allegedly identified the car after seeing the programme, although unable to verify that it was Phil who was at the wheel. Again the villagers passed through a period of unsettling scandals and Ellie was to play a major part.

The agitation surrounding the household did nothing to help Ellie cope with all the attention. The police were anxious to have her statement on record. The same tall burly constable explained gently that he would like to ask her a few questions. Whilst Phil was being held at the station convinced that he was the scapegoat, Ellie was comfortably settled in the lounge at home with a policewoman for effect. 'If we could just clear up a few little niggles,' the constable began. 'The night your Mother was in London was Mr Hughes at home all evening?'

She answered casually. 'Yes, I think so.'

'So you are not certain?'

Ellie bit her lip. 'Perhaps he popped out for a pint, maybe?' he persisted.

'No,' she paused. 'He always had plenty to drink in the house.'

'Was he drinking that evening? Did you see him take a drink?' She shook her head.

The policewoman inspected the Royal Doulton figure on the shelf. 'No, I was on my computer in my bedroom.' Ellie marvelled at his patience as he turned the notebook over in his lap. It was now or never; she laughed nervously. 'Oh, I remember now, he went out in the car. I thought it strange at the time. When I heard the engine I looked out of the bedroom window.'

The constable sat forward. 'You are certain it was him?'

'Oh, yes, I could see him clearly in the security light.' She was finding it easier to lie.

'What time was this? Please think carefully, this is very important.' The woman sat by her and put her hand on Ellie's arm. She pulled it away, she felt she was rolling down a grassy slope, a gentle fall into deception, but would the crash at the bottom jar her into reality? They waited.

'I think the news had finished on TV followed by the regional news, it was probably about a quarter to eleven.' A look of satisfaction passed between the officers. 'Just one more question.' Ellie clasped her hands. 'What time did he return home?' She dismissed the enquiry with a smile.

'Oh, I don't know. I'm sorry, I was asleep.' Yes, she thought. Phil said I was chaste and virtuous but holier-than-thou? He would never mock her again.

At the police station she repeated it once more. The newspapers were chiselling away at village life, leaving a sculpture of confusion. There was no escape. By the side of the road at the scene of the crime an indisputable piece of evidence had been found. Or so the postmistress informed her as Ellie was about to enter the shop. Adjusting her spectacles, she continued, 'According to sources Tracy may have died earlier. Won't that upset the applecart?'

'I don't see how,' queried Ellie.

'Well, it might not be Phil, might it? They,' she nodded towards the station, 'have been known to get it wrong.' Ellie decided that now was not an ideal time to change her story. She would wait a while longer.

It was soon plain to see that Moira was not coping very well. She had been absent when Ellie had been questioned and the analysis of police procedures was blotted out; most of it bore no relation to her Phil, it was all a terrible misunderstanding, she insisted. The normal routines of her life were breaking up, her Manager took over the running of the shops and her muffled sobs disturbed Ellie's sleep. Something had to be done. She would retract her statement, it was the only way. What sort of life was Phil having, what was he going through? He should have learned his lesson by now.

Then a reprieve for Ellie. Moira regained her composure with the help of Prozac and red wine. It held her together, she said. She was back in tune with business and spent hours listening to the music of the Three Tenors. They were helping her through her worst crisis, she insisted. Perhaps she was mellowing, thought Ellie.

Many people had likened Moira to a trendsetter and she was certainly sophisticated, smart and a little haughty. Gran's religious fervour did not reach Moira and she was rebellious and wayward. Ellie was the result of a one-night casual fling and at 16 posed an awkward situation. There was anger and disappointment and the unborn baby was unwanted and unloved. Gran took on full and devoted responsibility for Elise when she was twelve weeks old and Moira resumed her life as if nothing had happened.

It was only when Moira returned to Durham after living some years in London that Gran had to take a small flat and

Ellie moved in with her mother. Moira, hard-working and intelligent, was consumed with ambition and there was little time in her life for a daughter she had never wanted.

There was nothing much to show on the bright Sunday morning in August that Ellie was about to celebrate her 16th birthday. A solitary card, in a pink envelope, lay across her breakfast plate. In it a Pansy Potter type character which doubled as a fridge magnet ballooned "Happy Birthday" with a scribbled "From Moira" underneath. Moira was nowhere to be seen. Not even the fundamental niceties existed between them. Ellie had passed through the stage of being brushed aside, she was one year stronger and nearer to moving away, maybe to university.

Smoke came twirling up from the pocket handkerchief square of grass behind the chapel, and the air was filled with the smell of barbecued steaks and sausages. Gran moved slowly towards her and hugged her. 'Happy Birthday. We have organised a treat for you.' It was a lovely surprise. Ellie screwed up her mouth to stem the tears and the children swarmed round her with cards and gifts like bees round a passion flower.

Then came a fleeting thought of Phil; she searched her mind as to what she should do. What if he was found guilty? He protested his innocence, he was facing a long wait. It was a harrowing time for Moira; they had no security, she said gravely, she would have to consider other options. In spite of herself Ellie was ready to overlook the hypocrisy of the present and enjoy what little time was left before the trial.

She walked Gran home, linking arms, the older woman leaning heavily on her stick. 'I have a surprise for you at home,' she smiled.

'Another?' Ellie squeezed her hand. The ability to plan ahead was her strength, without it Ellie's future would have been in jeopardy. As she steered her from babyhood to a healthy eight-year old she concentrated on honesty, good behaviour and respectability. Most of all she wanted her to be happy. Moira, on the other hand, would consider obedience, external appearance and high achievement to be the main priorities. Happiness was a bonus. The cheque from Gran was sealed in a plain brown envelope. 'It's an endowment. Put it with your other savings and use it wisely. For university, maybe.'

****

The city had excelled itself with decorations, creating a sensation of light and warmth in the Victorian market. The spirit of Christmas surrounded her but she felt alone. Silence had replaced curiosity as the death of Tracy faded into the background. Other news had taken its place. Moira insisted that the police were groping in the dark and her visits to Phil confirmed it. 'I am shutting up the house over Christmas,' she informed Ellie briskly. 'I am sure you will find something to do.' Thank heaven for Gran. Thank heaven she no longer felt that she was being pulled into the quicksand of guilt and that being able to think of a stream of excuses would mean that she could sleep at night.

The trial began on the first Monday in March. It was a still, dark morning with heavy cloud and Moira was up at first light. 'We must appear well-groomed,' she said. 'We must beware of becoming blasé. I have no intention of being the target of pity.' In contrast there was a tenuous look about Ellie. They sat together in the corridor watching court officials wheeling and darting. It was warm and Ellie felt sick. She was not called to the stand.

On the second day the sun broke through. Ellie had been kept awake whilst the skies changed from black to grey and the breaking of dawn brought more anguish. It was beginning to register, the charge of dangerous driving, the witnesses for the prosecution, the responsibility she had brought upon herself, but she neither saw nor heard anything of the trial. Outside Court Number 2 the changing scenes of laughter and tears passed her by. Feeling remorseful and afraid, it occurred to her that perhaps there was still time to change her mind.

She was called after the recess. It appeared that the trial

had opened on an exceptionally quiet note and she felt alone and fragile as she faced the man in the black, silk gown and repeated her name. It was almost as if a fog had descended and was floating round the courtroom. The murkiness clouded her judgement, the oath was taken but would the truth be told? The bewigged, odd-looking man with the protruding lower lip was fatherly but firm. The sombre colours of the courtroom, shades of green, brown and grey, were lifted by intermittent flashes of sunlight. The same questions were put to her but the friendly atmosphere of the station seemed a long way off. The same answers were repeated but this time a more detailed explanation was required. 'Was he drunk when he got into the car?'

'I don't know.'

'Did the car drive away at speed?'

'I can't remember.'

'Just think about it.' His manner sickened her.

'I can't remember,' she repeated.

'Am I to understand that the accused left the house at approximately 10.45 pm?'

'Yes.'

'But you have no idea what time he returned to the house?'

'No,' I was asleep.' He coughed and turned over the papers in his hand. 'Were you there when the accused banged his head on the ...' he hesitated, 'kitchen cupboard?'

'No.'

'But you were together all evening?'

This changed things; she hadn't been asked this question before. She felt her face turning pink. 'I'm hot, may I have some water?'

'Of course, would you like to sit down?'

'No thank you.'

He smiled. 'Did you have a meal together in the evening?'

'No, I helped myself to something from the fridge, after school!'

'About what time?'

'4.30, maybe.'

'So when did you next see the accused?' She was trapped. Should she say he had driven away earlier on her return from the stables? He didn't see her. It was her word against his. She swallowed hard.

'When I saw him leave at a quarter to eleven.'

'I'm sorry, would you repeat that?' She did. Louder.

'Thank you.' He sat down.

Ellie helped herself to more water and sipped slowly; she was dry and nervous. The counsel for the defence was harsh and inscrutable. 'Now, on the evening of the alleged hit and run by the accused, what exactly did you see from your bedroom window?'

'I saw him,' she nodded towards Phil, 'get into the car and drive away.'

'I see. You give the approximate time as 10.45 so it would be dark?'

'No, the security light was on.'

There was a pause. 'You say in your statement that you heard the car engine and looked out of the bedroom window. I presume therefore that whoever was driving that night was already in the car?' Ellie remained silent. 'How could you be sure it was the accused?' He paused. 'I put it to you that you were mistaken.' Think this through, take your time, she thought.

She faced him with youthful defiance. 'He started the engine and returned to the house; he must have forgotten something. I saw him get into the car and drive away.'

How could she lie? She had sworn on the Bible to tell the truth. She was disgusted with herself. Throughout the cross-examination she had avoided eye contact with Moira; the trial had never been a subject of discussion between them, Phil's account had been all she needed. 'Tell me,' the questioning continued. 'Do you resent the accused sharing your home? Living with your Mother?'

'No.'

'Do you have friends visit, do you stay overnight with friends?'

'No.'

He leaned forward. 'You haven't been entirely candid, have you? You see, I think you have been brought up in a solitary, friendless environment and you are creating a place of fantasy; you have made an imaginary solution for yourself and have come to believe in it. Your whole story is a fabrication. I strongly suspect that you are confused.'

It would be impossible to prove otherwise; it was a puzzle how suddenly he had turned her testimony into nonsense. Yet Ellie was not going to miss this opportunity of answering back. 'You are wrong, Sir, and I will be proved right'. There was strength and passion in her voice but inwardly she was afraid. Could she safely assume that she was not suspected of damaging the car?

For a few moments as she returned to her seat she was aware of murmurings and she fidgeted to the end of the chair. With dramatic suddenness the prosecution called the doctor who had dealt with Phil's head injury. He was young and confident, standing with his hands folded in front of him. 'Yes,' he answered. 'I treated him for a laceration to his head, on the temple to be exact!'

'Was the wound deep?'

'Fairly; it needed stitches.'

'Did the accused give an explanation for the injury?'

'Not at first, but he mentioned later, um, bumping into a cupboard.'

'Anything else?' The doctor frowned. The prosecution continued. 'Any other injuries?'

'No, not that I could see. He did complain of buzzing in his ears.'

'Can we be certain that it was indeed the sort of injury he described?'

'Not exactly.' Ellie felt the colour drain from her face. There was obviously a theory to be tested here. 'I would suggest that it was caused by a spike, a tapering spiked heel on a woman's shoe, a stiletto, perhaps?'

There must be a limit of honesty and intention that a doctor might be prepared to give in evidence and it was obvious by the look on his face that he was uncomfortable. 'It is possible,' he answered.

'Just one more question, Doctor. Did Mr Hughes smell of drink? Was he drunk?' A slight pause preceded 'He had been drinking, yes, he was unsteady on his feet'.

There was a vulgar coarseness about Doreen Lane. She took the stand wearing a low-cut sweater and tight jeans and fingered the three rows of gold necklaces with French manicured hands. However she spoke so sadly and sincerely about the night Tracy died that the court warmed to her. 'I'll spell it out for you,' her chin jutted forward. 'I was travelling on the top road towards the village when this BMW drove straight in front, cutting me off. He was all over the place. I yelled at him, my language was a bit strong, and jammed on the brakes. As he turned into the lane by the woods he slowed down. The young lady struggled to get out and ran along the grass verge!' She paused and adjusted her sweater. The counsel nodded for her to continue. 'She was limping and I thought she had stubbed her toe on the stones.' Doreen's voice wavered. 'She rounded the corner well away from the car, then I heard the engine roar as he drove round the bend after her.'

It was obvious to Ellie that someone was guilty of Tracy's death but was it Phil? Doreen Lane, when cross-examined, could not identify him to the court. Ellie tried to shake off the nervousness and stop her body from trembling and chose the end of the trial to scrutinize the jury. Ordinary people with unremarkable lives about to make a notable decision and her thoughts returned to the victim – young, attractive and everything to live for.

She was only half-listening. Moira was very quiet and still. Her skin had taken on a grey pallor and she had made a deliberate move away from Ellie. The afternoon sunlight touched the walls with gold as the Judge faced the jury. There was a suspicion of contradictory evidence, he said, but then went on to refer to the fact that the car which was involved in the crime did belong to the accused and there was tangible evidence of gravel from the scene of the crime in the tyres and damage to the bodywork of the car. No importance was attached to the accused's apparent affair with Tracy as no evidence of sexual activity within the car had been detected. It was to be disregarded as hearsay.

Ellie was not an experienced observer of court procedures; she was caught up in a feeling of anxiety and awe. She prayed for the life that had been taken and the life that was about to be changed forever. Maybe he was innocent of this crime but he was guilty of molesting and reviling her and for this alone he had to pay the price.

The jury retired. Everyone here has a job to do she thought. They returned in less than two hours. GUILTY. Moira cried out. Her mouth and eyes opened wide simultaneously and then she sobbed quietly.

CHAPTER NINETEEN

"Silence is the door of consent." (Proverbial Moorish.)

There were four rounds of toast, cornflakes, a selection of jams and marmalades and fresh coffee on the breakfast trolley outside the hotel room. It was obvious that Gary was in a deep sleep. He was lying diagonally across the bed and breathing easily. It should have been a champagne morning, the world should have been a sweeter green, but once again the contours of her world were blemished by this illness she didn't understand.

It was the clink of china that woke him and the smell of coffee that enticed him out of bed. 'Hi, sweetheart.' He had never called her that before. 'Happy Christmas.'

About eleven o clock, as they left in a taxi for No. 68, dark clouds hovered and snow fell gently on empty streets. Again he apologised for spoiling their evening, especially one so full of anticipation. The symptoms were so degrading to him, he sighed, but added, 'Have you ever heard of anybody who amounted to anything who didn't have a few hardships in his life?' For Gary it appeared that suffering was not surrendering but he didn't have to do it on his own, without love, whilst Ellie was close by.

It was a clear, crisp winter morning when she visited Cassie. It was all written down, questions that needed to be asked, answers that could fill in the gaps. It was no accident that Cassie came to mind, it was a strong feeling of providence. Coincidence is God's way of staying anonymous, Gran had told her.

A short flight of steps led down to the cellar and Cassie guided Ellie carefully on the broken slabs. It was well lit and kept warm by a Calor Gas fire in the corner. 'It is a long, drawn out process of cheesemaking,' Cassie smiled. 'From sour milk. Hardly worth it, but satisfying. This isn't a purely social visit, is it?' The notepad changed hands. 'Come on, this calls for a glass of elderberry wine.' Cassie could not indulge in a confession, not on Gary's behalf, he trusted her. It was the appealing look of frustration which concerned her and Ellie was determined to get some answers. Cassie's long hair was loose around her shoulders and a tortoiseshell cat buried its nose in the dark curls as she carried it up the steps.

They settled in opposite chairs in front of the fire above which wet cheesecloths hung on a line across the mantelpiece. 'Do you still have the turquoise stone? Some day it will prove its worth.' Cassie plumped up cushions around Ellie and held her hand. 'I can't answer all your questions. I can't provide the complete answer but I will try. Gary was abandoned as a baby and put out for adoption. He came to live with my parents; I was 14. He was a good baby, a well-behaved boy and an intelligent young man. I mothered him. I learnt my nursing skills when he went rock climbing and came home with scraped knees and a broken arm. I consoled him when our puppy died, and I taught him to ride a bike. I loved him like a brother. Sometimes he would ask about his parents, at other times he would sulk but he was never mardy, never nasty.' The cat slid down onto Ellie's lap. 'Sometimes when you are young you push past everything that stands in your way, don't you?' Cassie continued. 'Gary wasn't like that. He was easy-going, amiable. And clever. He attended Nottingham University and started his career with the Cultural Heritage Society.'

Ellie had wondered whether a carefully-guarded secret had been centred on his boyhood but concluded that it couldn't be so.

'The date of his first appearance on stage,' Cassie went on, 'was when he was about 17. He had spent the summer fruit-picking and bought a guitar. He is self-taught, you know. It was central to his life at that time.' She ran the comb through her hair. 'Let me get you some more wine.' Ellie shook her head. 'I would love to tell you what you would like to know, was there ever a woman in his life? What is this sickness all about? I don't have the answers, I'm sorry.'

Ellie kissed Cassie warmly. She was now firmly resolved in a number of things; firstly she would concentrate on her career, secondly she would never tell anyone the truth about her past and thirdly, and most important of all, she decided she would do anything in the world to help Gary.

****

Perhaps there is no other time in the designer's calendar that generates pride and jealousy more than the show. Against a backcloth of a rich crop of white clover, the new designs of "Giselle" were born. Isabella hurried from one group to another, gathering models and escorting them to the catwalk like a teacher at a nursery school. Birdsong was all around and the breeze lifted the leaves as Milan welcomed spring. The conception that fashion models do very little but strut and pout is false. In fact, Athol Picora pursued Ellie with renewed vigour, waving contracts in his fat little fist. The Marazzoni brothers rubbed their hands. Here was a model in demand, full of self-confidence, climbing the stairway of success and still retaining the mystery of silence. The design of language was in her movement and in her smile. There would be no lack of suitors in the months ahead but she had stored up a reserve of wonderful memories of Gary and the gentleness of his nature.

Happy faces and furrowed brows, a mixture of delighted models and envious competitors encircled the stage on the lawn. A baby cried and sitting on a grassy bank enjoying the breeze a young mother rocked gently to the music. Ellie could well imagine Fab doing the same in front of a log fire, on the sofa against the wall which hid the damp patch. Suzy, named after the Banshee babe, was born in late February, a healthy seven pounds.

A tall sprightly figure hurried towards Ellie as she was about to climb into the mini coach. He wore a long-sleeved polo style shirt over blue jeans and from a distance looked quite young but the shortage of breath and the lines around his eyes belied his true age. 'You must be Elise,' he panted. 'I'm Erich Sava. I wonder if I could tempt you to an evening at the ballet? Oh I know it is very presumptuous of me, but please, it is "Coppelia".' Who told him she loved "Coppelia", she thought. From the back pocket of his jeans he produced a card. 'Please consider it and ask Isabella to ring me. She will vouch for me.' This was music to her ears. "Coppelia" in Milan.

Isabella approved but had reservations. 'There is something you should know.' Ellie sighed. Married? Playboy? Maffia? He didn't look Maffia! 'He's a consultant,' Isabella divulged. 'Ear, nose and throat. He is after your larynx and most likely your body.'

He was honest from the start. 'Of course you are a pleasure to be with, that goes without saying, but I would also like to help you. I specialize in traumas. I would recommend you come for a consultation.' At the ballet they drank cocktails in the crowded bar and she tried to focus on his accent. It was a mixture of all she had heard in Eastern Europe, Czech perhaps with a smattering of Polish.

To reach the clinic there were steps to be climbed and corridors to cover. Erich Sava's consulting room was marked by a blue square and a red cross. Letters from all over the world were framed and displayed around the waiting room and his receptionist was seated behind the slimmest of computers and unusually, she thought, male. Now she faced the white-coated, professional Erich Sava. The physical examination was thorough, the questions unnerving. 'Elise, if when you were able to speak I was to impose a rule of silence on you, how would you cope? What would your reactions be?' "Same as now", she wrote. This was not her first lesson in self-reliance and she had to see this through. 'What were the last words you spoke aloud?' He was trying to trick her. He knew physically she was able to speak but he wanted her confession. Well he was no psychiatrist and she wasn't ready to write a letter of commendation to add to his collection. She was bright and guarded. He took the chair opposite her, reached out and took her hand. 'When you are ready, Elise, come and see me again.'

It was hard to believe how easily they had become good friends, but he had the uncanny gift of making conversation which required no answers. They were linked by gossip columnists as an item, some said, but Ellie was quick to stem all the rumours and sent a prompt email to Gary. Gran received numerous letters over the months, painting pictures of Italy and the people, describing her love of the countryside and the cold and bare aspect of the interior of the Cathedral.

Holidays were snatched in between shows. Athol Picora wielded the whip. His methods were too dictatorial to be popular but he believed in hard work, well-disciplined models and solid contracts. There were aspects of the profession which made her feel uncomfortable but when she was approached with sleazy options her lips would stiffen in a grin, she would not be asked again. She would rise each day aware that her thoughts were far away and that only the pressure of work prevented her from going home.

On her 19th birthday, along with the usual swarm of models and retinue, she arrived in Austria. In the Schloss Belvedere, the palace outside Vienna, a film was in progress in the ornamental-filled gardens. The scented flowers blended with the perfume of Egyptian oils and the smooth, sensuous feel of the material clung to the models as they paraded past the museums. Flowering creepers added a touch of gaiety to the greyness of the walls. Cameras rolled. Why was it we couldn't convey a smell in pictures? Ellie wondered. Even ancient wisdom didn't have the answer.

They were barely 20 miles from the airport when their

fleet of cars was diverted to allow a caravan of Zingaros to take up camp in the nearby field. The Italian gypsies cross the border to trade, Isabella explained. 'Look how good they are with the horses.' Now could be seen the fantasy of shapes and colours, the magnet for artists, the glowing countryside of Austria.

Suddenly the awareness of something familiar closed in. A bus in the dip by the side of the road and close to the stream of fresh water came into view. It was Dark Horse, scruffy and travel-worn. Ellie jumped up, releasing her seat belt. "Stop," she mouthed to Isabella. 'Stop,' Isabella yelled and Ellie knew that the moment had come when she could step out in confidence without explanation. There wasn't time, and she didn't much care. She would not waste her life worrying about what people thought of her. Sliding down the bank, she ran around the bus, banging on the door and windows. "Please let there be someone here," she prayed. An audience of more than a dozen people watched as she embraced a slovenly-dressed male with uncombed hair and a ginger beard. He stood back to admire her and kissed her and the onlookers piled back into the cars as she clambered up the bank with tears in her eyes. She dreamed of her friends on the flight to Milan. Mustard had told her she was a beauty but friendliness was beautiful and kindliness and warmth.

It was impossible to close the door on Athol when he had his foot firmly in place. When he could push his models to the limit he was happy. 'Judging from my own experience,' he would say in a snide voice, 'you only get out of life what you put into it.' However he did allow Ellie special privileges. She never asked for them, she took them. She would use calligraphy to write notes for time off, informing him rather than requesting, and although he would chew hard at his cigar and moan, he relented. She wasn't his favourite, at least it didn't appear so, he simply did not know how to deal with her silence.

Gary was always near. Here, in Paris, even more so. The December wind howled through the lights on the bridges

and twisted the water into spirals under the boats. Ellie's
eyes were smarting and her lips were sore. This was really
tough shooting. The fake tan shone ludicrously through
flimsy fabrics and the girls shivered in the cold. Imagination
flew back to the time spent here with Gary and despite all
notions of romance, remained in her head along with other
sentimental nonsense.

The house stood elegantly on top of a hill above a fertile
valley stretching towards grazing land with not another
building in sight. It was a massive house with iron gates and
stone pillars. The girls shuffled inside, shoulders hunched,
sniffling and complaining. It was to be their home until
morning.

It had big rooms, fine ceilings and it was warm. Again, yet
another privilege, Ellie was given her own room, whilst the
others had to share. They thawed out over mugs of hot coffee
and ate their evening meal by candlelight at mahogany tables
with a fire blazing in the huge inglenook. The meal, French
Provincial, included game pie with aubergine beignets but
Ellie chose a dish cooked with tomatoes, onions, dates and
black olives. She shared the black olives but not the lemon
flan that followed. By late evening everyone was slightly
drunk and sprawled around the two sitting rooms.

Her bedroom was delightful, with pink and white sprigged
wallpaper and matching curtains. There was a patchwork
bedspread on a carved oak bed. It looked inviting and as
Ellie was about to undress there was a knock on the door.
The last person she expected to see was Athol Picora. 'Let me
in,' he demanded. Ellie looked down onto the frilled white
shirt and the whisky stains spattered across the front, and
shook her head. 'It is of great importance, I want to have a
discussion with you.' His broken English was interspersed
with coughs from his cigar smoke. Again she shook her
head and pushed him away. By her standing firm, he finally
relented. He raised his fat hands in the air. 'Then come and
collect the papers and read the contract at your leisure.'
Maybe this was the way to break the impasse.

The door locked behind her. Damn. Athol stumbled onto

the landing and along a corridor gripping his cane. His bedroom was spacious with two comfortable armchairs and some Victorian furniture. Ellie entered gingerly. Glass doors opened onto a small balcony. 'Sit down,' he invited, throwing the cane onto the bed. The wind howled and she shivered. He sensed an air of refusal.

From the bedside table he offered her a sheet of paper. It was snatched from him and she made for the door. 'Don't run away.' The cold eyes scanned her face, angry and defiant. 'There is so much I can offer you. How far can you go without a voice?' He mixed himself a whisky and soda. 'You have me backing you now. Without me you may never work again.' Looking down on him he looked a pathetic figure. Ellie smiled and tossed her head. The deep-set eyes under heavy brows narrowed. He made a move towards her, touching her bare shoulder. Her knee made contact with his hand and the glass hit the floor.

What had she learned from the girls and Gary? Be defensive – streetwise. Athol was angry and he lunged at her with his fist, catching her chin. She recoiled but he was unsteady and the cane on the bed was within her reach. It was time to strike. As he turned Ellie swung the cane at his head and he dropped to the floor.

He lay still but he was breathing. His stomach rose and fell like a pair of bellows and a nasty bruise was forming where the handle had caught his forehead. Was it the whisky on an empty stomach that had immobilized him completely? Her jaw hurt and she flopped into an armchair watching him for several minutes until she pulled herself together. She used a paper tissue to retrieve the glass from the floor. Maybe fresh air would revive him? The doors on the balcony were stiff and difficult to open but once opened she wedged them with his suitcase. 'The difficulty I have in keeping body and soul together,' Ellie said out loud, stepping out onto the balcony and checking that there was no one about. Every window was ablaze with light and there was a party in progress on the floor below. What now?

The wind had died down; he should be alright half in

and half out of the room. He was too heavy to lift; she rolled him and pushed him with her feet and he groaned with each turn. 'Silly man,' she sighed, bending over him. 'You didn't realize who you were dealing with.' The contract was returned to the drawer unread. She wasn't even curious.

At the desk she apologised for locking herself out of her room and ordered a martini with lots of ice. Once she had managed to make herself understood everyone was always very obliging. Try to study people before taking the plunge, was Gran's advice although I don't think she meant deep reflection, Ellie decided, and in any case it wasn't that easy. Relaxing in a bath with a loofah filled with ice cubes held to her jaw she tried to put the incident behind her, and settled down to sleep. It wasn't the thought of Athol's well-being that kept her tossing and turning but the possible repercussions; she would probably be sent home with no job and no future.

Breakfast was a lively affair with a queue of young ladies casually dressed in jeans and thick sweaters helping themselves to rashers of bacon and fried eggs. Catwalk diets did not apply here. 'You look rough, do you feel alright? What happened to your face?' Isabella shuffled beside her. Ellie shrugged. 'Two days off now, try to get some rest.'

There was something unusual about the stance of the two men in the doorway and the announcement that followed. It was greeted with disbelief. They spoke in French. Isabella looked shocked, then translated. 'Athol has had a heart attack.' Ellie felt a sudden tightness in her throat. 'He's dead.'

It was easy to be swept away with all that follows an untimely death. It was easy to say nothing but Ellie was in deep in the murky sea of deceit. Going with the flow was the best thing to do. There was a confused air of disruption, a post mortem was mentioned, the models were distressed and Ellie sat in stunned silence. Far away the fashion world was preparing to name his successor. Isabella returned with the news. 'Apparently he fell on the balcony and hit his head. He was there all night. There is some talk of a heart problem.'

It was not a gift that Ellie had of masking her feelings, it was what others perceived in her. The lights of Paris twinkled beneath them as they flew home and the air was rife with speculation. The conversation was an unbeatable combination of spite and pique. Once she had harboured a contempt for liars, Tony and then Phil, but to withhold the truth is surely just as bad? 'You look upset,' Isabella sympathized. 'Don't worry, we are in London next week.' All but Sophie had run out of things to say and everything that related to Athol had run its course. The girls were catching up on sleep in their own beds and Frankie listened intently as Ellie relayed all that had happened, voicing out loud her concerns in concert with his purrings.

London was green and beautiful with luxurious trees and grass despite the December frost, for the Fashion Week was held in the Botanical Gardens and such a relief after the shoot in Paris. They swept along through the waving grasses in the brand-new spring/summer collections by the top designers, and there was a minute's silence for Athol. Ellie felt his presence; after all she was the last person to see him alive.

The lights were dazzling, the clothes minimal and the mechanical wizardry made it almost possible to imagine the sea shouting against the cliffs. Hope of seeing Gary here was fading; he couldn't promise, he wrote. No matter, Ellie had no intention of returning to Milan until mid January. Isabella was happy with this, she said. The Morazzoni brothers thought differently. 'There is a difference between the arrangement you had with Athol and your contract with us. Quite a distinct one in fact,' quipped Tony. Ellie adopted an injured look. They drove off in the car before any more was said. Nothing would prevent her going home for Christmas.

In the city rain means simply a shiny black pavement. With her knee-length skirt and high boots Ellie was wrapped up warmly against the driving rain. The train from London was late into Sheffield and after booking into the Hilton she caught the bus to No. 68, to her family. The bus symbolized a return to normality. It mattered to her what happened to her friends and to Gran but there was still that barrier of uncertainty between her and the future which couldn't be lifted just yet.

At the squat tiny garments were put out to dry on the clotheshorse by the fire. Suzy gurgled. Valentine fussed and sniffed, everyone talked at once. Here she was set down plumb in the middle of reality. Could there be a more welcoming sight than this?

There was a need for her to count her blessings; it was the time for handing round gifts of gratitude and appreciation and to make her needs known to Gary. His world had moved far away from hers. She pretended to be casual when he arrived just before noon, meeting up with Jason at the front door; but at that precise moment the cistern in the bathroom overflowed and Boo, rushing downstairs to inform Bas and collect towels, fell over the wood heap in the kitchen. It was the sight of Tiz, flour smudges and red-faced, struggling with the Yorkshire puddings, that turned smiles into hysterics with Boo inelegantly sprawled at her feet.

The meal was over, Suzy was settled, and everyone relaxed when Gary suggested a walk. Together they sauntered through the near deserted streets. 'We'll take it steady,' he suggested. 'It must have been a special moment when you saw the bus in Austria.' He held her hand. 'I am so happy for you, things are going well here too. Fab is back with the band and Bas takes care of the bookings. Jan is in charge of the general running of the squat and there don't seem to be any problems. And what about you?' Ellie mouthed "Me?" and squeezed his hand. There was no time to answer. Quite suddenly, as if prearranged, a group of revellers poured out of a house and blocked their way. There was a great deal of pushing and shoving and a decorated fir tree was uprooted from a garden and was left straggling the pavement.

'What the hell are you looking at?' Gary was being

challenged but the remark prompted a fight among the youths which could not have been bettered in a boxing ring. The situation was menacing. Ellie was grabbed and pinned against a wall and Gary was shouting and struggling to break free. She remembered the can of body spray in her pocket, slipped in her hand and loosened the top. Her attacker's long shirt was clinging to his body and the smell of stale beer sickened her. Deliberately Ellie aimed straight for his eyes and he yelled and released her. He staggered away blinded and in pain. She was unrepentant; had she been warned of his reaction she would have acted exactly the same.

The drunks were silenced, they had no idea what had happened. Gary was released. The youths had a troublesome situation to deal with and the pair were forgotten; they linked hands and made for home. The foundation of her love for Gary was built on his determination to protect her. Yet his illness made him weak and it was almost as if he had fallen sick of an attack of innocence refusing to admit to his frailty. He had some difficulty repressing a smile as they sank on the sofa together. 'They are all at the pub.' Jan smoothed Valentine's coat with her scrawny hand. 'I'm babysitting. Have a Brazil nut.' Mysteries are always beyond measure. Ellie's belief was that she was based here and that the trappings of a rich girl were on hold until she was ready to return.

'Well, the girls seem to be doing fine don't you think?' Ellie was a little tipsy, she snuggled up to Gary as he drove the white van towards the Hilton. It was after midnight and Gary was tired and anxious to be home. She wondered if he was actually uncomfortable to be alone with her but dismissed the idea when he stopped outside his flat. 'Come and look at the garden,' he suggested. Her heart quickened. His look lingered, it did not happen often nor did it last long, but it was unmistakeable. Was he now ready to love her? She edged away from him; she daren't, there was too much going on in her life, problems that needed to be disentangled. Gary sensed her unease; it was another of the countless little puzzles that disturbed him.

He had managed to create a winter wonderland with shrubs and conifers and potted bulbs of colour carefully arranged on a bed of smooth, pinkish shingle. Behind a trellis of evergreen she drank warm beer and raspberry juice, a reminder of Poland, and found herself flushing deeply when he touched her. She was stilled with the closeness of him but yet she had to let him go.

Boxing Day and they had given up their comfortable beds to a punk band from Leeds. That is, all but Fab who remained submerged between layers of blankets after a hard drinking session leaving Jan to act as nursemaid. Bas was trying to be as rude as he could with the girls but was secretly glad of the change of company. The gig was played before a huge crowd in the local pub and Ellie was a bystander. Gary was absent; without him she was lost, with him she was adrift. The vocals cut through the music and rang out above heavy backing. Tiz looked across at the beautiful girl sitting at the bar surrounded by men she chose to ignore and with a reluctance to explain why. Would anyone ever fully know what was going on in Ellie's mind? Tiz thought not. It was hard also to imagine that she was so young.

Ellie sighed. Why did she subject herself to worrying about Gary? He had informed the band with complete lack of enthusiasm that he wanted to take a back seat, ease up a little. They were all agreed on that. It was some time before Tiz joined Ellie for a drink. Her bright red hair, cut short, stood stiffly upright and her eyes shone under the curly fringe. 'You are worried about Gary, aren't you?' There was a familiar obstinate tilt to Ellie's chin. 'We call him the gentle wanderer; he's not offended by it.' The tot of rum was swallowed in one gulp. 'Come on, we'll drop you off at his flat, put your mind at rest.'

They rattled their way through the city streets, the van swung and rumbled as the cymbals broke loose, and Rev cursed. This, for Ellie, was the hard part; she had no idea what to do, how to behave, she was less certain of what she wanted than ever.

The doorbell appeared to reverberate through the whole block of flats. The van clattered away; she was alone. No one came. She tried again and a teenage girl in lime green pyjamas opened the door. She exclaimed with abrupt and cheerful interest. 'Come to see Gaz, have yer? Do yer know yer way?' Who can fathom the hand of fate? Ellie felt she was here from some instinctive curiosity.

The flat was in total darkness, the curtains were drawn. As she fumbled for the light switch she fell over something. It was Gary, face down, arms outstretched and very still. She had failed to notice the vomit around his mouth or the blood until she bent over him. She retched. He had a pulse, she needed help. The telephone was on the bedside table next to the empty pill bottle. Please God, she prayed, don't let him die. The receiver shook in her hand. She dialled 999. What greater need for the human voice? She spoke quietly and gave the address with a voice brimming with emotion, faltering after each word. Then placing a pillow under his head, she washed his face and held his hand until she heard the sirens and opened the front door.

Tears ran down her face and everything within her silently screamed. She begged for strength, remembering how he had sought refuge in her arms. She was dumb again; she had no option, she had been recognised and the papers were keen for a story. Although she had dropped to a point where nothing mattered but Gary's recovery she was refusing to be a part of any speculation about her involvement. Instead of the joyous celebration of Christmas she sat alone in Sister's office away from prying eyes, drinking endless cups of coffee.

The nightmare ended when, just before dawn, Gary regained consciousness. She followed him as he was wheeled into a side ward and waited patiently to be called. He had understood nothing, she told herself, he hadn't heard her speak or recognised the fear in her voice. Normal conversation was still on hold.

'If you don't mind my saying so,' pleaded Sister, 'I think you should try and get some rest. Come back later.' She put her hand on Ellie's arm. 'There is so much love and pain here but give him a bit more time.' The steady drizzle persisted as the taxi pulled up outside the Hilton. It was time to write to Gran, to thank her for having faith, for introducing religion in a beautiful way, not a demanding one, for showing her love. The rain poured as the words formed kindled anxieties until eventually Gran was made aware of everything that had become a trial in her life. Well, almost everything. Mutism was not mentioned.

A big, bronzed man touched her arm. 'You can go in now,' he boomed. 'Don't excite him too much.'

'That,' smiled Gary, 'is what I call ridiculous sympathy. Have you come to make waves and spread ripples? Oh, come on, you are not going to cry, are you?' He was a mass of tubes and wires, and machinery which sounded as if a bomb was about to explode. His face, white as chalk, was like a mask and Ellie leaned over to wipe the perspiration from his forehead. 'Thanks,' he breathed. Privacy had always been an issue for him and Ellie had arranged a private room. It hurt her to think that there would be a loss of dignity.

It was not easy to make sense of all that was happening. Don't be so naive, she told herself, here is a seriously ill man and she had to have answers. 'I want to make contact with his family, are you family?' Sister perched on the edge of the chair in her office as if she was on starting blocks. Ellie shook her head. 'I thought not.' Excitement and confusion was high in the corridors and people talked animatedly and children cried as staff tried to deal with the aftermath of a merry Christmas. 'They show us no respect, you know.' Sister jumped up. 'I'll be back in a minute!' Fifteen minutes went by; Ellie became restless. She was anxious to see Gary, hold his hand, wait for the colour to return to his face, see him smile.

Moving towards the door, she saw on the desk a folder bearing his name. Here were his Medical Records and beside them a list of drugs. CONFIDENTIAL. No, she paused. It would not be ethical and would be extremely dishonest to pry and yet she needed to know before returning to Milan.

Ellie fingered the folder. It would only take a minute to turn the page. RESOURCES ON HUNTINGTON'S DISEASE. It was almost as if an explosion had blown up in her face. She had sensed that he was concealing something but nothing could have prepared her for such a bombshell. The notes continued: Understanding Huntington's Disease, Facts about HD, symptoms, diagnosis, prevalence, treatment and genetic testing. Ellie was so absorbed in what she was doing she forgot time and place. Sister was visible in the doorway and in a few seconds Ellie collapsed in her arms in a flood of tears.

Staff Nurse came bustling in. There was no time for lengthy discussions. Ellie wiped her eyes and blew her nose. 'Look love,' the matronly figure opened the door. 'Go and see Gary, he needs to talk to you and if you like we can have a chat when I come off duty at 7pm. I must go.'

Gary's attitude was calm and positive. 'I'll soon be out of here, sweetheart. Soon everything will be under control, you just see.' They held hands. Slowly she met his scrutiny. 'I have yet to meet anyone more independent, spirited and honest. Or obliging,' he smiled. 'Will you move into my flat until I come home? I don't need you to do anything, just be there.' So great was his sense of relief when she agreed that he fell asleep.

Sister was yawning in the car as they drove the short distance to the station bar. Her days were long and she was ready for bed. But good nursing meant more than accomplishment or efficiency. It proved its worth in being caring and honest, and this young, bright girl needed to know all the facts. The cost of not speaking meant that Ellie had to execute other means and she had prepared questions even though she had no knowledge of the illness. 'We have been through the motions of determining if he had other diseases that would account for the symptoms but I am afraid it is HD. It used to be called Huntington's Chorea, did you know?' Sister sipped her tomato juice. 'There is no easy way to say this. It is a devastating degenerative brain disorder for which, right now, there is no cure.' Ellie stifled a sob. 'I am sorry. Gary tells me that you have seen him through his attacks of myoclonus seizures, that is when he has an involuntary contraction of a muscle. Slurred speech and difficulty in swallowing are also significant symptoms, and an unsteady gait. Some are violent, have rages, but each case is individual. Gary is a patient man, maybe I shouldn't say this but he loves you very much.'

Ellie's world had turned upside down. Sister glanced at her watch. 'I'm sorry, my family are waiting for me. We'll talk again. Look, here is a book on patient care and management. It will help, I'm sure. Where can I drop you off?'

At the hotel Ellie spent time pacing the floor. Backwards and forwards. Thinking out loud. The curtains were open and the moon slid gently between the branches of the oaks. What was her destiny? Superstitious Boo had recited to the full moon during their tour of Ireland:

'All hail to thee, moon, reveal to me.

Him who is my life partner to be.'

Silly to think of it now. What life will Gary have? Pain and worse. Robbed of his personality and his future. She wept and switched on the radio, preparing to pack. Music played softly, a piano concerto, she didn't know which one, it didn't matter. Music had brought them together, she would never leave him now.

All the members of the band arrived to visit Gary the following day. At the tail end Fab and Bas were involved in a noisy argument and Fab was declaring, 'You cannot go through life without offending but there is no need to be offensive.' They discussed bands and venues and good and bad reviews and there was no hint of sadness in the room as the invalid sat upright in the comfortable armchair by the window. Perhaps this was a pattern taking shape, a blueprint of friendship which could create a design for Gary's future?

Nobody would ever convince her that remarks about his illness had been brushed aside; he had never been one to ignore signs, but this ignominious disorder was beginning to take control of his life. It simply seemed to Ellie that he was postponing the inevitable. Above the chatter of the television she prepared a pasta meal in his flat. The winter mist drifted through the broken panes above the roof garden and she cried quietly; she needed time to enter this new and frightening world of HD.

After his discharge on the fifth day a pamphlet arrived, "Facing Huntington's Disease". He measured her reaction as he left it by her plate at breakfast. It had been a delight to see him home; he was weak but anxious to evoke happier times and reluctant to discuss how he was feeling. The booklet was sensitive and straightforward and informative. Then when he announced, 'Of course I don't care where I live, eventually, a Nursing Home I expect. I don't suppose it will be up to me,' Ellie eyed him with suspicion. Misgivings were beginning to grow. She rose from the table, fastening her robe tightly around her; what exactly was she supposed to do? She might fall short of his expectations, then what? He stood in the doorway of the kitchen watching her pour the coffee. 'You are so beautiful. When are you going back?' A loving impulse seized her. His eyes had a deep sadness, his hands were cold but as they hugged each other he managed a smile. 'I wish I could get the right words in the right order.'

Erich Sava was waiting for her on her arrival at the airport. He was smiling as the photographers caught them embracing and he greeted her warmly. 'I have missed you so much. I have a surprise for you and a question to ask.' He was treating her – as he always did – with his customary kindliness as he went in search of her luggage. He tipped the taxi driver extravagantly. 'I am a satisfied man,' he claimed as his fingers gently touched her face. 'Now that you are here.'

Alone in her flat, she slumped into the chair. Frankie was fractious and hungry, jumping up and clawing at the windowsill. There was an hour to go before their dinner date. Ellie felt drained of emotion; the detail and images of the last day spent with Gary were imprinted on her mind. Was it surprising that relations between them had grown strained?

His decision to take the test for Huntington's had been a brave one and for that alone he had earned her admiration but somewhere deep down lurked a suspicion. 'I think we have a special bond, Ellie, don't you? You know all about compassion and patience. You know, whilst I was awaiting the results from the six-month pre-symptomatic testing, all I could think of was you.' Was it a carer he wanted? She held all her fears and anger inside. Instead she handed him the medication and watched television whilst he prepared for bed. While he slept his breathing was often laboured and as she lay beside him she wondered if the foreboding would subside or if she would be swallowed up in a well of pity. She made no promises.

The restaurant was crowded. Erich steered her proudly through the bar. In her pale blue tweed suit and fair hair piled high she looked confident. Yet there was still a lot to accomplish in her private life. It would have been fairer to Gary to have answered honestly that the prospect of a long-term illness was scaring her to death and that the daily fight against the disease was petrifying. Then, stirred by the memory of spells in which he had groaned and writhed in pain, she felt only pity. They sat in the corner of the bar. Erich's expression was of anticipation. 'I have a surprise for you. Tomorrow.' Isabella and a young Italian model joined them. He wore an expensive mauve shirt and burgundy trousers and Isabella was very taken with him. 'You would be a joy to photograph together,' she smiled at Ellie.

Over dinner they discussed plans the Mazzaroni brothers had devised for them and everybody was talking figures. Under the table the model placed his warm hand on Ellie's knee. She yawned. "I'm sorry," she mouthed. Erich laughed openly. 'That's alright. Time for bed!' Isabella, one who looked for signs in all her charges, noted the dark shadows under the eyes and a peakiness about Ellie. The break in England, it seemed, had taken its toll. She wondered how?

It was after nine the following morning when Erich arrived at the flat. He appeared to be wealthy, thought Ellie. He drove a very powerful car and wore smart clothes and most of his patients were rich and influential. He was conventional, liked everything correct and expected high standards from those around him. 'Today,' he smiled as she stepped into the car, 'I am going to teach you to drive. The question is, are you ready?' They found a remote stretch of level road and Ellie took the wheel. How different to the bus. Having never driven in England there was no right or wrong side of the road for her, it was as if being a foreigner gave her an advantage. She coasted behind a tractor. A lorry carrying fruit and vegetables jangled close behind and she watched him in the mirror. 'Overtake. Now. Adesso.' The wind swept through her hair, making her feel fragile in the red turismo, but she did it. 'Well done,' Erich grinned.

They stopped short of the city. 'No more fun for you until you fill in the form.' Traffic whizzed by.

'All foreign cities are the same,' Bas had moaned. 'Full of traffic, cinemas, shops, priests and policemen.'

The settlement and transfer of Athol Picora's business had been completed. Ellie was relocated like a commodity but so were all the other models, except that her new flat was contemporary and set in a cobbled courtyard and away from the others. On arrival at her old flat it was to find that clothing had been flung wildly in all directions and Frankie was sitting on the draining board. She opened the window just enough for him to squeeze through and breathed in the March evening air. The sound of the city closed in. These were times when she cast her mind back to Ireland and the sea which had slapped sulkily against the concrete wall at Dingle. Instead, like ships, people steered themselves through Milan's fog during the winter months.

The fast pace of Milan continued. Shooting in the massive white megalith of the central station had been a nightmare but the hardy models had survived. Physical exhaustion could be overcome with sleep but Gary was proving to be less easy to deal with. He sent frequent emails, sometimes as many as three a day. He was having trouble remembering, he said. His mind would go blank for short periods and his speech didn't come easily. He frequently forgot important meetings.

"I manage," he concluded. "But I get very confused." Could his courage and her faith pull him through? She shared his suffering and had fears about his future but her kind of life was hard to give up. It made sense to take a holiday when there was a break in the programme and Erich suggested she spent it with him.

It was May Day when they set off – formerly the Roman Feast of Floralia, and one of the most magical days of the year according to Isabella. Another Boo, smiled Ellie, who had no inkling of where she was going. Erich arrived wearing a denim shirt and serge jeans and for the first time she felt a spark of excitement at the thought of being with him. Pulling the cream sweater over her trousers she locked the door of the apartment. Ellie had never been to Portugal and did not expect to be recognised but she received a warm welcome at Lisbon Airport.

They made their way to the Spa at Caldas de Monchique where they were to spend five days. It was exactly what was needed. The natural spring housed in glass and marble offered curative waters to anyone who wished to try them. They spent time in the sunny square, set on a slightly raised platform of patterned stones and shaded by the dense foliage of elm trees. Below the Spa sits the hospital and below that a bottling factory from which the waters of Monchique are distributed all over Portugal. 'I have been here many times,' proffered Erich, 'and send my patients here too. Maybe you will be helped here, who knows?' Was it sufficient for him that they were together? Ellie felt that the sensual overtures were never far away.

On the third evening, after dinner, they attended a party and right from the beginning a sense of adventure gripped her. Madeira and vinho verde appeared and quickly disappeared as they drank with their guests. Erich leaned forward and pointed to the noisy crowd across the square. 'Let's find somewhere more peaceful.' They staggered up the hill and looked down on the bright lights of the hospital. He pulled her down beside him on the grassy bank and kissed her. 'Will you marry me, Elise?' She looked up and smiled with a certain incredulity. His warm hands caressed her face. 'It makes sense. Your smile gives me hope. I love you.' The brooks below which should have purled and sparkled beneath the stars were silent. Her fingers curled round his outstretched hand, her head was swimming. He sighed. 'I heard a song way back when I was young. It went something like "love each other while the feeling's good". It is so good now, Elise. Don't let us waste it.' He lowered his eyes. 'I would like an answer.' She began to tremble. "I would like to speak," she mouthed. 'Then talk to me. Go on. Take a deep breath. Buono. Slowly.' Tears ran down her cheeks. He kissed her again. 'Enough, no more. Maybe domani, tomorrow.'

Ellie could have blamed the wine but the tears continued well into the night. Pain was something she had always been prepared to accept in order to gain an insight into her behaviour but it was cruel and insensitive to lie deliberately. Erich was kind but he was left frustrated and disappointed.

The next morning they rose early to visit the solitary, rugged beauty of the coastline of Alentejo. In her way she let Erich know she was sorry. 'You have nothing to be sorry about. Love is about changing thoughts and changing lives. If I could change how you feel about me then you would change my life but I need to know!' She stared at him wide-eyed. They were lying side by side on the long and sandy beach where at the southern end nudists paraded. 'We won't take that road,' he grinned. His tanned appearance made him look younger than his 40 or so years and the laughter lines around his eyes were hidden behind sunglasses. Together they ran into the sea. The veil of uncertainty was wearing thin for Ellie; she was confident that here was a man who would make her happy, and who had splattered the surface of her sensual pond.

Scots pines and eucalyptus trees lined the coast road to Cape Sardao and the sleek hired car hummed along until they reached the cliffs. Wild garlic grew on the steep crags and common gulls and herring gulls swooped onto their nests on the rock face. It was the sight of the lighthouse

which caught Ellie's breath and the spectacular views over
the cliffs. 'It is gorgeous, isn't it?' It was Hel all over again.
A red lighthouse, not octagonal but red all the same. 'If only
I could paint,' sighed Erich.

Within a month Ellie could be seen in homes across Italy.
Television had offered her the chance to promote the new
perfume, "Prudence", and laughing warmly and turning
shyly she was photographed among the peeling houses and
waterside views of the Bohemian centre. It gave her prestige
and a considerable increase in wealth.

The email was picked up halfway through the evening.
Erich was about to refill her glass and glanced at the
computer. 'You have a message.' Another message from Gary,
only this time it wasn't about him, it was about Phil. He had
been released from prison, he was free. "Thought you would
like to know. Love Gary." Ellie leaned heavily on the table.
'You are very thoughtful.' Erich detected embarrassment or
was it alarm? Suddenly she wanted to scream. The journey
through a world without words was coming to an end; the
intricate, conniving scheme of things could be finished once
and for all. It was so apt that Erich was here, the one person
who could help her the most. But there were other lessons
to learn, the rehearsed response, she couldn't give away too
much. How well-qualified he was to take all the credit. She
cleared her throat. He looked towards her, about to take a
sip of wine. 'Erich.' He heard this beautiful girl speak his
name, his heart leapt, was it possible that she would manage
a phrase or even a sentence? 'I have something to say.' He
held her close as she sat down beside him and he listened
to the lilt in her voice and watched the expression of her
new-found freedom in her eyes.

It would take time. Their relationship had been forged on
respect and trust; now there would be no need for signs.
Slowly, deliberately, Ellie explained. 'You know why this
man was imprisoned but that was not the reason for my
silence. He tried to hurt me. I was a prisoner of a terribly
complicated situation and the best thing to do was to say
nothing at all.' He did not expect a full explanation at this

point. He waited patiently. 'I am not ready to face the world just yet. Could we just keep it between ourselves for a while longer?' The heart to heart sentiments were on hold.

Milan was muggy in summer. On her days off Ellie wandered through the congested streets which resembled a spider's web with roads radiating out from the centre. Parking was almost impossible. Officially she could drive now although there had been moments when she regretted the decision; having to learn road signs was not easy. With Erich's help she was learning Italian.

In the church of Santa Maria della Grazie the mural of Leonardo da Vinci's "Last Supper" was displayed in all its glory. Ellie queued for three hours for just a glimpse. In her letter to Gran she wrote, "I have never seen anything more beautiful. It is so easy here to make peace with God."

After a half day of costume fittings the models met at Jola, an upmarket vegetarian restaurant. Sophie was trying hard to cope with stress, she grumbled. 'I'm gaining weight.'

'Rubbish, you look like a pipe-cleaner.'

'That is not what Carlo thinks.' Sophie turned to Ellie. 'And how is Erich? Have you met his secretary? You should, although he wouldn't appeal to you.' An odd remark, Ellie thought. 'Oh, I am looking after your cat, by the way;' she added.

Seafood Italienne was on the menu when Erich arrived at the apartment for dinner. Celery and spring onions were dropped into the wok. He came behind her and nibbled her ear. She added the seafood cocktail and creamy tomato pasta sauce to the wok and served it on a bed of pasta garnished with basil. 'I didn't know you could cook.' Erich smiled.

'I love cooking.' She went into great detail about Jan and the cafe at Victoria Quays. Words came easily now. After dinner, making the most of the firelight, they sprawled out on the rug and she produced the photograph album of the band. When he had taken into consideration all she had experienced he wondered if she would find him unexciting, a waste of time. 'Of course not. I have been there, done it, got the tee shirt,' she laughed.

It was good sense to keep the press in the dark. 'One day we should go away and just be ourselves. I am too suspicious of people, I think. I have been silent for a long time; sometimes the truth is distorted,' demurred Ellie.

She could never quite pin down what Gary was trying to say. "The flat seems very quiet without you," he wrote. "I miss many things about you and some days I feel like an emotional wreck. Where are you to massage my aches away?" Should she respond or turn a deaf ear? She read the pamphlet "Facing Huntington's Disease" from cover to cover and understood why the illness is so soul-destroying and why sometimes it takes months to get the medication right. There was a very different side of him emerging as a result of HD. For purely selfish reasons it was important that no shadow was cast over her relationship with Erich.

The curtains were bellowing like sails. The sun beat down on the square and glitzy cafes but inside the apartment it was wonderfully cool. Ellie moved quietly, dressed in a simple blue shift and barefoot. It was Sunday and the breeze had played around the potted ferns on the windowsill whilst Ellie read her poetry. The silence was broken by a knocking in the apartment downstairs; it was to be hoped that Erich would not be disturbed in the bedroom. The hammering stopped. The bedroom door was ajar; she glanced inside. He was undressed and lying on top of the bed; his greying hair was tousled and his tanned face youthful. He murmured sleepily, and she sat gently on the edge of the bed. Waking he moved towards her, lifting his arms to embrace her. His fingers caressed her nape and her back and he whispered her name. It was a tender moment but she withdrew. 'Go back to sleep,' she smiled. He was allowing her time and she loved him for that. He had a way of making her feel special, one person above so many. He was a satisfied man, he told her; in return she was content simply to be with him.

CHAPTER TWENTY

"If you keep your tongue a prisoner, your body may go free." (Proverbial.)

'What more could we want? We are in a city full of life which supports a multi-million pound industry, of which you are a part; we are healthy, I am in a profession of which I am proud and we have each other.' Erich wrapped his hand around her slim waist as they wandered by the lakeside in the Parco Sempione.

'Oh. I don't know,' she answered flippantly. 'In August it is uncomfortably humid and polluted and taxis never cruise the streets.'

Later they made up a picnic lunch of cheese, fruit and a tomato and anchovies pizza purchased from the street market. Ellie was responding as much as she dare to his questions but she was always afraid she would say more than she needed to. On the park bench he held both her hands in his. 'Do you never wear jewellery?' he asked.

She pointed to the gold cross. 'Just this and some my friends gave me for my birthday.'

'Will you wear this?' As soon as he produced the small box from his pocket she choked back a sigh. 'I love you,' he whispered. She didn't feel like a little girl any more; her decision now would affect the rest of her life. She was suddenly in control and Erich watched his future being held in her palm.

'Let me look,' Ellie's eyes widened. The sapphire sat between two diamonds. 'It is beautiful. Thank you.'

'Do I have to keep this quiet, too?' Erich asked.

'Not for long, I promise.'

****

'I am not likely to be frightened by a mere matter of money,' Ellie stated 'but I have a new accountant and he speaks very little English.'

'Want me to come with you?' Erich removed the headphones.

'If you don't mind. Perhaps you can throw some light on the Inland Revenue muddle.' Ellie had now both fame and fortune. She also had a past and that past crept into her night thinking, a time of brooding and agonizing over what she had done. Perhaps she had considerably more imagination than most or maybe she knew more about heart-searching. She waited anxiously for news from home and chose only to answer Gary's mail when she deemed it necessary.

It became necessary the day after her birthday. The models had been at work in the hub of the city, the Piazzo del Duomo. It was always noisy in this pedestrianized square and hot in August and some of the crew were amateurish and unpolished. It had been exhausting. After a short nap in the apartment she was woken by running water and Erich's deep musical tones in the shower. She sat up and a strong sense of disquiet surrounded her. An email from Tiz. "Sorry to give you grief. Gary is back in hospital. He needs help with feeding and dressing. He has asked us to put his flat on the market. He sends his love. Wonderful picture of you in the mag. Bye. Tiz."

It was impossible to stem the tears. 'Darling, it is a harsh, cruel world for some people. Every day I deal with the inoperable and the dying. I will never get used to it but I do what I can.' Erich held her close. 'You must go to him.' Together they sat in a darkened room watching the beams from cars flash through the noisy streets.

'Why does this man who has done so much for others have to suffer?' she cried.

'Did you love him?'

'Yes. I did,' she sobbed.

Erich had made things easy for her, arranging time off and lifting her spirits. 'Remember, tell him to have courage and to put what little energy he has into the effort of getting better. He has to live through today and for tomorrow. Tell him.' She would.

From the train the English countryside looked lush and flourishing with sudden glimpses of blue between the green foliage. Cows stood stomach-deep in rich pastures and station houses displayed colourful window boxes with fuchsias and honeysuckle. Why was there no joy in any of this? The loud music from No. 68 could be heard from across the street and the taxi driver eyed her with some bewilderment. Sophistication and expensive perfume was not commonplace around here.

Out of the haze of steam in the kitchen Jan appeared. There was more flesh on her bones and her scars were uncovered in stark contrast against her white top. 'Great to see you again.' This was the place Ellie once called home. Certainly it felt homely with bright yellow walls in the kitchen and a garden full of nasturtiums and ferns. Valentine was happily installed in a kennel, a compliment to Cheddar and his dextrous handling of wood. Suzy was confined to a playpen and making telephone noises. 'I know I shall never fully recover, Ellie, but the truth is my life is OK at the moment. How's yours?'

'I am rich and engaged to a man who is well connected,' she could have said but instead mouthed "OK." Somehow, whilst fate had dealt a cruel blow to Jan, she was bearing up well and explained the tight schedule necessary in order to keep everyone happy.

In the hospital Gary was huddled over his bowl, eating very slowly. He was propped up in a bed with cot sides and smiled at Ellie, slightly embarrassed. 'It is wonderful to see you, you have come a long way!' She bent over and grasped his hand. It was little more than a whisper.

'Gary.' The spoon dropped with a clatter onto the tray. He almost choked. 'I am learning to speak again. There is this doctor, you see, and he is confident that I will soon be back to normal.' Gary straightened his back. He was in a state of shock.

'Sweetheart, I am so happy for you. You speak as I imagined. From now on your whole life will change.'

She kissed him gently. 'I'm not going public yet. Only a handful are in the picture, but you had to be one of the first to know.' He lay back as she straightened his pillows.

'It is almost as if you have been sleeping all this time, and now you are fully awake,' he replied. Ellie talked, slowly and quietly; he listened and she spoke about the past and the uncertainties which he had driven away when there seemed to be so many obstacles. As he closed his eyes it was to hear her say here were her real family even if it wasn't her real home.

Sister could only spare her a few moments. 'He's coping. Of course he is not at peace with the situation, but who would be? What we try to do is instil in our patients a grain of hope. His friends, he tells me, are rare students of life, they can certainly teach me a thing or two.' She smiled.

After dinner a small group sauntered between snatches of cycle tracks running through the wood. Everyone had an opinion on what Gary should do next. 'There was a big rumpus as to whether we should have him live with us,' sighed Boo, 'and the argument might have lasted till eternity when Gary announced that he would go into a Nursing Home rather than be a burden to anyone. I mean, Ellie, what can you say to that?' Very soon, she decided, she would have a lot to say.

There were flowers scattered around the apartment when she returned to Milan. It was Erich's day for surgical procedures. He was simply too tired to visit and he had yet to stay overnight. He did not even trouble to compete with his younger partners, he argued; let them get on with frequenting the Ticinese quarter and the night clubs, it wasn't for him. What he was looking forward to was the hospital charity ball. Not surprisingly he and Ellie went shopping. He chose for her a long, sleek gown with authentic snake trimming and she whispered in his ear, 'I can never wear anything made from the skin of any reptile.'

'Of course not.' Instead she chose to shimmer in silver and gold thread with a gold bracelet as an apology for being so insensitive.

'Like a child she marvels at everything she sees. Have you noticed?' At the ball Erich's receptionist, Gianni, had cornered Isabella, who was keen to circulate.

'No, not really.' What she had noticed was the exquisite ring on her third finger. Would there be an announcement, she wondered? Isabella doubted that Erich was being strung along; Ellie wasn't like that. Others had tried no doubt and failed.

Italian doctors and their wives shared their table. All spoke English well and when the conversation turned to the beauty of the English countryside Erich knew that Ellie was champing at the bit and found it hard to contain his amusement. Her companion relayed a catalogue of his senior partner's achievements and she was sure that his politeness and admiration were obviously sincere. 'Your ring is beautiful,' smiled his wife. At which point Erich raised his glass.

'To Elise,' and breathing a sigh of relief, caught a spark of incongruity in the eyes of Gianni.

Why was it important to keep one step ahead of Gary, who was pursuing her with his illness? His messages were often questions. Should he see a psychologist? The neurologist thought he should. Did she not think that children who are being given up for adoption should be tested for hereditary conditions? Would it benefit him financially if he rented out his flat? He might have to return to hospital soon, he said. Perhaps she could encourage him to set definite goals for the future? He couldn't be playing around with it now.

Erich was pressing hard to announce the engagement.

'I want to be able to speak to the world first,' Ellie announced.

'In that case we shall have a plan of action,' he replied.

She smiled. 'You must take the credit; you have given me the motivation to speak. I owe it to you!' It was a half lie but she was becoming quite adept by now. He wondered about her hesitation. Was she still wanting to cling to her former life? She was still a mystery; there was something he could not fathom.

Irregular breathing and alternate snores emanated from the bed in the corner of the hospice ward. Erich moved quietly among his patients with a nurse by his side. Ellie was standing by the dispensary. 'He is a treasure.' Nurse smoothed her apron. 'He does so much for these people. See the small child over there? She was in a road accident; her larynx and vocal chords were almost destroyed. But you will recover, I'm sure.' Recover from what? Ellie wondered. The fraudulent way of life which had led her to deceive so many or the forlorn feeling of helplessness where Gary was concerned? The image of his charm and youth was disappearing. He was once the organiser, the one who could cope, the peacemaker. Huntington's had changed everything. Now he needed friends, he needed her.

Erich held her arm as they closed the hospice doors behind them. 'Do they know they are dying?' she asked.

'We are all dying, Elise, only we don't have a specific date on our calendar, a date with fate. If we live as if every day is our last then that is time well-spent.'

It was to be hoped that her dentist was running late. Ellie had chosen to drive and the ring roads were a nightmare. It would have been better to have used the Metro. She had taken a wrong turning and found herself in the Via de Castillia and had no alternative but to park in a prohibited zone whilst asking for directions. Proper was a word which fitted Ellie well, liking all things conventional and seemly of late and yet, as she entered the club and looked around, it became obvious that it was a gay bar. The barman shook his head from side to side; her Italian was making no impression.

While gathering up her bag a familiar face came into view in the corner of the bar mirror – the dark brooding features of Gianni. He was holding hands across the table. Curiosity forced her to glance at his partner but in the half light she could barely see. Then Ellie experienced an intensity of feeling that blotted out everything else. It was Erich and he was looking deep into Gianni's eyes. How could he breach the trust she held so dear? How could he say one thing and mean another? How did he intend to live two lives? This dangerous game he was playing meant only one thing, the ball was in her court, she would determine who the winner would be. She took a deep breath.

Her thoughts were shattered by the noisy roar of the traffic, and the motorists with their edgy fingers blasting their horns. How much of the sweet life he had promised her was she supposed to share? The flashes of passion, were they really meant for her? The surreptitious glances from Gianni at the hospital ball were for Erich, of course.

The encounter with the dentist had left her feeling sick but she had purchased fresh mussels at the mercato, the local market, and began to prepare a meal for the two of them. Would this be their last together? The onion and garlic sizzled in the margarine as Erich entered the hallway. She drank indelicately from the bottle before adding the dry white wine and lemon juice. She would make him squirm. He stood in the doorway. 'Smells good.' It was when he kissed her neck that she recoiled. 'This is the tricky bit,' she said.

When the mussels had been added she covered the pan and stirred the boiling liquid. Her face was very red. 'How has your day been?'

'Very good, how about you?' It was difficult to face him, would it appear transparent to him how uncomfortable she felt? Once the mussels had opened she transferred them to a dish.

'Can I help?'

'Yes, you may pour the wine while I make the parsley sauce.' Long lapses of silence were conditions she had grown used to but Erich appeared anxious.

'How was the dentist?'

Arranging her napkin neatly in front of her and sipping her wine, she paused. 'I got lost today. I took a wrong turning, well you know what my sense of direction is like. Actually I ended up in the Via de Castillia. Do you know it?' He put down his fork.

'Vaguely.'

'Well,' Ellie was beginning to enjoy herself. 'I wandered into this gay bar to ask the way and who do you think I saw?'

Erich looked nervous. 'I don't know.'

'Have a guess.'

'I have no idea.' Ellie tutted. The colour drained from his face.

'Gianni. Did you know he was gay? Any idea who his boyfriend is?' Before he could answer Ellie left the table. Stacking the dishes near the sink might give him time to recover, she thought. 'Did you enjoy the meal?'

'Very much.' Erich swallowed hard. 'Moules Mariniere,' she smiled.

Conversation had brought a new vitality to Ellie. In the past she had been too reticent to make friends, now in her eagerness to convey her feelings it was time to burst her bubble. It was decided that Erich would issue a statement that Ellie had fully recovered from her trauma and was now able to speak. There was to be no announcement as yet of their engagement. Could it be that Erich was like a ship swaying from side to side, unsure of which way to turn? Or was it that he felt sure that by temporizing he would somehow find a way of solving the situation?

Ellie did not rise to the bait that television offered her, nor would she be caught in the net of newspaper columnists. Life went on very much the same.

The air was so clear on the October morning; all the sounds from the street, the screeches from the traffic, the shouts of women and children echoed around her. Perhaps she needed to think through her next stage. Her contracts were coming to an end and she was homesick. Offers were pouring in but she found it hard to concentrate. The smooth running of her life was due to the efficiency of Isabella and Ellie was exceptionally pleased that the support was still there. Nothing more was heard about the demise of Athol Picora and the last thing she wanted was for the past to rear its ugly head.

To explore the world of speech seclusion had been deliberate. Now it was time to bring it to an end. It had made her aware that almost everything we do depends on conversation; in this way we plan and organise our lives. It is how we build friendships, learn to trust and understand people. How we get close to one another. Yet without words she had built bridges, influenced people and allowed them to influence her. And discovered so many important things about herself. She had listened and learned skills; by not interrupting she heard the whole story. In some mysterious way she felt gratified. All of this was recorded and posted to Gran. "In two weeks I am coming to see you. I can't wait. God Bless, Lisa."

It was a relief to escape from the heat of Milan. October had been stifling whilst in England the air was fresh with autumn breezes; a lazy wind Gran called it, because it went through you instead of going round. Ellie jumped out of the taxi at the top of the steep path and walked down the steps. She was back, at last, in this ancient and beautiful city where as a child she had played by the narrow, winding river and breathed in the sweet country scent of the cowparsley.

It seemed that her Gran would never let her go. The years had wrinkled her skin and dried the sheen on her white hair but her smile shone through the tears and she hugged her tight. A life which was woven with 20 years of memories was united with the one who had cared for her. It took hours to catch up with the news and in sheer weariness Gran flopped into bed.

Wrapped in a duvet on the sofa, Ellie sleepily listened to

drops of water drumming on the sill. There had been a ray of hope, a glimmer of understanding from Moira, Gran had intimated. She had been concerned and remorseful when her daughter had left but relieved when she knew she was safe. They had shared news of her exploits, it would have been cruel not to, and as Ellie became famous, almost impossible to conceal. Ellie steered the conversation away from Phil; she did not exclude the possibility of him snatching at the first opportunity of revenge. It would be unwise to stir up the winds. There was so much affection and warmth in the visit but it had to end. The old lady waved goodbye to the young girl full of ambitions and dreams and the grass muffled the sound of her heels as she walked towards the car. There were very few bridges to burn here now.

Whatever happened to change the degree of intimacy and harmony between Erich and Ellie was due to Gianni. This tall, dark young man was stealing what could have been hers and Ellie was still brooding over their esoteric relationship. He wasn't going to admit to it, she wasn't going to ask. Her version of what was right or wrong was important and valuable to her but she was experiencing a whole range of feelings towards Erich and she was hurting.

The post usually arrived mid morning and Ellie's routine was to put the kettle on and open the mail on her return from work. The airmail letter was from Tiz. The sentences were short. "Sorry to give you bad news. The owner has found out we're here. We have had a warning letter; it says we are trespassing because we are living here without permission. If we don't leave by a specified date the owner will take proceedings. If we receive a summons, Ellie, we're out. We are not fighting this one. Gary says not to panic but it is easy to say. He can't help us, poor sod, although we have phoned the Advisory Service for Squatters in London who will help us. I will keep you informed. Great you can speak. Luv. Tiz. xx"

A powerful flow of injustice swept over her. What had her friends done? They had turned a broken-down hovel into a home. They had dispelled and corrected misconceptions about squatters and helped build a community spirit which previously didn't exist. They had put so much energy into establishing links with their neighbours, and worked hard for others. Ellie had never felt so angry: what is more, she exploded, it was her home.

It was not the most primitive of existences. Gary had chosen a tough bunch to tour with. The place was clean, warm and sparsely cheerful, and nowhere had there been healthier foods prepared and served. For Jan it had been a sanctuary and for Suzy a modern kibbutz. To separate them now would be close to tearing a family apart.

All night long their plight was the focal point of her prayers and then, like a bolt from the blue, came her decision. She had brought nothing with her to Milan and other than what she had earned, she would take nothing away. In her hand she held her engagement ring enclosed neatly in its box. She knew exactly what needed to be done.

Gianni was not at his desk. The waiting room was empty. A sharp knock on the consulting room door was answered by Gianni. Bronzed and slightly agitated, his dark eyes flashed in surprise. 'Elise,' Erich had dreaded this moment. He rose from behind his desk and held out his hands; it was crucial that he remained cool. On occasions of life and death he was unsurpassable but now, at this moment, he was taking the coward's way out, he was leaving the decision to Ellie. Gianni left the room with a backward glance at Erich. In his manner was a touch of defiance.

'I am going away.' She took Erich's hand, leading him to the window, and showed him the letter from Tiz. Carefully the tiny box was placed on the table. 'I can't marry you, I'm sorry. I have to go where I am needed. My finances are being dealt with and Isabella is in charge of everything else!' He had a strong impulse to hold onto her, he might never see her again.

'Is there anything I can do to change your mind?' Ellie could not think of any sensible way to evade the question. 'I do love you a little,' she sighed. 'You have been very kind and exceptionally patient but, well, there are different kinds of love, different types of feelings. What is important is to be with the one you love.' He should be saying this, she thought. He was older, experienced. Yet with simplicity and tact she had told him the truth; for ethical reasons alone he could not be a part of her world. Holding her close he said goodbye. Gianni left his seat in Reception to open the door for her. 'Look after him,' she smiled tearfully.

Isabella did her utmost to persuade her to stay but Ellie was adamant. 'I have been overexposed anyway,' she insisted, although she knew that was not true. There was quite a way to go in her career and the London fashion houses were calling. After filling in intricate forms and telephoning Estate Agents, saying goodbye to colleagues and packing her few belongings, she settled in her seat on her flight home.

There was little pleasure to be had in mooning about at No. 68 but the girls were fascinated by Ellie now that she could speak, although years of abstinence had made her a better listener than most. Gary was discussed at length. 'Even small matters affect him now. He suffers actual physical pain and there is no way we can help him,' Tiz sighed.

'What I plan to do ...' Ellie sat upright. Boo laughed.

'It's so peculiar to hear you speak.'

'Go on,' smiled Fab, cradling Suzy in her lap.

'... is to buy a large house and we can all live together,' she concluded!

'Like here, you mean, only without the draughts and the grotty toilet and the rusty bath and the dodgy plumbing and the shaky winders?' Bas nudged Rev who was reading a comic and nuzzling Valentine.

'Yes, Bas,' Ellie answered softly.

'I don't suppose we can grumble. They gave us squatters' rights for a time, whoever they are, and it's cost us beggar all to live here,' Tiz remarked.

'Well,' Ellie paused. 'You are free to say yes or no but I will try to make sure that travel isn't a problem.'

Their faces said it all. 'Let's go and visit Gary.'

The quality of care Gary was receiving was good and the medication appeared to be effective to a degree. The visits between the hospital and his flat were less frequent. There was no delicate way of easing HD into the conversation and his friends' approach to his bad days was so diverse. They couldn't agree on anything. 'They are just airing their minds, they're not arguing,' Gary would insist.

It was quite an undertaking looking for a new home, especially as the operation was kept secret from him. 'I want it to be a surprise,' Ellie insisted. It was essential that it had five bedrooms and ground floor accommodation which could be converted. There had been a couple of interested parties for the flat and Ellie had moved in permanently. She welcomed the opening of old memories over the last meal of the day, and Gary casually remarked, 'So you have given him the elbow have you, the doctor?'

'I suppose I have.' His look softened.

'He was too old for you, anyway.'

The chimes of the church bells cut through the fog of the chilly November morning. 'Glebe Grange should be just around the corner,' Ellie informed Tiz and Boo, who had settled comfortably in her new car. Boo began to chuckle.

'One extreme to the other, this is, from the ridiculous to the sublime.' It was uncanny. The way the Georgian house stood on elevated ground looking over the Derbyshire hills was exactly as Ellie had imagined a future home. They were escorted round by a short, overweight man who found the stairs difficult. The kitchen was huge, with a Stanley range providing the central heating. On the ground floor was a shower room and on the first floor a bathroom. It was ideal. The lime and white dining room had French doors and two more panelled reception rooms had large windows. Tiz and Boo whooped with joy rushing into every room. There was a strained silence followed by a nervous cough.

'Shall we go upstairs?' panted the agent. They followed him along a winding corridor and up the elegant staircase with the white balustrade.

'There are only four bedrooms,' Tiz berated. The man coughed delicately.

'That's alright. Gary and I won't be living here.'

Ellie led them to the adjoining holiday cottage. 'This,' she exclaimed, 'is for Gary.' As she walked towards the cars she asked. 'Why Glebe Grange?'

'It was originally church land, Miss, granted to the clergyman as part of his benefice. You see the rough track to your left? That is where your boundary ends.' My boundary, murmured Ellie.

'Do you think we could finalize for Christmas?'

Perhaps it was expecting too much but Christmas was among the best yet at No. 68. Bas had acquired a motor bike and he was like a child with a new toy. The legal and practical advice for squatters came in droves from ASS. Anxious to be involved, Gary offered his help but the painkillers could pose a problem and often he was too exhausted to speak. At Outpatients his manner became sharp and uncooperative, snatches of conversation would unnerve him and he would begin to argue. No one was judgemental, he was merely given his medication and sent home.

Sobuj shivered at the front door, his coloured shirt flapping over his trousers. His miserable face reflected his concern as he handed over the petition signed by all the neighbours. He was invited in to share lentil soup and barm cake. 'We have had someone talk to us about your unfortunate situation and the meeting took on rather an angry turn. We were told about summary offences and practices which could mount in a crescendo of tension,' he laboured.

'What's he on about?' grumbled Bas.

'He is trying to help us,' snapped Tiz.

'But we've found another place.'

'He doesn't know that.'

'Then tell him.'

She did. 'We are not fighting this, Sobuj, we are not wasting our energy in a courtroom fracas. We won't be homeless. We do have somewhere to live.'

Sobuj gestured frustratingly with his arm. 'It reaches my soul,' he cried, 'that a young child should be treated this way. Please look at me and answer the question. Will you be alright?' It was time for Ellie to put his mind at rest.

There was no mention of their new home being a Grade 2 listed stone built period property as Ellie sat on the modern sofa munching biscuits straight from Golnar's oven. It was, she explained, a necessary haven where Gary could be taken care of. They would all live together as before. 'You have thought this through,' smiled Golnar.

'Yes, and you must visit us when we are settled in.'

On the 5th February the contracts were officially exchanged.

Gary had been struck down with a sickly headache which locked him in his own world and Ellie helped him to bed. She saw how pale he was, carrying the grey look of illness, and tucked him in. The birds in the roof garden swooped round the feeder and perched on the angel and she held his hand and prayed.

Skipping, raiding skips, was not on the agenda, salerooms were. 'I can't remember you behaving so pettily before, Tiz,' Boo pouted.

'I'm not. I simply do not fancy sleeping in a room draped with red silk and net.'

'It was just an idea.' Boo was driving the van up to the big house, as everyone called it, with a load of small items of furniture from the saleroom. The line of the hedges, the paths through the fields, the trees in single file and the grass were covered in a thin layer of snow. Boo kept a safe distance from the huge furniture van as it trundled its way along the narrow roads.

It was not a precious load. There were no antiques, no Regency or Chippendale, simply good, solid, well-made robust furniture which would complement the Grange. Ellie had not been mean with her money, just careful. Everyone had enjoyed the experience of the saleroom, especially Bas who, after seeing the house, had purchased a snooker table for the room he was to share with Rev.

Initially they had chosen to squat because they were fed up with greedy landlords and in the beginning it was not a bed of roses, Rev reminded Ellie. 'Before we knew you we were in constant attack from people; we were called deviant subversives among other things and forced into jobs that nobody else would do. Yet we made this place presentable, anybody could live here now.'

They were taking with them only personal possessions and necessities. Coal and firewood was neatly stacked in the shed and tulip and daffodil bulbs were sleeping ready to face the spring in the window boxes. Bas, who wanted to prove that he was still vigorous, hoisted up the stepladders and removed the chandelier, accompanied by agitated instructions from Boo. 'Careful, you are like a bull in a china shop.' It would have been impossible to squeeze anything else in the van. There were hugs and fond farewells and intoxicated memories of the party the night before when the neighbours had thrown a shindig.

Tiz handed the keys to Sobuj. 'Thank you for your help.' His eyes filled with tears; he nodded.

Suzy was fit and happy in her new environment. Everyone was back at work. Between them they had a van, Boo's car, a motor bike and when Ellie eventually moved in, her own car. Along the hedgerows the daffodils were pushing through and the kitchen garden, which was showing signs of neglect, waited for the abundance of summer fruits. Ellie put the finishing touches to the cottage – a single bed fitted nicely alongside the double in the large bedroom. It might guarantee her a night's sleep. She was of the belief that somehow she was meant to be there for him, that he had been dealt a terrible blow and that her faith would help see him through.

Gary was completely in the dark about all that had been happening over the past months. It had not been easy; he was still a key part of their lives and curious. 'I thought we would take a drive into Derbyshire,' Ellie suggested. 'Are you up to it?'

'Yes, fine. I'm tired, that's all. Fresh air will do me a power of good. Just don't expect me to go rock climbing.'

The countryside was livened by the sparse wild flowers and the car held the road well. 'Hey, steady,' he smiled. She laughed. 'You are not in Italy now, you know.'

Ellie glanced at him. 'I'm glad about that.' But still refused to slow down.

He had glimpsed a streak of stubbornness, of independence. 'OK, you win.'

Cows edged over to the field on the brow of the hill as she turned the corner and the Grange came into view. 'O, God, please let him like it.' Hand in hand she led him to the cottage; there was an expression on his face she would never forget, one of complete bewilderment. 'Is this yours?'

'No, ours.' He fell silent. She rummaged in her handbag and handed him the keys. Once inside he walked over to the wide windows.

'You are staying with me?'

'Of course.'

'Do you realize what you are putting yourself through?'

'I promise I will never leave you and that is the only promise you will get out of me.' He kissed her, a long, tender kiss. If he had any wishes he kept them to himself. This was a major move.

'Have the gang been here?'

'They live next door.'

Never had Ellie felt such deep content. 'You need structure and stability with HD but more than that you need love.' Sister had warned her. 'You will become resentful and feel cheated and fighting a war, but don't expect any medals.' She didn't.

'We must sort out my finances. The proceeds of the flat will go towards this place, of course!' Gary was adamant.

'There is plenty of time for that. Have a rest before dinner and I will let you know when everyone is home!' Ellie could be forgiven for thinking that life might be easier here as by morning his approval had become enthusiasm. He ate two hard-boiled eggs for breakfast with Suzy by his side offering him thin slices of toast. 'Soldiers,' she said with a strong lisp.

It was walking country and no one appreciated it more than Rev, but the measure of his happiness depended on Angelica; she was due in the next day on her first visit to

England. She told him continually in her letters how much she missed him, he confided in Bas. All he got in reply was a grunt.

The small estate which spread below Glebe Grange had almost the feel of a large village. The medley of houses, cottages and bungalows added variety and fitted in nicely with the two pubs, two churches (one a Wesleyan chapel), three restaurants and two takeaways. Close by the honey farm a pond glistened amidst the trees. Within two weeks Bas had joined the darts team and the snooker team and was able to generate enough interest in karaoke to initiate a competition. 'He is not in the least bit troublesome,' declared Fab.

'There's plenty of time,' rebuffed Boo, gulping down her lager.

Ellie and Rev travelled down to Dover to meet Angelica. He drummed his fingers on his knees and clenched his teeth. He had made an effort to please, spiking his hair and cleaning his boots, but he was nervous. There was little traffic on the road, it was coming up to 6.30am and the car was running smoothly, albeit at over 80mph. Suddenly a lorry, a German pantechnicon, pulled out in front and Ellie slammed on the brakes. 'Shit, shit, shit!' yelled Rev whilst Ellie, pale yet calm, replied.

'I can hold her without any trouble.'

'Maybe you can,' he gulped, 'but do you mind dropping down a bit?' So she purred along at sixty until Rev dropped off to sleep.

Thinking back to Mustard she remembered how his sandy hair and beard dripped over the wheel when the bus was sweaty with bodies and the midday sun beat down. Then they would stop and lay a mattress in the shade of trees and sleep. Those days had given way to gracious living but were a part of her life she wouldn't have missed for anything. With the picture of Rev hanging on to Angelica and struggling with her luggage as they approached the car tickling her humour, Ellie smiled warmly.

They clung to each other in sheer exuberance on the back

seat and chatted non-stop.

Jan had surpassed herself. The willow pattern dinner service, a bargain from the saleroom as it had a few pieces missing, was displayed on the long farmhouse table. The chairs were mismatched but expensive looking and there was a huge glass bowl of silk flowers as a centrepiece. Angelica silently hovered in the doorway. 'What's wrong?' Briefly Rev panicked. 'What is the matter?'

'I do not understand,' she voiced. 'This is a squat?'

'Oh no.' There was a sigh of relief. 'I forgot to say, we moved. We all live with Ellie now.' There was a burst of laughter as they were joined by the others.

Along with potatoes and vegetables Angelica was offered dumplings and sauerkraut followed by apple strudel. 'What is the national dish of the Republic?' Jan asked. 'Veprove,' she smiled. 'Roast pork and stew.' Bas grunted. Boo giggled.

The vast patch of land behind the kitchen garden was vigorously attacked by Cheddar when he came to stay for the weekend. The tall pink Rosebay Willowherb stays, requested Ellie. Her mother called it the nuisance wildflower but what did she know? Had she been the nuisance wildflower to her mother? Perhaps.

Isabella was taking good care of her. Ellie was now contracted to an Advertising Agency in London and she had bookings until well after Christmas. For the first time in her life she enjoyed fashion. Tiz would speak with pride of her achievements at Loxley College and of her knowledge of the world of the designers as well as the experience she had gained in her ambition to promote fashionable clothing. At gigs, on stage, the girls wore the clothes she had designed and a friend was encouraging her to broaden her horizons. 'You should be earning money as well as compliments,' she announced.

It took some time for Valentine to settle. When making his first visit to his new abode he spent a considerable amount of time sniffing, exploring, examining until every nook had been scrutinized. Now he was undergoing hydrotherapy and, wearing a precautionary life jacket, swam against the jets in

the controlled pool. 'It will help to build up his muscles.'
Rev absolutely swore by it. Angelica was mesmerised by the
whole thing.

Animals adored her. As she walked from the house and
into the lane the cows would slowly wander from the top
field and follow her the whole length of the croft. She would
murmur softly in Czech. Boo watched her from the sitting
room. 'The Indians believe cows know the direct path to
heaven,' she directed. 'They treat them like Gods.'

'Not more superstitious rubbish,' rejected Bas. 'That's in
India, this is South Yorkshire.'

'No, it is not, it's Derbyshire, actually. Aren't you going
to the pub?'

'Why?'

'Just wondered.'

'Fancy your chances with me, do you?' The intimation
surrounding that question caused her face and neck to
flush.

'You bonehead,' was all she could think of.

****

'What are you looking for?' Gary was searching through
mounds of paper. It had been over 15 minutes since he had
left his comfortable armchair.

'I've forgotten.'

'Come and sit down.' Ellie made a place for him on the
sofa.

'I think, well I feel sure, that it was something important;
I'll remember soon I suppose.'

'Shall I make a drink?' She placed a hand on his
shoulder.

He nodded. 'I get tired so easily now. I used to rise early,
do a full day's work, do a gig until two in the morning,
then do it all over again. Now everything I do is a real
struggle!'

'That is why I am here.' He sighed and held her hand.

'There was a time when I had ideas and ambition. I tucked

this illness away, tried to ignore it, deny it but it bites into me like a leech. You are the only bit of happiness I can cling to.' It was the gentle pull at her heart again, intimidation and he was not going to let her go.

'I would be inclined to think twice before changing jobs, Boo,' Tiz appealed. They arrived just as the hors d'oeuvres were being served. Open Day at Loxley College was a warm, sociable event and Tiz was celebrating her achievement in Art and Design.

'I would love to do Leisure Management now that my course is finished!' Fab revealed.

'Why don't you?'

'Because I can't expect Jan to look after Suzy. It wouldn't be fair.' They pushed their way over to the hall where the Director was making his speech.

'Ellie will help,' Boo enthused.

'Don't you think she has enough to do looking after Gary? I think she is marvellous. I only hope he realizes what she has forfeited for him.'

'I doubt it,' sighed Boo.

'He is like a crab shedding an old shell and growing a new one,' Fab philosophised. 'Only the new one is more delicate and could crack at any minute.'

It was a sombre time for Rev as Angelica prepared for home. It was inevitable but it didn't make it any easier. Most of the city had been surveyed and Derbyshire explored and her stay with Ellie in the cottage had been enlightening. Observing as she did daily Gary's emotional and sometimes aggressive manner she gained an insight into how much Ellie cared for him and yet suspected that a silent battle was raging beneath the surface. 'I was apprehensive about coming, but it is different now,' Angelica explained. 'I think I should like to live here.'

Gary accompanied them to London. He seemed fine until after a short nap he erupted for about ten minutes and grabbed Ellie, demanding to know where she was taking him. He began to shout. The nearest service station was miles away; she had to keep going.

Rev leaned over from the back seat. 'You're OK, Gary. We are all set for London.' He was causing chaos and Ellie was regretting this outing but realized that a patient's fear should never be downplayed. He was out of his territory and he was scared, his teeth were chattering. 'You are OK, we are stopping soon.' Rev's words had calmed him. How long could he carry this anger? How long before his rage was exhibited in public? How long before the pressure of HD became too much for his carer? Ellie questioned her own abilities.

Victoria Coach Station was bustling. Angelica had chosen to travel by Czech International despite the journey taking over 24 hours. 'It must be love,' Gary laughed as Angelica checked in. 'If he gets any closer he will end up climbing over her.' A light lunch and the medication had revived him and the tension and anger had disappeared. Ellie agreed readily when he suggested they listen to a Dark Horse tape. Music was an accomplishment he could take pride in.

The gently rolling moors gleamed in the evening sun but the calm serenity of the countryside ended at Glebe Grange. 'Are we glad to see you,' Boo wailed, pulling up a chair for Ellie. 'We have had a hell of a night.' Tiz was busy at the cooker.

'The press arrived this afternoon wanting an update, a profile, they said. Well, you know what Jan is like with strangers. She refused to answer the door and they climbed the fence at the back and Valentine was barking and Suzy was yelling and by the time we got home Jan was in hysterics!' Boo ran out of breath.

'Local, were they?'

'No.' Tiz handed Ellie a cup of herb tea. 'Tabloid.'

'I will have a word with them. Is there some tea for Jan?'

Clasping and unclasping her hands, Jan appeared distraught. 'I am shut away in this room,' she cried and burst into tears of self-pity. Ellie held her hands. 'If you were shut away anywhere how would all the meals be cooked, and Suzy cared for and Valentine exercised and other chores which you think go unnoticed be taken care of?' She stopped crying and dried her eyes. 'Why don't we have your friends from the Asian Centre come and visit? I am sorry I have been so involved with Gary. I didn't think.' Jan seemed prepared to accept this promising line of reasoning, smiled and drank her tea.

The press had, on the whole, shown consideration for Ellie. Once the rumours and scandal of the trial had faded she felt no longer exposed and had never felt defenceless in their presence. Now she had a voice. She would discuss tactics with the group that evening. Through the long windows of the sitting room they watched the sun dip over the hills and heard in the distance the faint cries of cattle. Bas wore an expression of deep concentration; Rev was teaching him the rudiments of chess. 'He would do better teaching Valentine the basics of quantum physics,' jeered Boo who was lying full length across the rug. Gary was dozing.

Ellie spoke quietly. 'Do you mind if I interrupt for a minute?'

'Sure,' Rev straightened his back.

'I've been thinking. If we allow the press to take a few photographs outside the house and in the grounds we could advertise the band. We won't have them in the house; it would not be fair to Jan, but we could smarten up the roses in the box garden and put tables on the lawn, and add a few drinks. What do you think?'

'Look!' Bas cried with infectious enthusiasm, 'that is a clever idea. Great.'

'Sometimes it is difficult to see which way the coin is going to fall,' Fab queried, 'but you could actually say we were a hit with the press.'

'Bas made an exhibition of himself,' uttered Boo, 'with the flighty reporter.'

'Doesn't he always?' The article, she hoped, would be fair but the important part of her life had been omitted, the everyday battle with HD. News had not yet percolated through the press hierarchy. It was Ellie in a hounds-tooth short skirt, pink sweater and long boots which made the

centrefold but it was the band which left a lasting impression
as they performed on the lawn.

****

Cassie arrived at her front door with a trowel in one hand
and a potted geranium in the other. With her hair pulled
severely back and trousers that ballooned from her waist she
brought a smile to Gary's face. He was reluctant to discuss
his illness, insisting that doctors who could be relied on
dowsed any pangs of success in any of the treatments he
was receiving. Cassie was happy to listen to Ellie, convinced
that she had been able to alleviate the cause of her inability
to speak with the aid of her crystal. Ellie hugged her. 'I may
have a buyer for your flat,' she smiled. 'I described your
Garden of Eden to him, he became quite excited.' Gary
agreed to show him round. Whether he could ever shed the
memories of his refuge remained to be seen.

The ache which started in his head spread through his
body like a plague until he could no longer stand and he
would cry out. 'Why the nightmares?' he would ask. 'I
am hovering, floating, the ground is a picture, you don't
see it as solid ground. I'm going right through. These are
hallucinations, aren't they? I am going mad, aren't I?'

'Most of the time you are dreaming, honestly, it's the
medication. Maybe we should have a word with the consultant
about it?' Ellie lay beside him. The bedroom was warm.
From his window he could see the magnificent flowering
horse chestnut and the wide leaves which gave shelter to
the host of sparrows and the tittering of magpies. Why was
there this powerful urge to blame God? she thought. Why
had Gary been robbed of the use of his hands, well almost,
when he loved playing the guitar? Why was his memory
impaired when his mind had once been as sharp as a razor?
Why could he not enjoy a meal without choking? She had
dealt the first blow by refusing to speak to him, now she
had to find the right words and how, Ellie wondered, was
being sentimental going to help them? Had the insecurity of

his early years in which he grew from child to man had a lasting effect? Now he had to be handled with patience, tact and infinite love. To survive she had to have knowledge of what could happen and Gary had to be prepared.

On good days they would drive onto the estate and sit by the pond listening to the bees swarming around the hives, then treat themselves to a drink in the pub's beer garden. She was often recognised. 'I dare not be slovenly or have a bad hair day. You never know who might see me.'

Gary peered into his glass. 'Someone is going to woo you one day,' he complained. 'Sweep you right from under my feet.'

'What a charming, old-fashioned word,' she laughed. 'Why don't you woo me?' His eyes widened, he took a deep breath. 'I wouldn't know where to start.' He rose unsteadily from his seat. 'In any case, what have I to offer you?'

Ellie took his arm. 'I am no longer interested in what you have to offer; just think what I can do for you.' They were learning things about each other that were new and exciting. He would mock her Italian and reply 'Non ho capito' ('I do not understand'). Sometimes when his pride was bruised he would become churlish and bad-tempered and on occasions show a hint of violence. They left the pub arm in arm.

The mechanic hammered vigorously and loudly under the bike. 'What's up?' Bas was not happy.

'They have this fault, this particular bike, nothing serious.'

'Planning on racing it? 'Valentine was poised on three legs, ready to chase.

'No, I fancied being an outrider once, you know, escorting VIPs.'

The mechanic sniffed. 'You have one here, haven't you? Pretty as as a picture.'

'Yea, well,' Bas divulged, 'my lack of wealth has restricted me in my choice of women.' The engine burst into life, and so did Valentine.

Boo, watching from the sitting room, doubled up with laughter as the dog jumped up in a series of somersaults and grabbed the leg nearest to him, snarling and pulling. Bas grasped the plump body in the middle but Valentine stubbornly refused to move. By this time five pairs of eyes were streaming with laughter as they watched the performance; the girls had never witnessed anything quite so funny in a long time. 'What if he draws blood?' Tiz choked.

'He'll need a tetanus jab,' Fab sniggered.

'Turn off the bloody engine,' yelled Bas. Suddenly the dog released its grip and Bas fell backwards. His expression was furious, his language unrepeatable. The girls, still giggling, curled up on the sofa.

'Better be safe,' grinned Fab searching through the bookshelf. 'Let's see, tetanus.' She thumbed through the medical dictionary. 'Tetanus, Risus Sardonicus.' That brought forth more peals of laughter.

'Sounds like Frankie Howerd or Michael Palin,' chuckled Jan and they laughed till they cried.

'It is time we had our old friends over,' Ellie suggested to Jan. 'What do you think?' Jan felt more comfortable with her body, she could face people she knew but strangers still spooked her out, she complained.

It was the arrival of the vicar in the middle of the food preparations that unnerved her and her face puckered in a frown. He was shown into the cottage after the short introductions where he and Gary discussed religion, healing and music. 'The flutes represent the sea birds in the music of Delius,' Ellie heard him say as she served them coffee and cream biscuits. 'They are the healing influences in his music.'

'Pleasant man,' Gary said and added, 'his wife has Multiple Sclerosis.'

Gary spoke across to the doctor shifting uncomfortably on the chair in the consulting room. 'I seem to be dazzled by bright lights and sudden noises and I feel myself being invaded by thoughts which normally would be dismissed as nonsense!' He paused. 'I know there are people worse than me but each time I visit I have yet another symptom to add to the others. I cannot allow this disease to ruin my life.' The young doctor leaned forward.

'There are still some avenues we can explore. More drugs?'

Gary shook his head. 'I don't want to see my body destroyed by drugs. I have always been vehemently opposed to them in the past.'

Perching on the corner of the desk the doctor announced. 'The past is behind you, we are here to take care of your future.'

Ellie waited patiently outside the room. 'I want you to wait here,' Gary had dictated. 'I will deal with this before I become hospital phobic.'

In her long, informative letter to Gran Ellie was optimistic. Gary tells me he feels trapped in his own body and he gets irritated. When the irritation turns to exasperation and then to frustration I step in. I pray for patience and understanding and my prayers are always answered but it is painful for us both. Yet there are times he cheerfully accepts my help with a certain amount of alacrity.

On the eve of Ellie's birthday they took a short stroll down the boundary lane, stopping to watch the cows as they plodded across the field. He touched her hair which shone golden in the sunset glow, and held her close. He kissed the corner of her mouth and her gentle hands stroked his back. 'Ellie.' There was a moment of indecision, then he passed his hand across his forehead.' I'm tired. We have a long day ahead tomorrow.' These were times when she felt frustrated and bitter but they passed.

Jan's spatula paused temptingly in midair over the wok. The trinity of green pepper, celery and onions was added to the moisture and left to simmer. She had prepared a wide choice of Indian dishes for the buffet and Golnar suggested she returned to work at the Centre. 'I don't think that's possible,' she replied with a sigh. 'I take care of Suzy.' But the notion simmered in her mind. 'Perhaps later.' Just after six the guests started to arrive. Sobuj had hired a bus for all the members of the Community Centre and a few neighbours along with Jason.

'I am very impressed,' bowed Sobuj, 'and the chandelier looks much more elegant here in the hall.' Gary had good news for them about the sale of the flat and had surrounded Ellie with red roses. He was also quite effective when called upon to interpose between Bas and Boo when she took offence at some lewd comment.

It wasn't until the last of the guests were ready to go that Bas exploded. For most of the night he had avoided Sobuj. He had never liked him, he admitted, but this was the last straw. Gary was in no mood at this late hour to appease him, he wanted time on his own with Ellie and she was busy being nice to people. Instead, Bas cornered Tiz in her bedroom which doubled as a studio for her paintings. 'Do you know what Sobuj has done, do you? Only rented the squat out to his friends.'

'Sometimes you are a pain, Bas, what's wrong with that?' Tiz queried.

'He's only charging rent, that's all. The squat is meant to be for the homeless, it just goes to show how greedy people can be. I never trusted him.' Muttering and admonishing himself all the way down the stairs he collided with Boo. The momentary look she gave him was both searching and brooding. He looked deep into the dark eyes. 'Oh, what the hell,' he ventured and gathering her in his arms, kissed her roughly and whirled her round and round.

'Silly sod,' she snapped, regaining her balance, and climbed the stairs.

Suzy had a thirst for learning. She would stare at the pictures on the corridor walls and Tiz would explain about the sea and the sand and the red lighthouse. Each of the girls would read to her in turn before she went to sleep and she was beginning to use her feminine charms to persuade Rev to push her on the garden swing. Gary lacked the energy for outdoor pursuits but he would play with the wooden jigsaws and sit with her when they were short of a babysitter. Tenderness flowed over Ellie whenever she saw them together. He would make a truly wonderful father under normal circumstances, but his situation was far from normal. There was a 50% chance that his baby would have HD and as his illness appeared in the mid twenties chances were that the child would most likely show symptoms even earlier. It was one of the most pitiless parts of the disease and if it ever became necessary, only he could make the decision.

Bas, who was always pleading poverty, had a regular job in charge of the karaoke at the pub on the estate. It was there he met Fran. She was presentable and had a pleasant personality.

They sang duets and entered competitions and got drunk together. 'Well she has plenty of go, no inhibitions, ready for anything,' he boasted to Rev. 'Thinks the world of me.'

'You are getting carried away,' spat Boo. 'Nobody would look at you twice.'

'Is that right? Well, get this, she has asked me to move in with her. Get it?' Menacingly he came close to her, placing his hands on her shoulders. 'Anybody fancied you lately?' Her eyes brimmed over. 'You know what, all this innocence, all this,' he hesitated, 'purity, it's all for show, a pretence. Time you got real.' The friends made a move forward. He backed off. Boo burst into tears and ran blindly from the room.

Sitting alone, she considered the prolonged hostility that existed between them. Over the years he had never changed, rumbustious, coarse, disrespectful, a hard drinker but a hard worker and loyal. She had never given him a kind thought, until now. Someone had spotted the niceties in him and he was leaving.

The evening was drawing in. Boo draped a coat around her and headed for the woodland behind the Grange. It was a mass of trees, ferns and acanthus. It would be easy to wrap this darkness around her and think about what could have been. Crying had exhausted her. She lay on the grass and slept. Her dreams were of the ferns that were all around her, the Devil's brushes reputed to be evil plants that would bring harm if cut. But she hadn't cut them and she was safe and Bas was here holding her hand. And her friends came with torches and there was something cold and sweet flowing down her throat and Valentine sniffing at her face. Then she was lifted up and carried home.

****

It was while Ellie and Gary were out walking one evening that he handed her the cheque. 'What is this?'

'Towards the house.'

'I don't want it. Is it from the flat? Then it's yours.'

'What is mine is yours,' he said.

'Really?' She looked curiously into the grey eyes. The flavour of the air was filled with her perfume.

'Do you remember when we fell asleep in the heavy shade of the tree in Ireland?' he murmured.

'We did it more than once.'

'Yes, we did, only this time we were alone.'

'What about it?' she smiled as he stumbled against her.

'I chose you then.'

'You chose me?' She laughed outright. 'That's an odd word to use.'

'I did. I selected you, desired you, decided on you.'

They leaned against an old oak tree, and a wisp of memory breathed warmly around her. 'But here comes the rub.' He squeezed her hand. 'The HD raised its head. Oh, I know it has been hanging around some time but it wasn't so important until you came along. The spirit is willing but well, you know the rest.'

'What exactly are you trying to say?' He kissed her and the desire she felt for him at that moment was too sweet to contemplate.

'Are you withholding something from me?' He hesitated; she stroked his arm. Ellie sighed. Could this be true happiness which she felt was slipping from her grasp? 'Why don't you ask me to marry you?'

'I can't.' There was the beginning of a smile around his mouth. Ellie braced herself, prepared for an argument;

perhaps the mistake she made was trying too hard. 'Not yet. There are still a few things left to do,' he said.

Her twice-weekly visits to London were coming to an end. The catalogue for "selective and Discerning Women" had proved highly successful but it was time now to stay closer to home. Tiz opened a small shop close to the market, so small that the washbasin was squashed between a rusty gas cylinder and a lino-lined cupboard which housed a large family of slugs. Bas was called in to make a few minor adjustments. 'Do I get paid for this?' Part of him was counting on a negative answer.

'Course.' The mosaic sign above the door spelt out simply "Tiz" and very soon with the help of Ellie and her albeit limited knowledge of marketing her customers were increasing.

If Fran was expecting a long-term relationship and constant devotion from Bas then it appeared to be a long way off. It had been over two months since he had left the Grange and to expect him to change was asking the impossible. Fran provided him with the ambience he most enjoyed, the company of the fairer sex and attention. Bas bulldozed his way through life; no one was going to stand in his way if his mind was set on what he wanted. Rev spent some time in the pub trying to explain this to her but as Fran watched him surround himself with women she strode over to the bar and dragged him back. Exclaiming loudly 'It's time to go' it was like a red rag to a bull. He could have walked away but he was drunk and obstreperous and swept his hand across her backside and yelled in her face. Fran lunged at his stomach and he pushed her away. She left as the women sniggered, banging the door behind her.

Boo treated him with a minimum of warmth when he returned, and the rivalry between them had disappeared. He missed her insults; she no longer told him he was smelly or rough or an idiot. There was a hesitation in their conversation and a new awareness in their expression. Once they were enemies, now they were friends and the contrast between then and now was striking. 'It is a miracle how we can live together,' Fab sighed. 'We are prejudged, prejudiced against, dismissed and often ignored but at least we know how to get on with our lives.'

In the high fields behind the Grange sheep were grazing against a backcloth of coppers and mustards, the autumn foliage was ablaze with vermillion under a blue sky. Ellie and Rev were enjoying one of their rare walks together. In the sharp feel of the turn of the year, as the sun descended and the chill came down, the air smelled of burning leaves. All of them had busy lives but four years on they had become fellow travellers without having the encumbrance of financial demands. 'I am seriously considering applying to the Brighton Institute of Modern Music,' Rev informed Ellie, 'for a place to study for a Higher Diploma in drums.'

'That's wonderful.'

'Yea, well, it could cost four grand but thanks to Gary and the squat and now to you I could do it. Then I could bring Angelica over here. They are the two things that matter at the moment, the ambition to teach and Angelica.'

They continued walking to the high ground where the hills dropped into a pudding basin and the wind tugged at her fair hair and brought colour to her cheeks. Money does not discriminate, she thought. It was not difficult to share his enthusiasm and he pointed out that a lot of her mystery had disappeared now that she could speak. He kissed her politely on the cheek.

Bas wiped the sweat from his forehead. It was Sunday morning and the bike glistened. He stopped the engine as the vicar propped his bicycle against the ornamental vase and nodded. It was a courtesy call, a few minutes with Gary before the morning service. 'Nice bike, young man.' Bas rubbished the remark.

'What I would really like is a Fat Boy Harley.'

'You are halfway there,' Boo quipped, leading Valentine towards the wood.

Bas leapt after her grabbing her hand. 'Miss Feisty is back is she? That's more like it. How about we go for a ride?'

His pride was not easily bruised but his look held a boyish appeal.

For a second she was vulnerable. 'Where to?' Valentine pulled at the leash.

'Scarborough. Here, shove some gear in the pannier.'

'You will like Scarborough,' enthused Tiz, helping her with the helmet. 'Two lovely bays, a castle and clean sandy beaches.' This was make or break time for Boo and Bas. Each had their own strength and weaknesses; Boo whose outlook was often lacking solid common sense, and Bas who demanded constant attention. The engine roared and sped down the lane.

'He didn't happen to mention the motor cycle races on Oliver's Mount, did he?' smiled Rev.

****

The setting sun was turning the leaves to gold. Gary and Ellie were curled up on the rug in front of the fire. 'Did you love him?' Ellie felt a rush of compassion for the person who once gave confidence and inspiration to others and yet was now so unsure.

'Erich? I thought I did at the time,' she whispered.

'What happened?'

'He disappointed me.'

He blew out his cheeks. 'I see.'

'No, you don't. I did not want that sort of relationship at that time.'

'Because you were unsure?'

Ellie made a grimace. 'Because he wanted the best of both worlds.'

Now that the sun had disappeared the room was in semi-darkness. Gary was deep in thought; it would be wrong to contradict and his instinct was to believe her. How could he doubt her when he loved her so much? He kissed the top of her head. 'Do you think we could be married before Christmas?' Ellie held her breath; she understood now why being in love is both ecstasy and pain. Neither of them knew what sort of life lay ahead. They could be overwhelmed and scared of the future; they could try to maintain dignity and struggle to control anger and disappointment; they could find strength in each other and share the painful moments and they would take a vow that the illness would never tear them apart. Above all they had to learn to live with the unrelenting progression of the disease.

'Sweetheart,' she whispered. 'Of course we can.'

Tiz shouted above the rush of the wind as it howled around the gable end. Valentine was on a walkabout. "He'll be in soon enough when he is hungry,' Bas declared. 'If not I'll go and find him.' Bas's world had been turned on its head. He confided in Rev. 'I've had enough of shenanigans; I dare say me and Boo will do OK.' The bracing air of Scarborough had done more than clear his lungs; it had unblocked his head, according to Rev and after three days away the relationship which at first had been frosty, thawed under sunny skies.

Ellie's wedding was booked for mid December. Everyone, especially the women, wanted to be actively involved. Bas was to be the best man, Rev was to give the bride away. Despite Gary's close friendship with the vicar, Ellie chose to be married in the Chapel on the estate. Dresses were designed and made and the Grange was a flurry of activity. There were moments of hysteria and delirious periods of panic but Gary maintained a calm exterior and shut himself away in the cottage. Ellie was reminded of her mother who described marriage as an idealized farce. Moira was hypnotised into a belief that love was destroyed by commitment. 'Don't think I wanted to get married because I didn't,' she told her daughter. 'And certainly not to your father.'

It would have been wonderful to have her father in her life but she had never known him and doubted sometimes whether he had played a crucial part in Moira's life at all. In her own life she felt that something had always been out of adjustment, perhaps it was a father figure she missed.

Carefully she wrote out the invitations in italics. Sitting alone in the neat lounge, the cottage seemed to mould around her. Gary was resting on top of the bed; he was very quiet. Yesterday, without depressing or alarming them, she alerted their friends about what to expect in the future. They were shocked, all except Bas who exhibited an air of polite indifference. 'He'll be OK, we'll look after him.'

Every room in the house was decorated with blooms, menus were discussed, guest lists finalized and transport arranged. Ellie ignored the confrontations between Bas and Boo, who were constantly at loggerheads with each other, and came to the conclusion that we all love differently.

Ten days before the wedding Gary was showing signs of nervousness. He had overbalanced on his way into the main dining room and was found hanging onto the door. Before anyone could reach him he had slid to the floor. With a cry Ellie ran towards him but his face reddened and he thrust out his jaw. 'Leave me. Leave me alone.' Pushing her to one side, he tried hauling himself up; he all but collapsed. It was Bas who lifted him and half-carried him back to his room. He was hurting, hurting also those whom he loved and who loved him.

The spasms began and the bed, wet with perspiration, shook with each onslaught. The doctor ordered complete rest. Nausea prevented him from eating and he developed diarrhoea after a change in medication. Ellie nursed him day and night. Physically and emotionally this episode had scared him to death. He wanted to cancel the wedding, he said. 'I can't put you through this, Ellie. Someone else will have to take care of me.' She stood before him, lovingly resolute. The idea was rejected. The soapy sponge slid across his tender stomach! 'Who else could give you a better bedbath?' she said.

The two attractive girls, Tiz and Fab, fond as they were of Ellie, refused to dress up as bridesmaids. 'I shall be playing a very important role in this wedding as a photographer and do not intend to be there for decorative purposes,' informed Tiz.

'Nor me,' verified Fab, 'but Boo will surely look stunning.'

'I must remember not to trip on my way down the aisle,' breathed Boo, 'or I am destined to remain a spinster.'

'There are worse things,' retorted Tiz.

On the fifth day Gary began to recover. He entered into the spirit of the preparations with renewed enthusiasm and Ellie marvelled at his ability to focus on key decisions. He spent over an hour on the telephone discussing urban villages in the city centre with a member of the town council. Ellie thought he was teasing when he suggested a honeymoon in Paris: and not wanting to dampen his enthusiasm hastily agreed. He had little time to dwell on his problems and his optimism, his spirit, were lifting the hearts of those around him. It was impossible to avoid the symptoms but he was endeavouring to ignore them.

Cheddar stayed for two nights, sleeping in the spare room at the cottage. He unburdened himself and the difference in him was remarkable. 'Have you noticed he doesn't sniff anymore?' whispered Boo at the dinner table. He had no ambitions, he told Gary, he was quite happy at the dairy and was sharing his flat with a girlfriend.

'Bring her to the wedding.' Gary was feeling benevolent, he was responding well to the new drug.

'You were curious about me, weren't you?' Cheddar asked Ellie as they opened a bottle of Chianti in front of a roaring fire. 'Remember when I left you in Ireland? You couldn't ask me but I knew you were worried.'

'I remember,' she affirmed. 'I went to visit my father's grave. Didn't want anyone to know. I was only a kid then.'

Cheddar stood up and stretched. 'You were my first love.' He made it sound like love's young dream, smiled Ellie, when actually nothing happened between them.

The forthcoming wedding had not gone unobserved by the tabloids. It was Isabella who offered to act as a go-between and smooth out the creases. As she explained, 'If you make a fuss they will make an even bigger one. It is only for an hour or two anyway.'

'Oh for a magic wand,' said Ellie, 'and a life of peace and quiet.'

CHAPTER TWENTY-ONE

"Nature gives speech, but silence teaches understanding."
(Proverbial Danish.)

'You are shaping up nicely.' Gran's greeting brought a
wide grin to Gary's face.

'She is, isn't she?' The setting sun threw shadows from
the straggly beech against the wall as Gran ushered them
into the cosy flat. Gary had found the journey to Durham
tiring but he was determined to play the illness down for
now. He had decided to ignore it, he declared, because it
got on his nerves. He wasn't ignoring the reality of HD but
regarding it as little more than an imperfection, but this only
lasted while the symptoms were at bay. Ellie was aware that
this mental aberration was a form of denial.

It was a still, fine night when they set off from Durham
on the return journey to Sheffield and the sky was awash
with stars. Gentle snores came from Gran tucked up in
a travel rug on the back seat, her head resting against a
cushion. 'Are you still praying, lass?' she had asked earlier.
'I am glad you chose chapel.'

'I have also chosen one of your favourite hymns, Gran.
"Loved with everlasting love".'

'Beautiful,' she sighed. It was midnight before Glebe
Grange came into view.

****

'I am finding you unbelievably annoying.' Fab turned to Bas.

'What's the matter now? You keep bursting in here. Can't you see we're busy?'

'This is my bedroom for goodness sake,' moaned Tiz.

Bas hesitated in the doorway. 'Gary's gone missing.'

'What do you mean?'

'He had been dozing in a chair and woke sharply; the next thing he's out the door.'

'Does Ellie know?'

'She's taken the car to look for him.'

It was Rev who found him, stumbling down the long lane on the approach to the woods; a bowed shape huddled against the bitter wind. He was put to bed, he had little to say.

Over breakfast he held Ellie's hand in his. 'I have listed a number of options. I want you to study them carefully and tell me what you think. I know that I am not the person you fell in love with. I can't help that. But I can prevent you from ruining your life. I don't want you to marry me out of pity or gratitude.'

She gave him a look of compassion. 'I am marrying you because I love you, I have always loved you.' Ellie could feel the tears welling up and saw his face twitch with agitation.

'There is one more thing.' She knew what was coming. 'I do not want to pass this disease on any further.'

'I know,' she sighed 'but we can talk about it later.' It had been a heart-searching moment but there was always hope. Ellie was made aware that there is research into the disease and new drugs, that there are scientists who try to unravel the genes and cellular functions of HD and volunteer donors for the gift of a baby. Ellie would discuss this with him in quieter moments when the time was right. She would pray that the foreboding would pass and hoped that he would have the sense not to say any more.

The finishing touches to Tiz's shop had been cleverly put into place in time for Christmas and Ellie, who had spent most of the morning sorting out accessories, was on her way home. She could proudly claim that she knew a little about fashion. At the traffic lights she stopped and on her right saw the sign for the hospital. On impulse she decided to call on Sister and inform her about the wedding.

Over a cup of coffee she was having a quiet moment and was delighted to see Ellie, but subdued and uneasy when she realized the wedding was so close. 'The results had not been too satisfactory when he was last here and there was a gap of almost a month before the drugs took effect.' Ellie straightened her back in the chair, immediately on the defensive.

'I know, but I watch over him most of the time and note his progress.'

Sister bit her lip. 'You don't think he is in danger of becoming detached?'

'No, honestly, part of his indifference is due to anxiety.'

From a drawer Sister produced a manual and thumbed through the pages. 'To save you jumping from the frying pan into the fire I have to prepare you for something else.' Ellie leaned forward apprehensively. 'It may not be relevant in Gary's case but it is as well to bear it in mind. In short, ISB.'

'Sounds ominous.'

'It is. Inappropriate Sexual Behaviour.' Sister watched the girl's response.

'No, this couldn't happen, it isn't in his nature.'

'We are not talking about nature here, it is not about disposition or temperament. It is about a life-changing illness and respect and consideration for others doesn't enter into the equation. ISB is like lichen on rocks, unmoveable once it has started to take hold.' Ellie rose, she couldn't trust herself to speak. She looked round the neat office and at the walls touched by the waning light and wondered. How many more symptoms does HD have hidden? She went out into the corridor and only then allowed the tears to fall.

Gran was overwhelmed with everything, from the cooker to the cottage, and she could not find words to express her delight in the countryside despite the barren fields. Jan would take her for walks to the winter garden near the churchyard and they practised their cooking skills whilst Suzy blackened the pastry with her tiny hands. 'Take a sniff at that,' coaxed Jan, offering a bowl of curry.

'It's a bit hot.' She blew as her eyes began to water.

As usual there was a lot going on; their working days began early and once the evening meal was over there was practice time and a number of chores to do. It was a case of early to rise but hardly ever early to bed. If medals were given out for sleep deprivation, Dark Horse would win it hands down. On the other hand Gran could be found nursing Suzy in the quieter part of the house, both fast asleep. 'Touching base,' whispered Fab to Ellie, the meaning of which escaped her.

The band which Gary had nurtured and developed had matured. They had remained silent when he manifested most of the symptoms – tremors, twitching and short temper – but now they noisily expressed their support and performed a charity gig for HD. 'They each have a heart of gold,' Ellie told him.

As the wedding drew near she became watchful of his every mood, mindful that stress was one of the keys that could unlock an attack. Occasionally there was the slurred sentence and the odd moment of toppling over but the pale, gaunt expression had gone and his eyes were clear. The black cloud had lifted for a while. There was no hope of sleep; Ellie was too excited. Like a child she clasped her hands together and prayed for a good day ahead, especially for the man she loved. Alone in the double bed he slept peacefully, no tremors, no nightmares. Why now did she think of her father? Would he have been the type of man able to guide her with concern and responsibility through life? The moon dipped and rose among the clouds, carrying with it a halo of frost.

'You are very well organized,' Gran complimented, sitting on a bentwood chair in the corner of the kitchen.

'It is a special day, not to be screwed up. Ellie is a big part of our life now,' replied Tiz.

'I used to call her Lisa,' Gran said petulantly.

Suzy, the flower girl, danced her way over to Gran, plumping out her peach taffeta and georgette dress before sitting on her knee. 'Try to keep clean,' ordered Fab.

'I was just saying how well you manage things,' continued Gran.

'It's simple really,' Fab explained. 'We are like a train in motion; we know we are on the right tracks and although we are buffeted from right and left we still keep going and get there in the end.'

Tiz nodded and offered Gran a cup of herb tea. 'Fab studies philosophy. Socrates, I think.' Gran sniffed.

Ellie was left alone. The girls had helped to dress her and Boo had curled her hair around the jewelled coronet. Who was this girl who looked back at her through the long mirror? Would this be the time when a father might say 'You look beautiful, I am so proud of you. If you have any doubts about this marriage for any reason I am here for you.' There had always been a sense of hope that they would meet one day. Not any more. Still she would hold onto Rev, walk with him down the aisle and move into the future without regret.

There was a flurry of movement outside the cottage and the girls breezed in, bringing the chill December air with them. One o'clock – in half an hour she would be in the chapel. 'They're going.' Boo pushed open the drapes and they watched Bas and Gary drive away.

Last evening he had submitted to an aromatherapy massage; he was relaxed and wanting to reminisce. Perhaps he was testing his memory. She was a symbol of the unattainable he told her, and he often wondered if she was unhappy or bored. 'Never forget,' he said, 'that whatever happens I will always love you.' Ellie was conscious that he had never actually said those words before.

The long, sleek car came to a stop beside a small group of women at the chapel gate. Cheddar waved the driver on. 'What's wrong?' Rev looked puzzled.

'We are a little early.' The driver drove around the

avenue. Ellie adjusted her long, white gown and arranged the flowers on her knee.

Rev squeezed her elbow. 'Are you OK?' Ellie nodded her head in such a way it was impossible to know what she was thinking.

'We'll try again.' The car purred to a stop. The small group had grown into an inquisitive crowd. Once again they had to move on. Rev was beginning to realize the urgency of it all. Ellie could have wept. Something dreadful must have happened to Gary; he wouldn't abandon her, not like this. Please God, let him be alright. The sun came out and shone on the Christmas roses in her lap as once again they pulled up outside the chapel. 'I'm getting out.' Maybe it was her natural composure, her spontaneous reaction or her inner strength, but she smiled as she stepped out of the car; and the newspaper photographers captured the loveliness of the glowing bride and the warmth with which she greeted her bridesmaid. Cameras were busy as Ellie stepped inside the porch.

'They are 20 minutes late,' Tiz fumed. 'Where the hell are they?'

'Here they are.' Boo hitched up her long, peach dress and ran towards them. There was congealed blood around Bas's nose and Gary had a nasty bruise under his chin.

'For goodness sake, look at the state of you,' Tiz remonstrated.

Gary gazed in admiration at his lovely bride. 'I am sorry, sweetheart, we got into a fight.' Gary's apologies came with a grin of satisfaction.

'We?' Ellie's eyes opened wide.

'I have dusted myself down as best I can.'

'There is one thing for sure, it is bound to charm the readers' eye,' quipped Tiz, taking her place in the pew.

There were no more distractions. 'I want you forever,' he whispered as they stood before the minister. 'More than that I want you to want me.' He was shaking but he had had a tough time getting there; years of fear and worry and months of anguish and pain. Yet despite this for Ellie it was a happy day full of hope, excitement, curiosity, devotion and expectation. She wanted to give a love that responded to his joys and his sufferings otherwise it would not be worthy of being called love at all.

They were photographed against the wrought-iron gate leading to the garden and blessed from heaven with a celebration of a ticker tape of snow.

'Did he care about Ellie when he started the fight?' demanded Boo, 'or think how it would affect Gary?'

'Look, I didn't start the rumpus and when have I ever run away from a challenge? Anyway Gary was up for it, he might he sick but he stuck it out. Look, they were itching for a fight the minute we entered the pub.'

'What were you doing there anyway?'

'Hell, Boo, it's what every hot-blooded male does before his wedding.'

'So who started it?'

'Fran and her moronic brother,' Bas carried on, not even pausing in his greedy consumption of food.

'I might have known,' Boo sighed.

'She's weighted down with jealousy, that one.' Bas swallowed.

'I can't see why,' she sniffed contemptuously and left him to his curry.

'It was careless of me. I'm not much good at street brawls.' Gary smiled self-consciously. It was hard trying to explain to Ellie. She was recalling the sadness in his eyes when he failed to protect her against the drunken youths. 'I have never heard such a shriek of mingled hate and rage from a woman,' he informed her. He hadn't met Moira, thought Ellie. Nor would he if she had anything to do with it. Her mother was out of her life for good, or so she thought. Gran, on the other hand, had listened to her granddaughter's symptoms of isolation and repression and prescribed affection and attention.

'Will you be alright until we return from honeymoon?'

'Of course, love, they will soon get used to my little fads.'

It was time to go. Ellie thanked all her friends, including Isabella and Cassie, whose bright, dark eyes flashed with perception. Patches of snow were visible on the highest peaks and Gary wrapped her cloak around her as they climbed into the taxi. He had waited so long for this moment yet found himself lost for words. He was feeling nervous; he had expected to be apprehensive but not shaky or weak. 'You have packed all my medication, I hope.' His tone was light but his eyes betrayed him.

'Trust me,' she clung to him. 'We are here for each other.'

There were sprays in gold vases and champagne by the bed and the honeymoon suite at the Hilton was ready for the young lovers. Huntington's Disease was on the back-burner. Ellie had questioned her faith but even the fleeting feeling of doubt disappeared when he was well and in control. In his life he had longed for some sort of equanimity but he knew that the disease would continue to progress. Would she be ready when he could no longer dress, shave or feed himself? Would she be ready when he lost his temper, his memory or his will to live? She had wondered. Is being in limbo better than knowing altogether?

In the very beginning of their relationship he had taken care of her, found her somewhere to stay, taken pity on her, looked out for her. It was not gratitude that had brought her to this position but a love so deep that she had no choice but to ride the emotional rollercoaster to the peak of ecstasy and to the depths of despair.

The lights of the city shone bright before him. From the bathroom he could hear Ellie singing softly. Why do they say that a man's life is a closed book? Of course he realized that some thoughts will always need to stay private, they might be hurtful if brought into the open, but Ellie might press for honesty and she deserved nothing less.

A thin blanket of snow had settled on the rooftops. He stood by the window and the Christmas lights which spread across the canal in the distance swayed in the breeze. Ellie stepped quietly into the room and held out her arms.

This was their time; the bond of commitment in sickness and in health would depend on courage and compassion. Tonight he had to get this right, no pessimism, no weariness, no self-pity, whatever happened. He would be in control. They dusted the confetti from the sheets and drank the champagne. Tonight HD would not rule his thoughts, he would be lifted by Ellie's beauty and her infectious laughter for every restriction put on him would be overcome.

He had drawn a line in the sand; the ugliness of his illness would in no way be allowed to encroach on her radiance. More than anything in the world he wanted to please her, for her to be proud of him; she had given up everything to share his life. Nestling beside him she sensed his urgency, how different to last time when his body shook with tremors and convulsions. Now it was pure emotion. She was glad she had waited for him.

In the first light of morning he watched her sleep. On the bedside table the bottle was still half full of champagne. They would finish it before leaving for Paris. He felt good. In the paleness of day the slight fall of snow stretched as a sheet of white across the canal basin and he took a sip of water, stretched and crawled back into bed. She had smiled a little at his seriousness when he had described her as the oasis in his troubled life and promised to keep a perspective on things.

Her lightheartedness at breakfast was irresistible; chatting with other guests she helped herself to apricots and yoghurt. 'Where are we staying in Paris?'

'It's a surprise.' In the heat of the dining room she unzipped her cream wool sweater folding it neatly over the back of the chair. With or without cameras, the panache was there and he hoped that he hadn't cut short a career which had given her so much.

A bustling airport crammed with travellers on their pre-Christmas rush, filling the air with French perfume and cigars, welcomed them to Paris. A uniformed chauffeur drove them through the heart of the city and into the countryside. A spread of blue sneaked between a film of cloud as the river

sparkled alongside. The turns in the road became familiar
and as the route narrowed to a track she exclaimed, 'I know
where we are, it's Reeve's home.'

'So I understand,' Gary smiled and released her hand, yet
reluctant to let her go.

Reeve had left a note. "Congratulations Ellie and Gary.
Gone to OZ. Monique will take care of your every need;
stay as long as you like. Take the car. Don't do anything I
wouldn't do. Luv. Reeve.xx" Night set in and dinner was
excellent. Isabella had made all the arrangements, Gary
informed Ellie, and he hoped she approved. They listened
to Reeve's sentimental vocals in front of a log fire and
curled their toes around the sheepskin rug. To Gary Ellie's
loveliness became more exciting as he understood her more;
now that she had found her voice his world had changed.

They had long talks and long drives into the country, and
they made love as they watched the last faint glow of pink
along the horizon. Gary was well and Ellie thanked God.
There would always be a need for invocation in her prayers;
she would always ask for help from Him but there was so
much to be grateful for.

From the plush box in the theatre, courtesy of Reeve, they
enjoyed the "Nutcracker" and visited as many Art Galleries
as they could fit in during one day. And they shopped for
gifts for friends who were contradictory, diverse, complicated
but loyal and caring. Driving home through a thick mist,
Gary stopped the car. He felt a euphoria so strong that it
made him tremble. Ellie embraced him and he felt suddenly
as if he was being held in a world of mystery and sympathy
and gently and spontaneously he made love to her.

Their last night was celebrated with a sumptuous meal
and prosceto. 'Italian champagne,' smiled Monique, 'to have
with Marscarponi Cheese.' I thought you might like a bit of
Italian,' she beamed.

'Charming,' whispered Gary. In the winter sun the pride
of peacocks waved goodbye with their colourful tails as
the couple disappeared down the drive to begin their short
journey home. Ellie's hair hung loose around her shoulders as

she snuggled up to her husband on the plane. He smoothed the top of her head with his hand. Why did he have this feeling that he was running free, with no limitations to his health? Why did he feel that illness could be kept at bay because he was so nourished by love and devotion? There was no compelling reason for it.

Glebe Grange had been transformed. "Merry Christmas" and "Welcome Home" banners swayed side by side and huge balls of cottonwool adorned the steps inside the front porch. The house was ablaze with lights, with candles and silver torches leading from the kitchen garden. Lanterns glowed among the straggly oaks. A huge decorated tree surrounded by parcels stood majestically in the corner of the hall and in the midst of all the noise they were welcomed back. Gran, nursing Suzy at the table, gave Ellie a knowing look. 'Lovely to see you.' Suzy pointed out her sunshine tray on which four egg-cups were filled with kiwi fruit with the top sliced off. She fed Ellie forcibly. One by one their friends came forward to hug or shake hands.

'Hi, Gary, you look knackered,' greeted Bas.

Gary grinned and replied boyishly, 'Cheers.'

Ellie tried to picture what the year ahead would bring. From across the sitting room she studied Gary, relaxed and absorbed in his poetry, his movements perfectly controlled. He appeared to be at ease, whilst she sat back on the comfortable sofa and longed to hold him. He gazed out of the cottage window. 'I have never seen a sky quite like that,' he sighed. 'It is so bright and clear.' He had focused on a bright, clear stratagem, he told Ellie. 'I want you to allow me a measure of control. I know when I am tired and I shall rest. I realize that I tend to overdo it sometimes and that my memory is getting more erratic so I will slow down. But just because I'm slowing down doesn't mean that I don't need people around me or that I don't want to try new things. I am sure that you will not need me to tell you if there is anything physically amiss!' She had a strong power of waiting, she could hang on to silences. He held back deliberately for a moment then held her close. 'I do not need you to nursemaid me all the time,' he whispered 'but look, I will do whatever you think fit.'

The honeymoon had been a success, the menacing illness silent. Ellie slipped into the bedroom where Gran was preparing for her journey home. 'Is it convenient tomorrow, Gran?' The old lady laboured over her suitcase.

'It is love. I'm ready for a bit of peace and quiet. It isn't necessary to use so many words to make yourself heard, you know.' Her presents were scattered on the bed. 'I have had one of the best Christmases yet,' she smiled, 'although how you manage to consume so much food and drink I'll never know. But the company was lovely.' There was a wistful look on her face. 'Remember what our old minister used to say? Life, like football, is a game of two halves but the referee is the only one who can blow the whistle and finish it. You have a lovely man there. Take good care of each other.'

The decline in Gary's health was gradual. Spring arrived at Glebe Grange with a show of daffodils and tulips and the bluebell wood behind the copse was painted by Tiz and later displayed in the Gallery. Gary was often too tired to rise before midday and Ellie would listen to his complaints and sympathize. The evenings were still cold but they would sit up late in front of the fire over a warm drink and discuss the exploits of the band. He was no longer able to travel long distances with them or tolerate the noise of a live gig. 'I will some day,' he vowed but he knew it was merely a half truth.

She watched from the window as he helped them pack their gear into the back of the van and slowly cross the path towards the hedges crouched in a haze of fog. He had to bear this illness alone but Ellie tried to embrace it, to understand it, to face up to it. There were nights when she went out and walked by the light of the moon, mulling over the perplexing looks he had given her or why he would leave the room for no apparent reason. Yet she was doing what she was told to do, instilling hope and encouragement.

March was moving into April as gently as a lamb. Bas and

Gary were inspecting the outbuildings half-hidden between flowering shrubs and bushes. Around its broken walls years of rain and wind had eaten away the stone. 'What do you think?' Bas kicked at the weatherbeaten door.

'About what exactly?'

'Well. Ellie seems to think that it has been a workshop or a stable, somewhere to store whatever but seeing me and Boo have got it together I thought we could make something of it.'

'Like what?'

'A place to live. I am sick to death of bed-hopping to be honest.'

'And you have a deep regard for ethics,' Gary added sarcastically. 'Have you mentioned it to Ellie?'

Ellie was amused by the news that Jan had adopted a tomato. Apparently, she explained to Fab, it is a particular species that is one of many which is in great danger of becoming extinct so the seeds are cultivated by a company called Hydra. She saw it on television. 'It's an aphrodisiac, you know,' smiled Fab. 'Single women were discouraged from eating tomatoes in Puritan England; it is known as the love apple.'

'You have been talking to Boo.'

'Yes,' Fab laughed, 'we had a giggle at the time.'

Now more serious thoughts were being put into fruition, the act of turning an open-plan shed into a habitable home. For Bas it was just a stepping-stone, for Boo it was a milestone. She had a curious instinctive feeling that this was something she had wanted all along and there was a semblance of gaiety about everything she did.

Gary drew the plans. The new venture had opened up another door and despite having the discomfort of a sore throat and tongue he was confident about the scheme. They removed the rubble by the barrowloads and dust by the bucketful and organized a skip. From the house it looked as if a giant dust storm had settled on the building. It was surrounded by cart loads of bricks, scaffolding, piles of cement, buckets, shovels and streams of mortar.

'You are not taking on too much, are you?' Ellie was cleaning her teeth. 'It is barely nine o'clock.' Gary continued shaving. He knew that this would take stamina and effort; he didn't need dejection; he shrugged off his thoughts impatiently.

The building site became a social gathering. A plumber with a swift turn of humour, a plasterer with a dry sense of the ridiculous, an electrician who made wild suggestions to Fab and a roofer whose ambition was to display his acrobatic skills wearing as few clothes as possible, came in force from the estate. Bas, domineering and confident, having weighed up the opposition, took charge.

By mid August the house was near completion. It had a small kitchen, a lounge, a bathroom and two bedrooms. There had been one scary incident when the half-built dividing wall to the kitchen had collapsed and Bas was buried. His legs and abdomen were trapped under bricks and plaster. After yelling out he lay groaning, his face strained and white, and Gary and the plasterer grabbed him by the waist and pulled him free. Bas was defiant. 'It's nothing.' Boo meanwhile was slowly succumbing to the mysterious ways of Bas and it would have comforted her to know that he was ready to settle down. Bas had gained in stature and credibility; his strident voice issued orders during the donkey-work and he matched his fellow workers pint for pint at the end of the day.

Yet for Gary it was all too much. A complete rest was ordered after a series of explosive outbursts directed at Ellie and he developed a hacking cough and a severe chest infection. Only half aware of his surroundings, his voice hardly more than a whisper, she could only watch and wait. In the first couple of days he refused to eat, remarking bitterly, 'What's the point? Give me one good reason why I should carry on? There is no end to this, each day brings more problems. You must promise me when I have had enough to help me.' Ellie could only squeeze his hand; he thought her silence might have been at a cost.

The friends were held together by their devotion to

Gary. Jan cooked him nutritious meals, Tiz attended to his correspondence, Bas took full responsibility for the band, whilst Rev kept him company in the short periods of amiability. With unrelieved regularity Rev resumed his long walks and sometimes Ellie went with him. The contrast between the two men prompted her to ask, 'How do you think he feels, Rev? You are about the same age, yet there is a world of difference between you. You can do anything, go anywhere, share a partner for life, have children. Gary has been robbed of all that is worth living for. I ask myself what I can do to alleviate the pain.'

Rev leaned against the drystone wall and kicked at the ground with his boot. He looked into the blue eyes brimming with tears. 'You can push him, Ellie. He is like a creaking windmill; if you put wind in his sails he will take off again, come into his own. He has such capabilities, he is intelligent and there will always be somebody around to spur him on.'

'Right.'

She stood before him, chin held high and hands on her hips. 'Let us throw rationality to the winds then.'

****

Seven complacent friends and Suzy looked out onto the scene across the newly-mown lawn and marvelled at their tenacity. The building was complete and in the distance a curtain of dust turned to gold in the August sun. Jan had prepared a pasta salad and they sat at the long table with their glasses of wine and bread straight out of the oven. It was a noisy, happy bunch and Gary, fully recovered, had to wait his opportunity and had to shout to make himself heard. He rose to his feet. 'I would like to propose a toast. To the B & B Lodge. To Bas and Boo. Good Luck and Good Health!'

'To paraphrase Socrates,' Fab began.

'Please,' Bas scratched his head.

Fab continued. 'Wealth does not bring goodness, but

goodness brings wealth and every other blessing.'

'Thanks, Fab,' said Boo, raising her glass.

'You had no trouble with planning permission, then?' asked Rev.

'What planning permission?'

Gary helped himself to garlic bread. The room fell silent. Boo pursed her lips.

'For the building work,' Rev continued. 'Gary, you have done a major conversion there and this is a Grade 2 listed!'

Gary took a sip of wine. Bas in a totally overpowering moment of madness brought his fists crashing down on the table, spewing obscenities, and Suzy screamed. 'Don't tell me,' he spat, 'that we have to pull it all down!' Ellie glanced at Gary and saw an unmistakable look of smugness on his face; he was enjoying this.

'It's OK, Bas. The outbuildings are not listed and in any case the Inspectors came yesterday and passed the work. I forgot to mention it.' It took more than an hour to convince Bas that it was a wind-up.

Something in Gary came to life quite suddenly on the fragrant September evening as hand in hand Ellie and he strolled through the avenue of trees behind the Grange. The lazy wind curled the palmate leaves of the horse chestnut and birds disappeared into thick bushes. They walked up to the highest point and he kissed her tenderly. 'I have reached a decision,' he said, with a distinct air of superiority. 'I think we should have a child.'

'But I thought ...' He interrupted her.

'No, not mine. I am not prepared to risk passing on HD. I thought IVF.'

She leaned her face against his chest, then looked adoringly into his face. 'I would rather have you as the father but I always imagined that love is something special between two people who are moving in the same direction. Let's go home and talk about it.' He fell silent, he was afraid he had gone too far.

Sometimes their nerves were put to the test, their nights terrible. Gary was disturbed by dreams; that his life was floating cut loose from its roots. But that night when the full moon had slipped quietly behind the clouds they talked of their decision to go ahead with in-vitro-fertilization. 'The procedure is relatively simple,' he assured her. 'All the doctor requires is a list of my physical characteristics and then the donor is chosen. Do you go along with that?' Ellie knew that she wanted children and if using donor sperm was the only way, then she felt in her heart this was the answer.

It was well into the morning when Ellie awoke. There was no view from the cottage except a grey sky and wet woods and a fresh layer of mud which streaked across the drive. Bas saw the light and waved as he remounted the bike and tore down the road. Boo had earlier confided in Ellie, 'He is like a big bear really; in a subconscious way he has been trying to please me all this time.' Ellie patted her hand. Meanwhile a new timetable was being drawn up to accommodate Jan's forthcoming stay in hospital for her final skin graft. It could be, thought Ellie, that permanence was part of all their lives now, a routine of work, gigs and ministering care.

It had been a Sunday like any other. The beginning of autumn was mild and the trees spread their leaves over the lawn in the warm sun. In the lounge everyone relaxed in front of the television and Suzy was fascinated with the small horned lizard covered in spikes with slanting eyes winking sleepily on the screen. Suddenly the peace was shattered. Slowly at first, a drone, a clatter of wheels, the din of a labouring engine and a crunch of tyres on the gravel. It sighed to a shuddering halt.

All eyes turned to see the familiar sight of the bus, Dark Horse, as it parked obtrusively in the shadow of Glebe Grange. Then things really started to happen. Mustard was given a hero's welcome. He looked older and there was a sprinkling of grey among his ginger hair. The group came alive but he was in need of sleep and after a meal and a bath Bas suggested, 'I suppose he had better doss down with us.'

It was Gary who observed. 'Distance fades the sharpness

of memory but there are some people you don't forget.'

'I must admit I've missed you guys.' Celebrations were planned and after a long sleep he was enjoying a feast with the rest. There were numerous tales to tell about the lead singer who had been left behind in Turkey, under arrest. 'He intended to dominate everywhere he went,' he grumbled, 'and had completely obliterated the drum kit by the time the bouncers had a hold of him.' He continued biting into a chunk of cheese. He was arousing their interest, encouraging them to look ahead, reminding them of the good times and surreptitiously planting the seed of wanderlust. They gathered round him as he unfolded a torn map of Eastern Europe whilst Gary and Ellie remained curled up on the sofa. 'You fancy coming along, don't you Fab, are you still game?' She laughed and her cheeks were flushed with wine.

'Can't Mustard, I'm a mother now; I have responsibilities.'

Gary tried hard to hide the envy in his voice. 'When were you thinking of going?'

'June maybe.'

Ellie turned to see the look of hesitance on his face. 'We could go, you know, and fly home at any time, if you really wanted to.' He checked his frustration with a grin and shook his head.

His physical abilities were, on the whole, quite remarkable. Apart from the bradykinesia, the slowing down of movements, and the need to chew his food carefully to avoid choking, he enjoyed his involvement with activities at the Grange. The waves of dejection had rolled away and often it was easy for him to overdo it. He would do anything he could rhetorically and it took no time at all to persuade Mustard to stay until the bus had been restored to a relatively reasonable condition. As usual everyone was willing to lend a hand.

As the end of November approached and the cold wind howled around the gable end Fab developed a bad cold. Quickly it spread until it worsened and everyone feared the worst. Ellie was concerned both for Suzy and Gary and moved Suzy in with her in the cottage. They nursed each other in turn, their roles defined as to the stage of the virus and it was mostly Ellie's inner strength that she managed to care for others whilst spending time being sick and fighting a fever.

Bas and Boo, surrounded by aromatherapy burners, remained in bed for a week. Ellie fed them hot, nourishing soup with plenty of garlic and only their heads showed above the duvet in the comfort of the Lodge. Surprisingly Suzy and Gary remained unaffected. Preparations for Christmas began in earnest. Boo was back to her self-assertive approach to Bas; he was often expecting an aggressive response and she pulled him into line with an attitude that said 'And what are you going to do about it?'

The wood fire crackled in the hearth and the Christmas tree sparkled in the lounge. The meal, on Christmas Day, had lulled them into the comfort zone and the mulled wine and lager had exposed their sentiments. Fab smiled engagingly at Gary. 'Come with us on the tour. It won't be the same without you.' He looked almost boyish in his crisp white shirt, his hair slightly tousled and his lean face flushed with wine.

'With respect I don't think you should have the responsibility of looking after me.' Gary raised his voice in order to drown the noise of the speakers. It was a brave admission to make. Ellie sat close to him on the sofa. 'The days of tossing restlessly on a bumpy mattress are over,' he replied. Ellie squeezed his hand. He had crossed the line from denial to humorous acceptance, at least for the benefit of his friends.

Ellie dressed slowly. The simple cut of her cream suit exaggerated her long legs and she checked her fair, shoulder length hair in the hall mirror. She could not remember when she had been so apprehensive or so determined. She would have agreed to the arrangement solely on grounds of self-interest but she was an honest creature and knew that this was a sexually undefiled act of love.

The duvet was well down the bed revealing his shoulders;

his thin chest was covered with perspiration. She reached out to muss the hair on his chest, rubbed the bristles on his chin and kissed him. Gary stirred. Today was special; she wanted him with her but he needed time to recover from his recurring nightmares. Her appointment was for 10.30 and the clinic was busy. After many consultations she and Gary had decided on AID (Artificial Insemination by Donor).

The journey had been disrupted by shoppers clamouring for bargains in the January sales but she had hardly noticed. Her mind was filled with flutterings like bats in roosts. The young nurse, friendly and efficient, was charged with enthusiasm. 'I doubt that you will be expected to stay the night. After the sperm transfer there is no need to stay in bed. Avoid sex for a couple of weeks and take it easy.' She watched the doctor closely whilst he conducted tests on Ellie, straightening the sheet under her knees. 'You can get up now.' The doctor returned to his desk. Ellie slid off the bed and pulled on her skirt. 'I'm sorry,' he said 'I cannot offer you AID, I'm afraid.'

Ellie felt the colour drain from her face. He continued. 'It is too late; you are pregnant, Mrs Danby.' How was it possible to feel exhilaration and despair at the same time? The baby she had longed for with the man she loved was now a reality, a truly remarkable gift and yet she had put the child at risk. It was not deliberate, it was obviously the virus that had upset the effectiveness of the contraceptive pill. But what should she do? Was she compelled to go on deceiving people?

Phil had forced her to live a lie; she had continued to live a lie and this was hard enough to live with but more deceit would be even harder. The decision she made now would change her whole life. In the car park she sat with her hands on the steering wheel and prayed. The truth could not be told. Not yet. It was nevertheless another challenge, some sort of test. In a desperate moment early in their marriage Gary had confessed, 'I never knew my parents, nor will I ever know if I have siblings. All I ever wanted was the comfort of blood ties.' Now it may come into being but at what cost? The pleasures of her imagination coloured her world. A baby. An individual for which she was partly responsible. A being that shaped her future, giving a deeper meaning to her life.

'Don't you think it is a bit excessive?' Gary's annoyance was obvious. 'I don't remember Fab charting everything she ate or taking so many vitamins.' Ellie sank heavily into the armchair, pulling the footstool towards her. 'I am carrying a VIP here. I don't want any mishaps.'

'Really.' It was a strained relationship that had developed during the pregnancy. Ellie was making an intense effort to remain calm, aware that Gary had no intention of becoming closely involved. His refusal to show concern was hurtful. Had she revealed the baby was his, maybe parenthood would have more appeal. The content of lies was resulting in a mixture of irritation and guilt.

Kisses and compliments were rare and there was an element of anxiety in everything she did. She was sick of pretending, almost driven at times to tell him the truth. He walked slowly down the hall. 'I need some air,' he snapped, taking care to slam the door as loudly as possible. She sighed. This was difficult but tolerable behaviour. Ellie was alone in her painful world.

The big house, deprived of loud music, laughter and lubricious language, housed just Jan and Suzy. Whilst Jan was immersed in her role as acting housekeeper and nanny Ellie prepared and cooked meals. The tour had three more weeks to run. For the first time ever Gary was not directly involved. He had always been the figurehead, the one in control, the administrator. Now Ellie sensed his lack of self-esteem and was faced with the daily anguish of reassurance.

Tiz sent several emails but it only added to his depressed state. They didn't need him, they were having a wonderful time. His pride was wounded; Ellie was the prime target of his frustration and all she could do was murmur into the silence. To relieve the tension Jan became her sounding block although her loyalty to her husband never wavered. 'You must no longer be the victim of emotional upheaval,'

Jan reminded her. 'Struggling with Gary won't help, you have to battle with the disease.' Sunlight streamed across the room and Jan moved into the shadow of the blinds, settling the scarf to protect her scars. Ellie could never hope to match this woman's courage.

The arrival of the bus was imminent. The phone call snapped Gary out of his morose trance and Ellie received a kiss on the lips and a helpful heave out of bed. Every movement was an effort now; she had dreaded the change in her body and failed to understand the frustration that came with it. She hated being fat and shapeless and felt isolated and clumsy. At least the model agency had taken advantage of her situation. There were compensations; she had an exclusive maternity wardrobe.

There is nothing quite like a reunion, thought Ellie. Suzy cried with joy and the girls complimented Ellie on how well she looked. There followed hours of excitable chatter, recriminations and profane curses from Bas. Fab had been a liability, Rev laughed.

'Making up for lost time,' Boo sympathized.

'More than a double F, if you ask me,' Tiz argued. Slim and bronzed, finding their praises fulfilling, Fab hitched up her short skirt.

'Blame the booze for my lack of willpower.'

'Do I detect a lack of self-restraint,' Gary enquired.

'Yes,' the united response. It was a case of organized gloating, interrupted by crude boasting and expressive gestures.

Gary had a way of getting things out of people and despite his fatigue managed to settle them down to discuss finance. Although it appeared his mind was racing his speech was slow. Ellie spent time with Jan in the kitchen as the lager and wine whetted the imagination and embellished the impromptu speeches. Gary's manner was extraordinary. Why suddenly had he come alive? Hyperactive? Was it that pretence takes up an awful lot of energy? He dragged his leg awkwardly as he crossed the room and dropped into an armchair. Fab offered him a lager. No; Ellie thought. He should not be drinking. Alcohol would cause problems but Tiz was buzzing with enthusiasm, trying to persuade Bas to fetch more drinks from the bus.

It was after midnight, music blared out through the open windows. If Ellie had hoped to impose silence she was disappointed. She was tired. She glanced at Gary. 'I'm going to bed now.' Fab swung her legs over the end of his chair, her impish face turned towards him. Gary smiled back at her.

'OK. I'll stay a little longer.' Ellie resented his words. Could jealousy be the reason? She stepped into the doorway of the deserted cottage. It was a scary feeling to leave him. Fab was on form, she recognised the signs. Surely he couldn't be manipulated, persuaded? Had she been too protective of her baby? They had not been intimate for months.

The hot milk soothed her throat but did nothing to ease her fertile imagination. Was it willingly or under compulsion that she stepped out into the warm night? Late July brought out the perfume of the sweet-scented roses and the stars were brilliant. Yet under the shapes of the trees it was very dark. The music had quietened down and Valentine was taking his unaccompanied night exercise, sniffing around the bushes. In the distance she heard Gary's voice and started to walk towards him. Then Fab's throaty giggle touched the night air, peppering her speech, and Ellie felt the first pang of fear. She froze as the two silhouettes merged behind the gap in the trellis and Fab was pushed forcibly against the wall. It was difficult for Ellie to move; she felt a sickness in her chest. 'I'm not exactly asking you,' Gary began, and struggling to catch her breath she heard only jumbled words and moans. Ellie realized that the one thing she dreaded most was about to happen and there was nothing she could do about it. HD had taken hold, depersonalized him, brought about the confusion of right and wrong, robbed him of all inhibitions. What was it she felt? Anger? Indignation? Humiliation? She knew she was losing the battle to curb a natural desire.

Sobbing, she returned to the cottage, spared from the burst

of explicit gutter language. The hurt was indescribable and the knowledge that her husband was not exclusively hers confirmed the notion that she was failing him. She knew that this was not a desire to destroy their marriage for that would be inconceivable.

Gary's sleeping tablets were on the bedside table. It was not her practice to take medication but a night without sleep was unbearable, lying awake with provocative images flashing through her mind. She swallowed the pill and fell into bed and dreamed of a valley where against the vast greenness, white-walled cottages hid in tiny clusters. The opposite sides of the room appeared to be leaning in contrary directions and the ceiling began to spin. Pain stabbed at her stomach, cramp gripped her legs. Suddenly startled from sleep she cried out.

Gary held her hand. 'What is it sweetheart?' He was back with her, her love was in torment but her emotional energy was high.

'I think we should go. What time is it?'

'Baby is early, surely?' he asked, helping her into the car.

'Just a little,' she lied.

They drove almost silently away from the Grange as the sunrise peeped over the hill, stretching golden rays over the valley. Gary chose to take the easier curves and longer stretches of road to the hospital. Between the contractions she felt a surge of excitement and a powerful urge to hold Gary, to have him reassure her. She was apprehensive about the birth but not fearful.

After six and a half hours Gareth Oliver pushed his way angrily into the world! 'What price do you put on a new life?' she whispered. Gary was proud. Ellie was exhausted. After a long sleep she awoke to find him in the chair beside her bed. He smiled and she felt the core of her jealousy slipping away. Everything she had loved about him, his patience, his tolerance and his gentleness, cancelled out his betrayal. How was he to blame? The inappropriate sexual behaviour was not his fault; it was the bestial facet of the hell they call Huntington's.

'If you are going to cry I'll wait outside,' Tiz, Boo and Jan arrived with balloons, bears, bouquets and boxes of chocolates. They threw their energy into talking incessantly and Gareth was passed around like a parcel at a children's party. Unshaven, but with clear grey eyes and articulate conversation, Gary held court. 'Where's Fab?' Ellie tried to appear casual.

'She has taken over the kitchen,' Jan smiled. 'She thought Suzy would get too excited; she sends her love.'

Two nights later they left hospital for home, to the sweet smell of the newly-painted nursery, and Ellie was anxious to be back on an even keel. The pain was all taken away from her as Gary held her close. It was like being handed a rainbow of butterflies.

It was time to confront Fab. She was entering deep waters but it had to be done. If Fab's seduction was just the tip of the iceberg then she was floating in dangerous waters. From the outside no one saw the pressure Ellie was under; it was important that she maintained a measure of calm. She liked to think out loud, a habit when it had been necessary to exercise her voice when no one else was around.

With baby in her arms she walked through the kitchen garden and through the back door of the Grange. From the sink Fab looked up, startled. 'Hi, I would like you to meet Gareth Oliver.'

'He's beautiful.'

'Here,' Ellie placed him in her arms. 'Have a nurse.' Fab sat at the table and touched his cheek. 'During my stay in hospital I have had time to think,' Ellie began.

'It must have been difficult for you with no one to support you – Suzy's father, I mean. I wasn't here but I did wonder.'

Fab sighed. 'Well, let's face it, I was surrounded by a brilliant, talented, caring group of people and you did set up a bank account for her. Honestly, everyone was great.'

Gareth opened his eyes. 'You know, Fab, when you have a new-born baby in your arms you are ready to forgive anything. I am so fortunate to have a man who loves me.

He is my world but his world is breaking up and we have to help keep it together, keep the bad parts of our life private and not put any strain on him. Sometimes he is like a child; he will take anything that is offered to him, and he must be protected. He is suffering enough.' Fab kissed the baby's head. Ellie felt the first rush of sympathy when Gareth was handed back.

'I understand.' Fab dipped her hands in the warm, soapy water.

'Thank you.'

Gareth made a world of difference to the household and Gary had a catalyst to slow down. Yet the HD was progressing at a steady rate and most of his gestures were spontaneous. He would utter cries of mingled surprise, anger and delight at inopportune moments and yet go days acting quite normally. On Gareth's second birthday in the Grange with everyone present at the party Gary announced with enthusiasm that he thought it time they had another child.

It seemed that he wanted to prove that he still had a certain amount of control over her life. So Ellie agreed. This time the AID was successful. The doctor and the nurse were the same but her first pregnancy wasn't mentioned. The secret she carried was safely locked away for now. As the pregnancy progressed Gary seemed willing to question every aspect of how he was feeling and his symptoms seemed less severe after a new drug was offered to him.

Fab faced a dilemma and it was Ellie that she turned to. 'He's my tutor; he wants me to move in with him but he is still married. I love him, at least I think I do. I don't want to uproot Suzy and then discover it was a wrong move.' They discussed the pros and cons quietly, enjoying the warmth of the early spring opposite the bluebell wood.

'We shall all miss you and Suzy.' On the day of her departure Ellie hugged and kissed her.

'I will leave you with a quote from Sophocles,' Fab smiled. 'Silence makes a woman beautiful.' Her reply could have been. 'Reprove a friend in secret but praise him before others'

– Leonardo de Vinci – but it was too sad a moment.

After opening another small boutique at Victoria Quays, Tiz was off to Milan at the invitation of Isabella. She had produced a catalogue of maternity wear and Ellie was delighted to help promote her designs. Bas and Boo continued their explosive relationship. Conversation was never easy for Bas. 'He starts being argumentative, then unintelligible and then drunk,' Gary announced. 'When arguments fail he tries abuse. But to Boo he is a prince and the new Harley has worked wonders for his prestige.'

****

The small group stumbled down the flight of steps leading to the pub. It was to be the last gig. They realized that at some point this would happen. Gary had been their kingpin holding them all together and without him, and with other commitments, Dark Horse had to fold. Bas strode to the microphone and put up both his hands. The musicians had taken their places on the stage. It was not an easy speech to make and there were howls of disbelief from the crowd but the friends were going their separate ways and somehow the time seemed right.

Ellie looked back on the days when Gary could kiss a chord and coax a tune, when he could lose himself in melodies and rhythm. Now the guitar stood in the corner. 'It's waiting for Gareth,' he hoped. Ellie grew indignant. She remembered the quiet, handsome man who played with dignity in the subway. She could see beyond the disease remembering the kindness in his eyes and the warmth of his smile.

Jason, who had been working as a masseur in Greece, returned to resume his unique exclusive partnership with Jan. It had taken years but her courage had pulled her through the trauma of the fire. At her worst she had clawed at the plaster on the walls of her room, but at her best she had shared with the Asian community her culinary skills and earned respect. Jason was there when she had lost what once had made her strong, her self-confidence, and replaced it with commitment and expectation.

It was Gary who suggested that she should be given a salary. In the early days when the house felt like a prison she hid in her room until eventually, bit by bit, she took on the responsibility of running the house and caring for Suzy. Now she ventured out, taking Gareth into the village, sharing the friendship of others.

HD was pervading every part of the daily routine, from memory loss to extreme moods. When the panic attacks threatened Gary would take a mouthful of air and almost pass out. But Ellie coped and Gareth was a welcome distraction. The pregnancy was relatively stress-free and Abigail Grace was born in the heat of a June day and delivered by an African midwife who called her Blossom. It was a name that would stay with her till she started school. Gary was very protective but there was nothing remarkable in that; he showered a great deal of love on both his children.

Changes in Gareth throughout his teens were significant. He was so like his father; his features, his colouring and his ability to perform musically surprised everyone. Gary laughed it off. It was not the case for Ellie. From his infancy she had watched Gareth with trepidation for any symptoms, however slight, and several times had buried her face in her hands when he had shown signs of clumsiness. At rugby matches she stood with her heart in her mouth each time he took a tumble. Was he simply fidgeting or were the movements involuntary? Were the moods a symptom or teenage tantrums?

After dinner one evening Gareth followed Ellie into the garden. The air was full of the scent of ripening apples picked from the orchard and laid out on a white cloth on the lawn. Dandelions were scattered over the grass. They reminded her of the borage, thistles, mint and nettles that invaded the squat at No. 68. 'Mom,' the slim figure stood by the garden seat. The white tee shirt hung loosely around his tanned body, his faded jeans fashionably torn. 'Would you say I was mature, responsible, well able to make my own decisions?' She found the question simply mystifying. He was 16. Her age when she had met his father. Could the same be said about her? Of course.

'Is it a career you are thinking about? You have to wait for your results first.'

'No,' there was a slight hesitation. 'I want to know about something that's been needling me, but I require your signature.' He handed her a slip of paper. Ellie swallowed hard. He continued, 'It's a test for Huntington's Disease. Come on Mom, I've already had DNA; anyone with half an eye can see he's my dad. I have dispensation because of his condition, it's usually 18.' She signed. White clouds were rolling over the lawn as he walked away. He looked back at her. 'It's a 50% risk, isn't it? Don't worry, I'm prepared.' Ellie sobbed bitterly as she watched the tall, brave figure stride down the hill.

Abbi sat at Gary's feet reading. Usually she was whizzing round the lanes on her bike or walking Valentine. She was unusually quiet for someone so energetic. Ellie wondered if Gareth had confided in her. She smiled at the crocheted caramel fishnet tights which clung to her sturdy legs. They were hardly summer wear; no doubt a present from Tiz. Gary was in his less defensive, more combative mood, and chose to start an argument with Gareth on local politics.

Ellie made a jug of lemonade. She was nervous, ready for the balloon to burst.

On the eve of his return to college Gareth was called to the clinic to be told the result of the test. Ellie prepared the meal, helped Gary shower and sat him in the armchair propped up with cushions against the open window. Abbi was at the youth club playing badminton. It was a case of letting the young make their own discoveries, she decided, as the slim figure of Gareth approached the lane. He walked into the hall, leaving the door partially open. 'Hi.' He avoided the questioning look his mother gave him. 'Dad, I have something to tell you, two things actually.' Gary looked up. Gareth appeared uncertain how to continue. 'I have had a DNA test; I needed to know who my genetic father is.' Gary looked bewildered. 'I always suspected, now I know for sure. You are my biological father.' Ellie moved closer to Gary and he reached out and touched her arm. His mouth trembled, his thoughts hadn't yet caught up with the bombshell. 'And,' Gareth went on. "I have been tested for HD and I am not carrying the gene, I am clear.'

Gary's emotions were almost out of control and he buried his head in his son's chest, and cried with relief. There was an invisible twist he should know about, Ellie explained. 'I was offered the obstetric procedure of pre-natal testing but as I fully intended to keep the baby there seemed little point.'

He stared at her in disbelief. 'You know I did have an intuitive feeling about Gareth but thought it was just wishful thinking and daren't imagine the consequences.' He smiled. 'And Abbi?'

'Oh Abbi, she's a gift.'

In her battle with HD Ellie was discovering and inventing survival techniques. Gary's mental and physical behaviour had deteriorated in the two years after Gareth's revelation. His ability to think clearly had been greatly reduced and it was difficult for him to concentrate. Rigidity in his legs prevented him from driving. His temper would flare up and he would lash out at anyone within reach. She had to dismiss any thoughts of moral judgements; his sexual desires were pure expressions of love, his actions the result of perfectly unconstrained feelings.

It was just as well that Gareth had moved into Rev's room. Angelica had persuaded him to stay with her in the Czech Republic for now, whilst Abbi was also in the Grange in Fab's old room. Information about HD gathered from the weekly visits from the District Nurse was invaluable but other agencies too provided inestimable help along with Occupational Therapists and dieticians. An intercom system was installed between the cottage and the Grange in case of emergencies and a permanent night nurse was employed.

In one of his rare responsive moments Gary told her that he had never expected such devoted love. Yet she had been warned; soon she would lose him. Life, she decided, was all about loss. Loss of youth, of innocence, of fitness, of energy, of control. It comes to us all. Gary had been a proud, private man but he was being robbed of his dignity. He would apologise when she had to clean up the messes. His vulnerability tore at her heart. She loved him more than ever and showed it at every possible opportunity.

Gareth spent hours with his father. With this kind of encouragement it seemed he was fighting hard for a life he was desperate to hold on to. He had taken quite well to his wheelchair; she expected he would be tired of it after the first few months but it allowed his children the opportunity to wheel him around the paths and lanes surrounding the Grange and to spend time in the shady retreats near the roses and the arbour. 'I do not like planted gardens, flowers should grow naturally,' he complained.

The vicar was a regular visitor who reminded him that religion is the assurance that life ultimately is not pointless. 'He seems to have no faith in anything,' he told Ellie.

Ellie was angry. 'How can you judge a man who is dying? May I tell you that he believes that poetry is the natural language of all religions. My husband is a good man; without religious grounding he cannot accept the need for repentance but he has harmed no one and loved many.'

At times she was questioning the very foundation of her feelings. They were shut in together, the invisible wall always between them. Huntington's was killing them both, it seemed. Gareth gave her strength, Abbi tendered comfort but each day brought further agonies. His life revolved around routine and pain yet he told her repeatedly how much he loved her. Ellie had reached a low point, the exhaustion was eating at her patience; her prayers lasted until she fell asleep and prepared her for the day ahead.

The trees were barely changing colour, brightening into soft yellows and gold. On the evergreens the virid cloud of leaves provided a comfort blanket for the birds fluttering in and out. Suddenly a splitting noise echoed across the garden, shattering the peace. Harsh discordant sounds at full volume.

Dark Horse at their peak. Jan spun round in the sitting room of the Grange, grabbing Ellie's arm. Abbi appeared in the doorway. 'I can't get Dad to stop, please, Mom hurry!' Ellie took a deep breath and ran to the cottage.

Vibration shook the windows; Abbi covered her ears. The wheelchair barred the way to the CD. Gary's eyes were menacing. 'You are destroying me, leave it, leave it,' but she leaned over him and pulled out the plug. In a hoarse shout he called out her name, over and over, cursing her and lashing out. It seemed that his intellect had declined into a funnel narrowing his sanity and he cried out in distress. His head had slumped forward. Abbi rang for the doctor and left a message for Gareth at the college.

When the hyperventilating had stopped and he had been forcibly put to sleep Ellie sat by his bed and held his hand. The doctor felt his pulse and lowered his voice to a discreet level. 'There is no point in dragging it out. The time limit on his body is coming to an end.' He was aware that Ellie was trying to get a grip of her emotions and put his arm around her shoulders.

'Don't you touch him,' she begged. He prised his hands off the decision and left.

Abbi sat in the front of the fire crumpled and confused. Her mother held her hands. 'In order to understand your father you have to understand his past. Music was a large part of his life, the band was something he could control and he loved all the trappings that came with it. It opened many doors. I became a part of it because he wanted me to be safe in an unsafe world. We have been so close. We have lived in grotty hovels with strict conditions; we were warned no wild parties, no blocked drains, and don't let the pipes freeze.' She smiled weakly. Abbi couldn't possibly understand. Her life had been one of privilege. She made her Mom hot milk and settled in the chair.

The night nurse arrived. 'Alright, love, I'll take over now.' Ellie stood her ground and Nurse retired to the Grange whilst the devoted wife prepared herself for a long night. Gary moaned softly. Ellie slipped into bed beside him and held him very tightly to her and cradled his head on her chest. Throughout his life he had dealt courageously with the continual change of this severe genetic disease and she told him how proud she was. She talked to him and kissed him, she wanted him to know that she would never leave him but there was no response. She had done her duty, to love, care for, and protect her husband. Yet she had been hurting all these years, the years of self- imposed silence whilst he had waited patiently.

He choked. The irregularity of his breathing was a strong sign that he was dying. Her cries of, 'Dear Lord, help him,' cut through into the stillness.

Gary took his last breath as the narrowing ribbon of rain hovered over the hills.

CHAPTER TWENTY-TWO

"Repentance for silence is better than repentance for speaking." (Proverbial Moorish.)

On the eve of the funeral Ellie called a meeting. She looked pale and drawn. The sitting room lacked homeliness and colour despite the log fire and magenta throws. Bas had difficulty in expressing himself. Sarcasm disguised his emotions and Boo sat silently beside him, her eyes like brown velvet. Tiz's tone was bitter and questioning. Mustard mumbled inaudibly into his beard and Fab offered an innocent, affectionate smile which Ellie returned.

Jan chose to sit near the window overlooking the lawn which held such pleasant memories. The children appreciated that devotion had been the most consistent purpose in their mother's life. She began by thanking them for their love and support. 'I can't believe he has gone. Nor can I believe that I never knew what it meant to Gary for everyone to have a place to lay their head. Wonderful letters have been arriving from charities. He is credited with opening 13 squats here and 5 in Bradford. But I'm sure you all know that. I have to accept that it is something he failed to tell me about.' She sighed. 'How are we going to put him to rest?'

It was over; the stifled sobs, the tears, the quicksand of grief pulling her down into oblivion. She felt he was calling her to pace herself, to disentangle the funerary essentials from her raw emotions and to stay close to him. Her soulmate who had directed her through her teens to womanhood had left her. Still, she had known only him and words have no language which can utter the secrets of love.

The mourners gathered to admire the flowers.

The elegant lady, hiding her tears behind dark glasses and dressed entirely in black, was embraced and offered sympathy by friends of Gary she had never met. Numerous band members came from as far as Japan and when she felt she had reached the very bottom, messages of hope lifted her. For those unable to find words she was benevolent. 'Saying sorry isn't important, feeling sorry is.' She hadn't asked herself what the future held. She was fearful of extreme grief, of lacking strength for her children, of being on her own. Feelings had been stripped from her; she felt cold. Where was the warmth that had helped her glow? A world without him was a world without light, lacking direction.

Ellie opened her handbag and produced the key to the bureau. The thunder was rumbling with scarcely a pause. The wedding photograph held her attention for a while, the picture was fresh and flawless. After two months she was ready to sort out the finances. Half of her wanted to postpone the paperwork; when papers had to be signed she did so with little interest. The other half realized that life had to go on.

Gary's filing system was neat, the bills methodically stacked. He had struggled with the accounts until his mind became confused. She wrote out a cheque to Huntington's, a large donation from the offertory at the chapel. Taped inside the drawer was a white envelope addressed simply "Ellie". The letter was handwritten.

"Ellie Sweetheart,

"Today was a good day. A rest day, one free from pain and morbid thoughts. I have found sufficient energy to argue with our son and slightly annoy our daughter. Yes, I know I am sometimes indifferent, inattentive and even hostile and it seems as if the day will never end for me but growing old is no laughing matter either, is it? I wish I knew what you really thought, but if you ever leave me I don't know what I would do. I know you have been so careful not to spoil our life together. The threads of my life are tightly interwoven with yours, strong, unbreakable, intermingled with love and compassion.

"There!!! But it is not poetry, is it? Poetry is music written for the human voice (says Maya Angelon). Sweetheart, this is the nearest I can get to telling you how I feel.

'So what is love? If thou wouldst know
The heart alone can tell:
Two minds with but a single thought,
Two hearts that beat as one.

'And whence comes Love? Like morning bright
Love comes within thy call.
And how dies Love? A spirit bright,
Love never dies at all.

Maria Lovell.'

"My life may be ephemeral, my love for you is forever.
Gary.xxx"

Ellie could not hold back the tears or dispel the gnawing grief as she sat in silence until darkness fell.

It was dated six months earlier. This is when real courage starts, she realized, when she had to move away from sentiment and pick up the pieces until the sense of peace grew stronger.

It was during the night when the demons came. The pain was constant, she couldn't get rid of it, couldn't reject it, couldn't deny it. But the nights grew shorter and the days grew longer and Ellie found consolation in their children.

There was a time when a night free from dreams was commonplace but it seemed so long ago. Ellie shared her room with Abbi for the time being and often woke with the feeling that bats were flying at her and around her, their shrew-like faces coming closer and closer, the sound frequencies audible and their wings would tangle in her hair. Abbi shook her. 'Shall I make you some warm milk?' On the way to the kitchen she heard the telephone. It was Moira.

Ellie took the call. Moira's voice sounded cold and clipped. Gran had died suddenly in the early hours. There was no pretence at grief, no reverence in her tone and although it had been several years since she had heard her mother speak she sounded as distant and austere as before.

'We never really liked each other,' she explained to Abbi at breakfast. 'She kept falling into ditches of disaster but kept reminding me that my advice was worthless!' Until a month ago Gran had been reasonably well despite her deafness, forgetfulness and her unwillingness to accept help, and Ellie still corresponded regularly. Moira agreed to make the funeral arrangements.

Through the lashing trees the wind howled as Ellie drove her family to Durham. All the terraces and bay windows and sweetpeas reminded her of her early days with Gran where nearly all the houses were models of cleanliness. When her small home had imitation leather furniture, a sideboard, a piano, an armchair by the hearth and a creaky bed.

It was not in Ellie's nature to cling to the past but she was afraid. And why not? Old ghosts were about to emerge, to reappear from the past to haunt her, bad memories from years ago ready to vent their revenge. There was a moment of panic when the cortege arrived at the chapel and Phil took his place by Moira. She had been putting on an act, giving her daughter a swift peck on the cheek, carefully avoiding contact with her children. But Phil cut straight across the formalities at the funeral tea and incensed caught her unawares. His eyes were hating her. 'So you have made something of yourself, I see. Quite the lady. But we know different, don't we?' He gripped her arm and escorted her onto the patio. 'I have not forgotten what hell you put me through. The lies you told. I have waited long enough. There is no way you are going to get away with it!'

The very words were like a knell. He was enjoying the

situation. 'I am about to settle old scores,' he threatened. His once handsome face was etched with the blotchiness of overindulgence and his eyes stared deep into hers. Ellie looked round for Gareth. Moira, well into her fourth glass of wine, had him almost pinned against the display cabinet and she burst into a strident laugh. It seemed wrong not to put up a fight but she wasn't as vindictive or as cunning as her mother and could not think of the right thing to say. She would regret it, she knew, one way or another.

After a few moments he let go of her arm and caught a glimpse of Abbi as she chatted with members of the chapel and almost immediately came the words, 'How old is she? Early teens? Interesting age, don't you think?' Ellie was seized by a sudden and powerful compulsion to strike him; she had done it before, she could do it again. She pulled up short. Hitting him would give instant satisfaction but it would be only temporary at best. With a condescending little laugh he moved away.

Moira, businesslike as ever, handed Ellie the key to Gran's flat. 'I believe there are some papers for you there. Letters or something. I have other keys; you need not return it.' In the heart of Durham they stopped at a point where the river gushed round sharply and saw the patches of sunlight dancing on the swirling water. Long ago Ellie had skipped along in sunshine along the river bank. 'God Bless, you Gran,' she whispered.

There was little left in the flat. It had been emptied, apart from a portmanteau which sat on a strip of matting on the wooden floor. Ellie was close to breaking point, she was grieving and on the threshold of tears. Losing Gary was still raw. How she needed him now.

The case was full of letters, newspaper and magazine cuttings, postcards, photograph albums and gifts which Ellie and her family had sent over the years. Each letter had been numbered and a reply had been written. Despite not knowing where her beloved granddaughter was she had taken the trouble to read and respond. There was a sampler, faded and worn, tucked in the copy of the Family Bible.

"Teach me to live that I may dread the grave as little as my bed". Missing were her jewellery and her bank books. It didn't matter. She had bequeathed a lifetime of love and Ellie had inherited a gift of compassion worth more than gold.

****

Jan and Ellie were tending the new growth on the hydrangea when the dark blue BMW pulled into the drive. Phil stepped out and looked up at the imposing house, turned and walked purposefully towards them. Jan, always wary of strangers, disappeared through the orchard. Reluctantly Ellie rose to her feet, her fair hair delightfully straggling over her blue eyes.

'Well now,' he raised his eyebrows. 'We have done well, must be worth a pretty penny!' He studied the tall, tanned woman before him and saw the deep suspicion in her expression. He realized once again that he had to curb his fancies. 'Is there somewhere we can talk?'

'We can talk here.' She held the secateurs firmly in her hand. Phil always set her nerves rattling. 'What do you want?'

'What does a man like me usually want?' he smiled sardonically. He hovered, then advanced slowly. 'Money, Lisa, money.' It was strange to hear the name again.

Ellie saw the past being re-enacted. 'You are getting nothing from me. I owe you nothing.'

'You owe me plenty. Years of incarceration, you call that nothing.' There was no formal pretence of defeat; he was optimistic. Looking around the grounds he pursed his lips. 'I thought 20 grand, you won't miss it. You know damned well I didn't kill her.' She dropped her eyes momentarily. Had he really been as innnocent as he would have her believe?

Ellie had to think quickly; he wasn't going to go away. 'The court decided. What I think doesn't matter. In any case I can't possibly get that amount of money right now. I will have to think about it.' She pulled the dead leaves from the pink cluster. 'You will have to come back tomorrow.'

Her calm exterior flummoxed him and her voice was steady. Inwardly she was shaking. Another man spelling out danger, another situation in need of a desperate solution. No way was she giving in to blackmail. Leaning over he brushed her bare arm. He could almost taste the perfume that smelt of its own expensiveness. His dark eyes flashed. She stiffened. 'I will accept less if you are nice to me.' She stepped back, her stare despising him. He shrugged. 'Tomorrow then.' He revved the car and sped down the drive.

As Jan was away for the evening teaching Indian meat-free cookery at the Asian Centre, Ellie was free to prepare the evening meal and she had thought of an effective way of dealing with Phil. After a rainy start in the morning the sky had cleared, clouds floated like whipped meringue against a background of blue. She approached her neighbour's land and climbed over the gate. It was an area which had always been out of bounds, especially to her children, as the wooded area housed the inedible fungus which could easily be mistaken for the common mushroom. Ellie knew the difference. Shielded by the trees, she entered the wood and carefully plucked the mushrooms from the sodden ground and laid them in the basket.

A foxglove, revealing the mystery of a natural world, added a speck of beauty amidst the barrenness of the woodland and Ellie stepped quietly through the trees and into the cottage. It was not that she was simplifying the act of protection; it was a powerful move but one only meant to scare him. Could she manage Phil?

The mushrooms slipped between the rubber gloves and into the saucepan, followed by an onion, tomato and garlic. Chilli sauce would disguise any suspect taste. The cooked food was sealed in a basin and the utensils bagged ready to be thrown out. She was going to take Phil down and her arrogance came with flair.

In the kitchen of Glebe Grange she cooked the same meal with edible mushrooms ready to serve to her family and friends. Phil had mistaken her hospitality for acquiescence but it suited her to see him relaxed. Her plan was taking shape. She had imagined the scene; she would paint a picture of complicated financial structures, joint accounts, securities, unit trusts and foreign investments. In other words £20,000 was an impossible dream.

After dinner she accompanied Phil into the garden. He was not impressed or convinced by her explanation. He would not be satisfied with anything less. Her instincts pushed her into rebellion; memories of events leading up to his demands angered her. 'I will do nothing without advice. I have spoken to my bank manager,' she lied, 'and my financial advisor,' she lied again. 'And there is nothing I can do. You will have to wait.' He ignored the icy look and the determined chin.

'You are a bitch, you know that. I mean to have it. I have the right to some security.' He swallowed hard. Was he feeling ill? Ellie had watched him clear his plate.

'What does Moira think?' she challenged.

'It has nothing to do with her. She thinks I am away on business. This is strictly between you and me.'

Ellie struggled to think of something to say. 'All I can suggest is that you go home and I will start the ball rolling.'

She wanted him as far away as possible before the poison took hold, before the sweating and the cramps and the diarrhoea attacked his body. The tension between them was aggravated by her confidence and his threatening behaviour. But he could do little else but leave. Ellie felt that she had dealt with the problem but it hadn't been solved, not yet.

Alone in the cottage, she opened a bottle of hock Mustard had brought back from Germany, and looked through the photograph albums, feeling devoid of warmth and comfort. In his last days Gary had had such a hunger for her that he had kept her by him for two whole days. He was jealous, he said, he wanted her all to himself and excluded all comers, even his children. All his demands were met and Ellie participated with patience and understanding but with an unforgiving condemnation of Huntington's. Jealousy was a curse they had to deal with. Now it was over, but she would do it all again to have him here.

It had been a day of changes and discoveries. Fab's old room, given over to Abbi, had been redecorated and refurbished and she had discovered a flair for interior design. Bas was planning to visit the States for a Harley convention and Boo was going along for the ride. Jan had made cashew nut pie with crushed cornflakes and grated cheese and Jason brought along some garlic hash browns. When the telephone rang it was with a feeling of helplessness that Ellie replaced the receiver. She looked at the excited faces round the table and could see no reason to give them bad news. There was no joy in this, just the pain at the concern in Moira's voice. Phil was very ill, something he ate the doctor said. It started after a business trip, she concluded.

Ellie had seriously miscalculated the effect of her action and could only wonder why she had taken such drastic measures to scare Phil. She prayed he would recover. Was her mother ready to lay to rest the mistakes of the past? Perhaps the seed that Gran had planted had grown and been harvested.

She would travel to Durham. It was early summer and the pale morning sun painted the hills and brushed the grass with golden threads as she left Derbyshire behind. Yet she was too late. Phil had died.

The horrible nightmares were coming back to her. She was now guilty of two crimes. Could this be seen as premeditated? She did not dislike men but she was not prepared to have them damage or destroy her. All men were faithless, even the one she loved. It had never been her intention to be destructive but she was not one to be taken advantage of. Flute had got away with it, he was lucky!

The autopsy revealed Amanatin – like poisoning most likely from the toxicity of fungi and the coroner recorded a verdict of death by misadventure.

Ellie had never shrunk from the demands of personal responsibility and was acting with a daughter's response.

She was a mother, she understood the significance of security. She would take care of Moira. Ellie was saved the details of Phil's lapse into unconsciousness and his death. Moira was overwhelmed by the disturbing events and most unwilling to discuss them. Yet she found it difficult to accept the hospitality offered to her at Glebe Grange and she had fallen easily into the assumption that all punks were anarchistic morons. 'I daresay it is an advantage if you are not too bright,' she crowed. Sophisticated but lacking in subtlety she pointed out that Bas was self-centred and a bore and when the language became too filthy she was filled with disgust, fostered by periods of anger. After two months, unable to repress her hatred, she left.

It was the warmth of the reception given to Tiz as she exhibited her latest creations in the London hotel that lifted Ellie. With her fellow models she joined in the applause and congratulations remembering that over the past year she had made hard and fast rules. She had forced herself to be physically and mentally strong, to re-enter with a flourish the world of fashion and to grapple with the imbalance in her life.

Isabella was instrumental in this decision, deciding that the essence of Ellie's beauty was no longer the sparkle of youth but the perfection of elegance. Abbi was not intending to follow this road and was to study medicine. Gareth had taken a year out to visit France and Italy.

Tiz wrapped the coffee clutch around the steaming plastic cup and scrutinized her companion as the train pulled out of the station. 'I want to keep things safe in their places,' Ellie told her. 'I have seen life and death, apart but inseparable. I doubt I could go through that again.'

Tiz held out a tattooed arm and grasped her hand. 'Look, you have held fear, anger and disappointment inside for too long. Let it go now. Start living because you can't hurt Gary no matter what you do. Remember what Fab told us? Life is a roundabout, you can't keep going round and round, you have to jump off sometimes. If you get hurt you pick yourself up and walk away.' It took a lot of effort to hold back the tears.

The steel city was holding on to the fine rain and mist. They linked arms as they crossed to the car park and Tiz's voice jerked Ellie from her brooding. Darkness immobilized her, freezing her into a stillness when she was alone, but in the heart of the city she breathed in the night air and discovered a new way to cope. She would break into life with a new vigour.

Tiz was right. A gentle vapour-like breeze ruffled the leaves and, caught in flight, a murmuration of starlings, rising in joy, a joy that awakens the soul and sets it free.